Wor

ALONG THE ROAD TO KEY WEST

(The Truthmaker)

Pull up a barstool or beach chair and settle in for an adventure as captivating as the Caribbean itself. In his best tale yet, Michael Reisig takes readers on a thought-provoking, heart-hammering journey through the islands, intrigue, and the power of truth. With likable and engaging characters and his ability to blend humor and drama, Reisig expertly captures the steamy but understated reality of Key West, where anything can happen and truth is almost always stranger than fiction.

Along The Road To Key West is a great new addition to his exciting series. It leads us around the world and deep into the collective mind of mankind, but in true Reisig style, the harrowing trek begins and ends in The Keys. So mix up a frozen concoction, hang on tight and enjoy the ride!

— *The Key West Citizen's* award-winning "Tan Lines" columnist Mandy Miles

Michael Reisig is well-known for his captivating tales of adventure, but this may be his best yet in a series of outstanding novels.

Reisig sends the reader on a wildly unpredictable spree of Southern Hemisphere exploits—crazy characters, furious action—couldn't put the book down until I had reached the last riveting page.

Kansas Stamps and Will Bell have done it again!

— Jay Strasner
Publisher, *El Campo Leader-News*

Kansas and Will are at their best, and never has the truth been so feared as in this captivating Caribbean caper. This one is guaranteed to keep you guessing as you fly through the pages with Reisig's crazy cast of unlikely heroes. The truth may set you free, but not in this page-turner. Intense, highly entertaining, and thought provoking!

— **John Cunningham**
author of Crystal Blue and the
Buck Reilly Adventure Series

Clever! Imaginative! Reisig's fast-paced narrative carries our reluctant heroes from one perilous calamity to the next while studying the height and depth of human nature —reminding his protagonists (and his readers) that oftentimes no good deed goes unpunished. Of all the books I've read in the last decade, this is the best candidate for an action-adventure motion picture.

— **Best-selling author Richard W. Noone**

ALONG THE ROAD TO KEY WEST
(The Truthmaker)

Michael Reisig

A Note To My Readers:
Much of this book was originally published as a novel called *The Truthmaker*. But with the growing popularity of my *Road To Key West* series, I decided to rewrite it and publish it as *Along The Road To Key West (The Truthmaker)*.

In addition, this book is a work of fiction. I have taken some liberty with the location of some facilities and their design in places such as Fernandez Bay in the Bahamas, and El Campo, Texas, as well as the hometown of President Reagan's grandparents, and the names of some high-ranking officials in the Reagan administration. I hope everyone will forgive the necessity.

— The Author

This book is dedicated to my lady, Bonnie Lee, whose diligence in first editing and perpetual honesty have never failed to improve the books I write.

"In a time of universal deceit, telling the truth becomes a revolutionary act."

George Orwell

FOREWORD

Sept. 17, 1954

A searing shaft of lightning cleaved the dark sky not fifty yards from the twin-engine Beech 18. The atmosphere ignited with sizzling ionic particles, illuminating the surrounding cumulonimbus clouds as they swept in panic across a starless horizon.

The lanky, stern-faced pilot flinched at the explosion of light and energy, and the resulting thunder pummeled the aircraft hard enough to rattle the wings. There was no copilot, just him and a couple of passengers, if you could call them that. Hell, this was supposed to be a milk run—slip out of the boss's private airstrip just north of Miami and drop into Cuba's José Martí Airport late at night. The orders were simple: Deliver five heavy, wooden boxes from Mr. Lansky to the big guy himself—Presidente Fulgencio Batista—greasing the wheels for another deal in boomtown Havana.

He knew what was going on. Hell, he knew more than they thought. They treated him like a damned busboy at a luncheon, like he was invisible while he flew them from place to place, but he knew what was happening.

Batista was in power again after a bloodless coup in '53, and Cuba was back on track with organized crime from America. He listened when they talked about how Batista had changed the gambling laws, granting a gaming license to anyone who invested a million dollars in the construction of a new hotel, or two hundred thousand in a nightclub. It was a free-for-all for underworld investors. If you had the required cash, you got matching funds from the government for construction, a ten-year tax exemption, and duty-free import on materials. The government got two hundred fifty thousand for the license, plus a percentage of the profits from each casino or nightclub. The glitch was investors were falling over each other to get a piece of the action, so inevitably it became a case of who could sweeten the pot the most to get one of the prized licenses.

Meyer Lansky was one of the big players. He wanted what

he wanted and he had a flair for getting it. He had already set up The Montmartre Club, which was one of the hottest places in Havana, but there was no such thing as too much for Mr. Lansky. He had approached Batista about putting a casino in the *Hotel Nacional*, which overlooked Havana's harbor. His plan was to take a wing of the hotel and create a battery of luxury suites for major players. But there was resistance from a few American expatriates, like that big shot writer Hemingway, as well as other casino owners. It took some sweetening to do it. Lansky promised Batista five hundred pounds of gold bullion—a currency good anywhere, anytime—under the table.

That's what he was doing tonight—delivering the deal-closer. But the damned weather was closing out. There were reports of bad storms forming west of Cuba and moving east, and had it been any other situation he would have begged out. But Mr. Lansky wanted this done tonight, and nobody said no to Mr. Lansky.

Another bolt of lightning streaked across the sky, exploding so close the plane lurched viciously and the pilot thought they'd been hit. As he struggled for control he realized the wind was rising, and the rain, which had begun as an annoying distraction, had grown into fat, hard pellets slapping the windshield in waves. He glanced at the man strapped into the copilot's seat next to him—cold eyes and dark, greased-back hair, narrow mouth twisted into a grimace, pale and sweating. The fellow was holding on to his fear, trying not to show it. *A guinea tough guy*, the pilot thought. That was more than could be said for the idiot in the cabin who wanted to know where they were every ten minutes, like a kid in the backseat of a car.

What little visibility they had was fading, and the plane was being rocked hard. The heavens were now completely buried in ominous sheets of coal-mantled clouds. He checked the VOR. It was behaving skittishly, not holding the radio signal that kept him on course. *Could lightning have gotten it?* The directional gyro tenuously agreed with his course, but it, too, was erratic. None of it felt right, and the knot in his gut agreed. They should have been clear of the Marquesas by now and able to see the lights of Havana forward of the starboard wing...but there was only darkness. He grabbed his mike and picked up Havana radio once again, but the scratchy, almost ethereal voice he heard told him that the city was being blasted by what appeared to be the first bands of a quickly developing tropical storm. Power was out at the airport and they could not assist Beechcraft N1288 with its location.

He was sweating and just a little more than concerned at this point. The storm Miami had reported as a "small disturbance" had found its footing. *Shit. Risking my life for a few bucks while flying in a quarter-ton of gold for Cuban fat cats.*

He knew where the gold came from, too. Hell, he was no fool. He read the papers. Lansky was a cheap SOB, but he was clever. He set up a heist and stole a shipment of bullion from some refinery in England, which was being delivered to Miami First National for an "undisclosed buyer." He'd stolen the damned gold two days ago in a daylight heist! The paper said it was an inside job—and it probably was—and now he was delivering it to Batista. Not a penny out of Lansky's pocket and the guy gets the casino license. Smart SOB, he had to admit.

Another terrifying fifteen minutes passed with the storm growing in intensity. The plane was wrapped in the clutches of the gale and being tossed about indifferently by the creature that held it. To add injury to insult, the port engine had begun to miss.

The guy next to him recognized the change in the engine's rhythm. He turned to the pilot, his dark eyes struggling to maintain their tough-guy demeanor, but he clutched the armrest with a death grip. "You gonna get us outta here and back on the ground before this piece of shit stops working?"

"That's the plan," the pilot replied harshly, riveted to the panel and the controls, checking fuel and magnetos, and tapping gauges in the timeless, useless ritual applied by desperate pilots who are praying for a simple solution to a bad situation.

A half hour later the storm was still raging and relentless. They were lost—long past their arrival time, and no lights or life below them. The earth was veiled by a torrent of racing clouds and hammering rain. The VOR was definitely gone, reading way too radically to be accurate. The only gauges that seemed to be working were the airspeed, altimeter, and the compass...maybe. He was certain they were being pushed northeast by the storm, and there were mountains in the northeast area of Cuba.

The guy in the back was starting to lose it, yelling every time the plane hit a pocket and cussing up a blue streak, more in terror than anger.

The fellow next to the pilot turned toward the back of the plane. "Shut up, Benny!" he yelled. "You ain't gonna make this any better by whining, so shut the hell up." He straightened in his seat and muttered to no one in particular, "I hate whiners."

Suddenly, there was a backfire from the port engine and a huge burst of white smoke exploded from the exhaust. It didn't shut down, but it was definitely missing a beat now. The pilot quickly drew off some of the engine's power, trimmed out the plane, and adjusted with the rudder to keep them straight and level, but "level" was becoming an issue, especially with the buffeting they were receiving. Benny was starting to panic, crying out about crashing, and thoroughly adding to the tenseness of the situation.

"We're too heavy," said the pilot to the man next to him. "If we're going to stay in the air we've got to lighten the plane."

"That's not good," the fellow said as he shook his head. "Lansky would be very unhappy if we lost his cargo. Would a couple hundred pounds help?"

The pilot nodded, grimly fighting the controls. "Yeah, anything's better than nothing."

The guy got up and worked his way over to the entrance of the cabin, yelling to the fellow in the back. "Benny! We got to lighten the plane some. Get the cargo door open so we can push some stuff out."

Benny immediately complained about how hard that was going to be with him being tossed around like a damned rag doll, but the hard look on his partner's face convinced him to try. He lurched over to the hull, working to keep his balance in the rocking aircraft, threw the latch and gradually forced open the sliding door. He held on for dear life as the hurricane-force winds clawed at him and the plane trembled under the change of aerodynamics, gradually descending into the darkness.

Benny turned, standing by the open door. "Okay, Tony, what goes?"

"You do," Tony said, deadpan, as he pulled a pistol from his belt and shot his companion twice in the chest.

The very surprised Italian clutched his breast and stumbled backwards, eyes wide, mouth open. He stepped cleanly out of the hatch into the dark, roaring emptiness of the raging storm and was snatched away in an instant.

"I hate whiners," Tony said as he forced the door closed.

By the time Tony had belted himself uncomfortably into his seat, the tide had turned against the faltering aircraft. Benny's weight hadn't changed the equation, and a moment later the wounded engine coughed out another burst of rich, gray-white smoke and began to fail. There was no time left for alternative solutions. They were going down. As another torrent of relentless wind and rain assaulted the Beechcraft, the pilot pulled off the power on the dying engine and feathered the prop, then trimmed her one more time, practically standing on the right rudder and grasping the yoke as it trembled in his hands like a living thing. The fear he had fought so hard finally breeched his defenses, crawling up into his intestines and clawing at him. He grabbed the microphone. "Mayday! Mayday! This is Beechcraft November, one, two, eight, eight, estimated position somewhere east-northeast of Havana. Engine failure, we're trapped in a storm and going down. Repeat! Mayday! Mayday! November, one, two, eight, eight, going down east of Havana!"

The pilot waited in quiet desperation for a reply from someone—*anyone*—for the impossible reprieve he knew wasn't there. Whispering words of encouragement to his faltering aircraft, and the briefest of supplications to whoever might be listening above him, he struggled to control the Beech as she plummeted through the ebony torrent. But the scratchy silence in his headphones was all he got. Even God was out of range that night.

CHAPTER 1

The old faiths light their candles all about, but burly truth comes by and blows them out...

—**Lizette W. Reese**

1983, The Florida Keys

The morning sun rose out of the ocean, casting a billion shards of glass across the still, summer water. The first wind whispered softly, brushing the golden incandescence, while the calm, backcountry water quivered sensuously from the touch. From the bow of his eighteen-foot skiff, Kansas Stamps laid the stroke of his fly rod forward with practiced ease and the line arched gracefully above him in a lazy, thirty-foot loop. The bonefish fly soared past overhead, flowing in an almost slow-motion roll as the tapered monofilament leader that held it succumbed to gravity and inertia, straightened out smoothly, and gently laid the small calf's hair and sparkling lace body on the surface of the glimmering water not three feet from a tailing bonefish. The wisp of a satisfied smile brushed his lips as Kansas pulled the slack from the cast with his left hand, watching for movement in the water where the fly settled, braced but not overly anxious for a change in the tenseness of the line.

He exhaled softly. It was a scene that never failed to provide him succor. The rest of the world could be going to hell in a hand basket, but at that moment it didn't matter. For a few precious minutes he was part of the wind and the sun and the sea, entwined with nature, at peace with the elements.

Kansas was still enjoying the serenity of the morning when, off in the distance, he heard the drone of an approaching aircraft. He had spent enough time in and around airplanes to know that the oncoming plane was in trouble. Its engine was missing badly, sputtering, catching, then sputtering again. Suddenly, with an ugly finality, the engine quit, returning the stillness to the egrets and herons feeding in the shallows.

The VHF radio on the consol hissed with static and a

metallic voice broke the stillness of the morning. "Kansas. Hey buddy, that you in the flats on the end of Big Pine? Huh?"

Uttering a soft expletive, Kansas moved over to the consol and picked up the receiver with his left hand, holding the rod with his right. "It's barely sunrise and I'm fishing. It better be important."

"I guess it all depends on your priorities. Hate to drag you away from your communion with nature, but to me this call is important."

He recognized his friend's voice. It was Will's usual banter, but there was a little tenseness around the edges.

"If you look to the northwest at about two thousand feet you'll see an airplane—you got it?"

Kansas glanced in that direction. The plane with the failed engine was clearly visible. It looked like a low wing, single engine Piper, trailing a thin line of rich, oily smoke, in serious trouble. "Yeah, got it."

"That's me. I'm going to be dropping in to visit. I ain't gonna make the strip at Summerland and there's too many freaking tourists on U.S. 1. Besides, the engine's got a little fire going and a water landing might be a good idea. Hope you don't mind the interruption, but that's nice shallow water there where you and your bonefish hang out."

Kansas shook his head with wonder at the coincidence. Will, of all people. "Listen, I'm in the process of coaxing a really big bone right now. Could you just circle for about fifteen minutes, then check in with me again?"

He heard the chuckle at the other end. "Screw you and the horse you rode in on. I'm coming down now. This piece of crap just became a glider—and not much of one."

Kansas knew Will was an amazing character, but in the back of his mind he also realized how dangerous this was—no power, a dead stick landing, coming in and hammering that hard water at no less than seventy knots. On top of it all, Will had been a licensed pilot for less than a year, although he'd sat right seat in an airplane with Kansas more times than could be counted, through dozens of tight spots over the last decade. Their friendship went back to college in St. Petersburg, Florida. They were both taking English Composition, ended up sitting next to each other, and struck up a conversation. They hit it off immediately, as if they had known each other forever. Will had a rakish, acerbic wit and yearning sense for adventure that matched Kansas's perfectly. When it came to graduation, their fellow students were looking for master's degrees, brokerage houses, or other respectable professions. Will and Kansas just wanted to rip open the fat orange of life with their fingers and gobble the flesh until the juice ran down their chins. They wanted adventure, and they found it in the Florida Keys. Both of them loved the ocean, so in 1971 the crazy duo made a trip down to The Keys to do some diving and partying. They never left. The adventures over the next decade came so fast they could hardly absorb them. They found sunken Spanish treasure, got chased by modern-day pirates, ended up in Central and South America for some very high adventures, became friends with a mystical Rastaman, raced across the Caribbean chasing their passions, and found the girls of their dreams— then lost them…twice.

In the oddest damned set of circumstances, the women they fell in love with, fell in love with each other. They lost their wives to their wives, and as if the gods were just enjoying the irony of it all, they lost the girls of their dreams again, later on, in nearly identical circumstances. So they went back to adventuring and it proved profitable. Kansas still had his stilt house on Big Pine Key and his Cessna 182 amphibian. He had become a bonefishing guide in the process, enjoying what he did immensely, but not making much of a living from it. Will and he had lived together for a year or so after their divorces, but Will had eventually purchased a large shrimp boat and converted it into quite comfortable living quarters. He kept the boat at a marina in Key West. Over the years Kansas had taught him to fly. He eventually got his pilot's license and was now rated for single and twin aircraft, just like his friend.

They still chased treasure and women occasionally, and hardly a week passed that they didn't end up in the bars of Key West. There was no question that life had never been dull, but today was turning out to be a tad more exciting than usual.

"Okay Will, no problem," said Kansas, trying to keep the anxiousness out of his voice. "You can do this. You can do it. Piece of cake."

Will knew what his friend was up to and he smiled through it all. "You got pom-poms down there with the cheerleading section?"

"Just fly the freaking plane onto the water and we'll be doing margaritas at Captain Tony's by noontime," Kansas replied with just a touch of nervous exasperation.

As Kansas quickly reeled in his line, he could imagine Will in the cockpit—puckered, sweating, everything coming apart at the seams around him, but not about to give up— long, blond hair pulled back into a ponytail, that damned fat, droopy mustache he thought was so hip, carrying on a sarcastic dialogue with himself like Woody Allen on steroids while he crashed an airplane into his partner's bonefishing flats. A hero he wasn't, but he was the most audacious damned individual Kansas had ever known. He smiled at the thought, regardless of the situation.

As the aircraft glided silently out of the sky, the rising sun caught and held it like a glistening silver pendant against the gilded horizon. The plane still trailed a slight wisp of gray smoke, like a broken cord that bound it to the ethereal blueness— beautiful and frightening in the same moment. It soared noiselessly downward, over Big Pine Key, just missing the tops of the tallest pines on the high ground near the water, and still aimed uncomfortably close to Kansas and his boat.

Kansas stood there, mesmerized but suddenly closer to concerned. "Cutting this a little close, buddy," he muttered anxiously as the faltering aircraft cascaded out of the sky, wings wobbling dangerously in the last hundred feet of descent.

The plane passed nearly overhead, close enough to make Kansas flinch, then continued airborne for another two hundred yards. At about twenty-five feet above the water, Will pulled the yoke into his chest and the plane obediently stalled, the nose rose slightly, and the aircraft flared in a textbook water landing. The tail touched first and the drag instantly slapped the Piper down onto the water. It gave a short leap, like an injured dragonfly trying to escape the bounds of gravity, then buried its cowling in the bright crystalline water. The nose dug hard for a moment, bouncing off the soft, sandy bottom, then came up and settled with a shiver, surprised and shaken, like a young mallard that's just made its first pond landing. At that point the plane slowly settled into the shallows, water gradually rising about halfway up on the fuselage.

By the time Kansas got his engine started and raced over to the craft, Will was sitting on the roof, dangling his feet in the water. He waved casually, as if he were on a beach somewhere, and yelled over, "I think the fishing's done for the day—too damned noisy around here. Maybe we could go home so I can change clothes and you can buy me that margarita you promised."

Kansas didn't know whether to spit or smile.

That evening, after a day of dealing with the authorities and filling out paperwork with the local Federal Aviation Administration representative, they sat in The Bull and Whistle in Key West, having drinks and celebrating luck, timing, talent, and numerous other elements that are required for survival when you do stupid or dangerous things and they don't go as planned— which is more often than not the case in the realm of stupid and dangerous things.

"Yeah, I know I should have said no, but McPherson wanted the plane to be worked on by his mechanic down here," Will said, exasperated. "It was missing a little, that's all. His charter business is nuts right now and he didn't have time to go get it, so I rented a car, drove up to Miami, and picked it up for him." He leaned back in his chair and smiled. "Well, the engine doesn't miss anymore."

They were interrupted by the waitress—a svelte little thing with long, dark hair, blue eyes, and a smile that could melt glass. "Would you gentlemen like another drink?" She glanced from Kansas to Will and back again, a definite appraisal in her eyes.

Kansas wasn't a bad-looking guy. He was dressed in a polo shirt and a pair of Dockers shorts—not tall, maybe five-foot-seven, but he had one of those genetically gifted physiques (augmented by hours in the local gym) that often required a second glance from most women. Like Will, his hair reached his shoulders. It was a rich brown, streaked with golden highlights from all his time in the sun. His eyes were a light green with flecks of hazel in the irises. He offered a warm, wide smile to the young lady.

Will was tall, right at six feet. His pale blue eyes reflected both mischievousness and passion, and he, too, wasn't a stranger to second looks. He had strong but not demanding features—a slightly hooked nose, a bushy blond Tom Selleck mustache, and a smile that carried a slight tilt, which could be either disarming or challenging, depending on the situation. Blue jeans and a flowered tropical shirt were standard mode with him. He had the height on Kansas but he was slender, with a tightly muscled body from the arduous activities of a professional diver.

As the waitress reluctantly departed to get fresh drinks, Kansas finished the remains of his *Cuervo* and limejuice on the rocks, crunching an ice cube in the process. "So, what's new with you? I realize a man of your many talents has to keep himself busy. Done any interesting 'flying' lately? I'm talking about actually keeping planes in the air to their destinations." Kansas grinned. He was enjoying himself. "And what about your latest treasure scam? Last I heard, you had a new project you were working on. Lost planes and gold in Cuba. How's that pipe dream coming along?"

Will smiled. He was used to the banter. It was what they did. He was just about to issue a retort regarding Kansas and characters from Elmore Leonard novels when suddenly a commotion erupted on the sidewalk out front. Two fellows—one a little on the burly side, Cuban, blue Guayabera shirt, white pants, slicked-back dark hair, and a heavy mustache; and the other, fairly tall and hard-looking, tousled reddish hair to his shoulders, paler complexion, mean eyes, and dressed in blue jeans and a faded tropical shirt—had a girl cornered outside their car. Apparently they had just pulled up and stopped her. There was an argument—the gist being they wanted her company and she apparently didn't want theirs. The young lady was tanned and tall, maybe five-foot-nine or ten, with long blond hair the color of summer wheat, drawn back tightly in a ponytail. She had on a pair of loosely fitting, light cotton beige shorts and a Captain Tony's T-shirt. She was willowy, but closer observation would have recognized the well-formed muscle groups in her arms and legs, as if she might be a dancer of some sort.

The whole scene took place no more than thirty feet from Kansas and Will. Kansas's eyes lit up. "That's Cass!"

Will, who hadn't been paying too much attention at first,

took a second look. "Don't think I know her. But it looks like she's got a situation."

Will was already coming up out of his seat. Kansas was uncharacteristically slow.

"C'mon man, let's go," said Will, a little exasperated.

Kansas rose and sort of shrugged his shoulders indifferently. "I know that girl. Don't think we need to be in a hurry."

By the time Kansas and Will were out of the restaurant, the big Cuban, still standing by the open passenger's door, got tired of arguing and reached out to grab the girl, which proved to be a mistake.

The entire demeanor of the lady changed instantly, and as the man's hand came toward her, rather than retreating, she grabbed it with her right hand, turned sideways and snapped him forward, using his own momentum against him. The guy's eyes opened wide in surprise as her left hand shot out like a snake over his arm and she flicked the back of her stiffened fingers against his open right eyeball, hard enough to pop a balloon. The guy screamed like a child, raising his hands to his wounded eye, which left other parts of his body woefully unprotected. The woman dropped to a crouch, made a hard, solid blade with the fingers of her right hand, and slammed that up between his legs into his groin with enough force to make the Cuban's eyes (the good one and the bad one) bulge like Daffy Duck's. The air rushed out of her antagonist's lungs. He dropped to his knees and rolled into a fetal position, at that point not knowing where to hurt first. But by that time the other guy was moving in on her from the front of the car.

Kansas stepped between them, facing the fellow with the mean eyes, holding up his hands, trying to diffuse things. "C'mon man, we don't need any trouble here."

"Don't need your help," the girl hissed from behind him.

Kansas grimaced, talking over his shoulder, still dealing with the man in front of him. "No, you don't. I know that, and you know that, but he doesn't." Again he addressed the guy. "Dude, just let it go, okay? Just pick up your friend and go. I know this girl, this is not going to get better for you."

Will stood a few feet away, taking a moment to check out the young lady. She was quite attractive, with gray-blue eyes, a wide, sensuous mouth, and a fairly nice figure—long, nicely shaped legs and perky, smallish breasts—but there was a tomboyish air about her that didn't necessarily add to her sexuality. Hell, with what he'd just seen, she was a little scary.

Suddenly, the long-haired guy relaxed some, moving closer. "Listen, we don't want no trouble, either," he said to Kansas, almost confidentially. "She got some things that belong to us. We want 'em back. It's not your business, man."

Kansas was watching his eyes. The eyes told you everything about an opponent. They told him this boy was a veteran of "hard arguments."

Mean Eyes took a glance over at Will, weighing him, then a quick look down at his friend, who had gotten to his knees and was just getting some color back, though he was still holding his eye. He had made a choice. "Okay, maybe we just come back another time."

But his eyes didn't say that.

Mean Eyes lowered his head a little, as if to signify this was over, but in the process he turned slightly and dropped his right shoulder, telegraphing that he was about to throw a punch. The girl was way ahead of him. Before the guy was halfway into the swing, she elbowed Kansas aside and slapped his opponent's arm away, automatically turning the fellow and exposing his side. Then she hammered him in the kidney hard enough to fracture a couple of ribs—he'd be peeing blood for a week. As the guy grunted, clutching up, she side-kicked his knee out from under him, tearing ligaments that would take a month to heal. The man cried out and collapsed on the pavement, groaning in pain.

The young lady turned to Kansas and sighed angrily, placing her hands on her hips. "You were about to get your ass kicked."

Kansas held up his hands, palms out. "Hey, I was just trying to help."

"Did I look like I needed help?"

Kansas smiled in surrender. "Look, why don't we find another bar and have a drink, and you can thank me for being so gallant. I don't want to be here when these guys get themselves together and call their friends."

"I'm not thanking you for shit," she replied indignantly.

Will, thoroughly enthralled now, stepped over to them. "Hi,

I'm Will Bell. If you promise not to beat me up, I'll buy the first round."

Cassandra Roundtree, Cass to her friends, leaned back in her chair, propping her feet on the base of the table inside The Green Parrot. She was just finishing her first margarita and was in a much better mood. It was still early and the rowdy evening crowd was an hour or two away. Ceiling fans swirled lazily, catching whorls of smoke from an occasional cigarette and twisting them softly into nothingness as the bartenders and barmaids readied themselves for another night in paradise. An old Jimmy Buffett tune, whispering faintly in the background, caressed the senses and captured the spirit of the coming evening with a song about a lady on Caroline Street. Kansas had introduced Will and related how it was that he knew Cass, explaining that she was part of a new wave of computer analysts. She had worked for the emerging computer company, Microsoft, on the East Coast. Now she lived in The Keys, and had a small house on Summerland Key, half of which was dedicated to computer analysis and programming equipment damned near comparable to what NASA had. She worked freelance for several major companies across the country, solving problems and creating programs. He mentioned that she did have a couple of hobbies, or "non-debilitating passions" as she called them—things that you enjoyed which "didn't consume you, or cripple your sense of creative freedom and become identity liabilities."

As Buffett quit crooning, Will leaned in on the table and focused on Cass with a sage grin. "I'm gonna take a wild guess and bet one of those 'non-debilitating passions' is a martial art of some sort."

Cass shrugged indifferently. "Yeah, good guess. Krav Maga and Jujitsu."

Will nodded. "I'm familiar with Jujitsu, but Krav Maga not so much."

"It's a martial art that was developed in Israel. It involves striking principles and counterattacks designed to neutralize your opponent as quickly as possible—aimed at the most vulnerable parts of a person's body. No bowing, no shaking hands, just get it over with—fast."

A small smile from Will carried new respect. "Well, apparently it works pretty well for you." He paused. "So, what was this thing about today—those two guys and the collective bad attitude?"

Cass finished her margarita and motioned to the bartender for another. Removing her feet from the railing under the table, she brought herself forward, putting her arms on the tabletop in a more serious pose. "Has to do with my other 'hobby.' Those guys are bunchers, and I decided to put a dent in their operation."

Will gave her a quizzical look. "Bunchers?"

"Yeah, people who round up or steal domestic pets and sell them to laboratories to be used in experiments. Ugly business, but big money. They got a friend's dog two weeks ago, so I decided to go after them." She paused for a swallow of her new drink. "My friend got a partial on their license plates and a look at their van. I went to the DOT office in Key West and sweet-talked the guy who worked there—got the rest of the numbers, and from that I got their location in Homestead. We scoped them out and I waited for them to leave. When they went out for another run, we backed in a U-Haul and took all twenty of the animals they were holding. They kept remarkably good records for assholes, so with the records and the animals' tags, we were able to find the owners for most of them inside a couple days. The rest are with the Miami ASPCA while they try to find the remaining owners. Somehow they figured out who did it—maybe a security camera I missed. That's why they wanted to 'visit' with me for a while." She smiled mischievously. "That, and the damage to the inside of the house."

When Cass finished her brief dissertation, she studied Will for a moment. "You're Kansas's partner, the guy who keeps the Cessna 310 out at the Summerland airstrip, aren't you? I heard about you—new hotshot pilot who works this treasure hunting business with Kansas."

"I don't know that either of those are really apt descriptions," Will said with a shrug, trying to be humble but failing at the attempt—his ego enjoying the offhanded flattery a bit too much.

"Which part was wrong?" Cass said, nailing him with her characteristic directness.

"Yeah, okay. I'm a pilot. I own the airplane."

"What about the treasure business? I've heard a couple of stories. I'd like to shake the fact from the fiction about Mr. Will Bell."

"It's really not much," he said, attempting the humble thing again. In truth he wasn't all that anxious to talk about it, because although it looked good from the outside, it actually wasn't one of his high points. But she was relentless.

"Oh, c'mon, pretend I'm one of those hot tourist chicks you're hustling on a Saturday night," she said with a baiting smile, those gray-blue eyes igniting with animation as she teased him. She pulled the band from her ponytail and shook her thick blond hair free. It fell across her tanned shoulders in waves and she turned attentively to him again. "The lights are low, we're in a bar, you've got me on my third rum and Coke, and I'm already getting that sensuous 'I can't wait to feel your hands on me' look. But I need just one more push to win my...heart."

The normally fairly collected Will was a little taken aback by this woman and her direct assaults. "Hey, I'm not like that...always," he said, bringing up his hands in typical fashion for emphasis. "How do you know I'm not married with two kids?"

The girl huffed in sarcasm. "You're married with two kids and I'm the Queen of England here on vacation looking to get laid. C'mon, tell me a treasure story." She did that Cheshire Cat smile again. "From the horse's mouth. Word on the street has it you found that wreck off the Marquesas last year," Cass said.

Will sighed. "Yeah, we did, but it ended up being a lot of work and expense for little reward. It had apparently been salvaged pretty well after sinking." He took a breath and smiled, somewhere between sage and snookered. "Let me tell you, treasure hunting is somewhat akin to the boats required for the endeavor—it can be a hole in the water into which you throw money. If that were the only business I had to rely on, by this time I would be standing behind a counter somewhere saying, 'Do you want pickles and ketchup with that?'"

Cass chuckled. "You wouldn't last a day at McDonald's. They'd boot you out the door for hitting on chicks and mixing up orders just for fun. I know your type. Not good at being told what to do."

Will was again impressed with the woman's candidness and intuition. If she just wasn't so damned...what was the word... *right*...all the time.

"Well, the maybe good news is I've been working on a lead for something that I think is promising," Will added, sitting up a little. "It's a challenging situation, but I think there's a strong possibility there could be a pot of gold at the end of the rainbow."

"Would that be the Cuban gold thing?" Kansas said, lifting an eyebrow with incredulousness. "Sometimes you just got to know when to fold 'em..."

Will shook his head, lips pursed in annoyance. "Aahh, ye of little faith. Let me remind you of a quote by none other than the esteemed Henry Kissinger: 'There comes a time in every rightly-constructed boy's life when he has a raging desire to go somewhere and dig for hidden treasure.' Rightly constructed or not, I'm getting that desire again."

"So, what's this all about?" Cass asked.

"I think it's a story for another time," said Will, making it clear he wasn't ready to talk about it, and the conversation faded, then shifted.

After one more drink and a little more history on each other, Cass begged out, saying she had things to do at home—two cats and a dog to feed. Kansas and Will reassured her that she could call them anytime if she had any further problems. Will provided his phone number and got hers. He wasn't sure what to think about this woman, but he wasn't ready to write her off either, and he needed to talk with Kansas first, anyway. She was a cute little thing, but as tough as a carbide coconut.

As Kansas drove him to his boat on Stock Island, Will turned to his friend. "So, what's the story with you and Cass?"

Kansas smiled, running the fingers of one hand through his long hair and around the back of his neck, then stretched, knowing the question was coming. "She had advertised a Coon cat free to a good home in *The Citizen*. I like Coon cats so I went by her place. Somebody else got the cat, just ahead of me. We got to talking and, I don't know, we just hit it off and I asked her out."

There was silence for a moment.

"Okay, then what?" Will finally said, exasperated.

"She's a nice lady," Kansas said with an impish smile, his green eyes lighting up with humor. He loved getting Will's goat, and in truth, it was an easy creature to find. "We dated for a while, and got along pretty well. Some parts of the relationship were very good."

"Yeah, I bet."

Kansas turned his head from side to side in a reflexive, stretching motion—something he did unconsciously when he was pensive. "Yeah, nice. But for some reason we just didn't click in the long run. I don't know...she's a very independent woman. Somewhere along the way we just became friends. Maybe I just wasn't ready to take any chances again." He threw a sideways glance at his friend. "You and I haven't exactly had the greatest luck with women. I'm sure I don't have to remind you it was less than a year ago that our crazy Rastaman buddy's 'magic love potion' backfired and we lost the girls we loved to the girls we loved."

"Well, in all honesty, we screwed up on the way it was supposed to be used."

Kansas shrugged. "That doesn't make me feel any better. The last I heard, Carina and Vanny had moved to Saint Kitts." He drew a breath and exhaled hard. "How about a change of subject? What's the deal with your latest quixotic enterprise— the Cuban gold situation?" he said with a grin. "Are you tightening down this pipe dream?"

"Glad you asked," Will said, eager to talk to someone he could trust. "Actually, it was our Rastaman buddy, Rufus, who offhandedly helped set this in motion. When I first started getting involved with this I was in Key West, having dinner at Aunt Rose's, and he shows up out of nowhere, like he does. Same old Rufus—long dreadlocks, those weird eyes that seem to morph from gray-blue to chocolate depending on his mood, grubby shorts, and a weathered T-shirt. He says something to me about having a new Hobbit quest comin' up—islands, caves, and truth. Then he gets this serious look and says something like, 'Truth is more valuable than gold, mon, and more dangerous than envy. May the great tortoise let your egg break cleanly and grant you a moonlit path to the sea.'"

"Yeah, that sounds like our mystical pal, all right," Kansas said with a wan smile. "But I can't say that makes me feel more comfortable."

Will ignored the comment and continued. "I know I've mentioned the story my dad used to tell me about his friend finding the plane buried in the cave in the mountain, but since then I've talked with him about it again, extensively. On top of that, I started doing some research about storms and aircraft lost in Cuba, and it's led me to a solid hypothesis. I think I know what happened now."

Will took a breath. "I told you a little about this, but I'm going to run through it again so you've got a good handle on the situation. As you know, my dad's best friend was Cuban-American. He was shot down over Cuba during the Bay of Pigs on the first day of the invasion, April 17, 1961. He was the copilot of one of the B-26s that were supplying support for the landing at Playa Girón. He survived the crash and by some miracle escaped being captured, but he was badly wounded. He would have died from his wounds but for a second miracle—he was discovered by a family supportive of the invasion, and they took him in and hid him. They were once a fairly wealthy family, but Castro had taken much of what they had. In a twist worthy of a made-for-TV movie, they had a daughter—a beautiful young lady, eighteen years old—who helped treat the wounded airman for the first week while his life hung in the balance, and then one more week while he healed enough to travel to a hideout in the mountains. In one of those strange things that just sometimes happens, they began to fall in love. Her father knew the mountains of southeastern Cuba well—the Sierra Maestra. They hid my dad's friend in the back of an old farm truck and drove deep into the mountains to a cave system. They left him food, there were streams for water, and he hid there for another three weeks while the family arranged for a fishing boat to carry him to Key West. The girl came to visit him, bringing him supplies, and their love grew. When it came time to go, she slipped away and joined him on the beach, where the boat met them."

Will paused as Kansas pulled up to the dock at Safe Harbor Marina on Stock Island, where Will's boat was moored. The moon was rising, casting a soft, satiny glow over the water, painting the converted shrimper's hull and forecastle in chartreuse and shadows. The wheelhouse windows gleamed with yellow incandescence from the truck's headlights as Kansas turned the key off and rolled down his window. The rich, tangy scent of the sea and the warm night air embraced them like the touch of a loving woman. Kansas turned off the headlights and shifted around in his seat. "Go on, you've got my attention. Sounds a bit like a John D. MacDonald/Travis McGee novel."

Will edged himself up on the seat a bit, relaxing, then continued. "Here's the interesting part. While hidden in the mountains of Cuba, my dad's buddy started doing better, and he began exploring a little. On a short hike the day before he was to attempt his escape back to the States, he found a large cave concealed in the dense jungle on the northern side of the mountain, maybe a half-mile from his hideaway. What caught his attention was part of a rudder from an aircraft tangled in the vines at the entrance to the cave. He forced his way in and discovered an old Beechcraft 18 had somehow threaded the eye of the needle and, in a one-in-a-million chance, flown right into the cave. As it hit, the wings had folded and collapsed around the fuselage, the impetus driving the whole plane into the cavern and burying the nose into the back wall. The aircraft was so badly damaged and it was so tight and dark, it was barely possible to get in, but he finally managed to work his way through. It was a mess. There was dust on everything with vines growing into and around the entire structure, but he remembers seeing wooden boxes of some sort inside the cabin. Some were intact, but most were shattered or broken open. To this day the guy swears he saw what appeared to be small, rectangular-shaped objects strewn around the interior, maybe three inches by six inches and perhaps an inch high, but that was a guess. As he stood there next to the wreckage, looking through a huge rip in the fuselage, the setting sun cut through the foliage and splashed the interior of the plane. At that moment he was almost certain he saw a golden reflection through the dust on several of those rectangles. But before he could do much else, he heard something outside the cave. It sounded like voices, and he got spooked, so he slipped out and hightailed it back up the mountain to his hideaway. He planned on going back, but he never got a chance. He did, however, get the call numbers from the tail of the plane—November, one, two, eight, eight. Those numbers stuck with him, and when he got a chance he wrote them down."

Will looked out at the dark water, then turned back to Kansas. "After speaking with my dad's friend this last time, I decided to do some investigation. I've got a buddy with the Federal Aviation Administration. I seriously saved his ass once, when we were really young and foolish, and he owed me a favor. Anyway, I had him research U.S. airplanes that were lost over Cuba, including the possibility of a Beech 18 with the call numbers N1288. He got back to me a week ago with some interesting information. That plane disappeared on April 17, 1954, after filing a flight plan with Miami Airport for Cuba's José Martí Airport."

Kansas started to say something, but Will held up his hand.

"It gets better. There was a tropical storm that moved through the straits that night between Key West and over Cuba. The plane never arrived at its destination. Key West's Naval Air Station records have a small footnote on receiving a barely audible Mayday from that aircraft, stating a last known position over the eastern end of Cuba. A brief search was instituted, but the plane was never found. Everyone figured it went down in the water."

Kansas shook his head, amazed, and just a touch enthralled. "Damn, you've done your homework. Now you've really got my attention."

Will grinned, satisfied his plan was working. The bait had been taken. "That's nothing. Here's where it really catches fire. I went up to Miami and checked out the ownership of N1288. It was owned by Stellar Corporation, set up in 1948, and when I waded through the protective bullshit in the documents one name stood out—Meyer Lansky. You know who Meyer Lansky was?"

Kansas nodded. "Oh yeah, big mafia player in the early to mid-twentieth century."

"Okay, we're on the same page," Will said. "Now, what we've got is a plane that crashed in Cuba that maybe had gold on it. I thought about this and began to do more research, primarily wading through old copies of *The Miami Herald*. About the time this plane went down, Lansky was trying to cut a deal with

Batista in Cuba to put a new casino in the *Hotel Nacional* in Havana. The other thing that jumped out and grabbed me was a robbery that took place two days before the departure of N1288. In a daring daylight heist, a shipment of gold bullion from the English gold refinery Johnson Matthey, being delivered to the Miami First National Bank, was stolen." He let that sink in and stared at Kansas. "Five hundred pounds of gold bullion. Five hundred pounds..."

"Yeah, I heard you," Kansas interrupted with a look of profound comprehension. "I heard you." He took a breath and expelled it slowly. "That whole story is nothing short of freaking amazing. Son of a bitch! I think you figured this out."

Will smiled, gratified that he had set the hook. "Now, of course, the question is how a person would find that cave; and then the big question is...is the gold still there after better than half a century? But I have one final ace on this situation, as well. My dad's buddy said that there was a granite-like cliff about five hundred yards to the east of the cave with the plane in it. In the center of the cliff there is an abutment that rises straight out almost in the shape of a Mayan-featured nose—heavy, sloped, and rounded with what looked much like nostrils on both sides. It's not really man-made, but it's prominent enough to give a landmark to start from. If we could find this—"

"Aaahhh, I heard 'we' in there just now," Kansas said cautiously.

His friend nodded. "Yeah, why not? I thought maybe you might like to partner with me on this one. You've been spending way too much time at this 'pretending to be a fishing guide' thing."

"Meaning you don't have the resources to do it yourself."

Will shrugged. "Well, I am running a little close, and this is a caper that would take some planning and some finances. I've given it some thought. We'd probably need a seaplane so we would have the advantage of mobility and could make a quick exit—maybe not have to worry too much about landing strips or customs if we find the crashed plane and the gold. I was thinking we might talk to Crazy Eddie. He's got that Grumman Goose."

Kansas flinched like he'd been hit. "Oh Lord, not one-eyed Crazy Eddie again," he moaned. "I mean, this is not the seventies anymore and he still thinks it is. You can't just fly and land wherever you want—and not clear customs—especially not in Cuba."

Will held up his hands, realizing that he needed to loosen the drag here. "I admit there are a few bugs to be worked out, and the finances...but man, five hundred pounds of gold. I mean, you could continue to live in the lifestyle you've become accustomed to. At the present price of gold we're talking around four million dollars."

Kansas fell quiet for a moment, running his hand through his hair and around to the back of his neck in that pensive fashion of his. The truth was, he and Will had come into some pretty good money a year or so ago, with their finding of a rare, golden Spanish cross and a chest full of coins. But for some reason money had a way of getting away from him. After renovating his home, buying a new bonefishing skiff, and doing a "prop to tail" refurbishing of his 182 Cessna amphibian, he was running closer on cash than he liked.

"Even if it was possible, we'd need a reason to be going into Cuba, and all the paperwork to make it legal. It's not easy for Americans to get into Cuba these days, even though the restrictions aren't like they used to be. We would definitely have to call in some favors to make this work."

"Yeah, I know. But I've been thinking about that, too. The easiest way to get into Cuba with the fewest headaches is to represent a professional research group. It allows you the most latitude. We could be working with the Federal Aviation Administration—maybe an organization that tries to close files on lost aircraft for families of missing persons. *Lost Wings,* maybe. We could have been contacted by the family of Robert McCanaly, the actual pilot of the Beech, trying to get closure over what happened to their father thirty years ago, and we could be working in conjunction with the National Transportation Safety Board. I'm sure I can get my friend with the FAA to give us a letter of recommendation."

"You've got this figured out already, don't you?" Kansas muttered with a cautious smile. "We would need some sort of bona fide history—information someone could look up that shows our existence for some time." Kansas paused for a moment, thinking of Cass, the computer guru. "However, there might be a way to embed enough information in the right places to get us by." He paused again and his eyes clouded with distress. "But Crazy Eddie!"

"He may be a little fried, but you know as well as I do, man, he can fly that damned airplane. That gig we did into Bolivia with him proved that. Look, he's pretty much under the radar, got no record to speak of, and we just need him to get us in, move us around, and get us out quickly." Will paused and smiled. "'You must trust and believe in people and dreams, or life becomes impossible.' Anton Chekhov."

"Yeah," his friend spat back sarcastically. "And, 'Don't let people drive you crazy when you know it's within walking distance.' Jackie Peterson."

"Who's that?"

"My plumber."

"Really?"

"Really." Kansas straightened himself up and tilted his head, fixing his friend with a quizzical, somewhat skeptical gaze. "So, give me a ballpark figure at what this might cost us—the paperwork, bribes, transportation, equipment."

"I'm guessing somewhere between ten and fifteen grand—maybe a little more."

Kansas inhaled deeply, holding his breath, looking out the open window at the huge, white-gold moon hanging in the heavens above them, and wondering how many pacts like this it had witnessed—how many dreams it had been privy to. Pipe dreams.... He exhaled slowly with a degree of finality. "Listen, I'll think about it. That's all I can tell you right now."

Will nodded noncommittally, knowing that you never try to force a big fish to the boat. You keep the drag firm, but relaxed enough to give the fish its head until it decides not to struggle anymore.

"I'm good with that," he said as he opened the door of the truck and got out. "I'll talk to you in a few days. Take good care, *amigo.*"

As Will watched the truck drive off, wheels crunching on the coral gravel for purchase, the corner of his mouth tilted into a small smile. He turned, quite pleased with himself, and gazed up at that ancient, understanding moon above him. "We're goin' treasure hunting," he muttered with a chuckle. "Oh yeah. We're goin' treasure hunting."

CHAPTER 2

Truth, like gold, is to be obtained not by its growth, but by washing away from it all that is not gold.

— *Leo Tolstoy*

That week Kansas had a couple of bonefish charters scheduled, and as flagging as his guide business was, he couldn't afford not to give them priority. One was a buddy from Dallas, with whom he had shared the passion of fishing. The second was a couple of former associates of his father's. Much of his business came from the circle of friends and acquaintances his parents had established—businesspeople who had shared his family's love of the outdoors and the ocean. It was the better part of a week before he got back to Will. During that time he considered the highs and the lows of the gamble that had been presented to him.

First off, he was more legitimate-natured than Will, and he was somewhat uncomfortable with the idea of entering Cuba under false pretenses and attempting to steal a fortune in gold. Then there was, of course, the chance of being caught in the process. Spending five or ten years in a Cuban prison was way down on the list of things he wanted to do in this lifetime. He spooled back to the charters this week for a moment. One had gone fairly well and they had boated two fish worthy of the trip the second day, but the other had been a bust. After two relentlessly sweltering days of poling the flats and staring at the blinding, glistening mirror of the backcountry, they had barely seen a fish worthy of conversation, and his parents' friends had gone home disappointed. He doubted he would get them back again. It wasn't that he was poor—he and Will had done some successful things that left him comfortable, for the moment. But there was a future to consider, and he knew how easy it was to go through money in The Keys. Still, the thought of Cuban jails…

Will was sprawled out in a lawn chair on the deck of his boat, beer in one hand and a Carl Hiaasen novel in the other, enjoying the early morning sun, when his phone rang. He struggled to put down the beer and the novel and find the phone in the pile of clothes underneath him, failing miserably. The chair turned over, the beer spilled, and he ended up sprawled out on the deck. After several brief but poignant expletives, he finally grabbed the thing and sat up, one jigger short of pissed, but a greeting from Kansas quickly assuaged his anger. "Hey, buddy. What's up?" he said casually, still keeping the drag fairly loose.

"Sorry I haven't gotten back to you before now, but I've been busy," Kansas explained.

There was a lack of enthusiasm in his voice that worried Will.

"I've been giving this Cuban thing a lot of thought and I gotta tell you that there's a large part of me that's just not comfortable with it. I mean, this is a long shot at best, and the chances of ending up in deep shit with the Cuban government are very real."

Will felt a huge wave of disappointment roll over him and another poignant expletive made it to his lips but didn't escape.

Kansas let out a long sigh and continued almost angrily. "But damn it all, I don't think I'm gonna make a living at this freaking 'famous Florida Keys backwaters guide' shit, either. This ain't a cheap place to live, and the way things are going, sooner or later I'm likely to end up standing in front of someone asking them if they want ketchup and pickles with that."

Will exhaled the breath he was holding and relaxed. He tightened the drag just a little. "Yeah, tough place to make a living, I gotta admit. I've seen 'em come and go here, when the dream faded and reality set in."

"But it's just that I don't want to become another one of the *scammers* down here," Kansas continued, as if he hadn't heard Will, locked into his own train of thought. "This place is nothing but dreamers and hustlers and a few folks in between trying to hold on to the vision they found here years ago. I just don't want to end up disenfranchised and disillusioned. I don't want to wake up one morning and look in the mirror and see a dreamer or a hustler staring back at me."

"Taking a chance on something that could change your life for the better doesn't make you a hustler," Will said softly. "This is a one-shot, one-time thing. Once this is over you can tie your flies and choose your clients for the rest of your life. No more pressure." In his head Will suddenly saw the image of a huge bull dolphin close to the gunwale of a boat, feathered trolling lure locked securely in the corner of its hard jaw. He could see the fish slowly rolling onto its side, floating to the surface, iridescent yellow-green and deep blue flanks reflecting the bright sunlight as the waters in the current of the Gulfstream held him—finally worn out, surrendering, but with pride.

There was a silence at the other end of the line for a few moments, then Kansas exhaled again with a reluctant acceptance. "Okay, buddy, I guess I'm in. Let's set this up. We're going to do a treasure hunt."

"Yep," Will replied with a satisfied grin. "We're goin' treasure hunting."

The following week Kansas and Will began to work out some of the details for the caper and lay the groundwork for the cover they would need in order to get into Cuba. But the first order of business was to find Crazy Eddie and his Goose.

The porcine, gray and yellow, twin-engine behemoth sat like a wounded, forlorn pelican on the hard coral flats behind Jake Frasier's house on the backside of Ramrod Key. It canted to the port side, that wing hanging down and nearly touching the adjacent mangroves, its large, boat-like hull blocked up on the starboard side, the landing gear assembly on that side removed and lying on a greasy tarp. The other wing jutted up like a finger, pointing wistfully at the pale blue horizon where it ought to be, rather than dissected, trapped, and at the mercy of the mangrove swamp surrounding it, in a place that looked like a graveyard for airplanes.

Frasier sold airplane parts. Thirty years ago he managed to clear enough of the mangroves to bring in some fill and built a respectable house and a storage area, quickly turning the grounds into an aviation junkyard. Frasier had cut a deal with Crazy Eddie, renting him the back bedroom/bathroom of his house and letting him keep his plane on the property, which had easy access to the water. But true to his eccentric nature, Eddie spent most of his time in his plane when he wasn't out and about.

Will and Kansas had gotten out of their car and had begun to weave their way cautiously through the debris of shattered fuselages, abandoned wings, and engines that would never grace an aircraft again, working back toward the old Grumman Goose, when they caught the rich, sweet smell of contraband floating over the tangy scent of surrounding mangroves and the prevailing odor of old engine oil. The cargo door on the crippled airplane opened and out stumbled Edward Jackson Moorehouse—Crazy Eddie to his friends. With the nearly perpetual doobie in hand and black pirate patch over his left eye, he turned and saw the visitors. His face lit up with a huge smile as he exhaled a bluish cloud and ambled toward them. "Will, my man! Kansas! Cool runnings to you, my brothas! What's happening, dudes?"

Now, Eddie wasn't Jamaican and he wasn't black; he just thought he was. He had spent a lot of time in Jamaica back in the old days—the cowboys and Indians days. All the pot and God knows what else he smoked, snorted, gulped or tabbed had somehow burned out a lot of synapses, leaving him with a fleeting stratum of gray matter that identified with the people in the islands and the life and times of the seventies. But almost everybody liked Crazy Eddie, because he did crazy things, and he always had good dope.

He had been a major element in one of Kansas and Will's most remarkable adventures a couple of years back, when they had journeyed to Bolivia in search of an ancient relic—a golden scepter with remarkable powers. In the process, a friendship had been cemented, but that didn't discount the truth in Kansas's words about Eddie being bona fide eccentric bordering on loony at times.

He was in his late thirties, early forties. Tall and lanky, dressed in a perpetual pair of Hang Ten shorts and a weathered Ron Jon's T-Shirt, he had the look and the casual movement of a teenager. There was a total lack of ego about him that was engaging, and strangely charming, but he was nobody's fool. The top of his head was starting to be crowned with a tanned, circular balding spot, and his sun-bleached blond hair cascaded down to his shoulders. The eyepatch was the result of too much tequila, a feathered lure, and a careless cast during the frenzy of a mackerel run just inside the reef. But his single blue eye carried a sufficiently roguish gleam to make up for the loss of the other, and he had a thin, slightly crooked nose that looked as if it might have been the product of a long-past "complication" with someone. The lines at the corners of his eyes and his mouth furrowed like dry gullies into the landscape of his face, telling of the good times and the hard times shared along the journey. Like his bald spot, the rest of him was browned by the sun in a soft, leathery fashion, creased in places like a favorite old jacket.

Rumor was, the Grumman Goose was a partial payment for a pot trip he'd made years ago. He'd lost, spent, or given away most of the money he made in the seventies heydays in South Florida, but somehow he had held on to the plane.

"Peace on you, brothers. Welcome to my humble abode." He immediately offered Will and Kansas the joint. "Attitude adjustment?"

Both the men passed, thanking him all the same. "A little early yet," Kansas said with a smile.

Eddie went back into the plane and came out with a blender of rum punch he had just prepared for breakfast, along with some paper cups. They grabbed lawn chairs and set up under the wing of the Goose. After they caught up a little, Crazy Eddie stretched and yawned, then his one eye, which had seemed a tad distant, focused cleanly and he leaned forward. "So, tell me dudes, what brings you to me? I know it ain't for my rum punches and you don't dig my herb. So, let's be cool, brothas. Talk to me."

Will grinned. "You're right, man. It ain't the rum or the smoke. We've got a gig we're working on, and we need a pilot and a seaplane. Kind of like the trip we did in Bolivia."

Eddie smiled at the memory. "That was a very psychedelic gig, dudes. Very psychedelic. What you got in mind? Talk to Eddie."

"We're going into Cuba—looking for a lost aircraft," Will began. "It crashed about thirty years ago somewhere in the Sierra Maestra mountain range. We have a handle on the location and I think we can find it. Kansas and I need someone to take us in and fly us around the area, to see if we can find a landmark or two. Then we'll go in and find the plane. After that we may need someone like you to get us out of the area plenty quick, probably no customs clearance on the way out."

Eddie reached into his breast pocket, pulled out another joint and lit it, taking a hit and casually exhaling upwards toward the wing above them. He looked at Kansas, and then Will, his mouth scrunching up like he was sucking a lemon drop. "What's in the plane, bros?"

"If we tell you that, we have to kill you," Will said, deadpan.

Eddie was in the midst of another draw. He choked, then coughed, slapping himself on the chest. "Dude, you're harshin' my mellow here," he croaked.

Kansas chuckled, patting him on the shoulder as Eddie caught his breath. "Listen, it's some valuable stuff, but it's not drugs, and we're not greedy. If we're successful, we'll give you seventy-five thousand U.S. for getting us in, being our chauffeur for a few days, and getting us out when we say go, no questions asked. All expenses covered."

Eddie looked at both of them again, pointing his doobie at the duo, his blue eye becoming animated. "You cats ain't jivin' me now, huh? You not workin' with the man somewhere, wantin' to pop Mr. Brotha Eddie for crimes of past passions? Because that would be seriously bogus, dudes."

Suddenly, Eddie's face lost its casualness, rapidly growing fixated, almost wrathful. He rose quickly, drew up his T-shirt with one hand and pulled a small revolver from his shorts with the other, eyes riveted between his two guests. "Don't move. Don't move a muscle!"

The two men were taken completely by surprise. Kansas threw up his hands, palms out. "Listen, it was just an offer, we're not Feds—"

But he was too late. The gun came up, and with a wild look in his eye Eddie fired three times in rapid succession. Both Kansas and Will dove off their chairs, rolling for cover. But the firing had stopped and Eddie was already bounding between them toward the back of the plane, eye gleaming with wild abandon.

"Rats!" he screeched. "I hate rats—the bloody bane of the freaking Keys! The little runamuckers get into everything, eat the wiring of the plane, chew up the freaking tires!" He reached down and picked up the remains of a large, fat vermin (apparently full of electrical wire coating and tire rubber), and slung it out toward the mangroves. "And tell your friends they'll get the same if they come back!" (Both men found some difficulty in the logic of that rat conveying anything to anyone, but neither felt it was a good time to argue the point.) Eddie was still stomping around, raging about "son of a bitchin', runamuckin' rats" while reloading his gun with shells from his shorts pocket and stalking around the perimeter of the mangroves like a big game hunter after a wounded leopard.

Will looked at Kansas and offered an apologetic shrug, tilting his head slightly, eyebrows up like Groucho Marx's. "That's why they call him Crazy Eddie. Well, it's one of the reasons. He has his…idiosyncrasies, I admit, you know that. But we've seen the things he can do with that plane—"

"Yeah, yeah, I know, like a kamikaze pilot," Kansas interrupted. He shook his head dubiously. "Gotta hope there's no freaking rats in Cuba."

After a few moments Eddie finally came back, apologizing about the interruption, explaining that the little furry bastards were at the top of his shit list. They talked for a while longer about timeframes on the operation and the importance of keeping it between themselves for the time being, and Eddie gave them a quick tour of the plane. The cabin had been "redecorated" since the last time they'd been inside. He had removed all but two of the seats, replacing them with an old, threadbare couch, a small table with two chairs, and a port-a-potty stall he had built at the rear. The walls had seventies paraphernalia and old photos duct-taped or screwed in place here and there, along with peace signs that looked as if they had been spray-painted in the midst of inebriated abandon. It didn't lend Kansas the confidence he would have liked, but Will reminded him there weren't that many legitimate pilots with large floatplanes that would take on a harebrained scheme like this. And there was the kamikaze thing.

The upshot was Eddie agreed to help, but he would need about two weeks to get parts for his landing gear and get it reassembled, which was no problem because it would probably be three or four weeks before all the paperwork for the trip was approved.

The next stop for them was a visit with Kansas's friend, Cass, the attractive martial arts/computer expert. Offering a bit more about their upcoming venture than they had explained to Crazy Eddie, they convinced her to create a corporate identity—

Lost Wings—and via her friends, embed it into an agency or two, create some paperwork—something that gave the organization a history of several years. Kansas had expected some resistance from Cass, but oddly enough she found the whole thing fascinating, attacking the task at hand with enthusiasm.

The following weeks were a whirlwind of meetings with officials from the FAA and the U.S. State Department, to the Office of Foreign Assets Control (OFAC) and the Cuban Ministry of Tourism. It was not an easy thing for Americans to get permission to spend time in Cuba. There were few actual tourism visas issued for Americans, but much of what they needed got fast-tracked because of the connections each of them had. Will contacted his buddy at the Federal Aviation Administration—the one who owed him a serious favor. He was an old college friend who had been caught in an indiscretion—a sexual foray gone way bad—that would have nipped his plans for a government career in the bud. At great risk to himself, Will had gotten the fellow away from the scene minutes before the police arrived. Will explained to his friend that they needed to get into Cuba to try to find a lost aircraft, and that they were part of an organization called Lost Wings, which offered closure to families who had lost loved ones in aircraft accidents. He said nothing about the gold, but the man was no fool. He knew his friend well enough to suspect there was probably an ulterior motive, but whatever it was, he didn't want to know about it. The fellow finally agreed to give them a letter of introduction from the FAA on the grounds that their company/organization was bona fide on all four corners, clearly adding that any debt to Will was paid in full.

They also met with a friend of Kansas's in the State Department, an avid fisherman who had been down to The Keys to avail himself of Kansas's services a couple of times. A free fishing trip was arranged, including airfare—along with the papers they needed. The Miami branch of the Cuban Ministry of Tourism was the final hurdle, and it proved to be the most challenging. Mr. José Pinera, with whom they met, found it somewhat incredulous that there would be interest in a plane lost so long ago, and how could they possibly expect to find an aircraft lost for over thirty years when immediate searches after the incident were unsuccessful? Kansas explained that previous searches had concentrated on the waters offshore. They believed, upon reviewing the information available, that the aircraft may have gone down in the mountains on the northeast coast. That seemed to satisfy Mr. Pinera.

Near the end of their preparations, Kansas and Will flew via commercial airlines out of Miami to the Cayman Islands and met discreetly with an official of one of the many banking institutions there. The good news was, inside a month they were ready to go. The bad news was, Mr. Pinera wasn't really as satisfied as they thought.

The old ceiling fans in the office of the Cuban Ministry of the Interior, Security Division, struggled wearily with the humid air, barely moving it enough to relieve the oppressive July heat. From his office, Security Director Miguel Juan Santiago watched a brief summer shower patter the coconut palms and the flat leaves of the huge gumbo-limbo outside in the courtyard below his window. It would hardly help, and simply added to the nearly unbearable humidity of this time of year. The phone rang and he picked it up. His secretary announced a call from the embassy in Miami—an employee of the Ministry of Tourism, working in conjunction with the Cuban Interest Section in Washington, D.C., felt he should pass on a piece of information regarding an organization that had recently requested visas. The group seemed legitimate enough, but for some reason he felt that the premise of their search and their interest in Cuba seemed somewhat of a stretch. It was probably nothing, but he was faxing the names of the individuals and their organization to Santiago's office as they spoke.

The following morning Miguel Juan Santiago picked up the telephone and dialed the main office of Cuba's National Revolutionary Police Force, the PNR, asking to speak with the director, Roberto Morales. He lit a small, thin cigar and waited, his dark eyes wandering to the trees in the courtyard for a moment.

"Hello, Roberto." Pause. "Yes, yes, I'm good, thank you, and you? The family? Good. Listen, I have some information for you. It may be nothing, but I want you to pay attention to some individuals who are coming into the country next week. The research regarding their organization checks out, but our investigation into the individuals themselves makes me less than comfortable. One is a fishing guide and the other is a part-time treasure hunter. Both of them have somewhat nefarious histories, and now they are locating lost airplanes and their occupants to assuage the grief of relatives and significant others. There's no military background on either—we've checked—but it's a wide swing in the pendulum of human nature. We are issuing them the visas they require, but I want you to put someone on them—to watch while they are visiting with us." He paused, listening, taking a deep drag of his cigarillo, and exhaling a blue cloud at the ceiling, watching the blades of the old fan draw the smoke in and twist it into pale, gray ribbons. "Yes, yes, I agree with you. Martinez would be a good choice. If anyone can get us what we need to know, that one can. Keep me posted."

The week before leaving, Crazy Eddie got the parts for his plane and installed them while Kansas and Will gathered equipment and supplies and stored them onboard, pulling out some of Eddie's home furnishings and reinstalling a couple more seats. They might stay in the plane some of the time while in Cuba, so they added cots and sleeping bags, a new Coleman stove to replace Eddie's old one, and foodstuffs, as well. In addition, they included two lightweight dirt bikes. The friend of Will's father told him the cave where he had been hidden was about a mile around the mountain from an old bauxite mining site, and there had been just enough of a path to the cave to maybe accommodate a dirt bike. He remembered only an animal trail from there to the cave with the plane.

Finally, with paperwork complete, the Goose loaded, and a flight case full of aviation and topographical maps stowed, they departed on a cool Saturday morning. Eddie eased the big plane into the water, straightened her out in the channel and pushed the throttles forward, a grin on his face and a psychedelic gleam in his eye, "California Dreaming" by the Mamas & the Papas thumping the oversized speakers on the interior of the aircraft. The belly of the great bird slapped across the blue-green waters of Niles Channel, the huge, air-cooled, nine cylinder Pratt & Whitney engines from atop each wing whining like greyhounds at the gate. The rising sun came up under the starboard wing, easing through a mantel of soft gray clouds on the horizon, turning their edges into a brilliant coral and kindling the somber early morning sky with pastels of pale blues and greens as the plane broke its bonds with Earth and soared into the sky. Eddie took it up to five thousand feet, switched off the music speakers for a moment, contacted Miami Radio and confirmed his flight plan, notified Key West of a flyover and a final destination, then eased back into his seat with a satisfied smile and snapped the speakers back on. He was on an adventure again—and not a rat to be seen. *Cool runnings, mon.*

It seemed they had barely gotten comfortable in their seats, lulled by the comforting, steady drone of the big engines, when the island of Cuba materialized out of the soft haze in the distance and the José Martí Airport tower began supplying instructions for altitude and vectors that would bring them in. Eddie handled the entire affair with the aplomb of a professional, and approach and landing were uneventful. After touchdown, Eddie was directed by the tower to proceed to the end of the airport where there were a number of noncommercial aircraft. The props had no sooner stopped turning when two armed, taciturn customs officers appeared. There was a brief inspection of the aircraft and a perfunctory search of the inside, then they escorted the trio to the terminal, where their bags and passports were checked. From there they were presented to a representative who claimed to be with the Ministry of Tourism, but appeared more likely to work for the Ministry of the Interior or the PNR. He reminded them that the permission that had been granted them was tenuous, and was predicated on their reporting every twenty-four hours to him with their location and the results of their investigation; most importantly, they were to file a detailed flight plan every time that aircraft lifted off the ground in Cuba. If they were to find the aircraft of their search, they were to contact him before proceeding with any operations of any sort. With that, they were free to go. They caught a taxi in front of the airport—a vintage 1958 Ford Fairlane which, failing in luxury and fanfare, succeeded in stalwart reliability and took them to Hotel Mercure Sevilla at the edge of Havana's Old Town, where they had reserved a large, three-room suite.

The plan was to spend the night in Havana, then fly southeast across the island to the town of Manzanillo on the Gulf of Guacanayabo at the edge of the Sierra Maestra mountains, where they had been told there would be room to land and keep the seaplane.

That evening, after spending part of the day contacting the list of officials they were required to notify upon arrival, the trio grabbed showers and a change of clothes, then set out for dinner at a restaurant recommended by the concierge at the front desk. They took their time walking to the restaurant, enjoying the majestic but weathered architecture of Old Havana and the bizarre "back to the fifties" contrasts in terms of automobiles on the street. As they walked and talked, taking in the rhythmic murmur of Latin music from window and door, alive with sensual tempos, enjoying the fragrant scent of bougainvillea and lime, and the rich smells of evening meals being prepared, the trio failed to notice a nondescript older man in a white, short-sleeved shirt and gray slacks strolling casually along behind them, keeping a discreet distance. When they entered the restaurant, the fellow located a phone booth and placed a call, then found a seat on a bench nearby and lit a cigarette, inhaling with enjoyment and leaning back to exhale into the sky. He pulled a magazine from his coat pocket and began to read.

The restaurant was a collage of small tables with red-and-white-checkered tablecloths, soft candles, and Impressionist art. There was a small, half-moon bar in the corner offering a reasonable variety of liquor and an indifferent bartender. An old radio next to the cash register painted the room with a soft Latin melody, and the air carried the warm fragrance of fresh flowers and native cuisine.

After a dinner of the Cuban classics Ropa Vieja and Picadillo—which, to the knowledgeable tongue of Will, was good but not extraordinary—they retired to a table near the bar to discuss some of the details for the following day. They had just received their drinks and were getting comfortable when the waiter seated a woman at a small table to the left of them. She ordered a drink and sipped on it periodically while the Americans talked. The lady was attractive, perhaps five-seven, long sable hair, large hazel eyes, and a nice figure. She was dressed comfortably in a modest skirt and a silky white blouse, which fit well enough to define her more exceptional attributes. The men couldn't help but notice that she seemed impatient, checking her watch and tapping the crystal occasionally, eventually drumming her fingers on the table, telling the waiter she was expecting someone when he checked on her. She exchanged glances and a polite smile or two with the fellows in the process.

By the time Kansas and his friends had finished their second round of drinks, that someone still hadn't shown. The woman tried the phone at the bar to no avail, then, obviously flustered, reached into her purse for a cigarette, but was having trouble finding a light. Will, ever the gallant one, excused himself and went over and offered a light, which she accepted gratefully. "Is there anything else I can do?" he offered tentatively in Spanish.

Recognizing his inference, the lady smiled, slightly embarrassed. "I guess I have been standed up," she replied in fairly good English. "It was a meeting with my boss, and he is somewhat absentminded."

Will chuckled. A little taken by this attractive but unassuming young lady, he asked impulsively, "Would you care to join us? No point in drinking alone."

She hesitated. "Oh, I could not, thank you."

"We're harmless, I assure you. And besides, we're not from the area, obviously, and we could use some advice."

Again she hesitated, tilting her head and rolling her shoulders slightly with indecision and nervousness. "I...I don't..."

"Aaahh, c'mon, where's this wonderful Cuban hospitality I've been hearing about?"

With a sigh, she finally acquiesced, and a moment later she was seated with the men at their table, introductions made and a fresh rum and soda before her.

Mariana Fueres proved to be excellent company, providing a wealth of information on Cuba and its inner workings. She was employed as an accountant for the Ministry of Agriculture, was single, and lived in Havana with her mother and a mutually attached cat named Fernando. She had large, communicative eyes, an infectious smile and a soft yet resonating voice that, in typical Cuban fashion, trilled the letter R in American words, as well. Kansas found himself thinking that conversation from those wide, sumptuous lips and that voice of hers, which carried such an eloquent cadence and turned commonplace phrases into melody, was just about as close to sexy as sexy got, yet she seemed totally unaware of her sensuality, which was incredibly refreshing. Apparently, the same could have been said for Will, who competed avidly with Kansas for the lady's attention. It was her soft, dark hazel eyes that caught his attention. They were alight with expression, delivering volleys of emotion in conversation. Eddie was no less taken by her, but sagely recognized this was a contest in which he could not even place, let alone win; so he sat back, sipping his rum punch, adding to the conversation occasionally and simply enjoying this cool new adventure.

Mariana was fascinated by what they did (or what they claimed they did), saying she had an uncle who was lost at sea and she knew how those people who had lost loved ones felt. When they told her they were headed for Manzanillo the next day, she lit up.

"How amazing! I will be in Manzanillo all next week, collecting data from the area farms for our yearly report on gross production. Perhaps we could get together again." She paused, then lowered her voice and spoke somewhat conspiratorially. "I have to admit that I am fascinated by America." She held up a hand. "I know that I am not supposed to be, especially working in the government and having a good job as I do, but it is like the land of El Dorado, so close and yet so out of reach. I would love to hear more about living there." A sigh escaped her. "Understand, I accept what I have with grace and thanks, and I am loyal to my country, but still..."

Kansas glanced at Will and that intuitive communication thing they had passed between them like a spark. Here was the ace they needed to give them an inside track, a local perception of the area and the country.

"We'd love to get together with you again," Kansas offered. "We'll be staying in that area at least for the next few days."

"I know it well," she replied, reaching into her purse and producing a card. "Here is my office phone number. Call me when you are settled into Manzanillo, and perhaps I can show you the area, if you have time."

As they all walked out of the restaurant into the early night, saying their goodbyes and departing in different directions, the man on the bench across the street lit another cigarette, strolled over to a phone booth, and placed another call.

Walking along the quiet street, Will said to no one in particular, "I caught a nice feeling from her. We hit it off really well."

Kansas turned with an incredulous look. "You didn't hit anything off. If anything, she just felt sorry for you, with that drooling, puppy dog look. Hell, you knocked her glass over trying to light her second cigarette—about as suave as Woody Allen on Xanax. Now, if there was a connection, it was between her and me."

"*Amigo,* you wouldn't know a connection if it crawled up your freaking leg and bit you on your ass." Will's hands flew up into the air, painting emotion. "This is a Cuban woman. She needs a man of passion, like me."

With a weary sigh, Kansas replied, "You need to remember the immortal words of Bill Grieser: 'If you love something, let it go. If it comes back, great. If it doesn't, it's probably having dinner with someone more attractive than you.'"

Eddie shook his head, bemused. "You two dudes sound like teenagers on Spring Break. Don't be harshin' my mellow over hypotheticals or I'll drop a tab of acid in both your drinks next time you meet that foxy little mama. Then you'll really have some bad impressions to compare. You dig?"

Kansas looked at Will, uneasy. "He wouldn't..."

Will shrugged. "Hey, let me remind you, this is a guy who has *crazy* in front of his first name."

"Man, you don't really have acid with you, do you?" said Kansas, head cocked slightly.

Eddie grinned evilly, that trademark psychedelic gleam in his eye. "Bro, you should always have a vacation in your pocket, even when you're on vacation. Can you dig it?" His eyebrows danced up and down a couple of times with the jibe. "Got to mellow sometimes, man. Got to feed your head."

The following morning the adventurers were in the air and

crossing Cuba by 10:00 a.m. under the watchful guidance of Havana Air Control. The four-hundred-mile journey took about two and a half hours as they traversed the spine of the island, basically flying east, following the nation's main highway from Havana to Camaguey, then turning southeast toward Manzanillo, one of Cuba's primary industrial ports for sugar. They found an inlet facing the town, away from the port, with enough beach to bring the plane out and up onto shore. The port was a fairly large, busy complex with fishing boats and small freighters, and what appeared to be a few pleasure boats docked on the most distant side nearer to the city itself. There were also a couple of Cuban gunboats docked on their side of the port near the point that formed the little bay where they beached. The air was filled with the cries of seabirds, the tangy smells of the bay, and the perennial odor of drying nets and diesel fuel. A curious, probably industrious taxi driver was waiting for them by the time they had the plane tied down. By prearranged agreement, Eddie was to stay with his Goose. It would be too risky to leave it alone at any time. Will and Kansas set off with the taxi driver to meet with local authorities and explain their purpose, as was required by their visas. Eddie pulled out a lawn chair and began a vigil for "freaking Cuban rats."

Before the end of the day Will and Kansas had succeeded in calming down the local authorities regarding the seaplane, securing permission to dock it there for the next few days, and satisfying their visa requirements by contacting Havana and letting them know of their location.

They knew the task before them, even with permission from the authorities, was daunting. In their research, Kansas and his friends had learned that the calcareous, cave-ridden Sierra Maestra mountain range, rising up to six thousand six hundred fifty feet at its highest point, was the result of the collision of ancient tectonic plates, violent earthquakes, and volcanic activity, long before man was even a gleam in God's eye. Some of the more accessible cave systems had become tourist attractions, but much of the range, still distant—and in some cases, nearly inaccessible—remained as it was when the first Europeans laid eyes on those distant peaks from the decks of their galleons.

The friend of Will's father remembered going through the

town of Manzanillo on his journey in the truck that took him to the cave hideout. He was certain the cave with the plane was only a half hour northeast of that. Nonetheless, they had nearly a hundred miles of mountain range to explore. It would have been an impossible task without the knowledge of the great granite-like cliff with the Mayan nose protruding from it, which the man said was only about five hundred yards from the plane. *If they could just find that cliff...*

Early the next morning they were in the air, aeronautical and topographical charts in hand, and mildly giddy with the thrill and anticipation of the hunt. They had set up ten-mile grids, east to west across the mountains, using their GPS to establish and maintain the gridding. They flew for five long hours, staring continuously at the green and brown panorama of tree-covered hills and valleys, including some areas that had been cleared for lumber or agriculture. Lazy streams cut ribbons through the verdant landscape. Peaks rose majestically, surrounded by lesser mountains that had been the victims of the inexorable march of time, weathered by ancient storms and ravaged by earthquakes. Hour after hour they gazed at the impressive but unyielding scenery and finally, toward afternoon, disappointed but not defeated, Eddie turned the great bird toward the airport at the city of Bayamo to refuel, then return to base.

Kansas called Mariana that afternoon and discovered she was staying at a local hotel in Manzanillo. He made arrangements for him and Will to meet her for drinks the following evening, speaking in a general fashion about the day's events. Unbeknownst to them, their taxi driver watched from a hilltop in the distance, near the city, smoking a cigarette in contemplative silence.

The following day, Director Roberto Morales of Cuba's National Revolutionary Police Force received a brief phone call. He nodded, listening. "Very good, Martinez, no news in this case may well be good news, but continue to keep an eye on them all the same. Keep us apprised."

That morning Will and his team were in the air by nine again, but an hour into the flight the equation suddenly changed. It happened effortlessly, as if the gods had lined up the cards for them. They had been searching for only a short time when, off to starboard as Eddie banked into a turn on the grid, stood the cliff—the Mayan nose so prominent in the center of it that it made them wonder if at some point, centuries ago, it might not have been man-made. Amongst cheers, Eddie made a couple more passes over it and locked down longitude and latitude readings. Then they made several forays just east of the cliff, trying to find any semblance of a cave in the heavy foliage, but there was nothing to be seen from the air. With a bearing to go from, they worked the area slowly and found the old bauxite mine, and the narrow, winding road that led from it toward the main road and the coast. Will plotted a course on a land map, managing to tie the old road to a newer one that worked its way back to Manzanillo. Now the hunt was on.

That afternoon they went into town and rented an old Ford pickup for a week, taking it back to their campsite and loading some of the equipment they would need into it. They had made arrangements for drinks with Mariana the night before, and didn't want to cancel, fearing it might seem suspicious, but primarily because they both wanted to see her again. Eddie would stay with the plane, left to the solace of one of the small doobies he had smuggled in. Their attentive taxi driver had shown up almost psychically on their return to the plane, and after they had cleaned up and put on fresh blue jeans, along with a tropical shirt for Will and Kansas's standard polo, he took the two men into the city that evening. After dropping them off at the prearranged location, he drove only a block away to where he could still see the bar, parked, found a phone booth and placed a call. Afterwards he got back in his vehicle, lit a cigarette, leaned back and blew the smoke upwards in a satisfied fashion. He took his magazine out of his pocket and began to read again.

Seeing her once more, attired in a simple, low-cut, summer floral dress, sitting at the bar as he and Will came in, Kansas realized that she was indeed a startlingly attractive woman. He heard her speaking with the bartender and was reminded of the husky, almost sensuous melody in her voice.

As before, she plied them with questions about America, about the cities and the countryside, about theater and movies, enthralled by the freedom Americans took for granted, yet supportive of her society, where law and order reigned and few people feared walking their streets late at night, and championing the quality of their socialized medicine. Mariana was interested in their progress in finding the plane, but they had decided to say nothing about their find. She seemed genuinely disappointed to hear of their lack of success.

Will and Kansas, in turn, asked Mariana more questions about herself and her country; mostly, it seemed, to witness the pleasure of her animation and listen to the sound of her voice. Unfortunately, Mariana, quite apologetic, cut the evening short, saying that her mother wasn't feeling well and she had to return home early. But she made up for it with a warm and somewhat lingering goodbye hug for each of them, wishing them well on their quest and hoping to see them again, and pleading with them not to leave without at least saying goodbye to her.

The taxi driver was waiting for the two Americans when they came out of the restaurant, and with courtesy and good spirits took them back to their plane. On his way back into Manzanillo, the fellow lit another cigarette and found a phone booth...

The men spent the remainder of the evening preparing gear and loading the truck with the rest of the equipment after dark, covering it all with a tarpaulin. Before dawn the next day Kansas and Will were underway. Once again, Eddie stayed with the plane, having been advised to have everything ready for takeoff.

The taxi driver watched it all from the top of the hill.

Shortly after that, Director Roberto Morales got a phone call. He listened for a moment. "Okay, what we don't know, we don't know. But keep a vigil on this, in case your suspicions are correct."

It took two hours to reach the bauxite mine. They parked the truck there and quickly found the path that led east toward the first cave. It wasn't much more than an animal trail, probably accommodating Cuba's heavy population of East Indian mongooses, and the large, rodent-like hutias, but at least it was clearly defined. Staying with the path, just as Will's dad had told him, they had been hiking for about fifteen minutes, beginning to question the trail, when they came to the jagged limestone outcropping that marked the entrance to the cave his father had hidden in so many years ago. It was evidently part of an expansive underground system and the ragged, calcareous walls led back into darkness that furrowed into the bowels of the mountain. But this was not their destination. Now they could see the huge granite cliff to the east of them, with the Mayan nose protruding from it. They were on course.

At the mouth of the cave, Will paused. "My father told me his buddy said he picked up a path that led upwards and to the east of the cave he had hidden in. It ran along the base of a limestone rift about ten feet high, for about a hundred yards. He remembered that, as he continued along the game trail in the heavy growth that clung to the mountain, he saw a boulder the size of a Volkswagen Bug to his left, no more than five minutes from the cave with the plane." He paused for a second, thinking, then he snapped his fingers triumphantly in recall. "And there was a final ledge of limestone, maybe a hundred feet long, that bled back into the jungle just before the mouth of the cave! Let's go."

The tropical sun had neared its zenith and an almost cloudless sky gave it license to punish the earth at will. Sweat had already begun to stain their khaki shirts and the bands of their narrow-brimmed, floppy U.S. Army jungle hats. The brush along the mountainside thickened in places and they had to use their machetes, but for the most part they simply tried to stay with the small animal trail and watched for landmarks. They soon found the limestone rift, and from there they found themselves back in the jungle. For a while it seemed they had lost the trail, and the two had to backtrack to a subtle twist in the path they had missed. Ten minutes later the men came to the huge boulder on their left.

Will looked at Kansas with a broad grin. "We're on course, partner."

Kansas paused to take off his hat and wipe the sweat from his face, smiling back. "Sure looks like it."

Unfortunately, during the next part of the climb they lost the trail again for a few minutes, backtracking once more through the brush and climbing higher to pick it up again. Less than five minutes later they came to the final limestone ridge and followed it slowly now, the intensity and the excitement building in each of them. They were close. But when the ledge petered out there was no cave. They moved a hundred yards east of the spot, then backtracked a ways, in case they had missed it, but still no cave. Finally, the two sat for a moment, catching their breath, listening to the strident calls of birds and the buzzing of insects in the jungle around them.

Will sat deep in thought, struggling with their predicament. Finally, he looked up. "When Dad's friend told me the story of finding the cave, he said he heard voices below him and got spooked, so he headed up and back toward his hideout." He snapped his fingers again. "He headed up! The cave is below us!"

Kansas, who sat to Will's left about ten feet down the incline from him, offered a strange smile and said, "I know," as he pointed into the jungle below them.

Not twenty yards down the hill, the dull sheen of old, weathered aluminum could just barely be seen amid the tangle of vines and brush. Below a rounded edge were four numbers, still faintly visible after more than half a century—1288.

With the sweet flow of anticipation coursing in their veins, they shuffled sideways downward to the mouth of the ancient cave, moving slowly, torn by the conflicting emotions of great discovery and the looming possibility of failure. *Had someone been there ahead of them? Would the gold still be there?* The brush and vines were so thick it took a few minutes with machetes to make their way to the mouth of the cave. The rudder they saw was still well disguised; it would have been nearly impossible to view from the sky.

The cave was equally well disguised, its entrance probably thirty feet across and half that high. As they moved closer they could see, through the jungle growth, the old Beech, still tightly entombed, askew, and almost against the walls. It was a phenomenal happening—truly a one-in-a-million shot. But it had happened.

Kansas looked at his partner, the gleam of excitement burning in his eyes. "Let's find out," was all he said.

They slipped off their backpacks and began to slide into the cavern, backs against the walls, working around sections of the shattered wings toward the fuselage as bevies of bats hanging from the dark roof twittered and fussed angrily at the intrusion.

The aircraft was covered with dust and dirt and growth of all sorts. Vines weaved their way in and out of the crumpled silver fuselage and splintered wings, but there was less growth as they moved into the cave due to lack of sunlight. The men turned on their flashlights and slithered inward to a fracture in the side of the aircraft about four feet high and eighteen inches wide, behind the wing—just wide enough to get the long-awaited look inside. Will went first, kneeling down and sticking his head inside. There was an eternal moment of silence.

"C'mon man, don't be keeping me in suspense out here," Kansas hissed.

"Just a second, just a second, man. It's a freaking mess in here," Will replied as he pulled about half his body farther inside the opening and stretched. A moment later Kansas heard him sigh loudly—contented or disappointed he couldn't tell. "Help pull me out," Will said from inside the airplane. "Help me out."

Kansas grabbed his friend by the belt and eased him back. "Now c'mon man, what's the deal? You're starting to harsh my mellow—" but he stopped in mid-sentence as Will turned around, still on his knees, a triumphant grin splitting his face. In each hand he held a three-by-six-inch rectangle of solid gold bullion. Kansas slowly slid down the wall, his knees buckling, a rapturous, jubilant glaze in his eyes. "Son of a bitch. Holy freaking moly," he whispered reverently, reaching over and taking one of the heavy bars from Will.

The afternoon sun had crept down from its zenith to the rim of the cave and its warm rays bathed the gleaming bar in his hand, and in a single moment Kansas Stamps and Will Bell renewed their membership in the eternal fraternity of gold, joining an illustrious alumni that dated back to before the pharaohs of Egypt, moving forward across time, engulfing and consuming kings, queens, explorers, adventurers, bandits, thieves, and the dreams of common men and women since the eternally resilient, captivating metal was first wrenched from the earth with wonder and zeal.

It took an hour to sufficiently widen the gash in the plane to get in and out comfortably. The inside was a shambles—fractured pieces of heavy wooden crates along with gold bars were strewn everywhere, but more so to the forward of the aircraft. The nose and cockpit were decimated, having been driven into the rear wall of the cave and split open like a dropped watermelon. The remains of the two occupants were strewn into the devastation, skeletons barely recognizable, having long since become a feast for the jungle's residents. There was a musky, old smell of rotting vegetation and casualty.

For the next hour and a half the two men sorted through the craft, claiming all the bullion and stacking it at the mouth of the cave. Having planned for this contingency, they had purchased heavy, reinforced hiking backpacks. The plan was to take out just over eighty pounds each—about one hundred sixty-five pounds each trip. The gold would have to be backpacked to the first cave, where the trail was good enough to bring in the dirt bikes that were in the back of the pickup. They'd use the bikes to carry the gold the final distance back to the truck. Although the bullion had been packed in large, heavy boxes, it amazed them how little space five hundred pounds of gold actually took up—less than a cubic yard. The small gold bricks weighed two kilos each—a total of one hundred fourteen at final count. They thought they had it all, but Kansas decided to go back into the aircraft and have one final look while Will took a cigarette break before beginning the process of taking out the gold. Kansas moved forward into the shattered craft, up into what had been the cockpit, checking around the grisly remains of the occupants, when he noticed for the first time that the nose of the plane had not just slammed into the rear wall of the cave, but seemed to have punctured it somehow. Above and to the front of the craft there seemed to be a cleft in the rock and an opening of some sort behind it.

Purely out of curiosity, he shone his flashlight into the hole, expecting nothing, but the light caught a brief glint of brightness. *Had a handful of the gold bars been thrown forward into the fissure from the impetus of the crash?* He made his way over the debris of the cockpit and beamed his flashlight directly into the hole, peering in as he did so. And at that moment his life changed forever.

He stared incredulously, unable to take in what he was seeing and process it exactly. *What in the hell could this be?* He pushed on what now appeared to be only a thin wall of rock protecting the interior, and it gave way, enlarging the orifice even more so. Once again he shone his flashlight into the interior. It was a small, rounded room, maybe twenty feet across. The walls and floor had been cut and polished to a marble-like sheen, and there appeared to be a relief of some sort carved into those walls around the entire room. A dais or altar stood in the center, cut right out of the rock and buffed to the same brilliance, and there were artifacts displayed on top of it—brightly gleaming artifacts.

Kansas exhaled for the first time in nearly a minute, taking a breath and instinctively calling his partner. "Will! Will! Get in here. Now! You gotta see this!"

In moments Will was at his side, staring into the dimly lit interior with disbelief. In reverent silence, with the awe of children, they crawled over the broken stone and into another world.

CHAPTER 3

Truth is the property of no individual, but it is the treasure of all men.

— *Ralph Waldo Emerson*

There was a dry, ancient smell to the room, slightly acrid. The walls were cool to the touch and as smooth as glass, but there was a four-foot-tall, horizontal strip in the center of those walls that bore a remarkably detailed relief. It showed animals, birds, and reptiles intertwined with magnificent man-made structures, and strange vehicles without wheels, and devices the purpose of which the two men couldn't begin to conceive. And there were people, long of limb and leg, and firmly built, with supple yet defined muscles. Their faces bore a nobleness of character, with strong features, and many were endowed with the same kind of Mayan nose that they found on the adjacent cliff. Beautiful men and women in long and short, loosely fitting shifts were depicted at work and at play. There were rivers and fields and strange towering cities. This band of artwork ran around the whole room, but stopped behind the dais where the most magnificent carving of all stood, from floor to ceiling. The two men were drawn toward it, moving slowly with their flashlights, almost reverently, into the center of the room near the dais.

Hewn out of the stone and polished brilliantly, beautifully, in three-dimensional Michelangelo fashion, was a statue pulling itself out of the wall as if it were alive. It was of two women, backs melded into each other as if they were one. It was impossible to tell where one began and the other ceased. The shoulders of the first slumped forward slightly, oppressed and defeated, as if carrying the weight of the world, her face bearing a countenance filled with despondence, and she wore a blindfold loosely bound over her eyes. The other stood proudly, face to the sky, a countenance of pride and peace, with no blindfold, reaching outward and upward with her hands. It was profound and moving. The room also held statues in all four corners, carved from onyx or obsidian and what looked like ivory, of images that may have been gods, standing in wait. Who knew?

The rest of the room was empty except for the dais, which drew their attention next. They looked at each other, finding no words to satisfy the situation, and moved toward it. There, on top of the flat, four-foot-square platform was a cradle made of gold, welded into the rock and shaped in the image of two hands reaching upward. In each of the hands was a device of some sort—about six inches long, two and a half inches wide, and perhaps an inch thick, rounded on all sides, with miniscule vents in the front—resembling more than anything a television remote without all the buttons. It looked as if it might be made of silver, with a small, two-inch-square clear glass facing in the center of it, and strange inscriptions etched into the surface apparently inlaid with gold. Next to the hands and the devices was a stack of ultra thin, flat sheets of what appeared to be gold, each about ten by twelve inches in size, maybe twenty or so in all, and altogether not much thicker than a common notepad. They were bound with rings of silver. The top sheet was engraved with writing neither man could remotely identify.

Will exhaled the breath he'd been holding. "Mucking fagnificent," he whispered incredulously.

Kansas finally found his voice. "Go out and get your camera. We've stumbled onto something here that's way out of our league. We need pictures before we do anything else."

In a few moments Will was back with the camera he had used to document their aircraft find. "What in God's name is all this?" he whispered.

Kansas shook his head. "I can only guess, but I think there's a chance that we've come upon something that the scientific community would give their eyeteeth to have—some sort of connection to some pre-Mayan civilization, maybe farther back. Or maybe it's just an elaborate hoax, I don't know, but I want pictures of everything."

As they stood there, Will began to move forward, drawn to the dais. He snapped a couple pictures of it, then reached down and touched one of the devices tentatively while holding his light on it. He slowly put his fingers around it and lifted it from the cradle. As soon as it cleared the cradle, the air in the room changed. The hair on their arms prickled as if the particles in the air had suddenly been charged, and there was a slight hum for just a moment, deep and elemental, then both stopped.

"Dude, this is some heavy juju, I'm almost certain. But whatever it is, I'm taking it home with me," Will said, stuffing both of the "remote controls" in his pants pockets before starting to shoot pictures of the relief on the walls and the remarkable statue.

After scanning the room once more to make sure there was nothing else in it, Kansas went over to the golden notebook. He turned the top page, then the next, and the next. Closing the pages, he picked up the book. "We're taking this, too. Now c'mon, Will. As amazing as this is, we've got four million dollars' worth of gold outside and a long way to go with it, so one amazing thing at a time."

They spent the next two hours getting the gold and the artifacts to the first cave. Then they returned to the truck, got the dirt bikes, and began making trips back and forth with them. They had brought five heavy duffel bags in which to deposit the gold at the pickup. An hour later they had everything loaded and covered with the tarp. They started back, heady, exhilarated, but nervous to hives about needing to pull off a quick escape from Castro's Communist paradise. Both knew that this was now about more than just money.

As they entered Manzanillo, Kansas spotted a phone booth. He exhaled and looked at Will. "I'm gonna call Mariana and say goodbye."

"Hey, man! Why do you get to do that? It's me she's gonna miss when we're gone. She had them hot Cuban eyes for this *muchacho*. You know that."

Kansas shook his head wearily. "Okay, listen, you can talk to her too, okay?"

Mariana answered on the second ring. *"Hola."*

Kansas looked out at the glistening bay in the distance, soft cumulus clouds rimming the horizon in gentle gray and white pods. "It's me, Kansas."

There was an immediate lift to her voice and a soft sensuality flooded the line. "What a pleasure to hear from you. I was thinking of you and Will today. Have you had any success at this daunting task of yours?"

He didn't know quite how to respond to that. In fact, Kansas didn't quite understand why he had done something as sophomoric as this, given he would never see her again, but perhaps that's why he'd done it. Nonetheless, he still guarded his response. "Well, actually, we've decided to return to the States. It's been an interesting time," he said, with the intimation of a double entendre (or maybe triple).

"Why so suddenly do you leave now?"

"Well, I guess you could say life and fate call and there's little more to do here, but I want you to know that you have been one of the highlights of this trip, and—"

"You were successful with your quest, then?" she said, interrupting him.

He paused. "Well, I guess you could say that, in a fashion."

"Well, then," she said quietly, "I am pleased for you. It has been my pleasure to meet you. If you should return to Cuba, you will call, perhaps?"

At that point, Will's impatience boiled over and he snatched the phone from Kansas. "If he doesn't, I will!"

"Will!" she said with surprise and pleasure. "I am going to miss you, too! And if you come back I will be greatly disappointed if I get no call from you!"

After a couple more exchanges of pleasantries, Will reluctantly hung up and turned to his friend. "Might like to see that little *señorita* again sometime," he said wistfully. Then, straightening up, he growled, "Okay, let's get the hell out of here!"

Fifteen minutes later they pulled up at the plane, driving the truck around to the side of the aircraft that faced the sea where the cargo door was, away from prying eyes. Eddie had to have a quick look, especially when they told him about their most unusual find.

The taxi driver, sitting by a small bar on a hill that crested the bay, squinted at the plane and the waters in the distance, raising a hand to shade the sun from his eyes. The phone in the booth he was parked next to rang. He got out and answered it. There was a brief conversation, then he hung up and placed another call. Five minutes later the Cuban gunboat that was docked on the far side of the port fired up its engines and pulled away from the shore.

National Revolutionary Police Force Director Roberto Morales sat in his office, drumming the fingers of his right hand on the desktop, immersed in consideration. Finally, he stopped, picked up the phone and dialed a number. "You're certain there has been no flight plan filed?" He listened for a moment, then nodded with finality. "Send two cars to that location as well. Now."

The American adventurers had the plane loaded in another ten minutes. Kansas was rushing them along, driven by that sixth sense of his that was becoming more uncomfortable by the minute. They were working on the tie-downs under the wings when Will tapped his partner on the shoulder and pointed out into the bay at the gunboat that had rounded the point and was making a beeline for them. "I don't like that. Something's not right. We need to get out of here, now!"

Kansas nodded emphatically. "Eddie! Fire up the engines!"

They piled into the aircraft and closed the hatch as the starboard engine coughed to life with a rich burst of smoke from the exhaust. Eddie was priming the port engine when they saw two black sedans crest the top of the hill a quarter mile away. Whoever was in the cars assessed the situation and began to quickly wind their way down the twisting road to the bay.

As the captain of the gunboat kept a steady course toward the shore, still a half-mile away, his executive officer hustled up the walkway into the bridge. "You have a call, sir. Urgent."

"I'll take it here," he said, reaching for the phone on the console. "Captain Perez." He paused, listening. "Yes sir. I understand." Pause. "No sir, I have no problem with that." He put the phone in the cradle and turned to the first mate. "Prepare the forward deck guns."

Eddie ripped the big bird around like it was a Piper Cub and sent her plunging into the water as Kansas buckled into the copilot's seat and Will knelt between them, a hand on each seat for balance. They had a headwind coming off the ocean, right at them, thank God. Good lift and a quick takeoff were on their side, but the gunboat was closing fast, hoping to cut them off. The radio crackled.

"This is Captain Enrico Perez of the Cuban Navy Cutter *Heraldo*. We are on your bow. Shut down your engines and prepare to be boarded."

Eddie looked at his friends and muttered, "Shit on that idea! Eddie don't do Cuban jails." He got that psychedelic gleam in his one good eye and pushed the throttles to the walls. "Get ready to run amuck!"

The old Goose surged forward, lifting slightly in the water as momentum caught, but now they had an extra five hundred pounds of gold aboard. It was a guess whether they could get airborne before they ran into the bow of the oncoming cutter. The hull of the plane began to slap the water rhythmically, the gunboat still a thousand yards out. It had become a race—a miserable game of "chicken" that might not have a winner.

Captain Perez's voice again commanded their attention. "Cut your power now or we will fire!"

In the distance, Kansas could suddenly see men scurrying around the deck guns on the big gray cutter. He stared at the craft ahead, squinting through the shimmering haze on the water, then turned to Will. "You don't think they'd really—"

A puff of smoke on the bow of the gunboat emphatically answered his question and a towering explosion thirty yards off the starboard wing cast up a violent plume of water.

"Yeah, I do," hissed Will, clutching the dash with both hands as the plane rocked.

Eddie was staring ahead intensely, glancing at his airspeed, still holding his throttles to the wall. The belly of the plane was easing away from the drag of the water. They were only seconds away from lift-off. Another cannon round struck just to the right front of the aircraft, maybe fifty feet out, throwing up a maelstrom of water and shrapnel. The Goose lurched through the spray, rolling to one side and almost burying a pontoon, their precious momentum falling off a touch. Eddie cursed under his breath, a poignant expletive lost to the roar of the engines and the smacking hull. Still, they needed at least another hundred yards to be airborne. The ship in front of them was growing in size by the second. They could clearly see the forecastle and the gunners on the bow. They were opening up with a fifty-caliber machine gun. Pluming tufts of spray from the heavy weapon kicked up the water in a vicious, almost slow motion line, cutting sizzling furrows into the sea and slapping the airplane to the left of the cabin just as the Goose broke free of the water. They all jerked as the muted snaps of bullets popped through the port wing, not ten feet from them. Another cannon round literally missed the flying boat by a few feet, screaming under the starboard wing and exploding in the water just behind the tail.

The ship loomed up in front of the Goose, bearing down like an enraged, defiant leviathan, the deck machine gun chattering with deadly wrath. There was nothing that could be done—it was do or die now. As the bulk of the ship in front of them rose up and buried the waning sun, Eddie howled like a banshee and drew the controls into his chest. The old Goose strained and lifted clean as if she understood that her very life was at stake, soaring into flight as the clatter of machine guns filled the air, their screaming hot projectiles punching holes in her gray and yellow body with muted snaps, like popcorn exploding in a kettle. The bow of the gunboat passed only a few feet underneath her belly. Eddie cranked a hard right rudder and yanked the yoke to the right, throwing the plane into a hard bank, and the port wing missed the bridge by no more than inches.

"Whoashit!" Will shouted, following that with a poignant explicative about Eddie's dubious parentage.

Crazy Eddie howled again like a lunatic wolf, then leveled the wings and began to climb.

But the one thing that stayed with Kansas in those last seconds as they passed in front of and over the bridge of the ship was the brief but indelible image of his friend, Mariana, standing next to the captain, those huge, dark eyes filled with intensity and zeal.

As the plane soared over the cutter and climbed toward the southwest horizon, the captain snatched up his phone and viciously tapped out a number, putting the phone to his ear. "Give me Base Aérea Camaguey, now!" He waited impatiently for a moment, watching the airplane recede in the distance. Then he straightened. "Yes, this is Captain Enrico Perez with the Cuban Navy, ID number Delta, five, two, nine, nine. I need a MiG scrambled immediately, target is an American aircraft—a Grumman Goose amphibian, call numbers November, two, seven,

seven, zero, heading two, zero, zero, out of Manzanillo Bay. It has evaded interception and refused to yield. Force them around and make them return, or shoot them down. Do you understand?"

Everyone covers their asses in the military, no matter whose military it is, and the control officer at Base Aérea Camaguey wasn't going to leave his ass hanging out in the breeze. So instead of initiating a chase-down from a single phone call from a captain somewhere, he contacted the Ministry of the Interior to get a confirmation on Captain Perez, and that cost him eight minutes because the chief of operations was on another line when he called. Then he had to go through the base commander whom he had caught in the middle of a spat with some virulent diarrhea and was briefly indisposed before he could take the call, which bought the fleeing Americans another five minutes. It took another seven minutes for the pilot on standby to get to his MiG 23M and get it in the air.

Twenty minutes to those in the Goose, traveling at just under two hundred mph, meant sixty miles, but because they had to run out of the U-shaped Gulf of Guacanayabo in the curved underbelly of the island, it still left them within the Cuban ADIZ as they headed south-southeast for the Cayman Islands. The plan all along, if they found the gold, was not to fly back to the U.S., around or over Cuba, but directly into the Caymans, which was just about a two-hundred-mile run from the Cuban coast. They had flown into the Caymans a week before they left on the quest, meeting with the president of one of the very discreet banking institutions there. The bank would have an armored car awaiting their arrival at the airport and would "assist them through customs" before escorting them to the bank.

They'd been underway for almost twenty-five minutes and were certain they were nearing the perimeter of the Cuban ADIZ. There was nothing but blue water ahead. Eddie had kept the plane on the deck most of the way, but now he had taken them up to five thousand feet. Will had just begun to risk a small smile.

"Man, that whole thing was like a bad Harrison Ford movie, but I think we're—"

Without any warning, there was a deafening roar just above them and the plane shook savagely, lurching from the turbulence, dropping a wing and nearly rolling over. As Eddie fought with the controls, they watched the Cuban MiG rocket over them at over a thousand mph. The jet headed straight out about two miles and made a sharp, arching wing-over turn, then slowed down and brought itself straight and level, nose aimed at its target. Their radio, set on the standard 122.2 frequency, crackled.

"Grumman Goose November, two, seven, seven, zero, this is Captain Benito Balio of the Cuban Air Force. You are commanded to turn your aircraft around and return to Cuba now. If you fail to obey these orders, you will be shot down." To emphasize his point the pilot hit the throttle and roared across the nose of the Goose again.

"Freaking guy's playing with us like a cat with a mouse," Will muttered to no one in particular as the plane shook and lurched once more.

Eddie snatched up his microphone and snarled, "We are a private aircraft, outside of Cuban airspace. You have no authorization to demand anything from us, dude!"

The answer was another screaming pass as the pilot took his aircraft out about five miles, came around and threw the activating switch on the Russian-made Vympel R-3 heat-seeking missile under his wing. "You have one minute to comply."

There was no reply and in seconds, the warble in his headset went to a steady, insistent tone and the triangle on his targeter went from blinking to solid. He was locked.

"He's bluffing," Kansas said with less confidence than he felt. "We're in international waters, for God's sake. I can see a cruise ship down there."

And indeed, about three thousand feet below them and probably two miles out there was a floating white speck with small spirals of smoke rising from the stacks.

Kansas shook his head. "He wouldn't—"

But at that moment the conversation was interrupted by a puff of smoke under the wing of the MiG.

"Yeah, well, he just did!" Will shouted, backing up in his seat nervously.

Kansas had considered a plan when he first saw the MiG and the rockets under it. Crazy, probably useless, but it had passed through his mind. It was something he had trained himself to do—consider the possibilities in every situation all the time. He threw himself upright and dashed into the cabin, shouting for Will. "C'mon, Will! We've got one chance but we've got to be quick. Throw open the cargo door."

Will never hesitated. He didn't know what the plan was, but it was better than nothing and he trusted his friend's instincts. Kansas grabbed the closest dirt bike and ripped off the gas cap. He snatched a rag off the floor that Eddie had used to clean the windows, and stuffed it in the tank, then pulled it out sopping wet and stuffed it back in again, leaving a third of it outside the opening. As he shoved the bike toward the hatch, Will was already with the plan, whipping out his lighter and passing it over the fuel-soaked rag. When it blossomed in flame, they both shoved the bike outwards into the hurricane-like winds that screamed outside the cargo door. But the rear foot peg caught Will's pants, spinning him onto the back of the motorcycle as it headed out the open hatch. He cried out involuntarily and made a desperate grab at the side of the fuselage, eyes filled with sudden terror as he and the bike lurched outward into the wind. But at the last second, Kansas reached over and grabbed him by his belt, dragging him backwards with enough force to land him on his rear in the cabin, just as the bike was sucked out.

Kansas straightened up as much as the confines of the cabin would allow. "Who the hell do you think you are? Slim Pickens in *Dr. Strangelove?*" he said with a smile. "How many times have I told you about riding motorcycles out of perfectly good airplanes?"

Eddie watched as the missile curved in a deadly arch. Picking up the heat signals from the Goose's big radial engines, it straightened cleanly, like a hound that's found the scent, unalterable, riveted on a mission of destruction, a thin vaporous strip of smoke following, arching tightly then expanding across the sky like a soft ribbon tossed by a careless child.

Instinctively, Eddie threw the plane down and away, knowing it was a useless gesture, but drowning men grasp at straws. The move probably saved their lives because he inadvertently pulled them closer to the falling dirt bike. As the missile closed the final distance on the aircraft, the bike exploded in a fiery corona not two hundred yards below the Goose, and the searing heat from the explosion drew the sensors on the missile like a bee to the hive. The Vympel obediently switched course twenty degrees to the left, arched away from the plane and soared into the explosion, igniting in a fireball that rocked the old bird above and challenged all of Eddie's skill to keep her straight and level.

The Cuban pilot couldn't believe his eyes. There was an explosion but the airplane was still there. With the speed of his aircraft he overshot them by a couple of miles before he hit the airbrakes, chopped the throttles, and brought her sharply around. He wrapped his gloved hand around the trigger on his heavy machine guns—he was going to do this up close and personal.

A glance out of the rear windows in the cabin showed the jet slowing and turning. They couldn't fight; all they could do was run. As Eddie slammed his throttles to the wall, Kansas came up with one last idea. "Dive! Dive!" he yelled as he settled into the copilot's seat. "Drop us right down on that freaking cruise ship. The son of a bitch can't shoot us in front of a thousand witnesses!"

Will grinned at the crazy idea—he was right! Talk about an international incident—Cuban MiG shoots down passenger plane in international waters in front of five hundred sunbathers! There was just a chance.

Crazy Eddie got that psychedelic gleam in his eye again and threw the yoke forward, and the Grumman Goose became a rock falling from the sky. But they had to make two miles to get to those witnesses and the MiG was closing fast. The wings began to shake as the airspeed went from the yellow into the red and then just lined out, but the old girl just wasn't in the same class as a fighter that cruised at twelve hundred mph. The MiG fell on them like a vengeful hawk, taking them with its machine guns at the right rear quarter and up through the aircraft. As the bullets hit, it seemed as if everything exploded at once. The snapping noise of the rounds slamming the fuselage was terrifying as lines of holes appeared magically, cutting through the center of the cabin and into the cockpit. Interior lights took hits, bursting like firecrackers, and the air filled with an acrid, electrical smell. The windshield and the cockpit window on Eddie's side took several rounds, shattering and exploding. Crazy Eddie screamed like a pinched child, but never took his hands from the controls. There were a number of poignant exclamations in all directions, mostly regarding the dubious parentage of the Cuban pilot. The jet's speed in this situation probably saved them from another attack, because it took the pilot a mile just to start his turn, and by the time he'd executed it and started back, the old Goose was falling as if it were a carelessly tossed toy, wings askew and wobbling, the plane in a slip, coming in almost sideways at the cruise ship below.

Fred Thompson and his wife Georgia were splayed out in lounge chairs on the rear deck of the *Caribbean Journey*, slathered with suntan lotion, dressed in tropical prints and sporting Ray Ban sunglasses—all purchased specifically for their first real vacation in ten years. The waters around them were picture book—deep blue-green and almost calm, with the occasional offshore rolling swell moving through, glistened by the last of the afternoon sun. She was reading *Romance Magazine* and Fred had just settled into a Clive Cussler novel. He paused to adjust his glasses and glanced up. His eyes took on a curious look, which quickly bled into confused, then ran full ahead into outright concerned.

"Georgia. Georgia. There's a damned plane coming right at us."

Georgia didn't even look up. "Fred," she said lazily, unconcerned, still staring at her magazine. "There're planes everywhere. It's the twentieth century, dear."

Fred reached over and grabbed her arm, shaking her gently, still staring at the sky. "There's a damned plane comin' right at us, Georgia."

His wife looked up and suddenly her face gathered that same sense of intense concern her husband's reflected. "Damn, I hate it when he's right," she whispered, unconsciously edging backwards in her chair as she stared at the huge, gray and yellow aircraft plummeting down at them.

With Will in the seat next to him and Kansas crouched between them, Eddie was struggling with the controls, using rudder and yoke, forcing the plane into a tight slip, trying to get out of the sky and on the water next to the ship before the MiG could get around for another shot, but in his haste he had called it a little close. He wanted to hit the water in front and starboard of the ship, but he was coming down almost in the center of the huge craft. People below on the decks of the monster ship stood paused in awe, staring or pointing and yelling. The smarter ones had started to run. The Goose lumbered over the stern almost aimed at the huge smokestacks that rose up out of the ship like the Pillars of Hercules. Eddie yanked the controls to the right and smashed down on the right rudder while adding power, practically turning the plane vertical, and the left wing missed the closest big black stack by about three feet as they careened across the top of the vessel, damned near close enough to have stolen a cocktail from a terrified waiter's tray. Crazy Eddie howled, snapped her back level, chopped the power, dumped some flaps, and slapped the old girl down in the water not three hundred yards in front of the *Caribbean Journey.*

Kansas, dazed and amazed, just turned to Eddie and shook his head. "You really are a freaking kamikaze pilot! A freaking kamikaze pilot!"

Eddie smiled, holding up his hands and waving them slightly. "It's all in the wrists, man, it's all in the wrists."

As soon as they'd hit the water, Will had popped the hull hatch and was down below, looking for bullet holes. If the plane sank, they would lose everything. But by some miracle the jet had taken them on more of a horizontal trajectory and none of the earlier rounds had cut through the floating hull. However, the rest of the plane was a mess.

The MiG 23 pilot cursed loudly and vehemently for a good thirty seconds after the Goose touched down, but there was nothing he could do. After circling above for about ten minutes, he jerked his aircraft around and headed back to base to become the laughing stock of his squadron—the man who, while flying perhaps the best fighter aircraft in the world, failed to kill a fifty-year-old, unarmed seaplane.

The long and the short of it was, the captain of the ship ordered the throttles cut and they followed the ship on the surface until it came to a stop. It was a Norwegian, very neutral lines, headed to the Caymans. After Kansas explained the situation to the officials on board, they provided one of their electricians to wire off some superficial electrical damage and helped Eddie duct tape the windows that had taken rounds. By another small miracle, the engines and major electronics hadn't taken any direct hits and were still operational.

Two hours later the Goose was back in the air, and an hour after that the flat green and beige expanse of Grand Cayman rose out of the brilliant blue waters. Will placed a call when they were about a half hour out and by the time they reached Owen Roberts Airport at the edge of the perfectly circular bay enclosed by the island, a remarkably impressive armored car and a limousine were waiting for them. Customs was perfunctory at best, and inside of an hour their gold bullion was stored in a small vault in their banking institution of choice. The devices they had found, and the golden text, however, never left their possession.

They spent the night in Georgetown at a very nice resort and celebrated until nearly dawn. While they slept in the next day, mechanics did a thorough once-over on the aircraft, making sure it was flight worthy, securely repairing the windows as best they could in an expeditious fashion, and patching the holes in the fuselage. Then the plane was fueled and made ready to lumber into the sky once more.

The morning of the following day found them in the air again, headed toward the coast of Mexico. There was certainly no flying back across Cuba to get to The Keys, so they were forced to go the long way, across to the Yucatan, refueling in Cancun, then on into Key West. It was a long day, but as the sun began to burn itself into the rose-tinted stratum of puffy, gray and white clouds on the horizon, that scattered yet symmetric arch of slender islands known as the Florida Keys came into view. Those sandy, mangrove-fringed freckles in a shallow strand of sea had been home to scoundrels, adventurers, scammers, and dreamers for over three hundred years, and in truth, the crew in the cockpit of that badly beaten but proud old bird probably fit most of those categories. Eddie grinned from ear to ear, hit the switch for the speakers and "Smoke on the Water" by Deep Purple engulfed the cockpit with its sonorous, powerful rhythm.

"Cool runnings, mon," he whispered to himself. "Mr. Eddie comin' home."

Customs was a piece of cake, even with their pilot's prior reputation and the obvious damages to the aircraft. In addition,

Crazy Eddie had more secret hiding compartments in that plane than a paranoid packrat. They slipped the gold tablets and the strange devices into one of them, and the two hundred thousand dollars that they had taken from Will and Kansas's new bank account in the Caymans into another, and breezed through a customs search without breaking a sweat. Of the two hundred thousand, half was for Eddie, for his share, and to pay for repairs on his plane. Kansas and Will kept fifty thousand each for "running money." They flew back to Ramrod Key where the plane was kept and after a couple celebratory margaritas, they bade each other goodbye and headed home. Will and Kansas had agreed to tie up the following day. They both felt there were some interesting times ahead.

They were right.

CHAPTER 4

Whoever undertakes to set himself up as a judge of Truth and Knowledge is shipwrecked by the laughter of the gods.
— **Albert Einstein**

Will sat in a lounge chair on the deck at Kansas's home, sipping a beer. His partner leaned against the porch rail, studying the sullen-looking rain clouds coalescing in the south over Key West. There was a thin layer of gunmetal gray overcast pasted across the sky, which cut the heat but added to the humidity, and the air was rich with the scent of the distant rain—one of those dull, summer doldrums days. Still, all in all, they were some pretty happy fellows. Money for either one was not likely to be a problem for a long time to come. In one brilliant, albeit hazardous stroke, they had once again stepped from the ranks of schemers and dreamers to that unique fraternity where the air was more fragrant, the breeze was kindlier, the sun never glared at you, confidence was a way of life, and there was always a place of refuge. But then, someone should have told them that every place of refuge has its price.

Will held one of the strange devices in his hands, rolling it over, studying its design in speculative fashion. "All I can tell you for sure is that whatever this is, it's really freaking important," he said, still staring at it. "Nobody goes to that much trouble to display something that isn't paramount to their culture." He looked up with that characteristic cocky grin. "I'm thinking maybe it makes women impossibly horny. Load up on cologne and condoms, walk into any Victoria's Secret store and press the button."

About that time, Crazy Eddie showed up in his old Chevy van, accompanied by the growling lyrics of Jimi Hendrix bellowing about watchtowers and howling winds. He trudged up the stairs to the deck, a faded floral print shirt and his standard Hang Ten shorts dangling from his thin frame. "Wass happenin' fellow seekers of fortune!" he said, tossing a paper bag to Kansas. "You left some clothes on the plane."

Kansas caught it. "Thanks, *amigo*."

Eddie noticed the silver wand in Will's hand. "So, what do you think that is? A remote for the television of the gods?"

"No, Will thinks it makes girls horny," Kansas quipped.

Their friend's single eye lit up. "Eddie wants one!"

Will turned it over in his hand again, holding it up, noticing a slight indention in the side where one might place a finger. He wrapped his hand around the device and pressed the indention. Suddenly, that deep, sensuous humming began again—only for a couple of seconds—and the hair on their arms prickled momentarily, then stopped.

"What le fluck was that, dude?" Eddie said cautiously.

Staring at the wand, Will shook his head. "Don't know, but somehow I get the impression that whatever this is, I just turned it on."

There were a few moments of silence, then Kansas looked at his friends. "Are you guys feeling any different?"

"Funny you should mention that," Will said quietly. "Just a few moments after this hummed into life, I got like a feeling of calmness, relaxed...real relaxed. Still have it." He tilted his head quizzically, eyes pinched. "Not bad, just strange."

"Me, too," Kansas muttered.

Eddie straightened up. "Ditto, dudes. It's like I got all soft and fuzzy, like the walls of resistance in my head just sort of crumbled."

"Do you have any deep dark secrets you don't want to get out?" Kansas said with a smile, making light of it.

Crazy Eddie gazed at him with the strangest look in his eye. "Yeah, I do."

Will wasn't sure why, but he pressed it. "What, Eddie? What's your deepest, darkest secret? Tell us."

Their older friend took a deep breath and exhaled slowly. For a moment, confusion filled his one eye, and then it all just bled into a resigned compliance. He collapsed slowly into a lounge chair next to them, the strangest of countenances on his face, and he began to speak quietly, staring at the deck. "You know, Eddie makes a big deal about never doing heavy drugs—never running any. But one time Eddie run amuck bad. One time I brought in six kilos of cocaine from Colombia for a dealer friend

I knew. Got low on cash, the offer came up, and I just did it—a little twin-engine Cessna, over and back in two days, me and a copilot. The dealer's wife had just given birth to a baby boy. We got back, took the stuff up to them in Miami, and we got to doing a few celebratory lines. One hour bled into three or four. The baby would cry in the other room and the woman would check on him, take care of him, I guess. But somewhere in the fog of it all, I noticed she wasn't checking quite as much as she should, and that baby was crying more. But I was zoned, and finally me and my copilot got up and left."

He took a deep, shuddering breath and his face seemed to collapse inward, etched in pain from the memory. The cheek under his left eye began to twitch slightly, and that eye rimmed with tears. "I found out a week later that they just kept doing that toot for about twenty-four hours, then they passed out and slept for twelve to fourteen hours. When they woke up, that new baby was dead."

There were tears running down his face now, and he couldn't lift his head to meet the eyes of his friends. "I never did another run after that. I quit. I started doin' a few charters to the islands and I started doin' disaster relief work in Haiti and Guatemala." He paused again, lifting his head and staring out at the thunderheads rising over the distant sea, taking a slow, sorrowful breath, exhaling in anguish. "Eddie never forgot that. Never forgot what his actions caused. If I hadn't done that, that baby would be alive." The old pilot sighed heavily. "I never told a soul about that, not a soul. I just carried it inside, like a cancer that just ate at me, and many a night Eddie just drank and smoked himself away so he could sleep, and not hear that baby crying."

He turned and looked at his friends. "I never said anything about this to anyone. But when you turned on that damned thing in your hand and told me to tell you, all them walls came crumbling down and I had to say the words, dudes. I had to say the words."

Both Kansas and Will were shaken by the heartfelt confession of their friend, but moreover they intuitively understood what Eddie was feeling. That same strange, overwhelming vibration of comfort and solace had invaded them, too, climbing into their heads and bringing down the walls of resistance, and suddenly the desire to be baptized in truth seemed paramount. Kansas found himself thinking about the same question he had asked Eddie, about dark secrets, and he would have gladly told his friends about almost beating a kid to death with his bare hands—a young kid who had tried to force himself on his sister—the fierce, primitive pleasure of each hammering punch, watching the blood well up and out in spurts. Not wanting to stop, relishing it with every part of his being. He wasn't a violent person by nature, but the incident had uncovered that deeply primitive part of him, eons old and built into the genetics of man—the instinct to protect those you love, defense of the family, the pack, the pride. Even now his hands trembled as he remembered the violence that surged from him, the blind desire for mayhem. The boy spent two weeks in the hospital and his sight was permanently impaired in one eye. But at that moment he would have gladly talked about it. Hell, he would have told his high school graduating class about it. He wanted to...

Will looked up, eyes filled with confession. He opened his mouth slowly as if to start a sentence, then glanced down at the device in his hand and instantly shut it off. Seconds later the sensations he felt faded away, like the sun burning early morning fog from backcountry waters, and he knew unequivocally at that moment what this device from another time and another place was all about.

An hour later, Kansas and Will sat in the living room, having moved inside from the deck to the solace of the air conditioning. Eddie, uncharacteristically subdued after this soul-rending experience, said his mellow had been severely harshed, that he had places to be, and left.

Will looked at Kansas. "Are you aware of what took place today? What really happened?"

There was a poignant moment of silence, then Kansas nodded. "Yeah, I think I am. The bad news is, that wand of yours doesn't make girls horny. But I experienced something similar to Eddie today while that thing was turned on, and I'm guessing you did, too. That little son of a bitch that you're holding somehow affects how a person reacts to truth and lies and the space in between. Now, maybe this was just a fluke." He straightened up and twisted his head back and forth, cracking his neck in that nervous fashion of his. "But if we're right, the possibilities with that thing are limitless, dangerous, and a little frightening, and also pose extraordinary potential, if it actually makes you...tell the truth. I think we need to put it to some tests, and we need to take that golden notebook to someone who can decipher it. But first, here's what I have in mind..."

Key West was abuzz with a high profile murder trial. William Foster, a heavy hitter in local art circles and a serious patron of the arts in South Florida, had been arrested for the murder of his live-in girlfriend, Celia Longsworth. About a month ago, Celia had gone missing. Foster called the police, claiming they had an argument, and she stormed out of the house, never to return. Her car was located on Simonton Street a day or two later. A week later, Celia turned up floating off Smathers Beach, all bloated and nibbled on by denizens of the area waters—very bad for the tourist business. When the police questioned Foster he professed innocence, but the police got a search warrant and investigators found blood splatters that matched Celia's type on the kitchen wall and floor—all of which had been meticulously cleaned, but certainly not well enough to fool crime scene specialists. Foster claimed she had cut herself preparing dinner several months before.

Upon questioning, one neighbor said he was pretty sure he saw Foster stuffing something wrapped in a blanket into the trunk of his car on the night in question. Neighbors near enough to the quaint mansion off Simonton Street also confirmed a loud argument on that same evening. Rumor was, Celia may have been seeing someone else while spending Foster's money. In addition, Foster had scratch marks up and down his arms and neck, making it look like Celia might not have gone gently into the night. Foster was a pompous old fart, but had more money than King Croesus, and the best attorney it could buy. The big money wasn't on the DA pulling this off. On Wednesday, Foster was feeling cocky enough to take the stand in his own defense.

A soft morning sun filtered through the old windows of the courthouse and drifted in smoky, vaporous trellises into the room of great and small decisions. The courtroom was nearly filled to capacity with reporters, Foster's art cronies (some wishing him well, and some smiling at him with sketches and oils of gallows in their eyes), and the balance of the crowd made up of folks who just love a genuine reality show. Will borrowed a press pass from a buddy at *The Key West Citizen* and told the guard at the courthouse metal detector that the truth device was a recorder. Kansas just shook his head in wonder when his friend's story was accepted.

The standard preamble took a few minutes, but the judge was a no-nonsense type of guy and a few minutes later Foster was sitting smugly, quite confidently, on the witness stand, dressed flamboyantly in a mauve silk shirt, a bright floral scarf at his throat, and white cotton pants. He was portly, in his early sixties, with a shock of distinguished, well-manicured gray hair, an aquiline nose, arrogant pale blue eyes, and thin lips that seemed to be continuously suppressing a mouthful of disdain.

From their seats in the third row, Will turned to Kansas and whispered, "'And the truth shall set you free,' John 8:32," then pressed the indentation on the machine. There was that brief hum and the wave of subtle vibration that followed, and the crowd seemed to sense it—but hey, the circus was about to begin; who cared about prickling hairs? Kansas thought that all this really needed was popcorn, hot dogs, and beer.

The prosecuting attorney did a brief dance in his questioning regarding Foster's full name, what he did, and what his relationship was with Ms. Longsworth, then he went right for the throat, hoping to rattle Foster and make the following questions more relevant.

"Mr. Foster, did you and Ms. Longsworth have an argument on the night of July 22?"

Foster adjusted himself in his seat, paused, and answered slowly and clearly, as he had been coached. "Yes, we had a disagreement."

The prosecutor expected it to get more difficult from there. "What was the argument about?"

At that point a strange thing happened with Mr. William Foster. His eyes got a somewhat confused gaze. They blinked a couple of times as he tried to push himself farther back into the witness chair.

The prosecutor stared at the man on the stand. "Mr. Foster, shall I repeat the question?"

Foster blinked a couple of times and his mouth moved a little without issuing any words, then gradually he just sort of relaxed—maybe surrendered would have been a better word. "Yeah, we argued about her seeing that shithead artist Barry Belfont. Couldn't paint his way out of a friggin' tin can! Not qualified to paint road signs! Indolent symmetry, expressionless composition! I found out they were having an affair and followed them to a hotel that afternoon."

A deep murmur rolled over the courtroom like a summer wind across a wheat field. The prosecutor's jaw dropped and he struggled quickly to recover. "Aahhh, did this argument lead to the harm, in any fashion, of Ms. Longsworth?"

Foster blinked a few times, struggling, then just surrendered once more. "Yeah, it did. We got into it a bit and I slapped her a couple times. The bitch scratched the shit out of me, so I whacked her with a hammer that I was using to put up a new picture." Then he settled down from his animation and whispered, "Didn't mean to kill her. I really liked Celia. I might have even loved her, but Barry Belfont! What a shit! No sense of color or perspective. How could she?"

The judge's gavel came down, he called for counsel with the attorneys, and the trial was pretty much over. In the midst of the furor, the snapping of pictures and the buzz of voices, Kansas turned to his friend. "'The truth will set you free, but first it will make you miserable.' James A. Garfield." Then, with smiles of a job well done and the possibility of a new future in the business of truth, they got up quietly and left.

While all this was going on, about ninety miles to the south of them, Detective Mariana Martinez was meeting with Security Director Miguel Juan Santiago at the Cuban Ministry of the Interior. After the Grumman Goose had escaped, Cuban Intelligence had used Russian satellite images to trace where the Americans went while in the country. Security forces had then found the cave, the wrecked Beechcraft, and the hidden room behind it. Obviously, it was a find of huge importance, and equally obvious was the fact that something had been taken from it—something without a doubt incredibly valuable from a number of standpoints. It was decided that they would announce nothing to the world regarding the incident. They would take care of it discreetly.

Director Santiago leaned back in his chair and exhaled the cigarillo smoke from his nostrils in a slow, deliberate fashion, like an angry dragon, while fixing Martinez with his dark, almost impenetrable eyes. "You have, as the American's say, 'dropped the ball' here, Martinez. I expected more from you. I could pick up this phone and have you working a beat on the streets of Havana by nighttime. But I know what you're capable of, so I am going to give you a chance to redeem yourself. You're going to go after these two. You will be given new identification papers as a Cuban-American who lives in Miami. You will track down these people and you will find out what they have stolen. Am I clear?"

Martinez nodded, feeling no answer was the best course.

The director took another drag of his cigarillo, exhaling less forcefully this time, and brought those hard eyes back to her. "And you will keep me apprised continually, you understand?"

"Yes, sir," she said. "I understand completely. I will not fail you again."

He nodded. "I know, Martinez. I know."

CHAPTER 5

All great truths begin as blasphemies.
— **George Bernard Shaw**

Now that they were certain of what they were dealing with, there were two other stops for Kansas and Will that day. The first was a psychiatrist friend of Kansas's. Sunni Beach had practiced in The Keys for over ten years, starting out as a psychologist and going back to school to get an additional degree in psychiatry. She was about forty years old, lived alone in a nice little hibiscus-shrouded home tucked away beneath two huge rubber trees, and had converted the back bedroom into a study, where she held her sessions.

Sunni was small and thin, with large blue eyes that carried a soft sadness about them—as if perhaps she'd heard too much of the secret distress of the world. She wore a comfortable, light summer dress in a bright floral pattern—something a younger girl might have worn—yet it seemed to fit her personality well.

Dr. Beach invited the men in and offered them tea in her living room, which was decorated in soft old couches, fresh flowers, and photos of family and friends, and carried the subtle, fragrant aroma of her perfume. After a few pleasantries and Will's introduction, she settled back in her chair. "So, what is it that I can do for you boys today?"

"Sunni, we need you to tell us about the brain," Kansas said without preamble. "Not to take up any more of your time than necessary, explain to us what parts of the brain are affected by frequency and vibration and what parts determine the control of truth and lies. Doesn't have to be too technical, just an overview."

The doctor sat up and placed her hands in her lap, like a schoolteacher beginning a lesson. "All right, first of all, a good portion of the brain can be affected by vibration. Vibration has apparently been used to some degree by a number of ancient cultures and has been studied and applied to influence minds in modern times far more than most people realize. Recently, a consortium called Princeton Engineering Anomalies Research, studying the field of archaeo-acoustics—merging archaeology and sound science—set out to test acoustic behavior in megalithic sites such as Newgrange and Wayland's Smithy in the United Kingdom. They found that the ancient chambers all sustained a powerful resonance at a sound frequency between 95 and 120 hertz. In additional testing, it was discovered that stone rooms in ancient temples in Malta were found to match the same pattern of resonance, registering at the frequency of 110 or 111 hertz, which has been determined to be a significant influential level for the human brain. The concept of patterns of resonance has been documented in the Great Pyramid of Egypt and in the pyramids of the Mayans, as well. Scientists have determined that, at certain frequencies, there are 'standing waves' that emphasize and de-emphasize each other. Applied in the right sequence or combination, it appears these waves may have been used to create a trance-like state in certain religiously significant rooms for the ancients."

She paused and took a sip of her tea, then sat it down slowly and deliberately. "Taking us to modern times, a group at UCLA conducted an experiment in which regional brain activity in a handful of volunteers was monitored by EEG through different resonating frequencies. Findings indicated that at 110 hertz, the patterns of activity over the prefrontal cortex abruptly shifted, resulting in a temporary switching from left to right-sided dominance related to emotional processing. The study indicated that people regularly exposed to resonant sound in the frequency of 110 or 111 hertz begin to exercise or apply an area of their brain that relates to empathy and mood. Basically what this means is that there may be many frequencies or vibrations out there that manipulate our actions in broader and more dynamic fashions. Furthermore, there is some scientific speculation that certain vibrations induce the release of the body's natural opiates, encephalins and endorphins, in larger than normal amounts, creating a marginal euphoria. Ultimately, the sympathetic resonance created from this combination can even make a subject more susceptible to suggestion."

Sunni adjusted herself in her seat and then began again. "As to what part of the brain is related to truth and lies, scientists believe it is primarily the frontal cortex, which is normally involved in making decisions, and more specifically, the dorsal lateral prefrontal cortex, which is apparently the most active when deception is involved. The correlation here is that it is also the prefrontal cortex, which is most affected by vibration and frequency."

Kansas looked at Will and their eyes met with mutual understanding. It all made perfect sense. Their device invaded the prefrontal cortex with various vibrations/frequencies and disabled the lying mechanism by shifting from an intellective to an emotional resonance. If that wasn't enough, the vibration/frequency forced the release of endorphins that relaxed you like you'd just mainlined a Xanax. It wasn't so much that it made you tell the truth, it just destroyed your resistance to lie. And, as a bonus, it made you susceptible to suggestion.

An hour later they were at their second stop—Cassandra Roundtree's house. Cass greeted them exuberantly, dressed in light cotton pants and a colorful Sloppy Joe's T-shirt, pleased that they had survived their Cuban ordeal, and even more amazed that they had found the gold. When they told her the rest of the story she was astounded, but not convinced. "A golden notebook and a device that makes you tell the truth...yeah, right."

With that trademark mischievous smile, Will just turned on the machine in his hand and asked Cass where she kept her valuables. That pretty much took care of all doubt, and left Cass needing a new place to hide things.

They were sitting in her airy, sparsely decorated living room—a couple of seascape paintings, a handful of tropical plants and a few pieces of furniture the Spartans would have been proud of. Most of her money was in the other half of the house, which held wall-to-wall computers and related equipment. Cass sat in her single lounge chair, stroking Simba, her favorite cat, still flabbergasted. "I can't believe it all—it's like a Robert Heinlen and a Kurt Vonnegut book combined."

"Yeah, I know," said Will, finding a strange, almost disconcerting pleasure in seeing this attractive, highly independent woman again. Her blond hair was unencumbered, flowing down over her tanned shoulders in soft waves, and those bright, gray-blue eyes were filled with animation. "I wouldn't have believed it if we hadn't lived it. But now we need the second half of the puzzle—the part that hopefully will have a few answers. We need to decipher this golden notebook." He handed Cass the solid gold book with both hands and she balked at its weight. "We really need to know what's written here. You're the computer expert, Cass. Surely you must know someone with a computer program that could help us."

She answered thoughtfully as she studied the gilded pages. "You know, there's a strong possibility I do. Just recently an associate professor in MIT's Computer and Artificial Intelligence Lab, along with a couple of her colleagues, developed a system that possesses a remarkable synthesis of logic and intuition, enabling it to decipher ancient languages with more efficiency than anything in the past. Archeologists from around the world have come to them for help in this field, and what they've been able to do is just amazing. It so happens I know a member of the team—not well, but well enough to get you through the doors, I think. I'll make some calls today." She paused and exhaled, shook her head, then looked up at her friends in near disbelief. "Jesus! Do you realize what you've found here? This may well be the connection to the antediluvian world that existed before our recorded time. Unbelievable! Possibly the connection to what we have called 'Atlantis' for so long. The area where you found this is the same region where the second civilization of Atlantis was founded after the great breakup of the main island, according to the famous psychic, Edgar Cayce."

"Now you're sounding a little science fiction," chuckled Kansas.

She looked up at him with a defiant glare in her eyes. "Science fiction, huh? You're standing here with a device from an ancient world that forces people to tell the truth and a golden parchment that may well define and document their civilization, and you're calling me science fiction?"

The following morning, Kansas got a call from Cass. "Tell Will to warm up that airplane of his. We've got an appointment at MIT with a bunch of really smart people tomorrow afternoon."

"We, huh?" Kansas said as he took a sip of his coffee and looked out at the sun-gilded ocean from his deck.

"You're damned right, we. I missed all the fun on the first round. I'm not missing out on this part."

They were in the air two hours later and flew most of the day, refueling a couple times and getting out of the small cockpit to stretch and eat. It would have been easier to go commercial, but it wasn't an option with what they were carrying. They arrived in Cambridge, Massachusetts, late that evening. The following afternoon they found themselves in the language laboratories of the Massachusetts Institute of Technology's computer department, meeting with Myra Cunningham and her team of linguistic computer experts. Myra was a tall, relatively thin woman with inquisitive dark eyes, short blond hair, and a to-the-point personality. She was smartly dressed in a white blouse and a dark blue skirt covered by a white lab jacket. After introductions she came right to the issue at hand, and Kansas presented her with the golden notebook. Kansas and Will had decided not to bring the truth machines with them to the institute, and they had agreed in advance to say nothing of them.

There was the anticipated wonderment when the notebook was produced, and, of course, there were many questions regarding its origin. The group from The Keys politely declined to offer any information, saying at this point it was paramount to know more about their situation before they divulged anything.

Myra paged through the book in awe, face alight like a child with a new toy, dark eyes filled with both intense scrutiny and the joy of a new challenge. Finally, she looked up. "The writing is similar to cuneiform, like the ancient Sumerians, which goes back as far as the thirtieth century B.C., intermingled with what appears to be characters similar to Mayan, Incan, and even Egyptian texts, but there are many characters here that are unfamiliar. The good news is, since we developed this computer we have received ancient writings from scientists and archeologists around the world, developing a huge database, and by cross-referencing with other writings I'm betting we'll be able to fill in many of the blanks. But we'll need at least forty-eight hours to run this through 'Big Mother' and see what we find."

Kansas was hesitant to leave their find with someone, but as Will said, "We're going to have to take a chance somewhere with this. Remember, in the words of the immortal Ernest Hemingway,

'The best way to find out if someone is trustworthy is to trust them.'"

Kansas looked at him deadpan. "And in the immortal words of Jackie Peterson, 'Never trust a dog to watch your food.'"

Will cocked his head. "That's your plumber again, isn't it?"

His friend smiled. "Yeah. I guess we'll just have to see which one applies."

The morning of the second day Myra called. There was a suppressed excitement in her voice that even the elemental side of her personality couldn't conceal. An hour later they were all gathered in a meeting room outside computer operations. Myra looked around at them all as they settled into oversized couches set in an "L" shape with a mahogany coffee table in front of them, and without any further ado, began: "What we have here is absolutely remarkable. Our computer was able to decipher ninety percent of the text and I have to tell you, it is beyond fascinating. The people were called Alanians. The Alanians apparently thrived on a small continent in the center of the Atlantic Ocean for over a thousand years before a cataclysm of some sort destroyed the main island, but there was sufficient warning that many groups of Alanians left their original home for other parts of the world. Now granted, all this sounds a great deal like the speculation regarding the continent of Atlantis. You can draw your own conclusions. I'm not in the business of conclusions regarding ancient civilizations."

She paused and looked around at her audience, assuring their attention. "Now, you must remember that in our most recent Ice Age, from about 50,000 B.C. until 10,000 B.C., water from the oceans was incorporated into the snow and ice on glaciers around the world, and as a result, the Atlantic Ocean was at least three hundred fifty feet lower than it is today. Consequently, much of the area that the Alanians migrated to was above the surface of the ocean during the last half of the Ice Age. This apparently includes much of the Bahamas and a good deal of the northern Caribbean basin. The text explains that a large portion of this migration began about 18,000 B.C. by our calculation, and the culture thrived for the next 8,000 years in their new locations. Unfortunately, when the last Ice Age ended about 10,000 B.C., North American glaciers rapidly melted and the seas in the Gulf of Mexico began to rise rapidly. By 8,000 B.C. the rising waters, coupled with a series of violent earthquakes, put an end to the Alanian culture, but not before some surviving remnants had fled to Central and South America, I would assume to found the cultures we know as the Incans, the Mayans, etc."

"Incredible," Cass murmured. "Absolutely incredible."

Myra nodded. "Yes, but that's not the best part. The crux of these golden tablets tells a story about the culture itself and how it evolved—because of a gift given to them by a group of people called the Etherians. Now, I don't know if the Etherians were indigenous to the region or came from someplace else. The reference, the intimation of the word in this language is more 'from high' or 'from above,' but it doesn't explain who they were. The gift was called the 'truthmakers.'"

A sudden shift of eyes around the room didn't escape Myra. She took a sip of water and continued. "Evidently these truthmakers were some sort of device that, when activated, forced an individual to tell the truth. The concept, according to the Etherians, was that there was no greater deity than truth, and no nation of people could truly find peace and social continuity until their world revolved around truth. They convinced the leader of the Alanians—his name was Vandar—to put to use these truthmakers, which would ultimately do away with any standard court system and judicial structure other than the most basic legal networking. Long story short, this didn't sit well with a large segment of the society—some of the various secondary rulers of the country, magistrates, litigators, and second and third levels of ruling castes, along with state and national council members—because I'm assuming graft was equally as rife then as it is now, and they would not only be divulged for what they were, but most would lose their jobs, as well. There was very nearly a civil war, but in the end Vandar prevailed, and the nation began the use of these truthmakers."

Pulling a wisp of blond hair away from her forehead, she asked, "Can you imagine a culture, a society, where truth reigns supreme? Where it does no good to lie or to practice deceit in any way, because eventually you would come before a magistrate with a truthmaker and you would tell the truth? The long and the short of this is, with Vandar's strength of purpose, the entire culture eventually morphed from a chaotic, pretentious, deceitful society, like the one we have, to a serene people who accepted honesty as a way of life—a totally scrupulous society. It didn't happen overnight. But it happened. They became a people who worshiped truth."

It was obvious Myra was moved by the concept. She took a breath and exhaled softly. "But as honorable as the culture became, they couldn't prevent the cataclysm they eventually saw coming. So they took some of the truthmakers the Etherians had given them and built mausoleums to the truth they feared would die with them. In fifty different places throughout their known world they created hiding places for these devices, for whoever would come after them, so that they, too, might have...truth..." Myra stopped and smiled. "Is that an amazing story or what? Can you imagine?" She paused to catch a breath, then her expression changed slightly as she looked around at the group. "You didn't find anything else with these tablets, did you? Anything like what I've been deciphering?"

There were some hasty glances, but Kansas recovered quickly. "I wish we had, sounds incredible—devices that would make everyone tell the truth. Wow."

Myra nodded complacently, but her eyes didn't seem convinced. "What a shame. What a find that would be."

They thanked Myra profusely for her time and Will told her he would be in touch if they learned more or needed more information. Their new acquaintance watched them leave the building from her office on the third floor. She walked over to her phone and dialed a number. "Hello, this is Myra Cunningham, from MIT. You told me if I came across something...unusual...I was to call. I have a little information for you that may be useful." She paused, listening. "Yes sir. I understand sir. I'll do that immediately."

The flight back was one of excitement, introspection, and speculation. What do you do with a device from another world that makes you tell the truth? Will was piloting, Cass sat in the copilot's seat, and Kansas had the back of the plane to himself, reading the printout on the information Myra had given them. While he was lost to speculation, Will and Cass chatted, learning more about each other. Cass admitted to herself that she found this handsome, slightly off-center fellow intriguing—the long blond hair, those mischievous blue eyes so filled with spirit and life, and his sharp wit—but he was a little cocky, and she enjoyed keeping him off balance. They talked about interests and past history, and, of course, about the truthmakers.

She eased back in her seat and tucked herself against the door, turning to him as he managed the plane's controls. "The truth is, a device like this let loose on this country—well, you could either have a hell of a lot of fun stripping the charades from people, or you could use it to your own benefit and probably divine the numbers for every wall safe, credit card, and bank account you had time to pinch. Or you could go big game hunting, like Vandar did, and force an integral change in our system, as well as how we relate to each other, but that would take serious *cojones*, and I think that would have less than a fifty-fifty chance of being successful before somebody popped you and the truthmaker disappeared. I think personally I'd start with the civil courts. Our judicial system isn't based on who's innocent or who's guilty, but rather who can tell the best story or which attorney is best at the finding and application of judicial loopholes. If used discreetly, judiciously—more like a scalpel than an ax—a person could fix a lot of things."

Will turned his head back toward Kansas and they exchanged a quick glance. "Yeah, no question there," Will said with a chuckle.

"Damn, no one would be able to cheat on their taxes ever again. Talk about an elemental change in this country!" Cass added quietly, in an off-the-cuff realization.

"And no one would ever be screwed again on a real estate deal, or on the purchase of an automobile, or a stock exchange," quipped Kansas from the back.

There were a few minutes of silence, the people in the cabin lost in their own thoughts, then Cass turned to Will and said, "Well, have you worked up enough courage to ask me out yet?"

Will jerked in his seat like he'd been stabbed with a pin. The woman had caught him off guard again. "No, aahh yes, I mean yes, I guess I could...I have..." *Damn, she made him feel like a freaking schoolboy.*

"It's okay, just take your time," she said with a smile, those gray-blue eyes dancing with mirth. "Doesn't have to be a fancy place. The Sands in Key West would be fine—on the water, nice view. I'm not a hard woman to please." Then she got that mischievous smile of hers. "And if I find you're having trouble, I'll give you instructions."

Kansas just grinned knowingly from the back seat.

Their trip had been a success, but unbeknownst to them, much had happened while they were gone. Crazy Eddie had gotten himself seriously drunk the night after his experience with the truthmaker—too many memories. He had driven into Key West and started at Sloppy Joe's, then just worked his way down the street, inebriation chasing him like a pack of hounds. They caught him by the time he reached The Green Parrot. Sitting at the bar, elbows barely supporting him any longer, he got to telling the bartender what had happened to him. It just all came pouring out—about escaping Cuba with a device found in the mountains that could make you tell the truth. He told of his experience with it, and as bitter as it seemed, it was like an exorcism for him. He told of his friends, as well, and how each one of them had one of these devices. The bartender was a man who had heard lots of stories. It was fascinating, but he believed about a third of it. Hell, he had a busy bar to tend. But the guy on the other side of Eddie was really taken with the story.

Wilson McKenzie II—light brown curly hair, about five-foot-six, pudgy build, somewhat inscrutable, lazy hazel eyes, and a generally disarming appearance—had experienced a broad spectrum of life in his twenty-seven years. Wilson's father had been rich, very rich, but the house of cards on which he had built his fortune collapsed overnight to charges of insider trading, and a number of rash gambles with computer stocks in a desperate attempt to recoup. The final straw was an indictment for sex with a minor when he was caught in bed with the maid's fourteen-year-old daughter.

McKenzie's father blew his brains out in the study while his son played canasta with his mother in the living room. At the age of twenty, Wilson went from rich to poor overnight. He had grown up being given everything—silver spoons, nannies, and

Porsches at sixteen—but little love, attention, or affection, which is probably why he turned out to be a compulsive liar, slightly sociopathic, and the victim of one other significant psychological manifestation. After the loss of his father and his wealth, he tumbled through life for a while, living by what wits he had, sliding down the food chain until he was doing a little breaking and entering work from Miami south to The Keys, scamming tourists, stealing an occasional purse or wallet when the opportunity presented itself, moving a few pounds of pot when he got the chance, and eventually managing to create a circle of acquaintances from bookies and fences, to fixers. Still, he probably wouldn't have made it without Ralph. The problem was, Ralph was just so damned annoying—he butted into everything, but he was so... entertaining.

In his storytelling, Crazy Eddie had been descriptive, using both Kansas's and Will's names. Wilson McKenzie didn't have a flipping clue who Kansas Stamps was, but he knew of Will and his boat at Safe Harbor Marina. It just so happened that he lived in a small, ramshackle houseboat in that very same marina. Visions of sugarplums started dancing in his head when he thought about the possibilities of a device that would make someone tell you just about anything you wanted to know. About that time, Ralph showed up.

The pudgy fellow with the curly hair and uncertain eyes sitting next to Eddie slowly, gradually straightened up, and his whole countenance changed. His eyes suddenly cleared, his head cocked to one side and he got that same goofy, sort of cocky smile Mel Brooks garnered in *Silent Movie*—a brash, confident, but somewhat perfidious demeanor that makes you want to count your fingers after a handshake. As the change completed itself, a leering grin was added to the package, along with eyes reflecting the bright intensity of release, like a ferret that's just escaped its cage.

"Fark! What a story!" the new Ralph/Wilson McKenzie exclaimed, slapping Eddie on the shoulder in compatriot fashion. "What a story! You must be quite a fellow! Nearly a folk hero of some sort! And you own your own airplane! Tell me more about yourself...and these devices." He moved in closer, put his arm around Eddie in a conspiratorial fashion, brows narrowing. "What exactly do they look like?" But before Eddie could answer, Ralph/Wilson swiveled around sharply in his barstool and snapped his fingers in the air. "Barkeep! Kind sir! Another round for my friend and me here! And don't spare the rum!" Then his arm swung back over Eddie's shoulders, eyes bright with mischief. "You were saying, my friend?"

Later that night Ralph/Wilson strolled quietly from his little houseboat down to Will's converted shrimper and slipped aboard. It took him a while, but he found what he was looking for. For the next five days, during the time Kansas, Will, and Cass were gone on their sojourn to MIT, Ralph figured out the truthmaker and wreaked havoc. He began at bars, just turning it on and talking to people, asking them personal questions: "Hi, my name's Ralph, what's yours? What was the most important thing that you ever stole in your life? Did you ever peek in the bathroom and see your sister naked? Did you like it?"

Pretty soon he graduated to more important things: "Hey, nice to meet you. I'm Ralph. What's your name? Having a nice stay in the islands? Where're you staying? What's the room number? What's the combination on the lock for your room? Did you ever see your mother naked? How was that for you?"

From there he took a drive up to Miami International Airport, to the area where the rental lockers were located. He pulled his longish light brown hair up under his hat, put on a dark pair of sunglasses to hide his crazy eyes, and added a limp to his walk just to conceal his identity a little more, then sat out in the concourse chairs and watched people put things into lockers. He paid attention to those who looked around cautiously too long after closing the door—those who checked the door two or three times before walking away. Then he went over and sat by them. The conversations went something like this: "Well, hello there! Lovely day for flying, huh? My name's...(shrug) oh hell, my name isn't important, what's your name? Got kids? Wow, that's great. Where you headed? Yeah, nice place. What do you have in the locker here at the airport? And, by the way, what's that combination?" Then, sliding over, putting his arm around them in that too close, conspiratorial fashion of his and staring at them, he'd say slowly, "Oh, and by the way, you really just can't remember much about me, okay? Can't remember." Then, with a big smile, eyebrows popping up and down like Groucho Marx's, he'd give them an overly amicable slap on the back. "Have a great day!"

After pocketing several thousand dollars, five ounces of pot, and a handful of porn magazines that he just couldn't leave in one locker, Ralph/Wilson headed for the dog track. He knew a couple of the hustlers there, people who were in the know on what races might be fixed, and who the big hitters were betting on. They would, of course, have handed him his head for even asking in normal circumstances, but...

The *pièce de résistance,* however, was when he learned of a visit by State Senator Stan Schulte, the porkmaster of politics, having found more ways to funnel money into the hands of corrupt business and industry (and, of course, his own hands) than any other senator in the history of Florida. But his connections, rumored to run into the big house on The Hill, had so far kept him unencumbered by steel bars and concrete. Having just beaten an indictment for insider trading, he was in Miami on, of all things, a fundraiser for his re-election. He was speaking in the ballroom of the Fontainebleau about the possibility of a new Center for the Arts.

Wilson McKenzie II would have been quite content with his new life and its modest new wealth, but Ralph wasn't. Ralph wasn't happy unless he was screwing somebody, figuratively or otherwise. Ralph hated politicians and carried a powerful disdain for the figureheads of religion. Wilson had seen politicians come and go from his father's house, selling their influence and walking out with paper bags filled with money—the greedy smiles, the soulless, conscienceless conversations he'd heard in whispers as a child. And he'd been an altar boy who once found himself alone with a priest who had forgotten what should have been the eleventh commandment—"Thou shalt not grope children." When he heard about the senator, he smiled like Jim Carrey on bennies and Ralph really kicked in. He bought himself some new clothes and a larger pair of dark sunglasses. He pulled his hair up under his sporty hat again and stuffed cotton wads in his cheeks to change the appearance of his face. Then, with the truthmaker, he talked a reporter out of his press pass, which put him in the front row for the speech. Just beforehand, he singled out the senator's two aides—watchdogs, really, who were always with him. He had a brief conversation with each, with the truthmaker turned on, planting a suggestion to, "Just relax today and let the senator answer all the questions." He wasn't sure that would work, but it was worth a try.

Applause filled the room when Senator Schulte came on stage—tall, dignified graying hair, the same swagger, the same counterfeit smile, and the same gleam of conceit, deceit, and power in the eyes that Wilson McKenzie had seen so often. He let the senator perform his speech about the arts and their value in Miami, then it was time for questions. Ralph started raising his hand. After a few tries the senator pointed to him.

"Helllooo, Senator!" Ralph/Wilson said with a broad smile, as he clicked on the truthmaker in his pocket. "Just a couple of quick questions. First off, how much money did you receive under the table from organized crime for arranging approval on the licensing of the new Grande Mariose and Harrison Elite hotels downtown, sir?"

The senator blinked a couple of times and his eyes became confused with struggle. His mouth moved, but nothing came out. His aides in the wings of the stage blinked a few times themselves, rising partially out of their seats, but pausing.

"Could you answer the question, sir?"

Schulte blinked again and then just sort of relaxed, his face deflating of animation like someone had just unplugged his cord. "They paid me two hundred thousand. I wanted more, but that was the best they would do."

A confused murmur ran across the crowd, and there were gasps of astonishment and incredulousness. *Surely this was a mistake...*

Ralph nodded. "And how much money did you take from the Miami Iron Workers Union for your efforts in securing their contracts with the U.S. Navy for its Fourth Fleet refitting work?"

The senator drew a deep breath and expelled it slowly, confused, concerned, but trapped in the talons of truth. "Another two hundred thousand. Cheap bastards. What I did for them was worth a lot more."

The audience was abuzz with chatter, and people were starting to stand. News reporters were scribbling notes, shooting pictures, and holding microphones outward. Ralph almost had to shout the last question as the aides were finally rising out of their seats, as if struggling through pudding, knowing something was dreadfully wrong.

"And finally, sir, the insider trading charge you were just cleared on—were you guilty of that?"

The senator's eyes were hollow blue pools of confusion and confession. He nodded. "Yes. I was. Of course I was. Hell, I know half a dozen people who played that game with me. There's…"

At that point the Mayor of Miami Shores came out of his chair like a linebacker and snatched the microphone out of Schulte's hands, addressing the audience. "The senator is obviously not himself today. I think we will end this conference now and continue at another time."

Ralph was still shouting over the crowd. "Did you ever see your sister naked? Did you like it?"

Afterwards, as the lone figure with his wide hat and large sunglasses exited the Fontainebleau Hotel, his shoulders slumped a little and his posture became less erect, and there was suddenly less confidence in his stride. Wilson McKenzie found himself alone again. Ralph was gone. He had never stayed that long. It was disconcerting and somewhat frightening. On the other hand, he had considerably more money in his pocket now, and the potential for much more.

The next day, papers across the country headlined the remarkable public confession. The senator's press team was trying desperately for damage control, citing the possibility that Stan Schulte may have ingested a hallucinatory drug. But it was probably too late. Two ranking members of the Miami Steel Workers Union were already rolling over to protect themselves.

As Ralph was taking a hiatus from Wilson, detective Mariana Martinez was arriving in Miami from Cuba via Mexico, booking reservations at the Holiday Inn in Key West.

By the time the 310 Cessna touched down at the Summerland airport and its three occupants had returned to their homes from their trip to MIT, a number of things were apparent. Will had come home with sugarplums dancing in his head, looking forward to his impending date with Cass. But when he stepped into the cabin of his boat, all of that got slapped onto the back burner. His living and sleeping areas had been brutally ransacked—tables turned over, drawers pulled out with the contents everywhere, mattresses torn off beds, goods tossed out of cabinets, refrigerator contents emptied onto the floor, and books and knickknacks strewn everywhere. But most of all, worst of all, the vase in the corner of the room, where he had hidden his truthmaker, was shattered, and the device was gone.

Kansas had put his truthmaker in a small wall safe in his kitchen, but his arrival home was no less disappointing. It was evening. The sun had fallen off the end of the world and only the last feathers of soft blues and grays graced the corners of the sky. He walked into the house, turned on the lights, and there was Mariana sitting in a chair in the living room. She held a pistol with a long, menacing silencer in her hand. Kansas smiled, not terribly surprised. "Mariana! I missed you too, but I didn't expect you to come all this way to visit me." He was once again taken with how simply attractive she was, the long dark hair and those hazel eyes—not the fireworks kind of pretty, more like the beauty of backcountry waters in late afternoon with the sun casting Degas tapestries of reds and yellows across the mirrored surface.

"It's not a social call," she said. "It appears you left my country in a hurry. We'd like to know what you took with you." Kansas started to say something but she waved him off with the gun. "Don't bother trying to be too clever here. Satellite photos showed us exactly where you were. We could see the gold bullion. Our Intelligence people found the cave, but what we really want to know is what you found in the room behind the cave."

Kansas shook his head. "Empty. It was empty. Amazing and unusual, but empty." He was standing by a cabinet just inside the house. There was a spit from her weapon and the glass in the cabinet exploded. Kansas flinched, holding his ground, but beginning to consider alternatives. "I take it you're not really an accountant for the Ministry of Agriculture?"

"I'm going to ask again," she said, "and if I don't get an answer I like, I'm going to be less polite."

Kansas sighed, realizing he needed to buy some time.

"Okay, I'll make a deal with you. I'll tell you a story about an ancient civilization if you'll lower the gun and let me have a seat."

She thought about it, then nodded and motioned him to the seat across from her in the living room.

He decided he might tell her about the golden notebook, and leave out the information about the truthmakers. Perhaps he could buy his way out of trouble with that. He had just finished the story when lights appeared on the road by his stilt house and a car pulled up underneath in the driveway.

She pointed the gun at him. "I'm going to put this in my purse next to me. Don't do anything stupid. I rather like you and I don't want to have to shoot you, but I will. So just act normal and get rid of whoever it is." She glared at him hard once more. "Don't be foolish here, Mr. Stamps. It could cost you dearly."

He nodded. "Okay, got it."

They listened as two people came up the stairs and knocked. When Kansas opened the door, two large men dressed in light gray suits, white shirts, no ties, hair military short, eyes very steady, right on the border of inscrutable, stood before him. "Mr. Stamps?"

Kansas nodded, already getting that uncomfortable feeling in the pit of his stomach. "Yes?"

"Mr. Stamps, we're with the Federal Bureau of Investigation. We'd like a couple words with you, sir, if we could," one said, flashing a badge but not giving Kansas much time to look at it.

Realizing that this was not a good thing, but it got him out of the immediate problem, he let them in. He walked into the living room and turned around to offer a seat, only to find one of the men had a pistol in his hand. The other pointed to Mariana. "Please get up and sit on the couch over here." Turning to Kansas, he said, "You too, on the couch."

Mariana hesitated, reaching for her purse. The gun in the man's hand came up. "Leave the purse."

Professionals, thought Kansas. *Keep your subjects together, no external possessions within reach.*

They positioned themselves in front of the couple, still standing. The taller one spoke. "We'd like some information from you about a trip you made to Cuba just recently. The Cuban government hasn't said a thing about it, but a Norwegian cruise ship reported a Cuban MiG attacking an American seaplane, apparently escaping from Cuba, northeast of the Cayman Islands. The plane is registered to a friend of yours, an Edward Jackson Moorehouse. We'd like to know what happened, and we'd like to know exactly what you found in Cuba."

Kansas shrugged. "Yeah, okay. We were in Cuba, looking for an aircraft that went missing several years ago—in 1954. We found the plane we were looking for, but we ran into a little trouble about leaving when we wanted to."

The taller one stared at Kansas silently. "I'm going to ask you nicely one more time. What did you find in Cuba? We're talking about ancient artifacts here."

Kansas sighed, his thoughts swinging back to Myra at MIT. "Yeah, okay. We found a golden tablet of some sort in a cave—had some history about an ancient civilization on it."

"What else?"

"That's it, man. Didn't appear to be anything else in the room."

The man's face went hard. "I don't believe you. Last chance, Mr. Stamps."

"Listen," Kansas said angrily. "I don't know what the hell it is you want…"

"Shoot the girl," the man said to his partner. "Don't kill her at first, just shoot her."

The fellow raised his weapon and aimed at Mariana.

"Wait! Wait!" Kansas cried as Mariana drew back in fright. "Okay, okay. There was a device in the cave, as well." His mind was racing ahead—no point in telling them there were two. "It was about the size of a television remote, made out of what looked like silver."

The two men glanced at each other with a degree of subtle satisfaction.

"What's it about? What does it do?"

"What do I know? It's just a device of some sort."

"Where is it?"

This time Kansas hesitated again.

"Kill the woman," the man said decisively.

"No!" Kansas shouted, throwing himself across Mariana. "I have it. I have it. I'll get it for you. Just don't hurt anybody."

The fellow finally smiled, but it wasn't pretty. "Now, Mr. Stamps. Now is a good time."

Kansas was allowed to get up and unlock his safe. He brought out the device and handed it to the guy in charge. The fellow studied it for a few moments, then put it in his coat pocket. He looked up. "Here's what I'm going to suggest: you and your girlfriend forget this ever happened. Forget you ever saw us. Forget your trip to Cuba. If that doesn't take place, we'll visit you again, and things are going to go downhill from there. Am I clear?"

Kansas just stared at him, seething inside, anger rolling in waves through him.

The men backed away, out the door and into the night. Kansas and Mariana watched from the window as the black Cadillac drove away.

Mariana turned to Kansas. "They were going to kill me for an artifact. And you call my government harsh and unyielding!" Then she paused and her face softened. "You saved my life tonight, and you gave up something I know is precious to you. I saw your eyes."

"Yeah, you're right, and I want it back," said Kansas with determination as he snatched the phone off the wall and punched out a number. It rang twice before Will picked it up. For the next five minutes the men exchanged bad news. At first they thought the same individuals had taken both devices, but in the process of sifting information, Will realized his clock had been smashed—it had stopped over four days ago, before they met with Myra, so it probably wasn't the same people. It could be their truthmakers were out there in two different directions, but how?

"Listen," Kansas said to Will, "we've got to worry about the one we know of. My guess is these guys flew into Miami, rented a car, and headed into The Keys. We've got to cut them off before they can get back to Miami. I know it's a long shot, but it's all we've got. They're driving one of those austere black Caddies—dark-tinted windows and equipped with those extra bright headlights. I got the first three letters of their tag. They'll be pretty easy to pick out. We need to get into your plane and get up to the strip on Tavernier. Better your twin than my single engine amphibian for this. Then we rent a car and wait for them on the highway. Maybe, if we're lucky, they'll make a pit stop somewhere before the airport and we can hit them."

"But you said they were with the FBI. That's the big boys, Kansas."

"The FBI doesn't indiscriminately kill people who don't answer their questions quickly enough," Will's friend spat back. "Besides, whoever they are, they've pissed me off and I'm going after them."

There was a brief pause.

"Meet me at the plane in fifteen minutes. Bring something that shoots," Will said.

"Oh, you can count on it."

Kansas hung up the phone and redialed. "Hey Cass, I haven't got much time, so I'll get to the point. I've got a situation and I could use your help. Might be a little touchy and require some of your...skills. Are you interested?" He grinned with satisfaction. "Thanks, I figured I could count on you. Meet me at Will's plane in fifteen minutes." Then he turned to Mariana. "I'm going to tell you the truth and you're going to have to make a choice to either work with me, or become a combatant. It's your call and we don't have much time."

She nodded in cautious acquiescence. "Go ahead."

"We found some curious things in the room behind the cave. One was a tablet that told the history of an ancient civilization. The other two items were small, strange devices, like the one you just saw, which apparently emit some sort of vibration that affects the human brain and forces an individual to tell the truth."

She scoffed at first, but then she looked into Kansas's eyes and suddenly she knew. "You're telling me the truth. This is actually true. That is what this whole thing was about tonight."

Kansas nodded. "Yeah. Now here's the deal. We can work together on this and get these devices back. If we do, you get to keep one, and in this case one is every bit as good as two, you understand?"

Mariana straightened up. "Let us go to this airplane of yours."

By the time they reached the plane, Will was in the cockpit

doing a preflight check. Cass was sitting in the copilot's seat. Will was tickled to see her again, but he knew this was going to be a little dangerous. Then he thought back to when he had first seen Cass—and what she did to the guy who took a swing at her.

Will was also pleased to see Mariana again, remembering why he was so taken with her—that full, inviting figure, those legs, the delectable way that voice of hers made conversation sensuous. But given the fact that she was on the Cuban gunboat, the reunion was a little cooler. Cass was introduced quickly and the two women shook hands, weighing each other, certainly wondering about each other's status, but there was little time for explanation.

They were in the air five minutes later. It took them less than a half hour to make the strip at Tavernaero Park in Tavernier. They landed and the car Kansas had reserved from the local Hertz people was waiting for them. A few minutes later they were perched on the side of the road, watching the oncoming traffic from the south. It was a summer weekday night and the traffic was fairly sparse. Fifteen minutes later the big Cadillac with the extraordinarily bright headlights came rolling past them.

"That's it," Kansas said.

Will, who was driving, smiled and pulled out, thoroughly enjoying the whole thing. "Showtime," he whispered. "We're comin' for you, boys, and we're gonna harsh your freakin' mellow!"

Kansas couldn't help but chuckle.

Twenty-five miles down the road, just as they were coming into Homestead, the driver in the Cadillac turned to his partner. "We've got lots of time. The plane won't be there until ten. Let's get a bite to eat."

His big partner nodded. "Why not? We've got this one in the bag," he said as he patted his coat pocket.

The Caddy turned in at Charlie's Seafood House and pulled into the corner of the parking lot. Will drove by slowly, still on the highway, watching the two men get out and head for the restaurant. Then he turned around.

Both men ordered the special, the seafood banquet, and were finished in twenty minutes. In the interim, the crew outside laid plans. Kansas offered a gift to the enterprise—a new device being used by police called a Taser. This one was smaller and more compact than the first models, but carried enough punch to drop a horse.

The evening air was heavy and sultry, and filled with the odor of fried things and auto exhaust. Clusters of insects danced around the dull yellow lights above the restaurant, and the evening shadows clung to the eaves like needy lovers. As the two men emerged and made their way toward their car, voices wrought with anger overtook them. Ahead, next to their Cadillac, a man and a woman were arguing violently. The guy, in blue jeans and a loose-fitting T-shirt, had long blond hair past his shoulders and smelled of alcohol. The woman was lithe and fairly pretty in a tight white blouse and a green miniskirt.

"You miserable bitch! You do that again and I will beat you till you can't walk. You understand?"

"Don't tell me what I can and can't do, you lousy prick. It wasn't my fault!"

The man suddenly reached out and grabbed the woman, pulling her in and slapping her across the face. They ended up stumbling into the black Caddy. "You'll do exactly what I tell you to do! Do you understand, bitch?"

He was reaching back to slap her again when the two men stepped over to them. "Hey, what's going on here?" the big one asked as he moved closer. "Get off my car."

"Sure," Will said as he turned around and without hesitation, Tasered him in the chest. The guy instantly went stiff and started trembling, mouth working into a yelping cry while he vibrated like a dash doll on a bumpy road. His friend started to reach inside his jacket for a gun, but the young woman, who seemed somewhat helpless a moment ago, stepped into him and, with a flattened hand like a blade, struck him in the throat, quick as a snake. The guy's eyes went wide with pain and surprise as he staggered backwards, mouth falling open, tongue on his lower lip, trying to get a breath. But the girl wasn't done. In what can only be described as a violent pirouette, her lithe body lifted off the ground, twirling, and one of those muscled, attractive legs from under that miniskirt came swinging around at the speed of light, the attached foot striking the man squarely on the jaw. His head snapped like Muhammad Ali had just smacked him with a right cross, and he collapsed onto the ground, out cold.

"Ooohhh, very nice," muttered Will with a bit of a grimace, more than somewhat impressed. *She really was just a little scary.*

Cass turned to him with the trace of a pleased smile, then her face got serious. "But if you ever slap me like that again, you'll be wearing your nuts for a necktie."

Will sucked air in through his teeth, eyebrows furrowing, then grinned playfully. "I love it when you talk dirty to me."

There was a conference then, while their former antagonists were still out. It was decided they needed to throw the bad guys off their trail, and in the process, the two men mustn't see Kansas or Mariana.

The two agents woke up, duct-taped hand, foot, and mouth, in the back of their Caddy, on a side trail off Card Sound Road. Cass and Will were kneeling over them. Will leaned forward in a sinister fashion with a knife. "Do we kill them?"

Cass pretended to think about it for a moment. "No, I think not. We'll cut out their eyes and their tongues, that way they can't identify us."

There was considerable shuffling and moaning of the beseeching kind on the floor in front of them.

"By the time anyone finds them we'll be back up north, with The Master. The plane flight will take four or five hours anyway."

"Seems very messy," Will said with a frown. "Maybe we could spare them the agony if they gave us some information."

More shuffling and moaning from the smaller one affirmed that idea, eyes suggesting that conversation was good.

Cass reached down and ripped the tape from his mouth. "Who are you and who do you work for?"

The man drew in a gasp of air and coughed.

"Well?" said Will as he moved closer with the knife.

"We work for the government," he said. "This was a stupid thing for you to do, whoever you are."

Will moved closer.

"Okay, okay. It's an agency that's under the net a little; it means nothing to you."

"The CIA?" Cass asked.

There was a grim smile through the pain. "No, not exactly.

More like its heir. We're assigned to check out any leads that might represent a jeopardy to…"

"To what?" Will said. But the man went silent, like he'd said too much. Will moved in with his knife and laid it on the man's cheek.

"It's nothing you need to know about," the man gritted out, eyes filled with fear and defiance, trying desperately to pull his face away from the knife.

Will's blade broke the skin.

"Okay! Okay. The…The Bright Circle," he cried.

Will looked at Cass questioningly, then he turned back to the guy and frisked him, finding the truthmaker.

Cass was about to ask another question when Kansas and Mariana pulled up in the car, blinking their lights at them. Cass got out and went over to them.

"C'mon, we gotta get out of here!" Kansas whispered harshly. "There are cop cars everywhere. Maybe these guys were supposed to check in and didn't. I don't know. But let's get out while we can."

The following morning they all sat around a table in the back of the Big Pine Coffee Shop, talking in hushed tones. "We should have used the truthmaker on them," Kansas said.

Will shook his head. "No, then they could have asked us something. The damned thing's nondiscriminatory. No, we did the right thing, and now we've got it back. I just wish we could have gotten more information. I wish we could have known it was nothing more than a bad accident that drew the local police. And I sure as hell would like to know who or what 'The Bright Circle' is."

"Yeah, me too, but at least you folks are safe, regardless," Kansas said, looking at Will and Cass. "They have no idea who you are, and the false info you gave may throw them off for a while. But I'm thinking Mariana and I are going to have to find a place to lie low for a bit until we work this out. One of the first things we have to do is to figure out who stole the other truthmaker. I think we need to talk with Crazy Eddie. I've just got a feeling…"

Cass looked up from the day's *Key West Citizen* she was reading. "You guys aren't going to believe this. In the last few days there's been a run of people in The Keys and Miami who claim they gave their hotel room information, credit card numbers, and safety box combinations to a guy. Just gave them to him when he asked, but no one can remember exactly what he looked like. Then, a hotshot senator with a reputation for playing fast and loose gives a speech at the Fontainebleau in Miami and it suddenly turns into a Jerry Springer confession to insider trading and illegal deals with mobsters and teamsters. Some guy in the audience kept asking him questions and the senator kept obliging. What does this sound like to you?"

They all looked at each other.

"Somebody's using our truthmaker," Will said quietly.

"Well, first thing's first," Kansas said decisively. "I'm going to call Parmer's Place over on Little Torch Key, see if they've got a two-bedroom apartment we can rent for a week. The owner is a friend of mine, and it's the slow time of the year. He'll keep quiet about me and Mariana being there." He looked over to the lady at his side. "If that's okay with you."

Mariana murmured an agreement, and he continued. "Then I want to run down Eddie and talk with him. Maybe he can shed some light on this."

"I also think we need to draw this Bright Circle bunch away from us, a feint of some sort," Will added. "If there was an obvious 'truthmaker event' somewhere well away from here, we could get them looking in the wrong places."

Cass and Mariana both grinned.

"Excellent idea," Cass said. "It'd take some of the pressure off of you," she said, nodding at Kansas, "while you try to find the other device." Shaking out a page of *The Citizen,* she handed it to Kansas and Mariana. "It just so happens there's something interesting going on with the state legislature and some developers in Ocala. I think this might be the next stop for the truthmaker."

The article was about the Florida state legislature convening for a mini session in two days' time, regarding the planned development of a new theme park outside Ocala, in Central Florida. In an area that had struggled with rabid, conscienceless developers and their greedy partners in local and state government, a final piece of pristine property still filled with many of the trees, plants, and animals that made Florida so unique was now earmarked for "Pirate Land Theme Park," complete with lunch-evoking thrill rides, huge lagoons with pirate ships, concessions of every imaginable description, wild animals in cages, and eye-patched pirates everywhere. The problem was not just the destruction of habitat and the loss of wildlife, and the immense amounts of fresh water needed to accommodate thousands of thirsty tourists every day, but the disposal of all the waste and by-products of the "Aaarrrreal Good Time" they were promised. It was the same old scenario—developers promising jobs to the community and environmentalists trying desperately to hold the line on conscience somewhere. State Senator Ted Westerson and State Representative Lamar Jones had teamed up with the developers and were pushing "a newer, brighter future for the residents of Ocala and surrounding areas," but there was much hue and cry about possible kickbacks and collusion.

Both Westerson and Jones were poster children for the corrupt politician. Lamar Jones was under investigation for soliciting bribes and violation of the Foreign Corrupt Practices Act. He was accused of taking bribes for services/votes rendered, and investing the money in shady business deals with relatives in South Africa. Westerson was a good ol' boy politician who had the "earmark" process down to a fine art, directing contracts to nonprofit organizations headed by both his campaign contributors and business partners. In the last four years he had managed to earmark almost seventy-five million in U.S. government contracts to over a dozen profit and nonprofit agencies that, ironically, had donated nearly two million dollars to the Southern Children of Need Foundation, of which he just happened to be director.

It would be nigh on impossible to get close enough inside the legislature to use their devices, but as it turned out, the article mentioned the two legislators were holding a news conference (trying to whip up the investment/approval frenzy they needed) at the luxurious Governor's Inn, located in downtown Tallahassee, the day before the determining session. It would be an informal gathering of supporters and, of course, the press.

After reading the article, Kansas looked up at Cass and Will with a mischievous smile. "Your mission, should you decide to accept it, Mr. Bell..."

CHAPTER 6

Those who know the truth are not always equal to those who love it.

— **James Russell Lowell**

By midday, Kansas had picked up a few things that he needed from his place and they had retrieved Mariana's suitcases from her hotel in Key West. They secured a room with two beds at Parmer's—there were no two-room apartments. There was an awkward moment or two when they settled into the room, but it wasn't that uncomfortable. A connection existed between the two of them, some fire and ice given the circumstances, but an undeniable attraction, and they both knew it. Kansas was finding it somewhat of a pleasant return to life, to feel his pulse rise slightly when she touched him, that slight fragrance of orange blossoms and cinnamon that wafted in and captured him every once in a while. It had been some time—since Cass, really—but that had never really developed into a relationship, so there was neither angst nor guilt to be assuaged there.

Mariana found it somewhat disconcerting to be attracted to this confident, rather good-looking American who had shown such courage in protecting her earlier—his thick, sun-lightened hair and deep tan, and those bright hazel eyes. He was certainly a gallant fellow, and she needed his help to succeed, but it wasn't part of the plan to like him. She supposed the worst that could happen was she would find this a more interesting assignment than most.

Kansas set down a hastily packed suitcase at the foot of one of the beds, nodding at them. "You have a preference?"

Those expressive dark eyes smiled just a little. "Why don't we worry about that later?" she said.

He couldn't tell if she was teasing him, or being coy.

"Fine with me. I'm easy." Then he shrugged with a whisper of a smile. "Well, not that easy. I usually expect a nice dinner at least."

She definitely grinned this time. "Don't get your hopes up,

American flyboy. We have business to take care of, remember?"

"Don't you ever mix business with pleasure in Cuba?"

She paused for a moment before answering. "In Cuba we dance; we have a dance for everything," she said musingly, turning to gaze through the patio doors at the docks and sun-glistened water in the distance. "Dancing is not just passion, but patience and timing, as well." Then she turned to him, her smile an alliance of mischief and promise. "Enjoy the dance, Kansas. Live for the song, not the crescendo of the orchestra."

As they unpacked and made some plans, they talked about themselves.

"Have you ever been out of Cuba before?" Kansas asked as he put his things in a drawer. He could see the hesitation.

"Yes," she finally said. "A couple of times—for work."

"Which obviously has nothing to do with Cuban agriculture."

She shrugged noncommittally, and said nothing more.

"So, do you actually live with your mother and a cat?"

"No," she replied with just a touch of sadness in her eyes. "Most of my family was killed in a hurricane when I was twelve. I was raised by the State. I did well in school and was fortunate to be picked to advance for training with the Department of the Interior."

"I'm sorry," Kansas muttered, not knowing what else to offer.

"It's okay. It was a long time ago."

"Not married? A significant other?"

Mariana shook her head. "No, not now. There have been…people in my life. But not the right ones, I guess."

"I'm willing to trade stories," Kansas said, pleased to hear she wasn't attached. "Would you like to know about me?"

She looked up with an intuitive glance. "I already do. I know where you were born, where you went to school, when you graduated college, when you moved to The Keys, and that you are not who you told me you were." Mariana saw the look that touched his face with the last sentence, and she stood, coming over to him. Putting her hands against his chest intimately but not passionately, she moved into him, staring into his eyes, close enough that the orange blossoms and cinnamon engulfed his senses. Her face was unchanged but her eyes smiled. "Come, my new friend, let us continue about our business. The dance has just begun."

Cass and Will had settled into the seats of his little twin, headed for the news conference in Tallahassee on the following day. As Will banked out across the shimmering azure waters of the Gulf he checked his airspeed, altitude, and the course for the Tallahassee airport, then settled back into his seat with a satisfied smile. "Thank God for airplanes—the greatest invention since fire and beer."

"And maybe truthmakers will fit in there someday," Cass added.

"Won't beat beer and flying for me. Not that truth isn't an important commodity—something we could certainly use more of."

Cass sighed. "In this world, the purveyors of truth are in for a tough time. Truth has a great many enemies—greed, envy, prejudice, hatred, just to name a few—but its value is immense. It's the undeniable bond in any relationship. It carries more weight than passion, fairness, or wealth, and in the end is more durable and more precious than love itself. You can have a deep and abiding relationship without passion, but you can't have one without truth."

Will looked over at his companion, suddenly struck by the depth of this lady as she continued.

"Yet, it's also one of the most malleable elements because it can be twisted, a fraction, by just a few words. Our senses are continually in a state of seduction, overwhelmed by a plethora of abstract truths and cloaked falsities from commercials, commentators, attorneys, and politicians, and any real truth is getting harder and harder to find."

Nodding, Will added, "And in that vein, we all have to be aware of the half-truth because we can never be certain which half we've received." He smiled. "Sometimes we're eager to swallow the half that flatters us, while at the same time sipping just a little of the truth we find bitter. That's a quote from someone, don't remember who."

"Denis Diderot. He's the guy who said that. He was a

French philosopher," she said quietly, without any sense of superiority because she knew, still gazing out the window at the grand expanse of wind-swept blue-green water below. "The greatest challenge to truth is that we all see it with different faces. What is an undeniable truth to you is little more than a guise to me. Ralph Waldo Emerson explained it best when he said, 'The truth is beautiful, but so are lies.' And sometimes we end up just having to sort between the two." She looked over at him. "This is a confusing time for truth. Sometimes opening your eyes doesn't seem to help. I think every once in a while you simply have to take a deep breath and close your eyes to see clearly. The answer you're looking for may not always be close at hand, but the truth is."

As Will and Cass soared across Florida Bay and the Gulf of Mexico, landing in Saint Petersburg to refuel and get a bite to eat, Kansas and Mariana paid a visit to Crazy Eddie. They sat under the wing of the Goose at Eddie's home base on the back side of Ramrod Key, while Eddie made rum punches. After he brought out drinks, he settled into a lawn chair next to them, looking over at Mariana. "Foxy lady, how is it that you escaped Cuba, too?"

Mariana smiled. "It's a long story, Eddie. You could say I'm on a *vacaciones de trabajo*—a working vacation."

He nodded, content. "If it works for you, mama, it works for me." Then he brought his attention around to Kansas. "So, what's up, my man? What brings you to my simple digs?"

"We've got a problem, Eddie," Kansas said in a serious tone. "Someone stole the truthmaker on Will's boat—tore the place up trying to find it."

"Ooohhh, that's a harsh bong, man, a harsh bong," Eddie muttered, frowning. But there was a brief blanch of conscience in his eye when he said it, and his gaze fell toward the ground. "A stone cold bummer."

Kansas waited for a moment. The anxious calls from seabirds in the distance flittered in the silence. "Eddie, they knew what they were looking for. You wouldn't know anything about this, would you?"

"Nahhh, man. I don't think so," he replied, forcing his eye upward. But he just couldn't hold Kansas's gaze. His shoulders slumped and he took a breath, exhaling hard. "Aaaaaahhh shit, man," he moaned. "I don't know nothing for sure, but dude, Eddie got wasted a few nights ago. He was bogartin' them bad vibes from that freaking machine, and got wasted." His face was lined with regret. "I got to talking to the bartender at The Parrot." He looked up at the sky in anguish and took another deep breath, exhaling slowly this time, bringing himself back down. "I just had to get it out of me, about that baby, and the cocaine, and the freaking machine, and this guy sitting next to me just found it all really far out."

On the way back from Eddie's, Kansas and Mariana began to lay plans. They had a description of the fellow—longish curly brown hair, hazel eyes, maybe five-six, and an off-and-on, exuberantly counterfeit personality. Their next stop was the bartender at The Green Parrot. It turned out that the bartender remembered the guy. He wasn't a real regular, but he showed up there more often than not on Wednesdays, and on Friday nights for happy hour. And it was Friday.

Wilson McKenzie II had every intention of going to The Green Parrot for happy hour, but while he was reading *The Key West Citizen* that afternoon he saw a piece on the city council meeting that night, and he felt Ralph nudging him. "C'mon Ralph, not today, huh?" he muttered. "Not today..." But there was a part of him, so to speak, that did think a city council meeting and that freaking truth wand might be fun.

The Key West City Council came to order for a special meeting promptly at 6:00 p.m. with Mayor Jimmy Dalley officiating. After a pledge of allegiance and the reading of the minutes of their last meeting, they got right to work. There were a number of issues, complaints, and petitions to consider. Hot Cheeks Men's Club needed a permit for additional parking. The Wok and Gong Chinese Restaurant wanted a license to build an additional dining room, and the Second Glance Hair Salon needed a permit to add a psychic/massage therapist to their entourage. In addition, Mrs. Sylvia Petersen and the Golden Garden Women's Club were there to protest the increasing disappearance of pets in Key West—dogs and cats mostly. She had recently lost Little

Chitty, her pedigreed poodle. She was heartbroken and enraged in equal proportions that her little "Chit" had disappeared and nothing had been done about it.

By the time Wilson McKenzie got to the meeting, Ralph was sliding in, taking over. It was going to be a fun night. He pulled his hair under his hat, put on his sunglasses, and stuffed some cotton wads in his cheeks. He really wasn't looking for justice, just entertainment. McKenzie wasn't overly observant, but Ralph was. Several of the girls from Hot Cheeks, dressed in miniskirts, tube tops and tattoos, had come to lend support for their boss. Ralph couldn't help but notice Mayor Dalley's brief flicker of, shall we say, acknowledgement, toward one of the ladies—a tall blond with cobalt, carnal eyes, and legs up to her armpits. There was also just a flash of something in the Chinese guy's eyes when they mentioned the disappearing pets. He also noticed that the mayor's wife, who was a highly attractive lady in her own right, and generally attended the meetings, took a second too long in her handshake with Councilman Hensley, who was a hotshot developer on the island in the Mercedes-cum-Hatteras-cum-mansion category. Their eyes connected and did that "it's really, really, nice to see you again," thing for a split second.

Ralph let the meeting get underway with the first piece of business being the Second Glance Salon. After a brief discussion, the license for the psychic/masseuse was voted on and approved. How could anyone be against rubbing out your demons and your aches at the same time? Ralph started getting bored about then and turned on the truthmaker. There was that slight, deeply elemental hum for just a moment, and the audience shifted in their seats uncomfortably for a second or two, then it passed. The next piece of business was the Chinese restaurant. The mayor, who was a fan of the restaurant, mentioned that he was there the night before, as was Mrs. Sylvia Petersen (who nodded in acknowledgement), and both had greatly enjoyed the *Kim Som Dim*. The owner, Yan Lin—a small, thin Asian with cautious almond eyes and a narrow mouth, smiled with pleasure.

"The meat seemed to have an extraordinary rich flavor," the mayor said. "Tell me, was that chicken or pork?"

Yan Lin's eyes suddenly went from pleased to slightly off focus. His face tightened and his mouth opened, then shut, then opened again. Finally, he just sighed. "Was poodle," he said. "Belly belly tasty, but not many around. White poodle seem to be most tasty."

Ralph simply couldn't contain himself; he just couldn't. "Hey Lin, did that poodle have a nametag?"

Lin pursed his lips, frowning, knowing in the back of his head this was not a good thing, but... "Yes, name was Chitty."

There was a huge, pregnant pause, and the mayor craned around in his seat, stunned, flabbergasted, agape, and suddenly a little nauseated. Sylvia Petersen gasped, paling. Then the look on her face turned from incredulous to revolted.

"My Chitty! You...you...! My God! I ate Chit!"

Lin nodded, trapped in confession, clutched in the baptism of truth. "Yes, you ate Chit." Then, taken by the preposterousness of it all, the double entendre, he smiled. "You ate chit!"

She was a ponderous woman, Sylvia Petersen, maybe five-eight and roughly two hundred twenty pounds. At that point, revolt slowly slid off her face and rage climbed right into the driver's seat. With a bloodcurdling scream she rose, knocking over her chair, and charged, climbing over the people sitting in front of her, ripping a hole through the bodies and chairs like a wounded rhino. "You bastard! You slant-eyed son of a bitch! I'm going to rip you to pieces!"

Lin backed up haltingly, a look of terror replacing amusement, raising his hands to protect himself, but it was too late. She was all over him like a cage fighter on cocaine, pretty much keeping her promise.

By the time order was restored and the paramedics had taken Lin to the hospital, Ralph was having such a good time he decided maybe just one more trick. He stood up. "Hey, everybody!" he shouted.

The room settled and pretty much turned in unison—the council members, the mayor, his wife, the girls from Hot Cheeks, the millionaire and his wife, and a couple of the councilmen's wives.

"Let's play a game," Ralph said, eyes sparkling with mischief and that crazed Jim Carrey smile smeared across his face. "It's a simple game. I ask a question and you folks answer," he said, throwing up his hands. "Sound like fun?"

The mayor started to stand. "Excuse me, sir, you're out of order—"

But Ralph cut him off. "How many of you have cheated on your wife or your husband in the last sixty days—with someone in this room? Just raise your hand if the answer is yes." Ralph smiled evilly. "C'mon now, don't be shy!"

The room stilled as if it had been covered with honey. There was lots of blinking and looking around in slow motion, lots of confused eyes, and slowly, haltingly, the hands began to rise—a surprising number of hands. The mayor, arm in the air, looked across at the leggy blond with the great eyes. She smiled, made a perfect circle with her mouth and winked, and three other girls from Hot Cheeks blew kisses at two of the councilmen, who were also doing their Statue of Liberty imitation. The mayor's wife, hand up, stared at the developer with a good degree of passion, but when she saw the hottie from Cheeks ogle her husband with the open mouth, fury replaced longing. Key West's mayor didn't miss the fact that his wife's hand was in the air. The young janitor, who was standing in the corner with his hand up, blew a kiss at one of the councilmen, whose hand reluctantly rested above his head. The psychic/masseuse, who should have known this was going to happen, raised her hand while turning to stare at her new boss, who was holding his boyfriend's hand, sitting in the seat next to her.

In seconds the room slid from confusion and confession into a good degree of enlightened belligerence—accusations, stuttering excuses, pleading, more accusations, a few chairs and punches being thrown, and basically just good, old-fashioned pandemonium. The council video cameras caught it all, the reporter for *The Citizen* got wonderful photos, and Ralph was just beside himself.

"Well," he said, as he put his thumbs in his belt like they did in the old Western movies, head tilted cockily, that glittering, demented gleam in his eyes accompanying a Mad Hatter smile. "I guess my work here is done."

That evening Kansas and Mariana shared an intimate dinner at Louie's Back Yard, learning more of each other, enjoying the dance. From there they went to The Green Parrot, but

Wilson/Ralph never showed.

Ralph was enjoying himself so much he decided it was time to go big game hunting. Enough with politics; he wanted a trophy on the wall that represented man's perpetual chicanery when it came to God. Let's face it; God had been good to him lately and he wasn't without faith. He just hated people who twisted belief, or religions whose hierarchy groped children.

Yesterday's paper had featured an article on The Tabernacle of Ethereal Light, a rapidly growing Florida-based organization that made Scientology look like Baptists on Demerol. It was a bona fide "grab your bag of quarters and meet me at the spaceship" sect that had somehow caught the attention of a lot of people in the Southern U.S. It had a charismatic leader, Reverend William Alontos—thirty-five years old, six feet tall, movie star looks, with longish blond hair, laser-like blue eyes, and one of those voices that just seemed to make certain parts of women (and some men) turn to butter. He hadn't come up with much doctrine that was truly original. He'd taken a touch from Buddha, a cupful of Christ, a pinch of Confucianism, a dab of spiritualism and rolled it all together into a package that shared communion with the leaders of a civilization from a distant planet. The focus of the philosophy was that man in his present state, with his present package of competing, violence-advocating religions, was no longer capable of interacting without aggression. Alontos was intent on starting a new nation—"Euphoria." He claimed he had a small island in the South Pacific somewhere in the Solomon Islands—"a paradise of still blue waters, lovely green mountains, verdant valleys and beaches that go on forever," that had been donated by one of his followers. He wouldn't disclose the location for fear of a flood of the uninvited, but he had lots of pictures of palm trees, ocean, small houses being built, and the offices for his corporation that was handling the construction. There were lots of happy, tanned people waving, blowing kisses, holding hands—Nirvana.

There were to be five thousand people chosen to go with him to start the new Eden, where he and his followers would live in peace and contentment forever, constantly in communication with the "gentle masters" of Lonoria. William was selling each seat on the train to paradise for five thousand dollars, and business was brisk. If all went well, the end result would be a clean twenty-five million. The fly in the ointment was that William Alontos, aka Billy Baxter of New York City, had a police record that included forgery and larceny. But he willingly admitted this. He would still be living that same life of "contemptuous artificial fulfillment" had it not been for Erano and Deborao from Lonoria, who now guided his every action. "Peace, brothers and sisters. Peace..."

Ralph/Wilson booked a seat on the 9:00 p.m. flight out of Key West into Miami, then on to Panama City—to be specific, the Hilton in Panama City where William Alontos was holding a religious convention over the weekend. *Bring your quarters, everyone, the ship is leaving soon...*

Kansas and Mariana waited at The Parrot through happy hour, and on until about midnight, then they drove back to their room at Parmer's on Little Torch. As they reached the threshold of the apartment, the summer moon escaped a battery of cottony gray clouds and cast its silver cellophane magic across the landscape, bathing them in soft, sheer brilliance, and "the dance" allowed a few moments in each other's arms, and a kiss or two that left them both with a surprising sense of urgency and passion, and keenly aware of a physical harmony neither had really anticipated. But Mariana withdrew slightly before it got away with them, looking up into Kansas's eyes and putting a finger to his lips, drawing it across them affectionately, sensuously.

"Kansas. Could we dance...just a little longer?"

He smiled, the passion in his eyes cooling to affection. "At your convenience, ma'am. Besides, I'm starting to enjoy the dance now."

That Saturday morning, about the same time Cass and Will and their truthmaker were ending the careers of Senator Ted Westerson and Representative Lamar Jones at their scheduled news conference regarding Pirate Land Theme Park (both readily admitting to receiving a hundred thousand dollars each from the developers of the park, and Westerson damning himself entirely when admitting to illegal kickbacks to his Southern Children of Need Foundation), Ralph/Wilson got himself a seat near the front of the stage at the convention room in Panama City. There were easily seven or eight hundred people in attendance and the event was being covered by NBC, which was doing a special on the charismatic but questionable cult leader. The place was like a Pietistic circus, the smells of popcorn, hot dogs, and sweaty, feverous faith pervading the air. Alontos came on stage to mad cheering—a rock star. He gave a benediction to the audience and the people of Lonoria, then spoke for about half an hour regarding his faith, his accomplishments, and his ultimate goal of "Euphoria," the new island in the Pacific. There was a fabulous slide show across the whole back wall to accompany the speech, and it showed amazing, wonderful, awe-inspiring, wallet-loosening photographs of paradise, all for just five thousand dollars a ticket. Then he did the thing he was known for— climbing down off the stage with his microphone and mingling with the crowd, touching them, one-on-one. Unfortunately, one of the people he touched was Ralph.

"Hello, young man!" said Alontos with his usual exuberance and force of presence. "Are you looking for a new life of peace and contentment? Will you be joining me in the world's new Eden?"

Ralph nodded enthusiastically. "Sure! Sure! I've got the money saved already. But I've got just a couple questions, then I'd like to sign up and pay right now."

Alontos realized he had a live one. "Sure thing, my brother. What is it that you need to satisfy your heart?"

"Well, this is what I'd like to know," said Ralph with deepened curiosity, suddenly straightening up, head cocking to one side, eyes gleaming wildly, with that Mad Hatter smile on his face. He pressed the button of the truthmaker and its vibration rippled through the audience. "Do you really have an island somewhere, and are you really planning on taking these people to this island to live in peace and love?"

Alontos started, as if he'd been pinched. He shook his head and his eyes blinked a couple of times. "I...I..." he stuttered, struggling with the force that was overwhelming him. "Well, I..." He exhaled sharply, and you could see his eyes surrender, engulfed by the power of truth. His face lost its counterfeit confidence, and he bowed his head and chuckled softly under his breath. "No, there's no island. Never was."

A collective gasp of incredulousness rippled across the

room.

Ralph picked up again. "You have been a charlatan most of your life. Are you still one?"

William Alontos stared out into the sea of astonished, questioning faces, then lowered his head again and shook it slowly. "A charlatan. Yeah, I guess that's as good as any definition." Then he looked up, some of his fire returning. "But I am a good one. Better than any of those assholes who taught me. I got it all—the looks, the voice, and I know how to get inside someone. I know how to find that place of weakness and vulnerability that each of us has, and twist it just enough to bend someone past caution, to open them up like a sardine can, until I can see everything there that can be used." He smiled and shrugged. "It's a gift. My father had it, but I'm much better than he was. He was just a carnie with talent who could free a dollar from a mark here and there. But I can make you want—I can make you *need*—to give me your money." He stared at Ralph and suddenly it was as if the trappings of grace and virtue had fallen from his countenance and all that was left was the ugly, tattered remnants of his soul staring back. He held out his arms widely. "Yeah, a charlatan, but look what I was able to do! I packed all these sheep into one room, bleating to be sheared…"

In the back of the audience stood a tall, quiet man—a somber man with large, passionate eyes, and a wide, full mouth that was as free with a smile as it was a rebuke. He had served his faith well through all these years. He knew that now, as always, there were those who offered false hope to many; those who would steal salvation from the needy, who would, without conscience, ferret away some of those at the edges of the flock. Like wolves, they were—thieves of souls. He had come today in plain clothes to witness another case of dupery, fraud, and trickery. But what he had seen, what he witnessed, set him back on his heels. What power was this? What was it that could turn a charlatan of this magnitude from his course with nothing but words? *Was it the Holy Spirit? It didn't feel that way…* He watched the man asking the questions and was reminded of the newspaper article he'd read recently about the state senator who suddenly, in the middle of a news conference, began to make such profound confessions.

What was it that could wrench the truth from such a dedicated mountebank—that could wrest the unfettered verity from a soul? He loved his faith and he believed unequivocally in its purpose, but he knew from his time at the Vatican that some things were better left unsaid, unfound, unknown. He would need to send a message. They would know what to do.

The following evening, just as the sun set on Big Pine Key and the no-see-ums and mosquitoes pulled themselves from their leafy hiding places looking for blood, two cars full of men in gray business suits and dark sunglasses hit Kansas's house, ransacking it when they found he wasn't around. From there they headed to Stock Island outside Key West and raided Will's boat, ripping it apart for a second time. Then they made a third stop.

This was all the result of a "business meeting" held at a very private residence outside Washington, D.C. It involved a small group of what could be considered fairly important men and women in American government and industry. It was a clandestine gathering of egos, intellects, and aspirations. There were no notes kept, and no schedules would reflect this meeting. It was an assembly of dissatisfaction, but it was also a congregation of vision and revelation. Plans for this nation were being presented; a new course was being set. But on this day there was concern, as well. Most of them knew that truth had found little place in government and civic affairs for some time, and what little of it that actually saw light was muffled, gagged, or contorted by a cooperative press and a bought-and-paid-for judicial system. But there was something in the wind—congressmen confessing crimes like choirboys at the knees of a priest, religious charlatans with huge followings dropping their trappings of dupery and surrendering to the truth on national television. Most significantly, at the apex of it all was the possibility, however remote, of a device that produced the truth. It was a good time to be wary. Unembroidered truth, free to scamper about the village of government like a capricious nymph, was just not acceptable." *Especially not now.*

The tone of the meeting was set by those words, but not all the power of the new group rested in the hands of those who were present. In very nearly every political entity—except for perhaps the great, ruthless reigns of the Hitlers and the Stalins—there have always been powers behind the throne; shadowy figures that have dealt in secret knowledge, intimidation, and the authority of wealth. America was no exception, and even this new congregation who envisioned a changed nation was equally indebted to, driven by, and in some cases, owned by, voices in the shadows—perhaps even more so.

The man most responsible for this gathering was not even present, but it was his ideals they were heeding as they laid plans to continue to reshape the American political landscape, to drift away from pure constitutional ethics, to bring it closer to the developing European concepts of an obliging Socialism, and begin the process of establishing a true, one-world government. The enigmatic but forceful presence of Ramone Torreos—international banker, power broker, and nation changer, son of a Third Reich general who escaped to Argentina in 1944 and built an enormous empire in South America and Europe over the next half century—had every intention of becoming the true power behind the throne. Torreos was confidant to presidents and kings, intimate to chairmen of countless consequential boards, venerable acquaintance of and mentor to congressmen, parliamentary leaders, and sons of revolutions.

It would be a slow process, but things were going to change. Nonetheless, there would still be power enough to satisfy all the needs of the members present, and their cohorts. Simply because democracy morphed into a slightly different form of government and the country ultimately surrendered more control to a global council, it wouldn't really affect the vast amount of money made by those near the top. On the contrary, those in attendance this day had begun to see themselves less as Democrats and Republicans, or conservatives and liberals (of which there were both), but more as the new global associates who would represent America in the coming "unification." Unfortunately, there was a theme that danced in and out among the words but was never really given voice: that little of this was about making it better for "the people," or improving life for the masses; it was ultimately about power, control, and money.

The difficulty they faced was the President of the United

States. Many of America's presidents had been groomed, financed, and funneled into the presidency with money that came from around the world, and they had been appreciative of that. But there had been a problem with this Ronald Reagan. In private conversations before being elected he had appeared to be receptive to the socio-economic and cultural changes that were needed to gradually lead the United States more toward the "European" form of government that Torreos saw emerging. Torreos put his considerable weight behind the man. But after the election it became obvious that the president had no intention of taking that tack with America. Torreos realized that he had been used, and that was something that rarely happened.

Instead of promoting some of the more necessary agendas that would bring forth a one-world government, the president was doing just the opposite. America's new leader had discovered that, regardless of its flaws, he had more of a desire to repair the system rather than change it. This didn't set well at all with Torreos.

Will and Cass were on their way back to The Keys, slightly euphoric after a successful mission in the business of truth and a night at the Holiday Inn together. After a romantic candlelight dinner laced with small intimacies, sensual overtones, and lingering eyes replete with promises, they had made it as far as the door of the hotel room before being drawn passionately into each other's arms. In the silence of the cockpit, with just the drone of the engine as company, both were lost to the visions and the melodies of the night before. In the soft glow of a single lamp, the couple had lain together, drenched with sweat, exhausted, still trembling in the aftermath of sensation and passion, as satisfied as either could remember. It had been a long time since Will had found himself so unleashed—he was usually the one in control, passionate but cool, just above it all. He could still feel that firm, lithe body against him—the sweet, rich fragrance of her honey-colored skin, the taste and the feel of her mouth.

Cass's blue-gray eyes carried the effervescence of a teenager. She was still experiencing an occasional irrepressible shiver of reminiscence and delight. She expected to be pleased, but she had never imagined Will's patience and skill at lovemaking—his firm body, the scent of his heated flesh and the taste of him, his tenderness, and extraordinary sense of timing. Cass found herself reminded that one of the great treasures in life is an unselfish lover, and she had discovered, with such pleasure, that Mr. Will Bell needed no instruction at all.

Unfortunately, as they neared Miami their reverie was broken by the crackling of the plane's radio. "Cessna November, one, zero, seven, Tango, Echo, come back."

Will picked up his microphone. "November, one, zero, seven, Tango, Echo."

"It's Kansas," his friend said without any perfunctory greeting. "I'm at the Marathon Airport FBO. We have major problems. Last night, whoever it is that's after us got to Eddie. They nearly beat him to death. Frasier, the guy who owns the property where he keeps his plane, came home to find Eddie hanging out of the cargo door on the Goose, bleeding out. He got him to the hospital in Key West and they saved him, but he's in bad shape. Turns out they hit my house and your boat as well, and tore things up looking for—"

"Jesus Christ!" Will hissed in anger. "Is he going to be okay?"

"Yeah, he's going to make it, I guess." There was a pause. "Will, now they've made this personal, so they're not gonna have to look for me anymore. I'm gonna find them. You don't have to get involved, I just wanted you to know—"

"I'm in," snapped Will. "He's my friend, too. I don't give a shit who they are, I'm gonna have a piece of 'em."

"Okay," Kansas said, pleased and relieved to know that his partner would be with him on this. "Did you get those hidden security cameras on your boat hooked up—the ones on the outside of the cabin?"

"Yeah. You know I was having trouble with the wiring and I had turned them off when the boat was hit the first time. But I fixed them before I left. I know where you're going. We should have pictures."

They all met at Fisherman's Hospital in Marathon and visited with Eddie, who was conscious but on the cusp of the nepenthe haze of narcotics—legal ones for a change. Mariana and Cass kept back slightly while Kansas and Will stood on each side of Eddie.

He opened his eye and gazed up drowsily at his friends, offering a lopsided smile through all the bruising, and slurred out a greeting. "Wass happenin', *amigos?*" Then he winced and recollection emerged in his eye. "Mean sons-a-bitches—three of them. Beat Eddie like a red-haired stepchild who stole their dope. Especially the one with the scar." He took a breath and exhaled sharply, just this side of misery. "Wanted to know about that damned truth machine. Wanted to know where it was." He drifted away for a moment, his one eye dreamy, closing for a second, then he resurfaced, offering a hint of a grin in confidence, a narrow ribbon of spittle escaping the side of his mouth. "They didn't know there was two of 'em, and I never told them any different. Shit, man, what did I know, anyway?" he muttered plaintively, as he brought up a finger and smeared the spittle in a palsied attempt to remove it. "Didn't matter. They just kept askin' questions then beatin' me. Didn't tell 'em shit."

Kansas put his hand on Eddie's shoulder. "It's okay, Eddie. I know you did good. You just rest now and get better." He sighed heavily. "I'm really sorry, man, that this happened to you. I'm gonna fix it; we're gonna fix it." Kansas got that terrible, hard sense of conviction in his eyes. "It won't happen again."

An hour later they were all at Will's boat, watching the surveillance video. There were three men—big guys, gray suits, white shirts, no ties—same as before. Two had dark hair, and one of them, who wore his hair heavily oiled and combed straight back, had a scar on his cheek that ran from just below his right eye across his cheekbone—like the slash of a knife, maybe. The third was larger, with military cut blond hair. As the big, black Cadillac pulled out, they got a solid read on the tag. The next stop was Cass's place and her computers.

While the other three sat in Cass's sparse living room, she made some calls to heavy friends in computer/ government circles and got return calls/faxes with the information they wanted. She came out and tossed a piece of paper on the table in front of Kansas and Will. "No surprises here. Car is government owned, registered to a congressional security bureau in D.C. Not FBI or CIA apparently, though I'm not absolutely sure about that, but looks like somebody else. I dug a little deeper and got a name—John Macken, maybe head of the agency, or at least one of the lead players. She gazed at her friends, eyes narrowing. "You're stepping into some heavy shit here. Before you decide to get all quixotic you need to know these are serious dragons."

Kansas's eyes got equally hard and he held up the truthmaker. "Yeah? Well, I got a serious dragon slayer here. Besides, we only have two choices: We simply give this to them, whereupon I imagine we'll all just disappear—probably a boating accident, or a group Kool-Aid suicide; or we beat them at their own game—find out who this Bright Circle is and maybe expose them. But what we need now is an ally in their league." He thought for a moment. "I have a friend. Actually, he was my father's friend, Congressman Stan Meyers. Dad's contracting company did a lot of business with the government and he always said Meyers was just about the most honest man he knew, and well respected, regardless." He smiled at the pun, then became serious again. "I think he might have run for one of the big positions, but his wife was killed in an airplane crash in Mexico. That just pulled the wind from his sails. But he knows everybody you should know on The Hill and he's got a great reputation. I think he needs to be our next stop, because right now we're real short on powerful friends."

While Kansas and his friends planned for the next stage of what was truly becoming a monumental challenge, there was another meeting taking place in a small, stately council chamber at the Vatican.

Soft lighting cast a pleasant blush across old paintings lovingly brushed by long-past masters—van Gogh, Picasso, da Vinci. Heavy, ornate curtains were drawn against the night chill and prying eyes, and scented candles added to the ambiance. Gathered around an aged, elaborate, cherry wood table were ten men whose names would be easily recognizable in the present hierarchy of the Church. They were men of substance, decorum, and power, but tonight they were men of question. Before them stood the Bishop of Tallahassee, and in front of each of them were papers documenting the bizarre incidents of "truth" that were taking place in Florida—congressmen and state representatives, leaders of religious sects, all confessing their sins willingly, without any coercion; city council meetings going wildly amiss as people surrendered secrets openly and destroyed their lives. There were articles about this phenomenon in area newspapers, and news videos of congressmen and charlatans surrendering to the truth. It appeared possible, given the locations and the times of these events (which the bishop had meticulously documented) that there might be more than one perpetrator involved in this.

There was a mutual consensus that truth, unabated and available for all, was not necessarily a good thing. For well over a thousand years the Vatican's power had rested on two things: faith, and somewhat of a containment of knowledge. It wasn't so much that the council felt they had secrets, but rather there were things that everyone didn't need to know, much like any other government or country. There were just too many potentially damaging intangibles floating around out there, from extraterrestrial life and evolution to the mysterious deaths of papal hierarchy in recent history. Catholicism and its dictates were already losing ground to science and intellectuality as it was. The impact of unbridled and readily available knowledge had changed the status quo that had remained in place for centuries. Followers of religious persuasions around the world were moving from blind acceptance to curiosity and question, and simple faith was being challenged by fact. No, truth had its place on the table of life, but it was like sugar—best served with discretion, and after some refinement.

Yet each of them in that room loved their faith and their church completely. They knew unequivocally of the succor and peace it provided millions of people around the world. They knew that faith was the most powerful, intangible force on earth. It abided in hearts and minds beyond the reach of proof, just past the grasp of reason, yet it was as potent as the sword and as comforting as a mother's touch. It was the mercurial combination of faith and religion that had given courage to those who had changed the world, and changed how we perceive each other. It was the faith we possess in ourselves, in each other, in our countries, and in our God, that indeed stood as the great hope for the preservation of mankind. They couldn't afford to have this foundation shaken by a conjurer of truth and a method or device from God knows where.

There was much conversation, and much solemn nodding, and finally a decision was reached. They would send Vitor. He would ferret out this abomination. Vitor would find the truth, so to speak, and if he found some substance to this, he would know what to do.

In the meantime, thirty miles outside Washington, D.C., at a very private estate, the international power broker Ramone Torreos sat in his mahogany-walled office with two members of The Bright Circle, receiving a report on their recent meeting, and the president's continued adamancy to do things his way. He was also presented with a narrative on what had been discovered (or hadn't been discovered) in the ransacking of houses and boats and the torturing of the pilot in the Florida Keys. He was not altogether happy on either account.

Torreos realized that democracy was generally not a sustainable form of government, because once voters discovered that they could vote themselves entitlements from the public treasury, the majority would always vote for the candidate who promised the most benefits. Eventually, government coffers would dry up in this quid pro quo competition, and democracy would proceed to entitle itself to death. Usually by this time the Caligula Syndrome began to emerge, and integrity in politics began to deteriorate, politicians in general becoming more interested in what their country could do for them rather than what they could do for their country. Once the nation reached that point, the people would be ripe for any system of governing that promised more than what they had. It was never an easy thing to change a system from the inside—it was much easier to invade and possess—but this way left the pieces of the prize intact, and it was the pieces of the prize that he wanted. The process of bringing about this "change" was a challenge, and his greatest weakness was impatience. If the president couldn't be brought around to this process, well…it wouldn't be the first time he'd "removed" a president.

Ramone Torreos was a clever man, if nothing else. His ability to think in 3-D, to find a way to use each situation to his advantage, had taken him to where he was, and this situation was no different. If a president could not be relied upon to achieve the ultimate goal, then perhaps his removal could prove to be just as consequential, providing a catalyst for the impetus Torreos needed.

One of the great challenges Torreos faced in the plan for bringing America around to a "one-world government," or maybe a more definitive social state representing a little more "authority," was the Second Amendment. He was a student of history and it had taught him that the two things you must remove from a country before you can control the populace are organized religion and guns (in addition to controlling the press). A nation short on faith and weapons was easy prey. He recognized that removing orthodox religion would probably not be an attainable goal—at least not in his lifetime—but the Second Amendment was definitely vulnerable, and it was by far the most necessary of the two. The powerful gun lobbies and the inherent sense of independence with much of America's populace regarding the privilege of possessing a weapon was a heavy challenge to overcome. But, there had already been one assassination attempt on the president this term. What if the president were to be killed with a handgun now? That might change the equation...

CHAPTER 7

The truth is beautiful, but so are lies…
> — *Ralph Waldo Emerson*

It had taken a couple of phone calls, but Kansas finally got Congressman Stan Meyers on the line. The best he could tell Meyers was that he had some information he felt was highly important, possibly to levels of national security, and he needed to see him in person. On the weight of their friendship (his father's, really) the congressman agreed to meet with him at his office in D.C. at 4:00 p.m. the following day. The group, gathered in Cass's living room again, knew they needed to track down the other truthmaker, as well. It was obvious from the newspapers that the fellow in possession of it was on a mission, but he was drawing too much attention to himself and the device. It would only be a matter of time before someone, legitimate or otherwise, found him. They decided to split up. Kansas and Will would fly up to the capitol and meet with Meyers. The girls would see if they could chase down any leads in Key West, because they were certain the guy was a local—and two lovely ladies were much better bait with which to draw him out.

Kansas leaned forward, looking at all of them. "To get to the people behind this Bright Circle, the ones who tried to kill us and beat Eddie so badly, we need to find someone on the periphery of the Circle, just above the hired guns, and use a truthmaker on him. That should help us get to the next level and hopefully get us a name in the Circle itself. It's a dangerous game, but I don't see any other way. Congressman Meyers may be able to shed some light on this, as well."

The others agreed. Will and Kansas packed a few things and headed for the plane while Mariana and Cass made plans for their evening outing.

About the same time Kansas and Will were lifting off in the 310 Cessna, almost five thousand miles away Vitor Montesand received a package by courier from the Vatican. There were no names on it, but he knew who sent it and he knew what it meant.

Montesand was a tall, gaunt-looking man with large, almost mournful mahogany-colored eyes and dark, longish hair. His mouth was broad, harboring heavy rows of slightly off-white teeth, like tombstones leaning next to each other. He had glacially pale skin, and his nose bore the true Italian curve, adding to the startling character of his face. His priest-like robe hid a body that, at a distance, would have been described as thin, but a more careful observation would have revealed the corded, hard muscles of fanatic exercise and austere dieting. Montesand was not a man of indulgence, but he had his passions and his purpose. He brought the package back to the kitchen table in his small, plebeian apartment, which housed not much more than a few very ordinary pieces of furniture—no television, no stereo, only a number of bookcases with wearied texts on Christianity and other faiths. What adornment the walls bore was of a religious nature; images of Christ suffering on the cross, a few second-quality paintings of the Resurrection, and Dante's Hell.

As he sat down and opened the package, he heard a loud snap by the refrigerator. He rose slowly and walked over to it, kneeling down and extending a hand between the refrigerator and the wall, pulling out a trap that had pinned a mouse by its back legs. The creature squirmed frantically as Vitor Montesand's nearly expressionless eyes studied it. He grabbed it with one of his large hands, removing the trap with the other. He held up the mouse, less than a foot from his face, observing as the terrified animal squirmed and squealed and tried to bite him. Then he began to squeeze, watching the bright black eyes fill with terror and pain. As the pressure increased and the small bones inside the rodent began to snap, the tiny orbs went wide with agony and panic, then slowly, finally, surrendered to the stillness and the indifference of death. *It was a most exquisite moment, almost a spiritual experience—to watch life depart, and leave nothing more than a shell of useless flesh. How essential, how powerful this thing called life was, and how fragile.*

He went to a window and tossed out the mouse, then washed his hands and returned to the package. For the next half hour he studied the details and the photos. God had chosen another mission for him. He was pleased.

That night, as Will and Kansas landed at Dulles International in D.C., Mariana and Cass began their search for Wilson McKenzie. Cass had an epiphany. The two of them drove over to the Key West Airport, and claiming to work for a private investigative firm, managed to coerce a ticket sales agent into allowing them to view the list of people who had flown from Key West to Panama City over the last weekend, along with scanned identification photos. Within minutes they had found a pudgy guy about five-foot-six, with longish curly brown hair, and hazel eyes—the bartender's exact description from The Green Parrot. From there they went to the phonebook and found an address. Others who were looking for him had used similar approaches, but it was their thoroughness that had confounded them. Ralph was a clever entity and he purchased fake, removable tattoos to be used in obvious places like a forearm or the side of his neck every time he went out on a mission. Most everyone else was looking for a tattooed man.

Wilson McKenzie lived in a small apartment complex off Whitehead Street. His alter ego, Ralph, had taken a hiatus and Wilson was enjoying some peace and quiet again. He had just gotten out of the shower and was drying himself when the doorbell rang. Throwing on a robe he went to the door and peered out the peephole before opening it. Outside stood two lovely ladies—a svelte blond and a voluptuous brunette. The blond was holding a notebook of some sort. He shrugged and opened the door. *Two hot chicks—how bad could this be?*

"*Hola,*" said Mariana, turning on all that throaty Cuban sensuality in her voice and striking a sultry hooker's pose. "We're with Hot Cheeks off Roosevelt Boulevard. Cheeks is doing a promotion, offering coupons for a free massage…" (allowing the word and its implication to linger in the air for a moment) "…good through next week. Would you like one or two?"

Wilson instantly felt Ralph edging his way in. "Aaahh c'mon…not now, Ralph," he muttered to himself, but it was too late.

The girls couldn't help but notice the muttering and the transformation. The somewhat dowdy fellow in front of them gradually straightened up, his head cocked slightly to one side, and his eyes suddenly took on a lively, carnal gleam—like someone had just plugged him in. He swept back his slightly damp hair with the fingers of both hands in an unconscious grooming fashion and looked up with fresh enthusiasm. "Well, ladies, I'd be very interested," he said with a lecherous smile. "I'd be downright intrigued." He turned sideways in the doorway and with a flourish, swept his arm toward the inside of the house. "Why don't you come in and show me your wares, so to speak?"

Once the girls were inside, Ralph/Wilson noticed a distinct change in his guests.

"Actually, we need to talk with you about something else, Wilson," Cass said, moving a little closer and coming right to the point. "I think you have something that belongs to us—a small device with unique properties."

A look of surprise and understanding flashed across his eyes, even though he quickly buried it. He held out his hands plaintively. "Don't know what you're talking about, ladies. You sure you got the right guy?"

Cass nodded. "Yeah. We're pretty sure."

Realization dawned in Ralph's face. He wasn't getting out of this easy, so it was time for another technique. "You're a feisty little tidbit, aren't you?" he muttered with a confident drawl. Then he suddenly drew back into a classic karate attack/defense pose— feet apart, elbows bent, and fists balled. "Okay, ladies. I'm gonna give you one chance to leave, before I hurt you bad."

There was a moment of unimpressed silence. Mariana and Cass just stared at him. Not getting the desired effect, he pulled himself into the pretentious "crane" stance from the Bruce Lee karate movies, his hands above him and aimed outwards, fingers pulled together in pointed beaks. Struggling to keep his balance on one foot, he belted out the first thing that came to mind. "I'm a martial arts instructor for the Woods Hole Institute. I am a dangerous man!"

Cass sighed, eyes rolling up at the ceiling in languor and incredulousness. "Dude, that's an institution for marine biology research."

A flicker of confusion passed over Ralph's eyes, but he carried on. "Yeah, well…they're expanding their curriculum." He stepped forward aggressively and snapped into his pose again. "Now get out of here, before I strike! Eeeeiiieee! Yaaahh!" he screeched, pointed hands rising menacingly.

But at that moment his hastily tied robe came undone, exposing him in all his glory, or lack of. His face lost its Steven Segal narcissism, and as he scrambled to do himself up, Cass just shook her head.

"Okay, the hard way," she muttered as she turned sideways, and quicker than Ralph could spit, kicked him against the wall.

When Ralph came to, his robe was gone and he was tied spread-eagle to his bed. He could hear the two women whispering to each other as they searched his room, so he pretended to still be out. He heard the tall blond say something about getting back to "the guys" as soon as possible. The hot brunette added something about them probably just making Dulles Airport by now, about a room at the Holiday Inn, and something about a meeting and the other truthmaker. *The other truthmaker?*

As he fully came around and rose up, he noticed something else that was considerably more disconcerting. Tied securely to his penis was a line of packing twine. With just a little slack in between, the other end of the line was tied to the doorknob of the bedroom door.

Mariana glanced over at him and smiled. "Our karate *muchacho* is awake."

Cass looked up from a drawer she was rummaging through and grinned, going over and leaning down next to Wilson. (Ralph was long gone, having gotten out of town while the getting was good.) "Do you remember when you were a kid and your front tooth got loose enough to remove?"

Wilson was a quick study. The implication was way too clear. Cass nodded at Mariana and she grabbed the door and swung it in with just enough force to deliver the message. When Wilson quit shrieking, Cass leaned down again.

"On the count of three you're going to lose your…tooth…if you don't tell us what we want to know. One, two…"

Fifteen minutes later the girls were on their way back up The Keys. The willowy blond looked over at her Cuban compatriot, who was holding the lost truthmaker, and grinned. "I really enjoyed that idea of yours. You're devious. I'm beginning to like you."

Mariana smiled, watching the old silver moon play off the water as they crossed Kemp Channel. "The pleasure is mutual. It's been a long time since I had this much fun, *mi amiga.*"

That evening several things took place. Kansas and Will settled into their room at the Holiday Inn outside Dulles International. Cass called them to tell of her success in finding the other truthmaker, and Mariana returned to her room and placed a call to her boss, Director Miguel Juan Santiago. She told him that she was making progress on tracking down what appeared to be a few ancient artifacts found in the cave in the mountains. For some reason, she decided not to tell him what the artifacts were. Mariana told herself it would just seem too preposterous over the phone, or maybe too important, and she might get pulled from the investigation. She would wait until everyone was back in Key West and safe. Then she would return to Cuba with one of the devices. But in the deepest reaches of her mind, Mariana didn't want this to end yet. It was so different there, in America, and then there was this free-spirited American flyboy. She wasn't ready to return...so quickly.

Meanwhile, Ralph wormed his way back into Wilson, they untied themselves from the bed and doctored their mutual schlong. Then Ralph, fully in control again, packed a few things, went back to the airport, and booked a ticket for Washington, D.C. He'd lost one truthmaker just about the time he had grown really fond of it, but he had an idea now where a second one was.

Moments later another man—a tall, gaunt, somber-looking fellow dressed in a simple long-sleeved cotton pullover and dark brown pants, who was in line behind Ralph—booked a seat on the same plane.

At 4:00 p.m. the following day, Kansas and Will were ushered into the office of Congressman Stan Meyers, a heavyset man of medium height with graying hair and piercing blue eyes, probably edging sixty-five years old. After a hearty greeting and the introduction of Will, the two men took seats in front of the congressman's desk. A very attractive secretary came in and offered refreshments. After coffee had been served, Meyers eased back in his chair.

"Okay son, what is it that I can do for you? Sounded pretty important over the phone."

Kansas, in his Brooks Brothers shirt and slacks, cleared his throat and sat up, leaning forward with his hands clasped. "Sir, I'm going to ask that you just listen for a few minutes, then I'll answer whatever questions I can for you, all right?"

The congressman nodded. "Go ahead."

For the next ten minutes, Kansas and Will gave an account of their experiences—finding the cave and the truthmakers (they pointedly didn't mention the gold bullion), getting out of Cuba, and then a brief explanation of what had happened after that—the meeting with the people at MIT, a little of the history they revealed, and what had been done with the devices recently, touching briefly on losing one briefly to a zany Key West fellow who had made good use of it.

Meyers shook his head incredulously, then brought his steely gaze around to Kansas. "I've been reading about the bizarre confessions of congressmen and representatives, and religious cult leaders; so has everyone else," he said guardedly. "You're telling me you've been responsible for this? You and your...truthmakers, and this crazy asshole from Key West?"

Kansas exhaled. "Yeah, that's about the size of it."

The congressman's eyes narrowed. "You're saying that these things from an ancient civilization actually make you tell the truth? C'mon, that's got to be bullshit! It's just not possible."

At that point, Will, who had the truthmaker, interrupted. "Sir, with your permission, we could cut to the chase on this." He straightened the lapel of his tropical shirt, pulled the ancient device from the pocket of his jeans, and held it up. "This is a truthmaker, sir. I'm going to turn this on and ask you a simple, non-threatening question, and I'll bet you my airplane to your half-smoked cigar you're going to answer it. Okay?"

The congressman pushed back in his seat a little, staring at the small silver-cased device with the strange, inlaid inscriptions, slightly uncomfortable for the first time. Finally, he shifted his attention back to the two men in front of him and exhaled harshly. "Okay. One question. Let's see this thing work."

Will turned it on and there was the traditional hum and the prickling of hair as the device activated. Meyers felt it, tensing a little.

"Stan, what's the combination to your personal safe at your home?" asked Will.

For a moment Meyers just stared back defiantly, then his mouth fell open slightly, and his eyes struggled for a second or two, then just surrendered. "Eleven, thirty, sixty-nine," he said slowly. "My daughter's birthday."

Will turned off the machine and the congressman's eyes cleared, then filled with awe, but there was a flash of trepidation, as well, that skipped through them as he recovered.

"Son of a bitch! Son of a bitch!" he muttered with not a small degree of reverence. But Stan Meyers had been around a while and wasn't easily taken. With just a touch of skepticism returning, he said, "Okay, no offence, but maybe you found that out from someone. I'm an old dog and I've seen lots of tricks. Turn the machine on again. I want one more test."

When Will did as requested, Meyers clicked on his intercom and had his attractive secretary return. She came in and stood before his desk. "Yes, sir?"

He looked at her. "Marcia, I hope you'll forgive me, but are you having a relationship with Judge Standford while engaged to the city attorney? Because if you are, that's a break in protocol on a number of levels."

She started, eyes widening. "I…why I…sir…aahh…"

Then all of them watched her fall under the thrall of the machine—the change of expression, the ceding of control. She sighed, eyes fluttering, then reflecting resignation. "Yes, sir, I am." She shook her head, downcast. "I didn't plan it with the judge. It just happened, and I knew I should stop, and I was going to…"

The congressman nodded, satisfied. "This won't leave my office, Marcia. But you're going to have to make a choice if you want to keep my respect, and your job. You can leave now." When the secretary was gone he turned to Will. "Turn that thing off. I've seen enough."

Following the demonstration, Kansas told Meyers about being accosted by the government people, how they stole the truthmaker, what he and his people went through to get it back, and how the same government organization had nearly killed his friend trying to get information. He also explained in no uncertain terms that he intended to even the score. Finally, near the end of the conversation he asked the congressman, "Do you know anything about a sublevel government group called The Bright Circle? Or someone named John Macken?"

Meyers pursed his lips and squinted in thought. "Bright Circle? No, not that I know of, but I can look into it. I've got a few contacts in the nether regions of intrigue. Would be nice to know who these folks are, and if they're actually on our side. Macken...Macken. Yeah, I think he's the new head of Presidential Security. What's the deal with him?"

"Don't know for sure," Kansas said. "Just wondered if you knew him."

Meyers straightened up, then leaned his elbows on his desk, changing the subject. "What, exactly, do you see as long-range plans for this device?"

Kansas exhaled pensively, uneasy at the question. "Listen, this may be a little utopian or far-fetched," he said, "but the people who used these devices some ten or fifteen thousand years ago had an amazing society. I've read the transcript from the golden notebook. It was a struggle to get where they were because there was resistance, obviously, but they ended up as a society that lived serenely, in relative peace and security. Can you imagine a culture, perhaps a world, without guile? Without treachery, or lies, where truth is all-powerful? What if this device could be duplicated? We could change this country—hell, the world for that matter—into something extraordinary. It would be a life-altering event for mankind. Can you imagine a world like that?" He paused and took a breath. "I'm not so naïve as to not realize the challenges in something of this nature. Even just here in America it would take a leader—an extraordinary leader, like the Vandar of that ancient world—and beyond that, it would take an assembly of powerful, scrupulously honest people to make something like this happen. But it happened before, and it could happen again." Kansas put up a hand, palm out. "Look, even on a more realistic, non-spectacular level, if something like this were just used in our judicial and legal system. Consider that—no more lengthy, costly trials in America, no more intimidated juries or bought-and-sold judges and attorneys. Not one innocent person would ever go to prison, and not one guilty person would ever walk out the doors of a courtroom and thumb their noses at our system." He settled quietly for a moment and whispered with intensity, "If I could click my heels and make it so, that's what I would do with this device."

The congressman brought his hands up under his chin, a finger touching his lips, pensively. "There is no question it makes for a fascinating scenario, and I have to admit it appeals to me, if for no other reason than to see half of these lying bastards I work with forced by shame into honesty, but something like that isn't going to happen overnight. To begin with, we need to demonstrate this upwards in echelons, and see what a few of the people above me think. We have to move carefully and cautiously, because there will be people to whom this will not appeal—in spades. You need to avoid any more publicity with..." He pointed at the device. "...that. Just lie low for a while. Stay in town for another couple days, and give me a phone number where I can reach you." The older man shook his head in amazement, staring at the device in Will's hands, and smiled. "Son of a bitch. If I hadn't seen it with my own eyes I would never have believed it. That's a game changer for sure."

When Kansas and Will got to their rental car and headed back toward the motel, Congressman Meyers began a series of phone calls. His secretary sighed and made a discreet call herself.

Kansas had booked a ground floor suite at the Holiday Inn simply because he didn't like the claustrophobic feeling of large hotels. He was anxious to get back to the room, relax, and maybe give Mariana a call. They opened the door and walked in, carrying on a conversation about the congressman, but as they stepped in, the door slammed closed behind them, and there stood a man with a gun. A second man stepped out of the bedroom, pistol with suppressor pointed at them. Both were dressed like businessmen—light suits, ties, and dark, well-groomed hair, but Kansas immediately recognized the scar on the cheek of the one by the bedroom. He was obviously the same guy who had hit Will's boat, and beat up Eddie. A searing flame of rage surged through him, but he kept his composure.

They brought up their guns, coming in slowly at different

angles. *Professionals...*

"On your knees, now!" said the larger one.

Both Will and Kansas weighed the odds—not good. They complied.

While one kept a gun on them, the other pulled their hands behind them and snapped on handcuffs. "Get up slowly and get in the bedroom," the big one said. "One wrong move and I kill one of you. We only need one."

Ralph/Wilson had flown to Dulles and gone directly to the closest Holiday Inn. He gave the concierge one hundred dollars for a quick check on who had booked into the hotel from Key West, and what the room number was. He was waiting around outside, trying to devise the second half of his plan, when he saw a Domino's Pizza car pull up. He smiled and took out another one hundred dollars.

Not too far from Ralph, another man—tall and gaunt, dressed in a simple cotton pullover and dark pants—sat in a car watching, still and quiet as a wraith. God had granted Vitor the serenity of patience. Vitor had done much the same thing as Cass, using his exceptional resources (actually better than most law enforcement agencies, thanks to his friends at the Vatican), he was provided an analysis of flights into and out of Key West. His target had obviously hidden/changed his appearance, but Vitor had a remarkable sense of intuition, among other talents, and it appeared to have paid off.

The first punch almost fractured Kansas's cheekbone and he nearly lost consciousness. He came back around to see them hammering Will in the stomach. The two stepped back, and the one with the scar drawled, "We can do this all day long. All we want is the device."

The fools had never even checked Will's coat pocket, they just started hitting.

Unfortunately, at that moment, they decided to do just that. Kansas looked over at Will as one of them rifled his pockets and found the truthmaker. Suddenly, there was a knock on the door.

"Check it out," said the one with the scar, holding the truthmaker. "Get rid of them, whoever it is."

The other fellow went to the door and looked through the peephole. It was a pizza guy—bright smile, head crooked just a little like a barnyard chicken, and weird, shiny eyes, as if he were having a really good time. They must have ordered on the way back to the hotel. *Keep things as normal as possible in an operation*—that was the training. He opened the door. "How much do I owe you?"

"Well," said the pizza guy holding the ticket. "Looks like about fourteen ninety-five." But he accidently dropped the ticket as he handed it to the man.

Instinct took over and the fellow bent down to pick it up. When he did, the pizza guy pulled out a small but powerful stun gun from under the box and zapped the big guy in the neck. The fellow shuddered wordlessly for a second or two, collapsed to his knees, still shaking, then fell face-forward on the carpet. Ralph dropped the stun gun, quickly found the guy's pistol, put it in the pizza box, opened the door and walked in like he owned the place. "Hellloo, hellloo? Anybody home?" he sang out, all friendly-like.

The other guy came out of the room, stuffing something behind his back in his pants, and holding a truthmaker in his hands. "Who are you? What are you doing?"

"Delivering pizza. What's it look like?" Ralph answered indignantly. "Your friend didn't have change. He's getting it." Before the guy could digest that, Ralph added, "Here's your receipt," and reached into the box, coming out with a gun covered in cheese, and promptly putting the business end against the guy's chest. "Down on your knees!" When the fellow knelt on the carpet, Ralph muttered, "I hate this part," grimacing, "but business is business," and whacked him on the side of the head with the butt of the gun. Then he picked up the truthmaker and gave it a kiss, holding it at arm's length and gazing at it. "Helllooo, baby!" he cried.

At that point he noticed Kansas and Will, on their knees and handcuffed in the bedroom. He just gave them that eerie Jim Carrey smile, offered a small wave, wiggling his fingers at them, then tossed the pistol on the carpet, stuffed the truthmaker into the pocket of his jeans and walked out, stepping over the body of the guy in the hall. They could hear him whistling as he walked away.

From in the bedroom, Kansas caught most of what had just happened. Before Ralph was barely out the door, he and Will were scrambling over to the fellow on the floor, squirming around like a couple of epileptic snakes as they worked the handcuff keys out of his pocket. They got the handcuffs undone and Will quickly snatched up the pistol, then dragged the big guy from the hallway into the room, shutting the door. The fellow was still unconscious, but they put handcuffs on him anyway.

Will threw the other pair of cuffs to Kansas and motioned to the guy with the scar, who was just starting to come around. "Get his gun and get the handcuffs on him."

Kansas turned the man around and snapped the cuffs on him before he recovered, but there was a look in his partner's eyes that Will had rarely ever seen. His friend glanced around the room, mouth pinched in concentration until he saw a heavy, short-necked wine bottle on the counter in the kitchen —a complimentary gift of the management.

When the guy's eyes opened and came into focus, he was propped up against the couch, hands behind his back, and Kansas was kneeling in front of him, gripping him by the front of his shirt with one hand, and holding a wine bottle by the neck with the other. "Remember me?" gritted Kansas, a strange half smile on his face. "I'm the guy you were just using as a punching bag."

The man's eyes narrowed, but he didn't say anything.

Kansas continued in that same conversational tone. "Moreover, I'm a friend of the fellow in The Keys you recently beat the shit out of." He pushed the man back hard against the couch and held him. "I'm here to remind you that every bad thing you do in life eventually catches up with you, and I'm going to leave you with that thought." Without another word, or a wisp of hesitation, Kansas brought the wine bottle up in a vicious hard arc and hammered the guy in the jaw with it. It was a heavy bottle. It didn't even break. But the man's jaw did, in several places. Kansas stood and looked down at the man with the shattered mouth and jaw, lying on the floor. "That's for Eddie, my buddy."

At an abandoned industrial area parking lot on a bluff about three hundred yards from the Holiday Inn, Vitor watched through his binoculars as Ralph/Wilson went into the Holiday Inn dressed as a pizza delivery boy. He knew he was close now. From the moment he had finally determined his target and watched him leave his house in a hurry the night before, Vitor had somehow sensed that his target was on a mission of some sort. He had been patient. Soon he would have his reward. When the fellow came back out five minutes later, there was a spring to his step. He was no longer cautious and guarded, and he appeared to be whistling. Good signs.

Vitor had rolled down the car windows for fresh air while he waited. He was bringing down the binoculars when suddenly there was a man at each window. A powerful-looking, young black man in a skin-tight sleeveless shirt and baggy sports pants leaned in at the window on the other side of the car, and his lighter-skinned   companion—wiry-looking   with   hard, conscienceless eyes and a halo of frizzy reddish hair, attired in an oversized Redskins T-shirt and baggy shorts—had his hands on the window ledge of the door next to Vitor, crouching down so he could see inside.

The large African American suddenly opened the door and boldly sat down next to Vitor, a small revolver in plain sight tucked in his waist. The muscles in the man's arms rippled like serpents beneath his dark skin as he settled into the seat and turned toward Vitor, eyes like onyx agates and a smile that was anything but friendly. "Yo, man," he said, sizing up Vitor with a glance, not totally sure. "You got any idea where you are, dawg?"

Vitor glanced down the rise at Ralph, who was walking across the Holiday Inn lawn toward the parking lot, then back to his new acquaintance. "It doesn't matter, I have to go now."

The fellow grinned at his friend. "He in a hurry. Thass too bad. He most likely gonna be late."

His friend grinned wickedly. "He need to chill. Bein' in a hurry bad for yo' heart."

The man turned his attention to Vitor again. "You can go, but you gonna have to leave us all the Benjamins you got, dawg. Thass the price, and maybe we might wanna borrow yo' ride for a while, too." He smiled again, full of malevolence, shaking his head slightly and speaking with a false, concerned intimacy. "You just in the wrong place at the wrong time. It happens like that sometimes."

Vitor took a deep breath and expelled it. Ralph was in the parking lot nearing his car and he couldn't afford to lose him. "This is your last chance. Get out of my car and leave, now."

The friendly façade evaporated from the mugger and he growled, "You ain't in no position to tell me shit, man! You understand?"

Just then his friend saw the golden Saint Christopher medal that Vitor wore around his neck. "Hey, dawg, he got some seriously shiny decoration, too." He reached in to take it.

At that point several things happened. The hostility quotient in Vitor's usually impenetrable eyes rose about ninety percent and a long, stiletto-like dagger slipped almost magically from his sleeve into his right hand. With his left hand he grasped the arm of the skinny fellow and jerked him inward, slamming his head against the top of the car door and stunning him. Still holding the skinny guy against the door, his right hand slashed out in a vicious, backhanded half circle, burying his knife to the hilt in the heart of the big black man in the passenger's seat.

The fellow grunted and his eyes widened in surprise, mouth falling open, then he sighed and his body just slumped, eyes still staring outwards with incredible disbelief. Vitor jerked out the knife and shoved his door open, knocking the other antagonist to the ground. The tall Italian was instantly out the door and moving in on his assailant with the fierceness and purpose of a lion. The fellow scrambled backwards on the concrete, hands out, pleading. Vitor never said a word. He just lifted the man to his knees by his hair, buried the knife in his throat just behind the jugular, and ripped outward. He held the man away and down while the blood spurted out onto the old, cracked pavement, turning it a bright, sticky red. As the arterial flow slowed, he turned the man around and drew his face upward. He watched in fascination as the eyes went from terror and pain to the resignation and indifference of death. Then slowly, almost reverently, Vitor laid him down on the wet, bloody concrete.

Two minutes later, Vitor was driving into the Holiday Inn parking lot, a hundred yards behind the whistling, unsuspecting Ralph/Wilson as he drove away.

In the meantime, Will and Kansas realized they had a

situation. They had two Bright Circle personnel but no truthmaker, so Will called Cass. She picked up Mariana, and the girls were on a flight out of Key West an hour later. By midnight they were on the ground in Dulles and were at the hotel. It had been a rough day. It had also been a rough day for Ralph/Wilson.

CHAPTER 8

Truth comes as conqueror only to those who have lost the art of receiving it as friend.

— **Rabindranath Tagore**

When he left the hotel, Wilson's first impulse was to get right on an airplane and get the hell out of there, but Ralph was on a high from the success. The sun was just setting. He wanted a whiskey and water, a strip club, and a lap dance, not necessarily in that order. Ralph dumped the Domino's Pizza outfit and slipped into some nice slacks and a bright yellow pullover in the back of the car, then headed out on a night of adventure. Vitor followed patiently.

It was 6:30 p.m. and Phandango's Adult Entertainment Lounge was just swinging into gear from the daytime work crowd. As the steady bass thump of hip-hop music inundated the room, dancers slithered and writhed against poles and clients, and waitresses scurried from table to bar providing refreshments for the palates and the libidos of customers. Cigarette smoke swirled through sensuous lighting—sultry blues and reds enveloping all the undulating, imbibing, and dancing of laps in a Caligulan ambiance that just touched Ralph in that special place, and it wasn't his heart.

He followed a shapely, scantily clad waitress to a corner table close to the stage and ordered a drink. Moments later it was in his hands, and so was the waitress. He never noticed the tall, gaunt man with the strange dark eyes enter the lounge and slowly scan the room before finding his way to a table not too far from Ralph.

Vitor ordered a Pellegrino and lime, took several deep breaths and tried to spiritually insulate himself from the decadence around him while watching his target. *The man was debauchery incarnate—a soulless creature, self-satiating carnal filth.* He would enjoy this. He would take his time. God would be pleased.

For the next hour Ralph and Wilson lived up to the image,

working their way through half a dozen whiskey and waters and two lap dances. Then, with their individual libidos and their mutual schlong satiated, they felt the need to use the restroom. Ralph was enjoying himself, but being the more observant one, he had noticed a tall, thin guy sitting in the corner staring at him. The guy's eyes didn't carry amusement or interest, he was just staring, the way you might watch a bug cross the floor. It was disconcerting, even in his present, somewhat snockered state.

As he got to the hallway where the restrooms were, he glanced back. The spooky guy was getting up. Ralph was a little unnerved, but he needed to pee, so he opened the door to the men's room. There was a vanity with two sinks and mirrors on one side of the room, along with a row of five stalls ending with a larger handicapped stall against the wall, and a handful of urinals on the other side, where one fellow was relieving himself. Ralph's instinctual sense of preservation was starting to kick in. Something wasn't right with the dude outside. He went to the end of the room, entered the handicapped stall, locked the door and crouched on top of the commode, feet off the ground. The only other person in the restroom finished his business and left. Seconds later the door opened again and he heard a quiet, deliberate set of footsteps. They stopped in the middle of the room. Then slowly they began again, moving toward him as the stalls were being checked one by one. His heartbeat stepped up to a mild tango. Open, close. Open, close. Open, close. His heartbeat bounced up to heavy rock. The footsteps got to his door and there was an attempt to open it, but to no avail. Then the door shook, but the lock held.

"Give me it," growled a deep, menacing voice. "Give it to me and I will let you go."

Ralph almost shrieked at the sudden harshness of the utterance. *Sure you will, and it never rains in Southern California.* He bit his lip, heartbeat surging into the heavy thump, thump, thump of hip-hop. He was in deep shit and he knew it; he was going to have to take a chance. He saw the feet outside the stall back up and instinctively he knew this guy was going to kick in the door, so he reached over quietly and undid the latch, then grabbed the cheap coat hanger on the stall door. As he heard the man take a breath and lunge forward, he quickly swung open the portal. Anyone who has experienced something of this nature knows that all the momentum and inertia goes into the leg of the kick, and when it touches nothing, the body just comes up almost horizontal and goes down hard—the Charlie Brown football syndrome. This was no exception. Vitor, a very, very, surprised look on his countenance, came flying through the door almost horizontally. The stiletto-like dagger he held caught the doorframe and was jarred from his hand, clattering to the floor outside the stall. He hit the cold tile hard enough to knock the air from his lungs and incapacitate him for a moment. Ralph clambered over him and out the stall like a neurotic spider, but realized that his antagonist was already getting up, so he grabbed the knife from the floor and drew himself up, suddenly getting that Ralphish cockiness—eyes gleaming, head tilted.

"Now who got the knife, big boy. Huh? Huh? What chu gonna do now, you skinny mutha plucka? Huh? Huh?" Ralph was really getting into his Latin imitation of a bad guy, waving the knife around in a menacing, weaving pattern.

The fellow just stood up and stared at him for a moment like he was an insect. Then his mouth twisted into a malicious grin, and he reached behind his back, pulling out a knife twice as long as the stiletto and curved like a scimitar.

"Son of a bitch!" Ralph/Wilson shrieked, thoroughly terrified again, starting to back up.

Suddenly, the door to the bathroom burst open and four seriously besotted football jocks stumbled in, arms around one another, yelling a mixture of encouragement and profanities to each other in ribald camaraderie, most wearing some sort of Redskins football attire. Both Ralph and Vitor quickly hid their weapons as the group barged in. Ralph recognized the chance he needed.

"Hey, dudes! Go Redskins!" he shouted, prancing over for high fives all around and immediately mixing in with them. Then he turned to Vitor and pointed at him. "That's my buddy, Frank. He's a backfield coach for the Redskins! He's got free preseason tickets!"

That was all the drunken sports fanatics needed. They were all over Vitor like he was their mother coming back from the war. They buried him in bear hugs and high fives, slurring glorious testimony to the team, practically pinning him against the wall of the restroom. Ralph did his imitation of a neurotic spider again and was out the door in a blink. But as he headed down the hallway, he began to wonder if he really had enough time to make an escape. *Is this guy alone? Is there someone outside waiting for me to get in my car?* He suddenly saw another door in the hallway that read:

Dressing Room. Customers Keep Out!

He pursed his lips, his eyebrows went up, then he smiled.

As luck would have it, there were no dancers changing at the time and the room was empty but for the makeup and other cosmetics on the long counter, and the clothes and wigs that hung on racks on the back wall. Ralph grabbed a blond wig, a short red skirt, and a white blouse. He found a purse, emptied the contents, and put his clothes and the truthmaker in it, then grabbed a razor and headed for a tiny restroom in the corner. Four minutes later, after a quick, fairly painful shave of his lower legs and a costume change, he stepped out of the restroom a new person. He adjusted his wig, carefully applied some lipstick, a touch of eye shadow, and a splash of perfume, smelled under his armpits, splashed a little more perfume, and stood up to admire himself in the mirror.

"Damn, you a pretty good lookin' hooker, Lucille!" he declared with a grin.

As he headed out of the dressing room and down the hallway, two Hispanic guys walked by. One paused and muttered with a rapturous smile, "Hey, mama. Chu got a little of that for me?"

"Kiss-off, asshole!" Ralph barked.

The guy jumped like he'd been jabbed with a cattle prod. The fellow shook his head and watched Ralph walk away. "Tha's a hot, mean bitch, *amigo*," he exclaimed under his breath, his nostrils flaring. "*Mi gusta mucho!*"

Ralph grinned smugly and kept walking, heading into the lounge, making a beeline for the bright red exit sign. Halfway across the room he began to relax. He was going to pull this off. He started to let Lucille out a little, rolling into a stroll, working those hips, getting into the part, almost enjoying himself.

Ralph was about two tables away from the exit when suddenly he was grabbed roughly from behind. Big hands pinned his arms to his sides, and a gruff voice whispered in his ear, "Not so fast. You're not getting away from me that easily."

Ooohhh shit...

But as he turned his head, he discovered he was being held by a huge biker-type guy—black vest, blue jeans, chains, tattoos, shaved head, and large blue eyes gleaming with misplaced lust. "You're not gettin' outta here without one more lap dance, baby. Come sit with daddy for a while and make nice with the lap lizard, and I'll make it real worth your while..."

Holy fark! "No, no, I can't," Ralph squeaked in a high voice, partly trying to stay in character and partly out of pure panic. "I can't. I have to go. My...my mother's sick. The dog was hit by a car! Have to...the vet..."

He was interrupted by a pair of large lips on his neck and breath that reeked of beer and cigarettes. "They can wait a little longer, baby. C'mon, now!"

Ralph was about to try for a groin kick and a bolt for the door when he saw Vitor headed toward them, eyes searching methodically. Ralph shrugged and surrendered. *What the hell. Can't be any worse than the guy with the knife.* "Okay, big guy. I'm all yours..." *Oh Jesus...*

Fifteen minutes later, there was some good news and some bad news for Ralph/Wilson. The good news was they were fifty dollars richer. The bad news was, they were now official members of the Phandango's Lap Dance Club, and their mutual psyches were still shrieking from it. Even worse, Vitor was still hanging out by the door, having gone outside (obviously checking on their car) and come back in.

Ralph shook his head in desperation. There was no choice. He stepped into Lucille again and snuggled up to the biker, whispering sensually in his ear, falling into a vernacular and a voice somewhere between hot street slang and Penelope Cruz. "Now that you got an appetizer, why don't you walk me outside and I give you some serious humpty dumpty—knock your eyeballs out, screw you till you can't breathe, make yo' dick think it died and gone to pussy heaven." He pulled back and gazed into the biker's eyes, then smiled lasciviously. "And I gonna do it for free."

Moments later they waltzed across the floor, out of the club, and into the night, leaving Vitor still wondering what happened to his target. Ralph double-checked as he stepped out that there were taxis waiting (afraid to try his car, in case it was being watched). There usually were in places like this. Once assured, he led his new friend into the shadows on the side of the building by the kitchen, the smells of French fries and burgers, and other people's sexual experiences in that same spot assailing them in warm wafts. He looked up at his date with as much lurid sexuality as he could muster without gagging, then took hold of the guy's leather vest and pulled him close, whispering with soft, sensual femininity, "Why don't you pull down them pants and spread your legs just a little, so I can get you warmed up."

He didn't have to repeat himself.

"Now close dem big beautiful eyes and think nice thoughts," he muttered provocatively.

When the fellow gratefully complied, eyes tightly closed, Ralph stepped back and kicked him as hard as he could in the *cojones*. The guy's eyes bulged out (just as Ralph had promised) and all the air escaped his lungs in a soft whoosh (which he had also promised). As the biker dropped to his knees, tangling in his dropped pants and falling flat on his face, Ralph grabbed his purse and zipped around the building toward the taxis like a lizard on speed. While the taxi sped away, Ralph slid out of Wilson like honey from a hot biscuit, leaving him alone and relieved to still be alive, but puzzled. *Who the hell was that skinny, spooky dude?*

Well, at that point it didn't matter. He was getting the hell out of Dodge.

While Ralph and Lucille were competing for Wilson's body, Kansas, Will, Cass, and Mariana were extracting information from The Bright Circle's heavies at the Holiday Inn. They had both handcuffed men sitting on the couch, but only one was really able to answer questions. The other's jaw was broken so badly he was useless and in serious pain.

"Okay, we have some questions and you're going to give us some answers," Kansas said, pointing at the one who could talk.

He shook his head, staring defiantly at Kansas and the

others. "I'm not telling you shit!"

Will shrugged and turned on the truthmaker. "Have it your way."

The hum passed over the room and the initial vibration skated across them.

"Who do you work for? Who is your boss?" Kansas asked.

The look of defiance suddenly wavered in the man's eyes and confusion became its epitaph. He blinked a couple of times and his mouth opened, then shut, as he fought the power of the vibrations overwhelming his frontal lobes. Then, as always, the eyes yielded and the tenseness in his face and neck faded. "I work for The Circle, The Bright Circle. My boss, my boss is Macken, John Macken."

Kansas looked at Will. They had heard that name from Senator Meyers—something to do with presidential security. Not good.

"What is The Bright Circle?" Kansas asked.

The man seemed genuinely uncertain for a moment. "I don't know all of it. But I know it is a group of highly-placed, powerful individuals from a number of countries, with 'chapters' in each major nation."

"For what? What is the purpose of the organization?" Cass interjected.

"Change. Major change, I think." He shook his head. "I don't know for sure. I'm just a soldier—to protect the integrity of The Circle."

"What kind of change?" Kansas pressed.

The guy took a breath and exhaled. "Some kind of government change—a unification, like in one-world government, I think. But I don't know much about that."

"Do you know the names of the people in The Circle here in America?" Will asked.

The fellow shrugged, appearing uncertain. "They don't tell us names," he said, but his eyes betrayed him.

Kansas picked up on that and approached it from another angle. "But you've seen people—faces—haven't you?"

The man nodded slowly, still fighting the truthmaker. He was strong. "Yes, when we serve as perimeter security. U.S. House Speaker Petrolli—saw him once. Secretary of State—saw him. One of the big oil men, Watkins, I think, is the name. Those are all." Then he caught himself. "No, one other—'shadow man' they call him—international power player. Big player. Just caught a glimpse at a meeting in Paris. Wasn't supposed to see him—no one was. A security slip on their part. Torreos. Ramone Torreos."

A serious look passed around the group. Ramone Torreos—a man who had changed nations and shattered governments with his power from the shadows.

"What are their goals?" Kansas pressed, trying to get more definition.

The fellow sighed. "Change, like I told you. But just recently, after the last meeting, my boss gave the impression that something big was going to happen, something huge. 'Gonna change the landscape,' he said."

"Is there another meeting planned soon?" Will asked.

The man shrugged. "I don't know. They don't tell us things like that."

Finally, Kansas asked one last question. "How'd you find us?"

The fellow smiled shrewdly, nodding at Will. "Your buddy over there filed an IFR flight plan and listed you as a passenger."

"Son of a bitch!" Will hissed bitterly, chastising himself for the stupid move.

At a dead end with the questioning, Will pulled Kansas to the side and whispered a suggestion. "Look, your psychologist friend said there could be suggestive powers involved here, and none of the victims that this Wilson guy hit could remember what he looked like. We've got nothing to lose. I suggest we tell them to forget they ever saw us."

Kansas thought about it for a moment, then nodded. "Worth a try." He went back over to the two men and stared at them. "You're not going to remember talking with us about anything. Do you understand? You're just not going to remember any conversation. In fact, you're not going to remember us at all. Okay?"

Both the fellows stared at him, eyes growing strangely distracted and bewildered, then settling into indifference again. The big one nodded slowly. "Okay," he whispered in a disconnected fashion. "Okay…"

Kansas glanced over at Will questioningly and his partner shrugged. "What do I know? It was worth a try."

At that point Kansas found some masking tape in the hallway utility room and they taped their recent antagonists' mouths and legs—they had already cuffed their hands—then put them in one of the closets. They had both the pistols from the two men. In addition, just on a chance, they took their car keys and went out into the parking lot. A big black Cadillac stood out, and sure enough, the push button on the key chain unlocked the car. They checked the vehicle and found a large, special carrier compartment in the back. When they opened it, everyone just stood there in amazement.

Kansas whispered, "Unbelievable!" Then, in imitation of Will, he muttered, "Just like one of those Clint Eastwood movies!"

In the compartment were two of the latest AT4 anti-tank/vehicle weapons, basically nothing more than smallish forty-inch metal tubes that fired a finned, extra powerful rocket grenade accurately up to two hundred yards, along with a couple of M-16 carbines with several magazines, and a 9mm Smith and Wesson semi-auto handgun, with several loaded magazines.

After a quick scan of the weapons, Will said, "From all that I've read it's not really unusual for these kinds of units to carry hardware like this, trust me. Reminds me of our crazy buddy Bobby Branch."

Branch was an ex-Vietnam vintage wild man who lived in a ramshackle place on the back side of Cudjoe Key. They had met him one night on a drinking spree that ended up in The No Name Pub on Big Pine. He was an adventurer, just like them, and they traded stories for an evening. It led to the three becoming friends, to a degree. Branch was a serious survivalist/wild man, with a house full of food, supplies, and enough weapons to challenge the Key West Police Department. He was entertaining as hell, clever, and absolutely no fool. But he was wrapped a little loose. He loved things that go bang, and in the process, he taught them to use just about every modern personnel weapon the Army had. He had worked in the arms depot at Da Nang, and had broken down and shipped a huge variety of weapons back to his girlfriend in the States. He lost the girlfriend, but he still had the weapons.

It was an interesting experience, but the more they got to know Branch the more they realized he was an accident looking for a place to happen. When Bobby got blitzed one night, took an RPG (rocket-propelled grenade) and blew the giant plastic dragon off the top of the Wok and Gong Restaurant in Key West (claiming it was run by Commie spies who were poisoning the public water supply), the friendship remained, the actual associations diminished considerably.

Kansas smiled. "Bring the car over. We're taking it all."

There was no way to know what happened to the crazy guy who stole the other truthmaker, and they didn't need to add another distraction at this point, anyway. So, they paid for an extra two days at the Holiday Inn, and put a "Do Not Disturb/No Room Service" sign on the hotel room door when they left, which they hoped would buy them some time before the two occupants were discovered. Then they drove to a quiet hotel in Bethesda, outside D.C., and booked two rooms using the girls' IDs. It was 3:00 a.m. before they finally got to sleep.

At 10:00 a.m. the following day Congressman Meyers called. He wanted another demonstration for a couple of important people—"A private demonstration away from curious eyes and ears," he said—at an empty warehouse on the west side of Dulles Airport, at 4:00 p.m. Kansas got an address and hung up, then he turned to his friends, explaining the situation.

Will shook his head cautiously. "I like your buddy, the congressman, and I think he's just fine, but after yesterday I don't trust anyone. We need to lay out some plans. We have one advantage that, hopefully, no one knows about—the girls," he said, nodding at Cass and Mariana. "And we now have weapons, as well."

It was a nondescript concrete and metal building, about eight thousand square feet, at the west end of the airport, actually only about a quarter mile from the FBO (Flight Based Operations) and tie-downs for civilian aircraft. It looked quiet enough as Kansas and Will pulled up in their rental car. The large, slide-up bay door was open. There was a gray government town car parked parallel to the building just down from the door, and Congressman Meyers stood just inside the entrance in the shade, dressed in a casual tan suit and a beige shirt. The Miami suit and his slicked-back graying hair made him look more like a mobster than a politician.

Kansas parked on the opposite side of the bay. As he and Will walked over they could see the interior of the building was littered with stacks of pallets and large industrial rolls of packing paper, perhaps three feet by four feet. There were no lights on, but the room was diffused with sunlight from the large window panels at the very top of the walls.

As they walked up to him, the congressman nodded. "Good to see you again, Kansas and Will," he said congenially with that standard political smile, but there was just a whisper of something in his hawkish blue eyes—nervousness, discomfort—that Will and his friend caught.

As they were shaking hands, a very expensive black limousine pulled up in front of the bay, and two security heavies in dark suits got out, did a quick, professional pan of the area, then one of them opened the back passenger door. A stately-looking gentlemen exited slowly—someone Kansas recognized immediately. It was the Assistant Director of National Security, Marvin Levens—graying, military-short hair, dark eyes, about five-foot-eight, and dressed in an impeccable gray suit in defiance of the summer heat. He made Kansas and Will look like paupers in their short-sleeved shirts and slacks. He moved to the opening of the warehouse flanked by his security. As the congressman introduced everyone, a third vehicle slid up quietly on the other side of the road by a similar line of warehouses, within view of everything. Another bodyguard-type exited from the front passenger's seat, and did a quick security/perimeter check, then returned to stand stoically by the car. The dark tinted windows offered no indication of who was inside.

"Okay, gentlemen," said the director, without any further preamble. "Let's get down to business." He stared hard at the two men in front of him. "I hear you've got something unique—a device that makes people tell the truth. You're going to have to prove that to me. You're going to have to make me feel it, believe it, before this goes another step farther, you understand? But this is how it's going to work." He nodded to his two security people and they pulled pistols from under their coats. "You're going to take out this device with your fingertips, slowly. You do not turn it on until I say. You will ask me one question. If that question affects national security or my personal integrity in any way, my men will shoot you on the spot. You will turn it off when I tell you to, or these men will shoot you." He glared at them again. "Do you understand, gentlemen?"

Kansas and Will glanced at each other, then nodded.

"Yes, sir," said Will, who was in possession of the truthmaker.

While the director had been talking, the back window of the dark limousine in the distance slid down and the man inside gazed impassively at them. Kansas didn't know the fellow and probably ninety-eight percent of the people in the world wouldn't have recognized that face, but Will, who read newspapers and magazines voraciously, did. The man was somewhere in his mid-sixties and tanned in that perpetual fashion of the wealthy. He had thinning blond hair combed straight back, pale, indifferent gray eyes, and a blunt Germanic nose, but the giveaway was the small, puckered puncture mark on his right cheek, which rumor had it was the result of a knife years ago. Ramone Torreos, "the shadow man," in person. Will couldn't believe it. Ramone Torreos and the Assistant Director of National Security? He was beginning to wonder if this whole thing was going to have a happy ending. If nothing else, he and Kansas had pistols tucked in their belts, covered by their shirts.

Will brought his attention back to the Assistant Director of Security, while slowly reaching back and pulling the truthmaker from his rear pocket. He looked at Levens and gingerly held up the device. "Okay, I'm turning it on."

The brief wave of vibration moved through the group and the deep hum was audible for just a moment. Everyone tensed.

"Given the circumstances, I'm going to ask you the same question, Director, as we asked the congressman," Will said cautiously. "Sir, I want you to tell me the combination of your home safe. Tell me that number."

The director's eyes went from confident and hard to suddenly distracted and bewildered. They could see him struggling against the machine, his mouth opening a little but nothing coming out. He took a breath and exhaled, resisting, then did it again. But finally, as always, the surrender showed in his eyes and his facial muscles relaxed. He looked at Will like a lost child. "Forty-seven right, twenty-two left, thirty-five right." He blinked a couple of times, still captured by the vibration, but forceful enough to end the experiment. "Turn it off now," he said as defiantly as he could muster. "Turn...it... off."

Will complied immediately and the pall that had settled on the group lifted.

The first thing the director did was turn to Torreos in the other limousine and nod emphatically. The big limo started up, waiting for the security man to get in. Then he turned back to Will, Kansas, and the congressman, who were about a dozen feet from him. He shook his head almost sadly as he looked at them. "You know, I'd almost hoped this wasn't true, on a number of levels—most of all on this one." He exhaled hard, eyebrows narrowing. "You realize, of course, we're going to have to take this from you." Then his face softened with a sense of honest regret. "I'm sorry, you're just in the wrong place at the wrong time, with something we just can't have anyone knowing about. We can't let you go."

The trio in front of him started in unison, staring in disbelief.

"I wish there was another way, but there's not. If you don't fight this, we'll make it painless, I promise."

"What the hell are you talking about?" shouted Will. "We're United States citizens! You can't—"

"Yeah, we can!" yelled Director Levens harshly, his face becoming hard again. "And there's nothing you can do about it. It's just the way it is! I'll be damned if I'm going to have a machine like that floating around the halls of government. Not now!"

At that point, Kansas wiped his forehead with the back of his hand; a prearranged signal. At the end of the row of warehouses about a hundred yards down, Mariana stepped out with one of the AT4 anti-tank/vehicle weapons on her shoulder, aimed at the director's car, not thirty feet from the group of men, then pressed the red firing button. There was a detonation and a decided "whoosh" as the enclosed rocket screamed out, streaking toward the rear of the black limousine like a giant, angry wasp. Everyone heard the release of the weapon and everyone saw it coming. One moment they were all postured with threat and defiance, the next second everyone was diving for cover as the missile struck and turned the limousine into a fireball, launching pieces of flaming metal in all directions. One of the security personnel was too close to the vehicle and a hurtling door struck him in the back, knocking him out. The other came up with his gun in his hand, and as he aimed at Kansas, Will, in a panic, drew his pistol and shot him in the shoulder. He spun as he fell, pulling the trigger of his weapon spasmodically in the process. One of the two rounds he released struck the director in the chest.

The limousine with Torreos inside screeched away in a flurry of burning rubber and squealing tires. As Cass and Mariana were pulling up in the rental car, Kansas kicked the gun away from the wounded security agent. Mariana held a gun on him while Cass staunched the flow of blood from his wound.

Will had the director cradled in his arms. The man was mortally wounded, shot through both lungs, and coughing up blood. Will turned on the truthmaker, and lifted Levens's head, helping him breathe better. "What the hell is this all about? Why did you do this?"

Levens gasped, rivulets of blood running out the side of his mouth—small streams of life escaping him. "Couldn't let you get in the way…not now. Change coming…"

"Why?" Will pressed. "What are you doing? How?"

The man smiled grimly, knowing his fate, trapped in the rapture of the truthmaker. "Fading out pure democracy… world control…the President…gonna take him out… uncooperative, idealistic shit. It's Torreos's plan…rewrite Second Amendment…"

Kansas, kneeling next to Will, couldn't believe his ears. "You planned to kill the president?"

Levens coughed again, choking on his own blood, and nodded almost imperceptibly. "Yeah, on his birthday." He stiffened in a wave of pain, then settled. "In El Campo. Fitting, I think…" His eyes were glazing and he was fading.

Will clutched him tighter and shook him. "How? How, for God's sake?"

The dying man gazed up at him, those once bright, hard orbs now distant, his system shutting down. He gasped again, shallow and desperate, eyes growing wide, and he grasped Will's arm fiercely in the throes of death. "Old sewer system...perfect ambush," he mumbled, the remnants of a final grimace touching his lips as his eyes glassed and the lassitude of passing claimed him.

Congressman Meyers was standing next to Will as he laid the director down on the asphalt. He had heard it, too. The look on his face said it all. "My God! They're going to kill the president."

"Holy shit," Kansas said. He took a deep breath, calming himself. "Maybe not. Now we know about it." He stood and looked around at the carnage, then over to Mariana. "I give you a new toy and you can't wait to play with it," he said. "Pretty damned good shot on your part."

Mariana nodded with a slight smile. "I like to make a lasting first impression."

"That you did."

Kansas brought his attention around to Congressman Meyers. "As horrible as all this is, it's going to get worse. My guess is that we're going to become outlaws overnight. They're going to need scapegoats for all this and I'm certain that's going to be us. Sir, you are the one element in this with the reputation and voice to tell what really happened. But because of that, they're going to want you most of all, and they aren't going to want you alive. We're going to have to get out of here, now—all of us. But we need a plan. Out of the country would be best."

Meyers sighed and looked out at the puffy, summer cumulus clouds suspended out along the periphery of a clear blue sky, then turned to them. "I would never have believed any of this. I knew, as everyone does on The Hill, that the divide between liberal and conservative ideology was becoming more polarized than ever— that there were voices encouraging a blending with Europe, a farther left direction for this country, but I would never have imagined—"

Will stood, drawing in a couple of deep breaths. His face was pale with the realization of what he'd just done. He'd been in more dangerous spots than most people ever experience, but he'd never killed a man before. He exhaled hard. "We've got to get out of here, now. Listen, Kansas and I have a friend who owns a resort in the Bahamas, on Cat Island. Nice little place called Fernandez Bay Village. I'm pretty sure Tony will help us out. He's a bit of an adventurer himself and he appreciates 'difficult situations.' I bet he could make customs clearance a tad easier for us, because we're gonna have to get some of those weapons in, as well. Life could get dicey in the near future."

He looked across the airfield to the private aircraft sector, where rows of silent airplanes sat like flocks of patient birds longing for the sky. "I'm all fueled. We need to get out of here now, before an all points bulletin goes out on all of us and every agency in the country knows about the 'terrorists' who just killed the Assistant Director of National Security. If we can make it down to Lauderdale on a tank of gas, Kansas and I know of a private strip just north of the Everglades where we can refuel, then hop across to the Bahamas. I'll call Tony on the way, so he'll be expecting us."

In the distance they could hear sirens. Kansas looked around at the congressman. "Sir, you're going to have to come with us."

Meyers spoke as if he hadn't heard him. "What about the authorities?"

Kansas squared off to him, eyes firm. "Sir, as of this moment you are part of a plot to kill the president. Before you could get to anyone who would listen, you'd be whisked away and you'd have an accident or kill yourself inside of twenty-four hours, and your legacy would be that of a man who lost his mind at the end of his career. Who are you going to tell? The head of Presidential Security, John Macken, is in on this! Our only chance is to run, and then try to figure out a plan. We have to go together."

Meyers shook his head slowly, eyes somewhere between disbelief and anguish. "My wife is gone; my daughter lives out of the country. No reason why I can't. Yesterday I was a respected member of American government. Today I'm on the run from the country I love, being pursued by those who would silence me in a heartbeat for what I know." He looked up at them, lost between desperation and irony. "Ain't life amazing?" But he straightened up then, eyes alight with purpose again. "Okay. Let's get the hell out of here. I always liked the Bahamas."

CHAPTER 9

God offers every mind its choice between truth and repose.
Take what you please—you can never have both.
                                    — **Ralph Waldo Emerson**

They left the congressman's car and took the rental back to the FBO. On the way, at Will's request, they stopped at a hardware store and he bought a canvas duffel bag and a small, battery-charged drill. While Kansas drove the car, Will broke down the M-16 rifles and stored them, along with the last tubular AT4 and all their pistols, in the duffel bag. They reached the plane without incident, loaded the duffel bag in the nose baggage compartment, boarded, and were in the air ten minutes later.

On the ground, John Macken was just receiving a report on the disaster. Anger and savage disappointment burned in his cold, slate-blue eyes. He stood up and paced the room for a moment, his big frame tense and rigid, hands clenched. He would have to chase them now, and he couldn't keep this out of the news, so his people would have to find them before the authorities. He ran a hand through his dark, gray-flecked hair, frustrated. *So be it.*

Will cut a course diagonally inland toward Charleston at first, at ten thousand feet, but before reaching the Appalachians he dropped to five hundred feet, pretty much under the radar, and changed course for the coast, hoping to confuse anyone who might attempt to track the plane. They ran low along Chesapeake Bay for nearly two hundred miles until they reached Norfolk. As they entered the Airport Traffic Zone for Norfolk International, they rose up and out like an aircraft just taking off, becoming indistinguishable from the hundreds of aircraft arriving and departing in the area. After that, Will took them up to ten thousand feet for better fuel consumption and they headed south.

They flew in silence for about an hour, each lost to their own thoughts, weighing new destinies and their chances, knowing that life for all of them had made a quantum change. In the interim, Cass reminded them that last night's news had mentioned the president's birthday was a week and a half away—not much time to lay out a plan to prevent disaster.

Mariana, dark eyes studying the coastline below as she sat in the back with Kansas and Congressman Meyers, told herself she was doing this so that she might eventually return one of these devices to her country, where it belonged...but there was a part of her that realized she had crossed a line protecting the people around her—something the old Mariana wouldn't have done before she met Kansas. She felt him touching her, the warmth and the strength that emanated from him, and she found herself wanting to hold him again, as she had in the moonlight at the motel in The Keys. She found herself wanting more than that. Mariana wasn't sure where any of this would end, but she knew unequivocally she was locked into the ride.

Kansas found himself lost to an amalgam of images and feelings. In just a matter of weeks life had irrevocably changed— the Cuban gold adventure, the truthmakers, the intrigue he and his friends had been cast into, and last but not least, this woman who sat next to him—this incredible creature of poise and allure, a melding of sultry Caribbean beauty and New York confidence. It was strange and somewhat disconcerting, but she had somehow found a place in him that he had kept sheltered, if not closed off entirely, and now, maybe for the first time ever, he wanted to open it.

Will and Cass sat up front. Cass finally relaxed, letting her head loll against the seat, her thick blond hair casually flowing over her shoulders and down across her breasts. She stole a glance at the tall, handsome man at the controls of the plane. Her admiration for him was growing continuously, and for a woman as capable as she, admiration was essential. Good looks and bright conversation only took you so far with Cass Roundtree, although his blue, mischievous eyes and long mane of blond hair certainly didn't detract from the package. She smiled to herself. The incredible lovemaking and the fact that he was junked like a Clydesdale added some serious points, as well.

Will felt her gazing at him with those gray-blue eyes, and his right hand casually reached down and discreetly found hers. *I'm like a damned schoolboy!* he thought. Then he smiled. *Who gives a shit? Somehow it just feels good.* Besides, he knew with the direction they were headed, life could well be short, or harried at best. He was going to squeeze out every drop of this teenage debauchery and this wonderful sensation of being "connected"—of wanting to be connected—that he could. He didn't care what anyone thought.

About four and a half hours later, Will dropped them into a small, nondescript airfield—little more than a concrete building with a corrugated tin roof, a windsock, and a fuel pump.

A tall fellow in a blue denim work shirt, jeans, and a weary-looking ball cap ambled out slowly, with a touch of curiosity, but when he saw Will and Kansas, his face changed to pleased recognition. "Well, hello gentlemen. Long time no see."

Will nodded as he grasped the man's extended hand. "Yeah, been a while. Just need to fuel up. We'll pay cash."

"Cash is okay with me," the man said as he started to turn back toward the building. "Gotta turn on the tank pump."

Putting his hand on the man's shoulder and stopping him, Will said, "Ed, why don't you just have a cigarette in there for about ten minutes before fueling us. I have to make some adjustments on the plane."

His eyes were all Ed needed to see. The man nodded noncommittally. "No problem."

As Ed entered his small office, Will went to the baggage compartment in the nose of the aircraft, opened it, and pulled out the duffel bag. Then, with the drill he'd purchased, he undid four subtly placed screws on the floor and lifted out what was a false top to a hidden compartment. He quickly placed all the weapons, including the AT4, into the hidden box and reattached the false top. He put some of the personal things, like clothes and toiletries that he and the others had brought with them, into the duffel bag and put it in the nose compartment, then closed it. Ten minutes later they were fueled and were lifting off again, course set for Cat Island. When they got set to take off, Kansas took the left seat, spelling Will.

The flight was uneventful, but the views of the islands, the clear azure waters, and colorful reefs were an uplifting experience, as always. They passed from the deep, dark blue waters of the Gulf Stream into the shallow banks that contained the Bahamas proper, then crossed the tip of Andros Island as the sun was setting. Kansas skirted Nassau—the staggered, orange-colored reefs surrounding it lifting up through the darkening crystalline water, protecting the deep harbors of the island that once held pirate ships and merchant ships from around the world. Kansas called their friend's base station at Fernandez Bay via the plane radio and gave Tony an estimated time of arrival. Sailing on over Exuma Sound, the 310 finally passed over the foot of Eleuthera Island, coming into the small airstrip on Cat at New Bight, just before midnight.

The airport was closed with just a guard on duty. Tony Armbrister, of course, knew the man well, and there was only a perfunctory check of passports and the baggage they had with them. The weapons were left in the secret compartment to be picked up later. After greetings and brief introductions, everyone piled into Tony's Land Rover and headed for his resort.

Armbrister was a tall man, over six feet, at about one hundred ninety pounds, with longish graying hair and wary but attentive gray eyes. He carried his sixty-plus years well—they had been kind to him. His family had owned a healthy piece of the island since the 1700s and he was a Caribbean man by lineage and nature. There was a little sailor in him and a little pirate, and he was a capable, if not daring pilot, owning a small twin that he kept at New Bight. He had taken a few chances here and there and fortune had smiled on him more often than not.

Waiting in the car was Tony's driver, maintenance man, and longtime friend, Zediah Watkins, a huge black Bahamian, probably six-foot-three, with a large, muscled frame, curly ringlets of black hair cascading down to his shoulders, and fierce, smoky yellow eyes with pupils the color of midnight. He was about ten years younger than Tony, and it was his commanding presence that often permitted the discretion of negotiation in tense "situations."

After finding a room for the congressman and a small beach house for each of the two couples, and allowing them to refresh themselves, Tony had everyone meet back in the main gathering room at the resort. Drinks in hand, they settled into the comfortable rattan and pillow lounge chairs near the windows, close enough to the water to hear the waves breaking on the beach in the darkness outside.

"Pam will be pissed she missed you two. She's in Fort

Lauderdale doing some shopping for us," Tony said.

Will expressed his genuine disappointment at not seeing his friend's lovely wife, and Tony moved on.

"As good as it is to see you, I'm guessing this isn't a vacation."

"Oh, but that I wish it was," Kansas sighed. "No, you're right, and because you are the friend that you are, I need to tell you the truth, and hope you'll believe it."

Kansas began his tale and fifteen minutes later Tony sat back in his chair, looked at Zediah for a moment, then turned back to Will and the others. "Unbelievable," he muttered, shaking his head. "A machine that makes you tell the truth, and a presidential assassination. Even for you two, this is hip-deep shit. You will, of course, have to prove this to me—this thing about the truth, but it can wait until tomorrow." He glanced around at all of them, then back to Will. "So, how do I fit into this? You guys just need a place to hide out for a while?"

Will nodded. "Yeah, that's basically it. Don't want to get you involved any more than necessary, but man, we need a 'hole in the wall' for a few days."

"Well, you know you've got it," Tony said. "It's the slow season and we're doing some repairs. We only have one bungalow rented to a Canadian couple, so I've got the rooms. I owe you both, anyway, for that thing you got me out of in Haiti. Least I can do."

Nobody asked and nobody offered any details there.

"Oh, by the way, we've got some weapons we need to get out of the baggage compartment in the plane," Will added.

"Why does that not surprise me?" Tony said with a sigh. "If it can wait until tomorrow night, I can take care of it for you."

"Fine. That'll work."

It was almost 1:30 a.m. before everyone made it to their assigned rooms. It was much later than that before either couple got to sleep, particularly Kansas and Mariana. She had decided that they had danced enough. The following morning they awoke to the sun cascading through open blinds, casting soft, saffron trellises across the room. They made love again, with the sounds of the sea rolling onto the sand in the background and the wind chimes on the porch whispering to the early morning breeze.

They shared each other without the urgency and the fervor of the night before, with tenderness, soft caresses and kisses, and the all-encompassing warmth of embrace beyond simple passion.

But nearly a thousand miles away the hunt was on for them, and the hounds had already found the scent.

From Congressman Meyers's original conversation with the Assistant Director of Security, Torreos and his people knew about Kansas and Will and the airplane. Their people began to check discreet fueling stations along the route from Washington to South Florida. A day later, two men in gray business suits visited Ed, the fellow with the wearied baseball cap at the lonely airstrip just north of the Everglades. That information went to a customs national flight path center, which maintained an overview of departing and arriving flights throughout the U.S., including ones that left heading toward the Bahamas on the day Will and his friends had stopped and visited Ed. It seemed a logical assumption they might try to get out of the country. From there it was a matter of sorting the flights that came off the mainland at that time and determining their destinations. But there were a lot of flights and destinations. If not for a small piece of preplanning, it might well have been impossible.

Vitor knelt on the floor of his dimly lit motel room outside Dulles, wearing no shirt, no shoes. The flittering light of ceremonial candles danced on the walls as anger and disappointment waged war inside him, his stiletto cradled in his palm, the cold strength of the steel urging penance. *He had failed! Failed! He had his target and the man had escaped him!* Pain was true penance. God understood pain. Vitor grasped the razor-sharp knife with purpose and brought it up, slowly, deliberately, pushing the point into his flesh, running it diagonally across his naked chest. Breathing heavily through his clenched teeth, he took a gasping breath and brought the knife up again. The crimson rivulets of blood sluiced down across his hard, rippled stomach as he stared upward in the rapture of attrition, the shadows on the wall flickering in witness to his suffering.

Later, after he'd cleaned himself, he considered the situation. He didn't truly expect his target to return to The Keys, but there was always a chance. He would follow that possibility. As a backup, he contacted the Vatican's resource center again. He reviewed the photos of the man and woman who had asked the incriminating questions of the senator and the state representative promoting the Pirate Land Theme Park in Florida a week or so ago—the debacle that had cost the politicians their careers. They were an attractive blond and a tall man with sun-bleached hair. Maybe they could be found, as well.

It was after nine the next morning before everyone made their way to breakfast on the veranda. They were greeted by Tony and Zediah, who were having coffee and reading the Nassau newspaper. Tony was sporting a company-logoed polo shirt and shorts. Zediah's huge frame stretched out a Margaritaville T-shirt and a pair of walking shorts. After everyone sat down, Tony tossed the front page to Will.

"Got the paper from the morning flight," he said, deadpan. "You guys are big news."

An article near the top told about the killing of the Assistant Director of National Security and about the pursuit underway for the individuals responsible. Kansas and Will's names and photos were at the top of the list. They hadn't identified either of the women and had no descriptions.

Congressman Meyers, standing over Will and Kansas's shoulders, grimaced. "Well, it's all in the fan now, and anything we do at this point becomes twice as difficult."

"You don't think you could just contact a news agency with this information about a possible assassination, to try to prevent them from acting on it?" Tony said.

"We've already been over this," Kansas replied. "No bona fide news agency is going to run something like that without checking sources, and all the sources are going to say it's bullshit—that we're trying to draw attention away from ourselves. You have to remember we've been accused of killing the Assistant Director of National Security. What news agency isn't going to call the authorities first thing? What are we going to do, show up in person? I don't think so. Besides, we actually know next to nothing." He paused for a moment, considering something, then continued. "You know, years ago, I had a good friend who worked for Channel 11 News in Dallas. He used to come down and fish with me. There's a chance I could get him to listen to me—tell him the truth about all this. But we can't do that from here."

"Sounds like a possibility," Will said. "But if all we know is true, we don't have much time. The president's birthday celebration is next Saturday, in the little town of El Campo, Texas, and all we know for sure is something about using an old sewer system. Right now I think we need details on where the president will speak and what his itinerary is that day. And we need a schematic of the old sewer system there." He turned to Cass. "Can you be of help on this?"

She tilted her head and her face pinched into a sarcastic frown. "Does a cat cover its scat? I'll call my computer friends at Microsoft and see what they can come up with—maybe they can fax us some info."

Will chuckled, fully chastised. "Yeah, okay. That'll help."

Tony smiled, as well. He liked the frankness in the tall blond. The rest of her wasn't bad, either. If only he wasn't so damned happily married. "No problem, you can use my phone in the office. And tonight we'll run back to the airport and get your weapons."

"Yeah, need to do that," Kansas added. "I don't think we have to worry as much about legitimate authorities as we do this Bright Circle bunch. You keep a few guns on hand, as well, I bet. Might want to make sure they're handy, but here's hoping we won't need them. In truth, I don't think there's a chance in hell they can find us."

"I've got a couple older model M14 carbines and a pistol or two in my office, and I'll put people at the airports here twenty-four/seven just in case," Tony said. "We've got the main airport on the north end, the one you came into here, and a small strip at Hawks Nest Resort south of us." He exhaled sharply, then focused on Will again. "Okay, I think it's time for a little proof in this pudding."

Will understood completely, taking out the gleaming, silver truthmaker and laying it on the table. He turned it on and asked a simple, not terribly incriminating question about Tony's income tax filing last year.

A few moments later, when the machine had been turned off and Tony's eyes had cleared, he whispered intensely, still slightly under the spell, "Son of a bitch! No wonder they want you guys." He blew out a sigh. "I can hardly count the business deals I've done where I would have liked to have had one of those on the table."

Mariana nodded, thinking out loud before she caught herself. "The interrogations I have witnessed—all would have been over in minutes. So much better for all concerned…"

Catching her drift, Kansas replied, "What a humanitarian change this would be for intelligence and warfare, and so many other things, all the way down to the office, the boardroom, and the bedroom." He grinned with a twinge of scorn touching the corners of his mouth. "You know what the irony of this is? I'm guessing the ACLU would fight this tooth and nail, calling it an invasion of privacy—the right of a citizen to guile."

Zediah, who had been subject to the spell as well, shook his head and muttered in his deep bass voice, "I remember watching a *Voudon houngan,* a Voodoo priest, in a ceremony years ago, forcing the truth from a man. He rubbed two strange-looking, flat rocks together for a few minutes, creating a vibration throughout the room. There were potions as well, and invocations, but what I felt then was the same as today."

"There are more things in heaven and earth, Horatio, than are dreamt of in your philosophy," Will replied quietly.

With business taken care of, and at least a temporary sense of security, the next couple of days were dedicated to enjoying the island. The two couples strolled the lovely, curved beach that contained Fernandez Bay, picking up seashells, playing in the water like children, and letting the wind and the sea wash away their worries for a brief time. Stan Meyers set himself up with a good book and a tall, cool drink in the gathering room, spending hours in conversation with Tony and trading stories from their different worlds. Zediah met briefly with Kansas and Will, telling them he would set up eyes at the airports. He had turned to the two men that day and told them in that heavy bass voice, those huge yellow-white eyes fixing on them, "You are friends of my friend. I will watch over you."

The first evening, they did go back to the airstrip, and while Tony kept the guard occupied, Will and Kansas slipped over the fence and retrieved their weapons from the plane. During their absence, Mariana called her boss in Cuba, explaining, honestly enough, that some of the artifacts she was pursuing had been stolen by someone in Key West and this needed to be resolved. Santiago was becoming impatient, threatening to send in someone else, but she managed to buy a few more days. When they hung up she stared pensively at the phone for a few seconds, torn between loyalty to her country and the discovery of the emotions that were building within her breast. She reminded herself, once again, that she was a professional, not a schoolgirl.

Cass spent several hours calling back and forth with her computer and government friends, and eventually received faxes with some interesting information on the President of the United States and the sewer system of El Campo, Texas. The president was born in Tampico, Illinois, but he spent his summers with his grandparents, who lived in the small town of El Campo, Texas. It was there that he would be giving a short speech on his birthday. The town originally went back to the late 1800s. It was actually incorporated in 1905. Its economy relied primarily on agriculture and petroleum—rice, cotton, soybeans, and oil. But as Cass searched for information about the sewer system, she discovered that in the mid-1970s the town had experienced some expansion in businesses and population. To accommodate this expansion, they closed off much of the old, cement-segmented sewer system and built a new, modern system adjacent to it. They never took out the old one, just left it in the ground. Apparently, with the old system, the engineers had used extraordinarily large-diameter piping from the water station to a handful of underground, four-way concrete junction boxes, perhaps four feet by six feet, then reduced flow to a more conventional-sized conduit after that. When she reviewed information on the president's upcoming visit to El Campo, she discovered he was to give a speech in one of the parks there. The city was erecting a large bandstand with enclosed sides especially for that event. Curiously, one of those old four-way concrete junction boxes appeared to be directly underneath the bandstand. Kansas and Will decided to keep this information to themselves—no one else needed to know.

The habitually determined, always in control John Macken was fried enough to spit nails. How in God's name had these people gotten away, and what did they know? He had spent the last eighteen months setting this up; it had taken him and his people a year of trolling Communist Party meetings and quasi Marxist bars to find just the right politically possessed malcontent with the correct balance of talent, experience, and blind, righteous intent. Then they had to go through the laborious process of winning his confidence, ever so slowly, carefully encouraging him, then implanting this plan in such a fashion that he became convinced it was his design, and his destiny to change the country. Everything had to be perfectly compartmentalized to the point that there were no threads leading back to anyone. And suddenly, out of right field, comes this montage of Pollyannas who want to save the world with truth. Torreos said he got the word from Director Levens, before he got himself killed, that the damned thing actually worked! *Did Levens tell them anything while under the influence of the damned machine?*

He took a breath and exhaled slowly, calming himself. Chances were they got nothing, and if all went well they would disappear before the president's birthday, anyway. Besides, who in the hell would believe a group of malcontents who had just murdered the Assistant Director of National Security? In an unprecedented move, Torreos was bringing in his own security forces to handle this, under Macken's command, quietly circumventing U.S. security. He was, at that moment, waiting for a call from them.

"Just stay on track," he muttered to himself. "Get rid of this idealistic bastard in the White House and get things moving toward a new plan." He had been promised big things—maybe a shot at a vice presidency down the road—and nothing was getting in his way now.

Cass and Will sat on a rugged outcropping of rock near the curve of the bay, watching Tony's aircraft soar into the heart of a magnificent sunset. He told them he had business in Lauderdale that couldn't be postponed, but he'd be back in a day or so. The domed sky was just taking on that pale clarion blue as a fiery sun melted into layers of soft mauve and gray clouds bruising the horizon. A quiet sea had just gone from emerald blue to still, blond honey as the sun's last rays brushed it. The wind settled politely in reverence to the passing of another day, seabirds stilled their voices, and for a moment, a hush fell over the world. Cass took Will's hand wordlessly as they stared in wonder at the magic of nature. When the moment passed and the hues began to darken, she spoke quietly, still staring outwards. "I wish I could click my heels and make this whole thing go away, this course we've set ourselves on—saving the world." Cass turned to him, just a touch of desperation in her eyes. "I'd just like to go home and get to know you without looking over our shoulders. I'm wondering if life will ever be the same." She returned to studying the sun as it was swallowed by the melding grays and purples, and sighed. "I don't have a good feeling about all of this. I wish I did, but I don't."

Will looked over at her, then put his arm around his new lady and pulled her close to him, touching his lips to her forehead. "We've got to see this through now. I'll admit, we need a little luck, but we'll be okay." But in the far reaches of his mind there was a hollow, anxious place that didn't feel good about this, either.

Kansas awoke early, just before sunrise. As pleased as he was with this growing relationship with Mariana, his sleep had been fitful and his dreams laced with confusing images and strange admonitions. He rose quietly, so as not to wake her, grabbed his shorts and his T-shirt, and slipped out for a walk on the beach to clear his head. The edge of the sun was just breaching the still darkness of the horizon as he stepped out onto the porch. The morning air held that cool, salty fragrance of the ocean and the tart aroma of gray mud and mangroves. He breathed deeply, relaxing for the first time in a while.

At that moment the distant throb of rotors intruded on his reverie. He squinted into the swirling mists over the sea and finally the shape became clear, soaring just above the water a half-mile out—a Blackhawk, just about the most popular transport/assault helicopter in the world. As it drew closer he saw it was painted a light gray-blue with no other identifying markings on the body. Instantly, intuitively, he knew what it was, and he was bursting through the door of the cottage, shouting for Mariana to get up. In moments, she had her clothes on and a pistol in her hand. He had the Colt automatic rifle, a couple magazines, and had slipped the tubular AT4 anti-tank weapon over his shoulder via its canvas strap.

They had barely made it out the door, headed for Cass and Will's bungalow seventy-five yards from them, already shouting warnings, when the helicopter crossed the beach two hundred yards out and hovered in position. Suddenly, one of the Hydra 70 rockets in the pod underneath the stubby port stabilizer screamed out, streaking across the beach and slamming into Cass and Will's cottage. The small building exploded in a corona of fire and flame. Kansas cried out involuntarily, stunned by the violence and its implications. His friends were gone, incinerated before his eyes.

"God! Will..." he whispered painfully, the anguish in his eyes like shadows in the mangroves.

But self-preservation took over as the nose of the Blackhawk swiveled a few degrees and a second rocket swept in at the cottage behind them. Instinctively, he threw Mariana to the ground and covered her with his body, but it wasn't enough. A maelstrom of shattered wood, glass, and fiery debris engulfed them. Ears ringing from the explosion and his body sliced in a half-dozen places by shrapnel, Kansas struggled to his feet and tried to get Mariana up, but a slim, six-inch piece of wood had buried itself about three inches into her thigh, pinning her shorts to her leg. She cried out as she tried to move. Kansas could see the helicopter settling on the beach. He ripped off his belt, pulled and locked it painfully tight above the wound on his lady's leg, and tore out the wooden dagger. Mariana screamed as blood rushed from the wound, but the makeshift tourniquet stopped most of the flow. He grabbed his rifle and pulled Mariana to her feet, while almost a dozen men dressed in black combat gear poured from the copter. As they spread out, moving toward Kansas and bringing up their weapons, a burst of rifle fire erupted from the heavy rock outcroppings above the curve of the beach. Two of the black figures went down and the others dropped to the sand for a few moments, returning fire. Orders were shouted and two broke off toward the shooter under covering fire. Given the distraction, Mariana and Kansas ran for the cover of the sea grapes, buttonwood, and scrub palms on the crest of the beach, heading toward the pavilion and main building. Kansas paused just long enough to gaze back toward the shooter who had just saved their lives. Behind the rocks in the distance, the rising sun gave him just enough light to make out Zediah, huge fist raised in salute, like a dark, fierce, guardian angel, and Kansas was reminded of his parting words, "I will watch over you..."

With bullets slapping the sand around them, they stumbled over the crest and ran down the soft sand path that led toward the main complex. As they ran, Kansas found himself emotionally savaged by his friends' deaths, yet at the same time he was filled with the bitter taste of betrayal and the desire for revenge. He fiercely wiped the blood from his face, where a piece of shrapnel had torn a gash above his right eye. *They knew where to hit us! How did they know? How did they find us?* But for now he and Mariana had to stay alive. Their pursuers had split up into two groups—three staying behind them and another four running along the widening curve of the beach, trying to get ahead and cut them off before they reached the resort.

Kansas couldn't have known, but of the two who went into the jungle after Zediah, one never came out. A few minutes later the other stumbled from the dense foliage onto the beach, no weapon in his hands, blood still draining from a jagged throat wound, turning the front of his dark fatigues a wet red. He lurched onto the beach, fell to his knees, sighed out one last breath and dropped face-first into the sand.

Even with the tourniquet, Mariana was bleeding badly, and tiring. Kansas had his arm around her, trying to keep up a pace, but the group behind them was gaining. He could hear her panting, breath coming in quick gasps. It had become a running gunfight, him pausing long enough to get off a few rounds here and there, trying to slow them, but they were professionals and it did little good. He was already into his last magazine. Finally, they reached the outskirts of the pavilion area that housed the main buildings, but the last exchange to gain that ground emptied the magazine in the weapon he was carrying. Fortunately, he had knocked down one more of them. There were just two left in that bunch. Kansas stopped and looked at Mariana, then glanced at the empty parking lot in front of them, dotted with miniature stands of palm trees and tropical flowers. The resort entrance was still some two hundred yards away.

"With these odds we're not going to win this," he gasped. "We're going to have to take a chance." He pointed at the four large trash dumpsters in a square near the center of the lot. "You keep going, try to make it to those. When you get there, show yourself—make sure they see you for just a second." He caught a breath and looked at his lady. "Now, you're going to have to trust me," he said, slipping the AT4 from his back and handing it to her. "I'm going to need your pistol."

She nodded, weary to exhaustion, her leg caked with blood. It squished between her toes in her tennis shoes as she moved, but the look in her eyes was still defiant. *"Sí.* Yes, I understand," she said, handing him the Glock.

The last two soldiers moved into the open area cautiously, using the first stand of palms as cover. Then they noticed the body, with several obvious wounds, lying splayed out on the asphalt, the M16 several feet away, breech open, weapon empty. As they advanced slowly, they saw the woman hiding behind the dumpsters, frightened and cowering. The larger one looked at his companion. "I told you I thought I hit him."

The other nodded, still not taking his attention off his targets. "Yeah, I heard you." They reached the body. The man's eyes were open, staring into the blinding morning sun. One kicked him lightly in the side. Nothing.

The girl cried out, diverting their attention. "Don't shoot me. I surrender. I have the device. I tell you anything you need to know! Just don't kill me."

They smiled grimly at each other and moved away from the dead man toward the woman. It had been costly, but they were going to get what they came for after all. They got about fifteen feet from the fellow on the asphalt, moving toward the girl, when the dead man sat up, pulled a pistol from the small of his back, and killed them both.

Kansas had barely gotten to his feet, picked up one of the men's weapons and headed toward Mariana when the other four soldiers who had taken the beach route came barreling into the pavilion/parking lot area and opened fire. He reached Mariana at the dumpsters, but they were pinned down again, and this time they could be circled easily. *Fish in a barrel*, thought Kansas bitterly as he checked the magazine on the Heckler and Koch assault rifle he had just taken. *Only five rounds...*

Kansas looked at the AT4, but it was almost useless as a personal weapon with their adversaries starting to spread out again. They were working their weapons just enough to keep him and Mariana pinned as a couple broke away in a flanking motion. A ricochet off the metal dumpster cut through the sleeve of Kansas's right arm, turning the cloth red. They both ducked back down between the metal containers. *Trapped!* his mind screamed. *Waiting to be killed like rabbits in a hole!* He wasn't going to die like this! He turned to Mariana. Fatigue and fear filled her beautiful, dark eyes. "I'm going to charge diagonally from them and run out this magazine—pull their attention away from you. When I do, you run for the resort. Run hard. Maybe you can grab a car or—"

"No! You can't!" she cried, tears rimming her eyes, knowing it was suicide.

He smiled softly, almost sadly at her. "I'm sorry, Mariana. I'm so sorry I got you into this." He brought his hand up and gently caressed her cheek. "But I'm not sorry I found you. If there's any truth to getting a second try at this world, I hope I find you again. I'd love to finish this..." He drew her to him and kissed her hard, with all the passion and love he had discovered in the place inside him that had been hidden for so long. Then he pulled back, the passion fell away, and his eyes went all business. "Now go!" he cried. "Run!" He rose and dashed out, firing as he went. Even at the end, when he could see the pavement being stitched with deadly rows of fire coming right at him and he knew he was dead, he uttered a terse, spontaneous prayer—something he hadn't done for a long time. "Let her live, God. Please, let her live!"

But at that moment there was a burst of semi-automatic weapon fire from the eaves of the resort, behind the enemy. From around the corner of the building came Will, charging at them like a madman, rifle in his hands jumping with precise, deadly flashes. Cass was covering him from the bushes under the eaves. Two of the soldiers went down, another fired back for a second before collapsing, and the final man turned and ran. But he was on his radio as he scrambled into the sea grape and buttonwood copses and back down the path toward the helicopter.

Kansas found himself astounded on several levels. First off, he was still alive. Even more amazing, there, coming toward him, were Will and Cass, back from the dead, like Lazarus! "How?" was all he could mutter for a moment, lurching forward, reaching out to grasp his friend's shoulder in both amazement and joy, and a somewhat clumsy attempt at an embrace. His friend was alive! And Cass, as well! "How did you survive? I saw the house destroyed!"

Mariana came running up and threw herself into Kansas's arms, all sense of decorum or pretense gone, thankful beyond belief that her man was still alive. As they held each other, Will replied, "We weren't in it. We were here, trying to find some medicine for Cass. She evidently ate something last night that didn't agree with her. It looked like food poisoning of some sort—throwing up violently, all the standard symptoms. So about 5:30 we got up and I took her down here to the store. They generally open about then for the charter-fishing people. We were hoping we could find some Pepto Bismol or something. When we heard the chopper, the shooting and the explosions, I started looking for weapons. I left mine in the cottage. I finally managed to break into Tony's office and found these." He held up one of Tony's M14 carbines. Cass, looking pale and drawn, but determined, had the other. "We saw the group coming up from the beach and trailed them until they got here. When we saw you and Mariana and those guys, we took 'em out." The seriousness fell away and he grinned in that typical Will fashion. "I hope you don't mind us shooting a couple of them. You looked like you were into some sort of Wyatt Earp, Teddy Roosevelt-San Juan Hill charge thing there—eyes all glazed and guns blazing—and I really hated to interrupt, but I thought maybe you wouldn't mind sharing a little of the excitement."

Kansas took a normal breath for the first time in several minutes, realizing his hands were still shaking. He exhaled gratefully with a smile of his own. "Yeah, well, next time ask first, okay? There were barely enough of them to go around as it was."

Will tried to keep a straight face, but he lost. Grinning, he said, "You know, looking around at the trail of bodies you left, I'm reminded of a quote by a guy named Robert Savage: 'You can measure an individual by the opposition it takes to discourage him.'"

Stan Meyers had shown up, too, coming over from the individual motel rooms across from the pavilion. The older man bore a frightened, cautious countenance. "What the hell is happening? What's all the shooting?"

Before Kansas could answer, something suddenly occurred to him. He looked at Will. "The truthmaker? Where is it?"

"Oohh damn! I knew there was something I was forgetting!" Will moaned, palm of his hand going to his forehead.

Kansas physically deflated. It was over. The truthmaker was gone—lost to the explosion in the cottage.

Will allowed his partner a moment's torment, then grinned and reached behind his back, pulling out the shiny object that had captured so many people's interest. "Sorry, I just couldn't resist. Man, I never go anywhere without this."

"I wanna hit you, you know that?" Kansas said with a half smile.

Will looked at him, head cocked, eyes filled with scrutiny and humor. "I'll let you take a rain check on that. You've been beat up enough today."

While they all stood there reveling in survival, one of the last members of Torreos's assault squad, the sniper, sat at the base of an old banyan tree on a sandy rise covered with casuarina bushes and wild bougainvillea about two hundred yards away. It looked like the game was lost; they weren't going to secure the prize. But, as if some higher power had willed it, the group they were after had somehow paused in a spot that gave him a clear shot. He was going to take out a couple of them, then catch his ride out of there. He had caught glimpses of the muscular man with the long, sun-bleached hair continually foiling his team as the fight had rambled its way from the beach, yet he'd never had a clear shot. Now, there he was, surrounded by his companions, so frigging pleased with himself. He cradled the scoped, bolt action Remington M-24 comfortably in his arms, butt securely against his shoulder, slipped off the safety, and settled his eye at the scope. He put the man in the crosshairs, moving carefully to a clean heart shot, and slowly squeezed the trigger.

But at the very last millimeter of pull, a huge, calloused hand covered his face and another grabbed the back of his head, wrenching viciously in a counterclockwise twist, then quickly snap-turned a second time. The gun discharged, its round racing impotently into the heavens. But by that time, it was a moot point for the shooter, whose startled, dead eyes were staring down at his shoulder blades.

As the rifle fired, Kansas and his people were immediately drawn toward the source of the discharge. Once again, Zediah stood like a dark angel against the verdant green hillside illumined by a brilliant rising sun.

Kansas just shook his head. "I don't know what Tony pays that guy, but it sure as hell isn't enough."

Suddenly they heard the rotors on the helicopter begin their cadenced, rhythmic throb. Everyone looked at each other for a moment, then headed in unison for the beach below. Kansas reached for Mariana to help her, and seeing the AT4 lying on the ground, picked it up and once again threw it over his shoulder.

The Blackhawk pilot and two surviving members of the team were evacuating, humiliated in defeat. A handful of civilians had kicked their asses. Frigging civilians! When the pilot saw the group come down toward the beach, his face went grim with fury. He drew the bird up and swung it sharply in their direction. "He who laughs last..." he muttered to himself between clenched teeth.

Everyone saw the chopper turn dramatically and head for them. They didn't need a playbook.

"Get back up over the beach and into the woods, now!" shouted Will.

No one needed further prompting, but the copter was coming on fast, and Mariana and the congressman were struggling with great effort up the sandy incline toward the higher cover.

Kansas called to Will, pulling the anti-tank weapon off his back. "I'm going to draw them off!" he yelled, starting to move back down the incline and out toward the beach.

"Not without me, you're not!" Will yelled back. "You're not gettin' all the great barroom stories on this adventure."

Kansas smiled, almost certain that was going to be Will's reply, but still touched by his friend's courage and loyalty. He also knew Will was a remarkable shot with a rifle, which couldn't do any harm right now.

Lost to pain and exhaustion, Mariana didn't realize that Kansas wasn't close behind her until she neared the top of the rise. When she turned, she saw Kansas and Will standing on the beach, braced and waiting for the oncoming helicopter like David before Goliath.

Will threw up his weapon and took aim carefully. The chopper was still a quarter mile out—a ridiculously long shot for a carbine. Adjusting for wind and distance, he let loose with a half-dozen rounds to draw the chopper pilot's attention. As luck would have it, a couple of them hit the windshield, not doing much damage, but the gauntlet was cast. The aircraft locked its direction on the two men on the beach. The pilot, choosing to make this up-close and personal, flipped the selector switch to his M240D machine guns, and lightly gripped the trigger on his cyclic stick as he bore down on his targets. As he drew in closer, he noticed one man kneel down and bring up a weapon, but at that point it didn't matter. He was going to have them regardless. Then he'd circle back and take the whole place apart before he left.

As the Blackhawk closed in, its machine guns opened up and twin trails of mayhem appeared magically, slamming the sand in two ragged rows starting out about two hundred yards from Kansas and Will and moving inexorably in at them. Mariana and the others stopped at the top of the sand ridge, captured by the horror and awed by the spectacle of courage. They stood motionless, like fearful, frozen statues, watching the inevitable fight to the death in the sandy arena below. Zediah had just shown up, as well, carrying the Remington sniper rifle. In an effort borne purely of desperation, Mariana snatched the weapon from him and checked the magazine. There were four rounds left.

Will calmly, determinedly, raised his rifle and punched out an entire magazine as fast as he could, cutting small holes in the fuselage of the behemoth bearing down on them without consequence. He snapped out the magazine and slapped in another. Next to him Kansas removed the safety pin and the sight covers on the anti-tank gun, released the first safety, then took aim, holding down the second safety and placing his finger on the red firing button as the dancing furrows closed in on him and his partner. Will knew this was it. Everything had notched down into a weird slow motion; a simple contest of life and death with nothing in between. He watched, strangely detached as the waves of bullets came in at them, raising his weapon and emptying it at the chopper again, but this time several of his rounds slapped the windshield, puncturing it and distracting the pilot a little, causing the deadly rows to waver off course slightly. At that point, Kansas fired. There was a tremendous resonance and a loud "whoosh" as the back blast of the weapon scorched the sand behind them and the rocket-propelled grenade screamed outward and upward at the Blackhawk, its hot, ribbon-like trail meandering behind it. The hail of bullets passed by them close enough for the pelted sand to sting their legs. There was no point in running. They were either dead or alive. They stood there waiting to die or see the copter explode. Strangely enough, neither happened.

The pilot jigged as the rocket-propelled grenade came at him and the deadly projectile passed about a foot under the belly of the aircraft, missing it entirely. With the same amount of fortune, both swaths of bullets missed the two men by about the same distance.

The big helicopter roared over the top of them and headed out over the water, swinging about quickly and coming back at them. Will turned to Kansas and raised his hands, palms up, in that typical fashion. "Hey, cowboy, what the hell happened there? If they'd been any closer you could have swung the freaking thing and hit them with it!"

Kansas shrugged, then glared back. "Yeah, well, look who's talking. You burned up three magazines and did nothing more than piss them off! You, who I've heard say could shoot the freaking balls off a cockroach at fifty yards!"

"Yeah, well the dammed cockroach wasn't shooting back at me!"

While they were arguing, the Blackhawk had come in off the

deeper water and was hovering just about a hundred feet off the beach, and about two hundred feet behind the two men, nose (and machine guns) tilted downward at them.

On the ridge, Mariana had thrown herself down behind a jutting of coral, snap-bolting a round into the chamber and steadying the black barrel of the sniper rifle on the rock, setting the gun into her shoulder and peering into its scope. She could clearly see the pilot, perched high and staring down at his antagonists (who had just decided to save their argument for later and run). As he surged the aircraft forward, the pilot closed his finger around the trigger of his machine gun. Kansas and Will were in full gallop across the sand dunes. Mariana aimed and fired.

There was a brief burst of fire from the chopper. The same deadly furrows raced at the two men, but then it was as if the aircraft hit a wall, shuddering in midair. Suddenly, the center of the copter underneath the port stabilizer exploded into a brilliant fireball, ripping the aircraft apart. Amidst the ear-splitting cacophony, sizzling hot, flaming fragments of metal rained down as the back fuselage of the machine, rotor, and boom, simply cracked off the fiery mass in front and tumbled lifelessly to the earth.

Kansas and Will stopped running at the sound of the explosion, then just turned and watched in utter disbelief as the burning, dismembered helicopter dropped into the sea, hissing and smoking, and sank into the shallow water.

"Whoashit," Will muttered, exhaling hard. Then he turned casually to Kansas. "You know, in my defense, cockroaches don't actually have balls, so it would be nigh on impossible to shoot them off."

Kansas swung around. "Hey, I'm not the one who made up the analogy. That's what you get for believing your own PR. Serves me right for believing you! Talk about harshing my freaking mellow!"

The two men had just renewed their argument about each other's abilities, or lack of, in the use of projectile weapons when they saw Mariana limping her way toward them with the sniper rifle still in hand. Cass was with her.

After a couple of much-needed embraces, reassuring a small

fraction of continuity in their lives, Kansas moved back, still holding his lady by her arms, and looked at her questioningly. "You did this?"

She nodded with a shrug. "*Si*. Yes."

Kansas shook his head. "Amazing. Absolutely freaking amazing. Brilliant. To aim for the rocket pod."

She grimaced sheepishly. "Not so amazing, *mi amigo*. I was aiming for the pilot."

Will went over, pulled her away from Kansas, and gave her a huge hug. "I don't give a rat's ass what you were aiming for. You're on my Christmas list forever!" He paused then, taking in the shattered fuselage of the helicopter protruding from the water and the still smoking remains of the two cottages down the beach, then turned back toward his friends. "Damn! Like a bad Clint Eastwood movie, huh?"

After Kansas and Mariana had been treated for their wounds, they called Tony in Ft. Lauderdale and told him what had happened, and he and his wife departed within the hour. In the meantime, there were some immediate concerns that needed airing.

"First off, we can't stay here any longer," Will said to the others as they gathered around a table in the meeting room of the resort. "We need to be out of here tonight. Even more importantly, we need to know how they knew."

Kansas's green eyes became hard and locked onto his friend. "I happen to like your buddy Tony, but I don't like the fact that he takes off for a 'business meeting' and we get hit a few hours later. May be a coincidence, but—"

"Out of the question," Will said, interrupting him. "I'd trust Tony with my life."

"Maybe he said something to somebody," Cass suggested.

"He just wouldn't. I know him."

Congressman Meyers cleared his throat. "I have to agree with Will. I just can't see a man like Tony doing something like that, and he doesn't strike me as the kind of guy who makes many mistakes. I'll tell you what I think. I think they figured us out. I worked with Intelligence for a while, before I got into serious politics. I think they did some good guessing and ended up getting a handle on where we went. The informational/deductive powers of certain aspects of our government are beyond astounding, especially in air traffic." He looked over at Will. "If I were you, I'd call the guy who refueled us at that little strip north of the Everglades and ask him if anyone showed up asking questions after we left. All they have to do is pinpoint us near the end of that journey and they can track us from there."

Will stared at him for a moment, then picked up the phone and called his friend. Five minutes later they were much more informed, but they still only knew half the truth.

Tony was back, and the first thing he did was meet with the constable on the island regarding the strange battle on his property. The story was delivered in such a fashion as to portray two groups of black-clad soldiers attacking and killing each other near his resort. Kansas, Mariana, and the others were left out of the version and kept out of sight. Then there was a gathering of the troops and some seriously frank conversations. Afterwards, it was unanimously agreed that Tony had nothing to do with the recent attack. In fact, he was screaming, spitting mad when he saw the two cottages that had been destroyed. But after he had calmed down, he admitted with a slight smile that he had been planning on renovating them at a huge cost. Now his insurance would pay for it. Furthermore, and most importantly, he agreed to help them get off the island undetected. "I can't afford guests like you," their friend said with a beleaguered grin.

They couldn't fly out. They realized the Feds and The Bright Circle people would be watching the airways, and every airport in the States would be looking for their aircraft and the "terrorists" who owned it, so they had to go by sea. Tony had a couple friends in occupations that required fast boats, large *cojones,* and not much conversation—it was the way of the islands and nobody blinked about it. For a few thousand dollars, he arranged a midnight run to the mainland. It was decided they'd cut through the Exuma Cays, around the southern tip of Andros Island, where they'd refuel, then make a long, straight shot for the Middle Keys. It was still a dicey affair, slipping through the Coast Guard and the Marine Patrol, but as Will had said, at this point there were no "non-dicey" solutions. They were taking a huge chance returning to The Keys, but for the next part of their plan they were going to have to meet with Crazy Eddie, hoping that he would be recovered enough and sufficiently receptive to what they needed.

Will and Cass relaxed in chairs on the resort veranda, watching Kansas and Mariana sitting on the beach below. The sun was setting, carving brilliant golden trellises through the darkening stratus clouds on the horizon. Small bands of white egrets skimmed effortlessly across the orange sky, heading inland, searching out a roost for the night, and the still, humid air held that rich, salty evening flavor. They would leave sometime after midnight, and they were enjoying the last few hours of peace they would have.

Cass gazed down at the couple below, watching as Kansas reached over and gently caressed Mariana's face, letting his hand move slowly across her cheek and trail down her arm. The tenderness and meaning in that simple gesture spoke volumes. Cass smiled knowingly, without envy, for she too had found what she was looking for. "Aaahh love," she whispered. "It's a brilliant, colorful, carnival ride that leaves you with the lights of the midway and the smell of cotton candy for the rest of your life. Never let the anticipation of disappointment overshadow the expectation of sheer thrill. Take a chance. Step into that precariously swaying bench and tell the carnie at the lever to throw it into high gear, because love may not be what makes the Ferris wheel spin, but it's what makes the ride memorable."

"Who said that?"

"I don't remember," she replied, turning to gaze at the handsome, blond-haired man next to her, who had somehow found his way into a place she, too, had kept secret and protected.

"Is it a suggestion?" he asked.

"Take it for what it's worth," she said with a beguiling smile.

CHAPTER 10

Pure truth, like pure gold, has been found unfit for circulation, because men have discovered it is far more convenient to adulterate the truth, than to refine it themselves.
— **Charles Caleb Colton**

The husky Bahamian with shoulder-length dreadlocks at the helm of the subtly modified forty-two-foot lobster boat told them they could call him whatever they wanted—names weren't important. He and his partner, a smaller man with a halo of frizzy hair and almost gray eyes, were dressed in Dockers shorts, hundred-dollar tennis shoes (no socks), and Bahamas Goombay T-shirts. They weren't necessarily unfriendly, but they were definitely all business. After a series of quick but heartfelt farewells to Tony and Zediah, everyone clambered aboard and into the forecastle. There was a cabin down below, simple but sufficient. Most of the rest of the hull was "storage area," large fuel tanks, and a couple of engines that belonged in Cigarette boats.

As the craft got underway, they watched the docks recede into darkness, then looked across at each other in the dim light of a single yellow bulb attached to the ceiling, still trying to get used to one another's new images. Their pictures were in most of the newspapers in the country, so during the day they had made some final, necessary alterations at the small beauty shop in the resort.

Much to his and Cass's dismay, Will now had short dark hair that barely covered the tops of his ears, and had lost his much-revered Tom Selleck mustache. Kansas now had dark brown hair—no longer sun-streaked—and had started a beard. Mariana's long hair had been shortened and curled, and was now a lovely, dark red; and Cass's golden locks had been cut above her shoulders and dyed sable. Even Congressman Meyers had consented to changing his stately gray hair to light brown.

Tony watched from the docks, his countenance somewhere near plaintive, his eyes carrying a strange, melancholy sadness. Finally, he turned and walked away. He had business to attend to.

One other soul had decided to return to The Keys, as well, knowing that he shouldn't. Wilson didn't know what else to do. Ralph was taking a hiatus and he was in control again, but damn—Ralph was much better at bad situations than he was. The whole dual personality thing just absolutely sucked. Sharing a body with an egomaniacal sociopath was hell on the nerves. But Wilson had to admit, at least life wasn't dull. And, like Ralph, he just loved this little device, which put everyone at his mercy. He just wished he knew who the hell the spooky big guy was. Most of all, he wished he knew *where* the fellow was. His intuition told him that this weird SOB wasn't done with him, so there was no going back to his house. The apartment he'd rented off Truman Avenue would work for now. He'd try to shake down a tourist or two to keep him in money, but not be real obvious—lie low for a while. He'd be all right if Ralph didn't show up.

Wilson took a beer from the small refrigerator and settled into the worn couch, flicking on the television—catching up on the news and making sure he wasn't in it. The reporter was telling about the big story this week. On his birthday, the following Saturday, the president was visiting his grandparents' hometown in Texas, to give a speech in the park where he often played as a child while visiting them. It would be a very personal appearance, with the president entertaining questions from the townsfolk briefly after the speech—people he had known for years.

Entertaining questions…entertaining questions…

Very subtly, Wilson felt Ralph, as if he'd awakened from a nap. They were showing pictures of the bandstand being built and the reporter was saying that perhaps some of the questions that were perplexing many Americans might be given attention in this more informal atmosphere. Ralph was nudging now, curious, interested. "Ohhh shit, Ralph," Wilson whined. "Not now. Not again. I need a break."

A few minutes later, Ralph's shiny eyes were taking in all that the newscaster had to say. He cocked his head jauntily and smiled, not all that pleasantly. Could you imagine? The President of the United States! Now that would be a prize for his little truth machine.

While the group motored noisily across a gently rolling, moonlit sea, they laid plans for the next part of this odyssey into which they had been so unwillingly cast. They only had the next week to figure out how to stop a presidential assassination while avoiding being killed or arrested in the process. For the time being, they couldn't worry about the other truthmaker and its somewhat flamboyant caretaker. The best they could hope for was that this Wilson McKenzie fellow might get stupid and actually draw some of the heat off of them. Both Kansas and Mariana were still recovering from a number of shrapnel wounds received in the gunfight with Torreos's people, and they needed a few days off.

"The good news is, if we can get to Texas, I have a couple friends there, not the least being my newscaster buddy," Kansas was saying as they sat in the small galley of the boat drinking coffee.

"Yeah, and the bad news is they all think you killed the Assistant Director of National Security," Will replied.

Kansas grimaced. "Yeah, that's probably true. We'll have to work that out when we get there." He paused for a moment, turning his head from side to side in that reflective, stretching movement of his. "But you know, the more I think about it, I feel we need to take a shot at contacting my buddy with Channel 11 News in Dallas. There's a chance I could get him to listen to me without dialing 911."

"Could you risk that? You take a big chance," Mariana said.

"I don't know, man," said Will with a sigh. "If we get caught before they make their attempt at the president, it's all over." Then he grinned in that typical Will fashion. "I'll tell you what's really screwed up. Here I am risking my life to save a guy I didn't even vote for."

Cass chuckled lightly, then became serious. "I did, but it doesn't matter. What you're risking your life for is the process of democracy. It's slipping away as it is. A presidential assassination would put us another notch closer to that third world mentality. We can't afford it."

"We'll just have to wait till we get to the mainland," Kansas added decidedly. "We've played everything else off the cuff so far. No point in getting ahead of ourselves."

"How do you plan on getting around?" Congressman Meyers asked.

"That's where Crazy Eddie comes in," Kansas replied.

Ramone Torreos received the news from John Macken while aboard his yacht in the Mediterranean. Their contact reported all twelve men lost and a ten million-dollar helicopter destroyed—after the bloody debacle at the Holiday Inn in Dulles! The usually very reserved Torreos was almost apoplectic. He threw a three-hundred-dollar bottle of champagne against the wall of his cabin and shouted for the captain to prepare his on-deck helicopter. Storming out of his suite and up to the bridge, fists clenched, he stared sightlessly at the crystalline blue sea, his face flushed, the puckered scar on his cheek livid. *Who in the hell are these people?*

After his evening of penance, Vitor had resorted to prayer and fasting for a day, then to investigation and intuition again. He took the security photos of the man and woman who had questioned the officials in the Pirate Land Theme Park debacle and compared them to the people who were on the front page of the paper—the killers of the Assistant National Security Director. They were the same. Then Vitor faxed the Vatican and had them check their facial recognition, military service, and collegiate alumni informational systems, confirming they lived in the Florida Keys—the same place he had found the little pervert who had somehow eluded him in Washington, D.C. He would pick up the hunt again there. The tall Italian smiled, feral and hard. He would have what he came for from all of these unbelievers. This world did not need instruments to divine the truth. It was in our hearts already and it was for God to find, not some machine. Besides, there were truths few mortals needed to know.

The weather had been exceptional, with calm seas and favoring winds, but the journey by boat from Cat Island to the Florida Keys had still taken nearly thirty hours. The president's birthday speech in El Campo was less than six days away. At the reef line off The Keys, Kansas and his people offloaded from the lobster boat into a small skiff that ran them ashore at the boat ramp on the northern end of Big Pine Key. The Bahamian at the helm took the balance of the money owed him, wished them luck, and was gone before their thank you succumbed to the breeze.

None of them could risk going anywhere near their homes, and there was no getting a motel without using identification. All they had was a small suitcase of personal items and a duffel bag containing a couple of the smaller Heckler and Koch assault weapons, plus extra magazines they had taken from the competition on Cat, and a couple of semi-auto pistols. Everyone carried a pistol now. Life was becoming increasingly more complicated. By pure luck, they flagged down a taxi van to get them to Crazy Eddie's.

Kansas opened the sliding side door and as they all scrambled into the back seats the driver, who hadn't turned around, spoke. He was a big black guy with dreadlocks down to his shoulders. "Hello, hello mons," he rumbled in a heavy, sonorous voice.

Will and Kansas stopped as if they'd been frozen, staring at each other. Glancing at the rearview mirror they could see the driver looking at them—mahogany skin, big chocolate eyes, a smile displaying big, square, white teeth.

"Rufus," Will whispered incredulously. "Son of a bitch. Rufus!"

Sure enough, it was their old soothsayer buddy—the crazy, mystical Rastaman whose prophecies had gotten them involved in a number of remarkable adventures.

Rufus was an incredible character who not only seemed to march to a different drum, but apparently knew the guy who made the drums. He claimed to be the progeny of an ancient race, and was gifted with the eerie disposition of oftentimes knowing what was going to happen well before it happened.

"Rufus…how?" Kansas stuttered.

Their old friend's smile grew wider. "The Gods, dey be bored easily, and sometimes dey make coincidences. Dey have a fine sense of humor and irony—these be some of dere favorite things." But then he became serious. "You little pinballs got yourselves in deep muckety-muck, mons. Even Rufus can't fix dis for you."

Kansas pushed out a hard sigh. "No shit, Rufus. That much we know." *The question was, how did Rufus know about it? But then the guy always seemed to have an inside line…*

"Where you need to go, mons?"

Will moved forward a little. "We have a friend—"

"De crazy one-eyed pilot," their driver said, finishing his sentence for him.

Will just shook his head in disbelief. "Yeah, that's the guy."

Rufus put the van in gear and pulled out onto U.S. 1, never asking for directions. "Okay, mon. No problem."

But as they drove, Rufus had a few words of advice. "Da coconut telegraph say you got more enemies dan a blue crab at a octopus convention. I tell you dis now. Do not linger here. You get dat crazy pilot to put you in his fat bird and get gone—you hear me?"

Fifteen minutes later they had said goodbye to Rufus, and found Eddie sitting in a lawn chair under the wing of his Goose, sipping on a rum punch and working his way through a fat spiff while watching the early morning sun brush the channel with a mellow yellow. He still bore a number of ochre-colored bruises here and there, and a couple of cuts that were scabbed over. His long hair was tousled, and his T-shirt and Hang Ten shorts clutched at his sparse frame, but that charming, roguish smile was still the same.

"Some things never change," Will muttered with a smile as they ambled over.

Eddie turned around when he heard them coming and his eye lit up. "Holy shit! It's the runamucking terrorists with new hairdos!" he blurted cheerily. "Greetings, bros, or should I say 'Allah Akbar'?"

"I hope you're not believing all our bad PR," Kansas said with a cautious smile.

"I don't know exactly what's going on with you dudes, but I ain't buying any of this bogus bullshit about you turning into public enemies and popping some director of security. You dig?"

Kansas relaxed. "Yeah, buddy. We dig."

"So, sit your asses down and tell me the un-jived version of what you been up to," Eddie said as he kicked around a couple of chairs and poured everyone a portion of his notorious rum punch from the ever-ready blender.

After they introduced the congressman to Eddie, they gave him a *Reader's Digest* version of what had happened since their last meeting. Their battered friend whistled softly. "You been some busy sons-a-bitches." Then he looked over at Kansas. "You kicked that bastard's ass, huh? The one that worked me over?"

Kansas nodded. "Yeah. I did."

"You have no idea," Will added. "The boy will be eating through a straw for the next six months—that's if they ever found him and his buddy, all handcuffed and duct-taped in the closet at the Holiday Inn. And Kansas told him exactly what the ass-kicking was about."

Eddie got an odd look in his single eye, somewhere between profound appreciation and deep respect. No one had ever done something like that for him, and the statement in that single act moved him deeply. Everyone liked Crazy Eddie, and some people appreciated his aeronautical talents, but he knew, somewhere in the reaches of his heart, that few people held him in high esteem anymore. It was just the way it was. He was Crazy Eddie, the older guy with good dope and an aging airplane that he flew madly. But here was a man who said, not just with inconsequential words, but with actions, that he was important to him, that he was his friend, and he was touched.

Near the end of the conversation, the congressman asked if there was a restroom handy, saying his old kidneys had dealt with all the bouncing they could handle after the boat ride. Mariana and Cass raised their hands in unison, agreeing it was something high on their list, as well. Eddie chuckled and pointed to the rear of the house—the section he rented from his friend, who was conveniently out of town. Eddie also warned the rest of them to use that bathroom, because the small toilet "closet" he had built into his Goose was not functional at the moment. He explained that a "freaking thoughtless rat" had crawled into the drain pipe the day before and died, clogging it up, and he hadn't had time to take the plumbing apart.

As Congressman Meyers headed for the house, Kansas got right to the point. "Eddie, we're in a bit of a spot." He looked over at Will, and the others, as well. "We've got to get out of The Keys. It's too small and there are too many people who know us. The chance of being recognized at some point is high. But we don't want to end up in El Campo too early—too high a chance of running into problems there with presidential security. We need another hole in the wall for a couple of days so we can plan things out."

It was then that he told them of a small town called Mena in the Ouachita Mountains of Arkansas. His father had been born there, and he spent many a summer in the area, particularly at a fly-in campground and RV park called River Bend Aero Ranch, which was owned by a cousin of his. It was well out of town in a beautiful, ranch-style setting, well away from prying eyes, and he knew he could trust the owners, Greg and Tabitha.

Finally, he looked at his friends. "What do you think, guys?"

There was a moment of silence, then nods of agreement.

"Sounds like a plan," Cass said, speaking for everyone.

Then Kansas brought his attention back to Eddie. "My friend, we need to get to Arkansas on the sly, and probably from there to El Campo in Texas. If we don't pull this off, they're going to kill the president. We need some help, *amigo*."

Eddie looked at them all for a minute, that single eye totally inscrutable. He finished off his rum punch, tossed the plastic cup on the ground, and stood up. "So, when do we split?"

Will called his bank in the Cayman Islands and had them wire twenty-five thousand dollars into Crazy Eddie's bank account so they would have running money. He couldn't use his own local bank, as they were certain their accounts were being monitored. By the time Meyers had eased the pressure on his old kidneys and returned, they were loading the plane and reinstalling some of the original cabin chairs in the old bird to make the ride more comfortable. Meyers seemed somewhat surprised at the new plan, but shrugged it off and began to help.

An hour later, Eddie ran the Goose out of the slick, blue-green waters of Niles Channel, Bruce Springsteen's "Born to Run" hammering the walls of the cabin as she cut her bonds with the earth and winged into the mottled gray horizon. He set a course for New Orleans, and four hours later they landed and refueled, and grabbed a bite to eat. By 3:00 p.m. they were back in the Goose and headed out once more.

They took a northwest heading for the next two hours and by 5:00 p.m. they were sailing over the gorgeous, verdant hills at the edge of the Ouachita Mountain Range, and were dropping onto the long grass runway at River Bend Aero Ranch. Kansas knew in his heart this was as safe a place as he could find. He would have felt less comfortable, however, had he known that not fifteen minutes after they left The Keys, three black Cadillacs had screeched onto Eddie's property, disgorging a dozen big, very disappointed men.

As the Goose rolled to a stop in the tie-down area, Greg, Tabitha, and their two young children came driving out in their golf cart. Tabitha's sparkly blue eyes brightened when she saw Kansas standing with his friends by the plane. She shook back her sandy, shoulder-length blond hair and waved. They had always been close, and the summers he had spent there as a child had given them a bond as strong as most brothers and sisters. Kansas liked her husband, as well. Greg was a pilot, like Tabitha, having spent most of his life around airplanes, and much like Tony Armbrister of Cat Island, he was a little on the daring side—having his share of great barroom stories. He was tall, with dark hair that he wore on the long side, just over his ears, and had smart, brown eyes. Both were dressed in blue jeans and T-shirts. He and Tabitha were grounded, capable people who loved the wilderness they lived in—modern people with survivalist instincts. Both were exceptional bow hunters and were qualified with other weapons, as well, but they were just as comfortable at a business luncheon in Little Rock.

They came up and gave Kansas unqualified hugs, but when Tabitha stepped back, the look in her eyes begged the question, "Kansas, what the hell is going on with you? What I'm reading in the papers just can't be true."

"It's not, Tab," he said quietly, sincerely. "You know me better than that. It's a long story. Take us to the house and I'll tell you the whole thing."

A couple of hours later they all sat around in oversized sofas in a living room that was contrasted by modern art and mounts of deer, elk, and smaller game. Kansas had lived up to his promise, giving them a tale that started in Cuba and rambled from Florida to Washington, D.C. and back, then out to Arkansas, complete with a demonstration from Will regarding the truthmaker. But they excluded the information about the president and El Campo. That was need-to-know only.

When they finished, Tab and Greg were just short of astounded and certainly in awe of the device from another time. Greg shook his head and smiled with just a touch of genuine anxiety. "Man, keep that damned thing off in this house. I'm in enough trouble with this woman as it is!"

Everyone laughed and Tab playfully spiked him with a look. "I'm going to borrow that little machine and wait until you go to sleep, then ask you questions all night long."

"Oh, dear God," Greg moaned.

After the laughter settled, Tab got serious and said, "Kansas, you're my cousin. Hell, you're closer to me than most of my brothers. I believe you. So, what can we do for you?"

"The truth is, we need to hide out for a day or two," Kansas replied. "Make some plans on how to get ourselves out of the mess we're in. Hopefully we'll get all this resolved and it'll just become a great story you can tell the kids someday."

She nodded. "You got it. We'll put you two couples in the extra bedrooms and the congressman and Eddie in the guest cabins. Your timing is good. It's the middle of the week and business has been miserably slow, so there's only a family who flew in yesterday camping at the far end of the airstrip."

They had a late dinner, then everyone retired for the evening. Eddie did a final check on the plane and Congressman Meyers begged off after dinner to take a walk and "commune with nature" for a while. It had been a long several days, and for the first time in a while they felt almost safe. Through all of the trauma, the resiliency of love flourished, and Will and Cass were like teenagers. They could hardly wait to get upstairs and "be alone" once again.

That evening, Kansas and Mariana stood on the small balcony of their second floor room, watching a fat, chartreuse moon work its way across the heavens, its luminescence bathing the hills and the forest around them in satiny greens and yellows. Contented frogs croaked out nocturnal messages from the nearby pond, the evening birds chattered and cried, and the cicadas offered their all-encompassing hum to the orchestra that was the night.

As they stood there, watching and listening, holding each other, Kansas asked quietly, "If we should be so fortunate as to survive this, what will you do?"

The question hung in the air, the greater meaning clear to each of them. She sighed. "I do not know. There have been changes in my life since I arrived here...since I met you. And wrapped around all this...new experience...is so much uncertainty. I can only apply hope and faith, and ask God to guide me."

"Hope," he muttered, somewhat disappointed in her reply. "It's a subspecies of happiness and when it's hungry it feeds on anything. You can lose perspective. Which is why it's best applied in reasonable doses and tempered with reality."

She shrugged noncommittally, still staring at the moonlit landscape. "That may be true, but to me, when the world says 'surrender,' hope says 'one more time.'" She turned to him. "If you don't hope, you can't win at the game, whatever it is. Hope is the sister of faith. In the middle of misery or uncertainty, faith provides the spiritual inertia to continue on, and hope provides the emotional and intellectual sustenance to believe victory, or even just survival, is attainable."

He gently pulled her closer, conscious again of the depth in this remarkable woman. A night bird cried and the wisp of a cloud cleared the moon, allowing its brilliance to bathe them. "You keep the faith polished for us and I'll keep the weapons cleaned," he whispered. "And maybe between us we can hope for a future." Then he turned her and she drew into him like a magnet to steel, and their kiss was like fire, all-consuming, burning out all the images of doubt and fear, seething and sizzling into nothing but the taste and the feel of the moment. Conjecture limped away into the night and passion fiercely claimed its place.

The next morning everyone gathered at the breakfast table, refreshed and once again ready to face a world that wasn't ready to accept what they were offering. *Who would have ever dreamed that truth would be such a hard sell?* Tabitha and Greg decided to take the kids to her sister's place, just to be on the safe side. When the two returned, like any good team in the midst of challenge, they all took stock of their weapons, discussed the next steps, and studied the terrain around them. Even though they would only be there a day or so, and even though anyone finding them there would be nearly impossible, Kansas decided he wasn't going to be caught flat-footed again. They made sure everyone had a weapon at all times. Cass, Mariana, Congressman Meyers, and Eddie had handguns with extra magazines. Kansas and Will took the Heckler and Koch assault weapons and a pistol each. Tabitha and Greg armed themselves with their favorite handguns and put their compound bows with extra arrows within easy reach. Eddie had rummaged through the Goose and found three Vietnam vintage handheld military radios. Kansas and Will took one each and the third was given to Greg and Tab—to be kept with them at all times.

They sat at the kitchen table, going over the property—access points, tourist trails, and lesser-known paths. The housing area and the airstrip were set between Highway 88 and the Ouachita River. There was a long, paved road from the highway that led into the airstrip and living areas. Along that road was a large hangar and a few storage facilities. Kansas asked to have a look at them. About an hour later while he, Will, and Greg were going over the accesses, they stopped at one of the storage buildings. Kansas noticed a couple of heavy-looking, small boxes in the recesses of a crowded shelf near the back of the building. He had worked for a construction/mining company for six months before going to college and he recognized the boxes.

"Dynamite?" he asked, gesturing at the weathered, old containers.

Greg shrugged. "Yeah, been there forever. We used some to clear out trees and boulders when we were extending the runway years ago. Don't even know if it's still any good."

Kansas stared at the shelves for a moment. "I'm going to ask a favor of you," he said to Greg. "I need you to get together with Eddie. I'd like a few sticks of that."

A good part of the afternoon was spent with just the original group, deciding on an approach to El Campo. They had five days before the president was to give his speech. It was decided that when they left Arkansas, they would fly into the airport in Wharton, Texas, which was about fifteen miles from El Campo, to avoid drawing attention to themselves. They would have Eddie rent a car for them there, and they would slide into the president's hometown like tourists, Eddie having rented three motel rooms in

Wharton in advance.

During the day, they studied the faxes Cass was able to get by calling the City of El Campo—which included the layouts of the park where the president would speak, the location of the city water facility, possible access routes, escape routes, and other pertinent information. They also discussed the old sewer system and the line that ran to the large junction box, apparently right under the president's bandstand.

"From looking at the diagrams here, I'm guessing they're going to put a shooter with a silenced weapon in that junction box," Cass explained. "Think about how perfect it is—they go in ahead of time and cut a small manhole in the concrete top of the junction box, exactly below the president's podium. The soil is probably not more than six inches deep there. The shooter pops up through the ground like a bad Halloween prank, spits a half-dozen silenced bullets at the prez while he's speaking, gets back in the hole while everyone's trying to figure out why the Commander in Chief fell dead, and crawls back to the old water plant, or maybe another junction box or manhole cover that he's arranged for a getaway."

Kansas shook his head incredulously. "Damn, girl, you've been reading too many James Bond novels. But I think you've nailed it on the head. Someone's going to have to go into that sewer line after the assassin and stop him before he shoots. You see, the thing is not to just stop him, but stop him in a fashion that the rest of the world doesn't know what he tried to do. If the whole thing gets big publicity, then the Second Amendment is still jeopardized, and they win post-mortem." He paused for a second. "The other issue is, I'm betting their plan is to kill the assassin. They want a dead president and a dead shooter to wrap this package up nicely, so somewhere they're going to be waiting for him—if we're right about all this. The real trick here is to get the shooter before he gets into the ductwork, and I'm betting he's going in the night before. So, we have to figure out where he's going in and be there, watching."

"We're right," Cass said emphatically. "I know we are."

"So," said Kansas. "We're dealing with two fronts—getting the shooter before he gets the president, and getting our person out before they find him and find out what we've done."

For the next half hour they ran scenarios, but nothing could be set in stone until they got to El Campo and had a look for themselves. There was much debate on one other issue, and Kansas finally convinced everyone that before they decided to run the gauntlet, they needed to make an attempt at bringing in his friend, Scott Mosby, from Channel 11 News in Dallas.

"If we can convince Scott that the device is real, then perhaps we can convince him that the threat to the president is real. Maybe he could blow this thing open for us and we wouldn't have to do it ourselves," he explained.

Each of them wanted desperately to believe that they might not have to risk their lives—that they could walk away from the challenge of saving a president and fighting an organization with resources and manpower that dwarfed them. With reluctance that hid their true relief, they all agreed it was worth a try. In the afternoon, Kansas placed a call to Scott Mosby and made arrangements to meet with him in Dallas the following day about 1:00 p.m. The mood at dinner was perceptibly lighter. There was a flicker of hope in the air. Maybe—just maybe—they were going to get out of this alive. That night, they all got mildly lit and toasted each other's health, the lovers loved, and Tabitha and Greg sighed in relief with the prospect that maybe their lives would return to normal soon and they could bring the kids home—if the television news guy would just come through.

Will and Cass had made love that night with less passion and more feeling, slowly enjoying each other in swirling eddies of emotion, basking in the raw delight of a dawning love. When they had ridden those new sensations to the ground, they weren't quite as exhausted as they had been in the past, and Will—who, despite himself, was becoming somewhat of a romantic—recommended a moonlit walk along the river. They dressed, and Will offhandedly tucked his pistol in his belt, then reluctantly grabbed the handheld radio. They snuck out quietly and headed down the trail behind the house that led to the river.

That huge, silvery moon hung above them, casting soft shadows along the trail and reflecting off the placid water of the swimming hole as they reached the river. Crickets chirped in chorus, and as a whippoorwill whistled out its questioning call in the stillness, another answered. It was like magic. They sat on the sand by the water and talked a little. Then they kissed, and gently touched each other. Slowly at first, then with more fervency, their clothes slipped away and they slid into the water. In the cool caress of the river they found each other with eager hands, and finally joined together in a slow, deliberate rhythm, moaning softly, the passion coming in waves. But as they neared a crescendo, Will heard it…voices—curt, muffled, and terse.

Cass was suddenly aware, also. "Who is—"

Will put his hand across her mouth, his eyes shouting silence, and they slid quietly into the bushes that overhung the river at the bank. They watched as two groups of dark-clad soldiers converged at the trail that led back to the house and the cabins—men with black gear, fierce weapons, and faces smeared with dark camouflage paint. It appeared one team had trekked in from the east, the other from the west, stealthily entering the properties on each side of the aero ranch, working their way to the Ouachita River, then stealing along the banks toward Tab and Greg's property. After a moment of hushed conversation, they moved forward as one. As soon as they were out of earshot, the lovers quickly slipped from the water.

Will snatched up the radio while they slipped on their clothes, and whispered tensely, "We've got to warn the others!"

In moments he reached Kansas and gave him the news.

"Have you got a weapon?" Kansas asked.

"Yeah, my Glock."

"Okay. Follow them at a discreet distance. We'll set up a surprise for them at the throat of the trail, just as it opens up into the campground. When they get near that spot, if they don't come out together, you open up from behind and force them into us."

"Gotcha," Will replied. Then, with just a touch of a smile in his voice, he said, "Don't be doing any of that Teddy Roosevelt/Wyatt Earp/kamikaze shit, okay? Just stay behind something and shoot them this time."

Kansas couldn't help but laugh. "Yeah, that's a good plan. I'll do that."

Will turned to Cass. "You can't help me here. You have no weapon. I want you to stay with the river another hundred yards, to the trail that comes in from the airstrip campground. Beat a path to the house and grab a weapon. They'll need your help in the ambush."

There was fear in Cass's normally cool eyes. "I can't leave you here!"

"Yes, you can!" he hissed forcefully. "You have to. I can't do what I have to do and worry about you, too. Do you understand? You can help us survive by doing this!"

She sighed, consternation giving way to logic. Her eyes dropped. "Okay," she whispered. But then her eyes filled with that quintessential fierceness and strength, and she grabbed him by his shirt. "But don't you do anything stupid. You understand me? Follow your own advice—no freaking Teddy Roosevelt shit. You hear me?"

He chuckled and her eyes softened.

"Because I can't afford to lose you. It would screw up a lot of my plans." She went into his arms and they embraced with an intensity borne of need and fear, and love. Then she was on her feet and gone into the somber darkness.

Rousing Tab and Greg in one of the adjacent bedrooms, Kansas quickly explained what was happening. "Listen, this isn't your fight," he said adamantly. "Just arm yourself and keep your distance. Stay at the house—or better yet, head out to the road and wait until it's over."

The couple looked at each other. They weren't warriors. They had children with which to be concerned.

Tabitha finally shook her head. "No, we won't run. We'll hold the house for you—someplace you can fall back to if you need it. We won't let you down, cousin."

Through all the trepidation and anger, Kansas's face softened into a smile. "Thank you," he said quietly, the passion of respect and pride showing in his eyes.

Tabitha moved to the closet and pulled out two compound bows, then looked up at him. "In the dark, this is the weapon of choice; no noise and as accurate as a rifle at seventy-five yards."

Kansas nodded, a smile lifting the corner of his mouth as he remembered his youth in this very area, and compound bows. "I miss that weapon," he said. "Still one of my favorites after all these years." He paused, hating to leave them in this predicament. "Get someone over to the cabins and let Eddie and Meyers know what's going on. Take care, cousin, and you too, Greg," he whispered. Then he was gone.

He knew Eddie and the older man would be a few minutes getting to him because the cabins were built along the airstrip, several hundred yards from the house. The trail from the river, which his enemy was using, wound through the woods and came out between the big house and the cabins, but not necessarily close to either. A storage shed, a workshop, and a copse of large oaks stood near the entrance to that trail.

Kansas had grabbed Will's Heckler and Koch assault weapon and a couple of magazines, and had given it to Mariana. They rendezvoused in the darkness with Myers and Eddie, who had their pistols, and took positions on opposite wings of the ambush, behind the oak trees and a shed. Kansas and Mariana positioned themselves more toward the center, behind the workshop and the trees. The old yellow moon was waning, slipping into the horizon, drawing longer shadows on the thick, charcoal and ebony foliage. The night birds had stilled, aware of the intrusion. Even the crickets held their chatter. Only the drone of the cicadas remained, and even it moved with uncertain rhythm, as if they, too, knew of the impending conflict. They were barely in position when Cass showed up, out of breath from her run up the other path. Kansas gave her his handgun and an extra magazine, and she took a position with Eddie on the far side.

The cool, early morning air carried a wisp of honeysuckle, and a light touch of breeze caressed Kansas, cooling the perspiration on his face as he crouched silently against the trunk of a tree, staring at the killing field in front of him, hands sweating and trembling. Motion pictures and television made it look so easy, even exciting. But he realized it was never comfortable facing another human being, knowing you had to kill or be killed. It was a gut-wrenching, terrifying experience.

After what seemed like an interminable wait, dark shadows began emerging from the mouth of the trail. For professionals, they had made a critical mistake, coming out together on the trail rather than branching out ahead of time, and it cost them dearly. Kansas waited until it appeared they were all out and moving cautiously forward, the last of the moonlight holding them like gray wraiths against the dark ground. He took a deep breath then aimed and fired. Suddenly, the air was filled with the thunder of weapons. Muzzle flashes seared the night, and the shouts and screams of combatants and wounded added to the cacophony. Several of the twelve antagonists went down immediately, the others broke right and left. Two stumbled back into the darkness of the trail to be killed by Will. A third got past him in the melee and he chased the man along the trail for fifty yards before shooting him in the back as he fled. There was no mercy in this game—only winners and losers. Mariana, with the H & K, took out two that broke to her side, practically cutting them in half with the fierce weapon on full auto. Cass and Eddie ambushed two more that practically ran right into them, but Cass took a round on the ball of her shoulder in the exchange. It was more of a graze, but it was bleeding badly. It seemed like hell on earth for a few minutes, then, suddenly, it was over. Stillness fell across the killing field. There wasn't a sound from the night creatures. The only thing that could be heard was the harsh breathing of those who were still alive.

But during the confusion of the firefight and the darkness, a couple of the assault troops had escaped, breaking off into the woods and circling back toward the trail that led to the river.

Will was just beginning to think they had, by some miracle, pulled it off, when the men stumbled from the heavy summer brush onto the trail about thirty feet behind him. It took them, and Will, a moment in the darkness to realize who was who, then it was just a matter of reflexes. In the melee of rapid fire and muzzle flashes, Will killed the first one with two rounds to the chest as a line of bullets stitched the ground next to him. He got off two shots at the other before the slide on his Glock snapped back and locked in the empty position.

The last round he fired had struck the trigger guard of his opponent's H & K assault rifle just as he was raising it, smashing the guard and the trigger and cleanly taking off the man's index finger at the second knuckle. The fellow grunted from the pain and in reflex tried to find the trigger with another finger, but the gun was, at that point, as useless as a stick. He was a heavily built man, probably six-foot-one or two. In the moonlight he could see Will's pistol was locked open. He dropped his damaged weapon and pulled a K-Bar combat knife from his belt, moving forward with deliberate confidence. As he neared, Will saw blood squirting from the dismembered finger on his right hand, pulsing out onto the dark ground. The guy acted as if he hadn't even noticed it.

Ooohhh shit, Will thought. *Mean son of a bitch.* He considered running back toward the house, but charging at the compound in the dark, he was just as likely to be shot by his friends. *Damn! I should have...* But then it was too late and the big man was on him. The fellow swung a vicious, backhanded cut at his opponent's throat, hoping to end it immediately. In pure instinct, Will brought up the pistol in his hand. The blade of the knife struck the barrel and the trigger guard hard enough to slam the weapon into Will's face, striking his nose, smashing his lips, and loosening his front teeth. Reflexively, he pulled away and backhanded the man in the temple with the butt of the gun, stunning him for a second. But in truth, he wasn't a soldier, he was just a man fighting for his life. In the flurry of adrenaline, Will made a huge mistake. Instead of hitting the guy again, he moved in and grabbed the wrist that held the knife. They grappled, each holding the other's weapon hand. However, the man was too big and too strong, and Will found himself losing ground, being forced backwards. Worse, as they struggled, he was losing the battle of strength, and the knife blade was moving inexorably closer and closer to his throat, while his hand that held the empty pistol was immobilized in the powerful grasp of his antagonist. Blood was running from his broken lips and mouth, and still squirting from the man's shattered fingers, splashing in sticky, dark spurts over both of them. He could smell it and taste it, and it added to the menace and dread that surrounded him in an almost suffocating embrace. They had become like two nearly rigid statues, struggling in the moonlight, trying to wrest by strength and willpower the life from one another.

Suddenly, from the corner of his eye, he saw a figure approaching cautiously with a pistol. It was Congressman Meyers. *Thank God!* his mind screamed. *Thank God!* The point of the knife was nearly touching his face. But Meyers suddenly slowed, then stopped, and let the muzzle of the pistol fall.

"Meyers!" Will hissed through clenched, bloody teeth, the blade now at his neck. "Meyers!"

But the congressman did nothing. In fact, he got a sad, almost detached look on his face and let the gun fall to his side. The blade began to bite into Will's neck just above the collarbone, and he couldn't stop it. He could feel the cold steel digging into his flesh, grating along the collarbone, then burying itself deeper, almost an inch into the muscle of his throat. Rivulets of blood ran down his chest, and he was helpless to prevent it. Fear was crawling over him like sugar ants on a candy bar. He wasn't a "fighter." He had no training for something like this. He was running on adrenaline and terror. His muscles trembled in their effort to stop the inevitable. The man was so close Will could hear his coarse rasping and smell the foul odor of his breath. The giant's eyes gleamed madly with the realization of victory and the intense pleasure of the kill.

At the last second, Will did the only thing he could think of. He hocked in a mouthful of blood and phlegm and spit as hard as he could into the man's eyes. Totally surprised and blinded for a moment, his opponent slacked his grip for a millisecond. That was all Will needed. He broke the man's grip on his gun hand and hammered him in the jaw with the weapon. It stunned the fellow just enough for Will to pull back and deliver a groin kick with sufficient force to crush any opportunity for progeny in this lifetime. As the man shuddered and collapsed to one knee, Will kicked him again. It was a wild thrust, but it caught the guy in the throat. As his opponent grunted in agony, involuntarily bringing up his hands to his neck, Will ripped the knife from his bloody fingers and walloped him on the top of the head with the heavy pommel. The guy dropped as if he'd been pole-axed.

Overwhelmed by exhaustion and terror, heaving in gulps of life-giving air, Will dropped to his knees and brought his head up, gasping, suddenly realizing that Meyers was still standing off to the side. His gun was raised again and pointing at Will.

Meyers shook his head. "I saw these two double back and followed them. I thought it might be a good time for me to make an exit." He nodded at the dead man on the ground, speaking in an almost detached, melancholy fashion. "I thought for certain he would kill you, and here you go and survive." He sighed. "Now I have to do it."

"Why?" Will gasped. "Why?" Then suddenly his face lit

with understanding, incomprehensible as it was. "It was you! You're how they found us each time." Then again there was puzzlement in his eyes. "But at the warehouse in D.C. when we met the Assistant Director of Security…when they were going to kill us all, and you didn't say anything…"

The congressman sighed and replied in a condescending fashion, as if addressing a confused child. "They were never going to kill me. I was just getting ready to step over to their side when your people blew up the goddamned car with the anti-tank weapon. You never gave me a chance. Afterwards, I had to play along. How else would we have been able to find you?"

"Why?" Will asked again. "Why?"

Meyers shook his head again in sad reproach. "Worshipping truth is an errand for fools, son. People don't want the truth. It's too damned uncomfortable in the long term. They'll take a sweet lie to an inconvenient truth every time. They want to be coddled and taken care of. They want to be told that it's gonna be all right. Where have you been all your life, son? The mortar of government is lies. Do you think the populace out there could be controlled if they knew the truth—about the food they eat, or the water they drink, or the people that govern them? God! In my lifetime alone I've seen backroom deals cut by politicians and corporations that would have had the populace wanting the heads of every elected official in the nation. The duplicity, the misinformation you've been fed, and the real conspiracies—from Roswell to the Rockefellers, to the exotic energy technologies we've tucked away in hidden vaults, all the way to the people who really control this nation—hell, this country would come apart at the seams in a week." He took a breath and exhaled slowly. "It's simple, son. There's more victory in deceit than there is in truth. There's more money in it. Nobody really gives a shit about honesty. Put simply, unadulterated truth would just screw things up abysmally."

He sighed again, and almost reluctantly brought up his gun, aiming at Will's chest. "I'm sorry, boy. I don't have any choice here. You just got killed in the raid…"

But as the congressman's finger closed on the trigger, two brightly feathered arrows suddenly appeared to sprout from his chest, the bloody, razor-sharp points of the shafts driving out of his back with the "thwack" of a fist striking a gym heavy bag. His eyes went wide with shock and his mouth suddenly hung loose, as if unhinged. His head dropped down, eyes staring at the shafts in amazement, then those puzzled orbs suddenly lost all sense of purpose and he dropped like someone had cut his strings.

Thirty yards away Tabitha and Greg stepped out of the woods carrying their compound bows at their sides. They helped Will to his feet.

"We had to," Tab said apologetically. "He was going to kill you."

"You're damned right you had to!" Will huffed adamantly. "I can't believe it. He was playing us the whole time!"

Just then Cass came bolting down the trail, her face an amalgam of joy and consternation when she saw him alive, but his lips and neck bleeding, and the blood from the fight all over him. She threw herself into his arms, ignoring the gore, ignoring the bandaged wound on her arm, hugging him fiercely. Then she drew back abruptly and grabbed him by the shirt. "What did I tell you about the freaking Wyatt Earp shit?" Looking at his battered lips, her features narrowed to distress and she reached out tentatively, then drew back her hand and cried, "It'll be a week before I can even kiss you again!"

He was finally beginning to get used to this girl. He realized he would never quite be "in control," but somehow it was okay. There were many other benefits. He chuckled. "Yeah, well, you'll just have to make do with my other parts for the time being."

Cass thought about Clydesdales at that moment, and grinned mischievously. "Yeah, okay. I can do that."

An hour later, after everyone had cleaned up and the dead had been counted, they sat at the dining room table in the big house. "We can't stay a moment longer," Kansas was saying. "The Bright Circle people will realize there's been a problem when their team doesn't report in."

"Still can't believe it was Meyers—that the dude was one of them," Eddie muttered. "The jive-talking runamucker!"

While the others nodded solemnly, Kansas said, "I think we're going to have to split up. We've got a meeting with Scott Mosby and Channel 11 tomorrow. Mariana and I are going to borrow Tab's pickup and head to Dallas to meet with him. You guys are going to have to pile into the Goose, get out of here and fly on into Wharton, Texas, and stay at the motel rooms Eddie's already reserved. We'll plan on meeting you there tomorrow night, or the following day, depending on what I learn from Scott." He came around to Eddie. "Just remember that we put a half-dozen sticks of dynamite in your plane, okay? So keep the kamikaze flying to a minimum. I hope we don't need them, but the way things are going I'm beginning to like the idea of having something with a bigger bang." He paused and looked around at his companions. "We're coming down to the wire. Only four more days before the president gives his speech in El Campo, and now we no longer have anyone to back up the story of how we got into this predicament." He gave a long, slightly exasperated sigh. "But I guess we never did."

Kansas turned to his cousin and her husband. "Tab, Greg, I can't thank you enough, and I'm so sorry we drew you into this mess. If I had only known about Meyers.... But there's no point in Monday morning quarterbacking. Here's what you need to do now. You have to call the sheriff and tell them there's been some sort of gang warfare fight on your property—that there are bodies everywhere and you're terrified. Will is putting Meyers's body in the plane with them and they'll drop him out over the Ouachita Mountains on their way into Texas. It'll probably be years before anyone finds a trace of him, if ever." He paused again. "I'm sorry, that's about the best we can do. It should get you out of the picture. Then I'd recommend that you get the kids and you all go on a vacation to Mexico for about a month. Have your brother keep track of the place while you're gone." He set a stack of hundred-dollar bills on the table. "This will cover your expenses and your vacation. I'll get the pickup back to you as soon as I can. And thanks again for being there with your bow for my partner."

Tab got up, went over to the corner of the room and picked up her compound bow with its rack of arrows. She brought it over to Kansas and set it on the table in front of him. "A gift to remember the better times with. I saw your eyes when you got a look at it. I know it reminded you of the old days."

"I couldn't," he said hesitantly, knowing that he could— wanting to hold it and let it take him back to another time when life was so much simpler.

"Yes, you can," she replied adamantly. "Sometime soon this will be over and you can enjoy life again. Take it back to The Keys. Shoot at the fish."

He reached over and touched the limb of the bow, feeling the strength and power in the solid composite material, and the memories flooded back—memories of safe, good times. He couldn't resist. It gave him hope. Maybe even yet he would find his way back, along the road to Key West. Kansas looked up, eyes filled with gratefulness and affection. "Thank you, Tab. Thank you so much."

By 3:00 a.m., after handshakes and hugs all around, the two teams split up. Eddie's kept one of his military radios, and Kansas and Will each got one. They wouldn't work at a distance, but they would be fine for a mile or two radius when they got together again. Kansas and Mariana took the old Ford pickup out onto Highway 88 toward Dallas. Right behind them the Goose lifted off into the still darkness, Crazy Eddie howling like a wolf and Don McLean's "American Pie" pulsing the thin metal walls of the aircraft. The grand old bird passed over the highway, tilting a wing in salute and banking into the waning moon as the ancient orb wallowed in a river of gray and white clouds on the ragged horizon.

Ralph/Wilson McKenzie, tucked away in his apartment in Key West, was just about jittery excited. His bags were packed and he was headed for Texas, hopefully for a little question and answer session with the President of the United States.

Vitor was less than pleased at the moment. He had experienced no grace in the locating of the man and woman who evidently possessed the other truth device. They had not come back to The Keys, and the other fellow, Wilson McKenzie, could not be found in Key West. He had not eaten for nearly a day and had little or nothing of sustenance in the motel room he was renting, so he pulled on a fresh, white cotton shirt, tucked it into his pants, combed back his longish, dark hair with his elongated fingers, and walked out to his car, then drove to a small store near the main road.

It just so happened that, in one of those star-struck coincidences that the gods sometimes arrange simply for entertainment, Ralph/Wilson had just stopped at the same store to pick up some snacks on the way to the airport.

Vitor was pulling up when he saw Ralph/Wilson enter the little market. His stomach clenched and his knees went weak. Tears glistened at the corners of his eyes. God had answered his prayers! All thought of hunger and discomfort was forgotten. He parked off to the side, slid down in his seat, and grabbed yesterday's newspaper from the dash, burying his face in it, but peering aside enough to study his target. When Ralph left, Vitor followed, and soon it was apparent that his prey was flying out of Key West.

Fortunately, Vitor had his passport and his wallet with him at all times. His other few belongings meant nothing. He would find another knife.

CHAPTER 11

We do not err because truth is difficult to see. It is visible at a glance. We err because this is more comfortable.
— **Alexander Solzhenitsyn**

The morning sun rose over the mountains, gilding them as they gradually metamorphosed into green, tree-lined hills, then into the rolling, slowly flattening terrain of Texas. Once Kansas and Mariana reached New Boston and made a hard right onto Interstate 30, it was a straight run into Dallas.

Mariana sat watching the brown and green flatlands pass by her window, her now dark red hair curled down to her shoulders, those sultry hazel eyes distant in thought. A country singer named Johnny Lee was moaning out a tune called "Bet Your Heart On Me," and it brought a small, almost bitter smile to her lips. "I would have never dreamed a month ago that I would find myself on such a life-changing, confusing, yet intriguing adventure—in Texas of all places," she confided quietly. She paused and looked over at her companion, eyes burnished with affection. "With a man like you." She took a breath and expelled it softly. "I have never lived day-to-day like this. My life was structured before, my direction always clear. The State was my life. And I have never quite felt like this…about someone. It is a confusing time for me, as well as challenging." Again she paused. "If you are able to do this—save your leader—you will become a hero of the State, no?"

"I'm not sure we know what heroes are anymore," Kansas replied, slowly shaking his head with a degree of doubt and disenchantment. "In this country, we've juxtaposed the idea of heroism with celebrity. Just because you appear in every other movie on television, or you can throw a ball through a hoop with idiot savant accuracy, doesn't make you a hero. Real heroes most often put up with a lot of unrecognized effort, doing what they do because of who they are, not what they hope to receive or to satisfy some imprecise sense of ego. We have a tendency to confuse the Mother Teresas of this world with the Jane Fondas."

He paused to catch a breath. She had hit a nerve with him. "Today our heroes are chosen for us by our half-blind, politically correct media. Nobleness and character have been obscured by the feverish squeals of rabid fans, and the propaganda of television and the motion picture industry."

She nodded thoughtfully. "The concept of true heroism can be a lifelong commitment, or as simple as a split-second choice or a three-minute gamble with your life, and sometimes this thing we call gallantry or valor, simply, suddenly rises to the surface like cream. But wherever it's found in its purest form, we should respect it. We should never compare a soldier's courage or a nurse's sacrifice with the glamorous professions of sports enthusiasts or movie stars, but you do in America. I have watched and I have seen it."

"Damned right, we do," he said heatedly. "I don't really care if we admire culture, art, and talent in all their complex forms, but we should damned well never confuse them with the Winston Churchills, the Abraham Lincolns, and the Martin Luther Kings." He exhaled again and his face softened self-consciously. "Sorry for the sermon. It's just that I've known real heroes, and I've seen sacrifice, and I know the difference."

Mariana smiled almost sadly, as if the dissertation had passed through unscathed. "Yes, you could become a hero, I think." Then she turned back to the window and the rolling tapestry of Texas and whispered, "And I...I am not sure what I will become..."

They met Scott Mosby at a truck stop on I-30 just into Dallas. He was a tall, good-looking fellow in his mid-thirties with sandy-colored hair, brilliant blue eyes and one of those Colgate newscaster smiles. He was dressed to the nines, as always—crisply pressed beige slacks and a maroon, long-sleeved shirt—one of those people aiming for an eventual seat somewhere on the 6:00 p.m. show. Mosby was headed for the top, but he had a tendency to hang out with a slightly younger crowd. Kansas knew from their previous association that he liked the nightlife probably a little too much, but he did it on his own time; it was almost a hidden lifestyle. He played it very straight at work. In fact, he was the image of "strictly business." After introductions, the three of them walked around to a small patio behind the truck stop where they could have some privacy.

"It's been a while, Kansas," Scott said as they settled into one of the small, concrete patio bench and table sets. "I see you've changed your hair color. Tired of having too much fun as a blond?" After a few moments of chitchat and catch-up, he approached the whole concept with the typical skepticism of a good reporter. "All right, let's get to the meat of this. You claimed on the phone that you have a story for me—something that's going to 'change the world.' Okay. I'm listening."

Fifteen minutes later, when Kansas finished with a *Reader's Digest* version of what had taken place with them, Scott leaned back and shook his head, obviously unconvinced. "Great story. You should write it down and sell it. But Kansas, my friend, I think you're out of your freaking mind. Did you fall on your head lately? You been taking acid?" He looked at Mariana. "This can't possibly be true. C'mon, this is a joke, right?"

"It's no joke," Kansas said as he took out the truthmaker and laid it on the table.

"Aaahhh, the truth device," Scott said with a smile. "Fresh from Radio Shack. I've got pencil sharpeners that look more *Star Wars* than that."

"The proof is in the pudding," Kansas muttered as he turned it on. The result was immediate—the brief hum, subtle vibration, and prickling of the hairs on arms and necks. Scott certainly noticed it. He didn't say anything, but he was paying attention now.

"Scott, I'm going to make this simple," Kansas began, playing a hunch he'd had for a long time. "I'm going to ask you a question, a personal question, and I bet you're going to answer it. Are you ready?"

Scott was looking a little less sure of himself, but he nodded, dredging up some of that charismatic confidence of his. "Sure, why not? I'm game."

"Scott, how much cocaine do you do a week, and where do you hide it?"

His friend's startled eyes widened with surprise and he started to respond in his typical, glib fashion, but the words stuck in his throat, then others just stumbled out. "I...I don't...I wouldn't... I..." Then gradually his eyes changed from struggle to surrender, his shoulders slumped, and he spoke, staring at the cars zipping along the highway next to them. "Not very much, a gram maybe—sometimes on weekends a little more. I have a hidden compartment against the top of the cabinet that holds the kitchen sink. Has a sliding door. Nobody knows...knew...until now." A moment passed. He looked at Kansas and said very quietly, but with great certainty, "Okay, I believe you." After another moment he said, "You can't tell anyone about this. It would—"

"Not to worry," Kansas said. "We have much bigger fish to fry, and I have no desire to hurt your career."

Later, after they had been through the whole thing again, Scott exhaled heavily and frowned at them. "This is impossible shit. You know that? A secret organization, a presidential assassination, and a device that makes you tell the truth?" Then he smiled. "Jesus Christ! I'm gonna be famous! This is my ticket to the big time!"

Kansas and Mariana grinned at his effervescence, but Kansas's grin faded with admonition. "Remember, buddy, this is not a Hollywood movie. There are people trying to kill us. And by virtue of this shared information, you, too, have become a duck in this shooting gallery. We have to get them before they get us."

Scott scratched his nose for a moment, lost to a thought, looking out at the cars on the highway again, then he turned back to them with fresh animation. "What if I could arrange an interview with this guy, Macken? I happen to know he's already in Texas, preparing security for the upcoming presidential appearance in El Campo, so it's convenient for him. What if I could sucker him into an interview by suggesting I had heard that the group of terrorists he was after had some sort of device? He couldn't resist having to check it out. If I could get him alone for a brief interview and if I had that truthmaker there at the time..."

Kansas thought about it for a few moments. It was a huge risk, but what if it worked? What if they got him to admit everything? It would be end game. He looked at Mariana.

She nodded emphatically, then added, "What about a cameraman? You'd have to have someone you trust."

Scott smiled excitedly. "I know just the guy—a gutsy fellow who will do anything to get the big story, just like me."

"You're going to need a list of questions. You'll have to memorize them—nothing on paper," Kansas added.

Mosby brought his hands up, palms out. "Hey, no problem, man. It's what I do."

Kansas risked a grin. "Okay," he said, narrowing his eyes. "Buck up, kid. We're going big game hunting."

That afternoon Scott Mosby called in a favor from a buddy of his who was an anchorman in D.C., and got Macken's office number.

Macken was angry at first. "How in the hell did you get this number, you little piss ant?" Then he became intransigent. "I don't have time for a goddamned interview! I have a president to protect!" But when Scott mentioned the information about the terrorists and some sort of device being involved, the head of presidential security got quiet. "Where'd you get that information?" he replied sharply.

"Listen, sir, if you'll just do a brief interview with me on the upcoming weekend—five minutes—I'll tell you what I heard. I'll come to you and we can do the interview in your suite."

There was a pause. Seconds later, the harsh voice on the other end spat out the words he wanted to hear. "Ten a.m. tomorrow morning, at the Four Seasons in Houston. Just be at the front desk. Somebody will meet you there." Then the line went dead.

After they calmed down, Kansas took a breath and said, "Okay, we've got to get down to Houston. There are a few things we need to go over regarding this little device. You will be susceptible to its power also, but it works on a suggestive level, as well, so the first thing you need to do is to suggest to him that you ask the questions and he answers, not the other way around. Then—most importantly, or we're all dead—you must suggest that he doesn't remember the interview, but that he feels good about it."

That night Kansas called Will, telling him the extraordinary news. Will, Cass, and Eddie had rented a car after landing at the Wharton airport, and by the time the sun was setting on the chaparral and mesquite of the parched and dusty landscape, they had settled into the motel rooms that Eddie had reserved. The motel had been chosen ahead of time so everyone would know the gathering place.

Will hung up the phone, entranced by the emotion of real hope for the first time. *Good Lord! There was indeed a chance that they just might survive this!* He told Cass, and wordlessly she came into his arms, tears of relief in her eyes, crushing him to her. She was a strong woman, but living in day-to-day fear for her life, falling in love in the process, then becoming terrified she might lose what had become so precious to her, was taking its toll. He stroked her hair and held her until he felt it pass. "You know I love you," he said quietly, and the words hung in the air like summer clouds, offering neither shade nor rain, but the possibility of either. He felt her tense, just a little, and the silence was thunderous. He suddenly wished he could pull the words back. He should have waited…

Then she softened against him and whispered adamantly, "You damned well better, because I've slipped over the edge, and you better be there to catch me."

He smiled, his eyes filled with relief and emotion. "I'll always be there for you. I promise. I'll be there to catch you."

Eddie had just poured a couple shots of rum into a Yoplait yogurt and stirred it when Will knocked on his door. He was blissfully slurping from the container when his friend told him the news. He wiped the creamy rum-filled treat from his mustache with the back of his hand and grinned, his eye gleaming with excitement. "Far freaking out! Psychedelic, dude!" He snatched the rum bottle off the television and held it high. "Here's to kicking the runamuckers' asses!" he cried.

He took a solid hit and passed it to Will, who took a swig and added with cool vehemence, "To kicking the runamuckers' asses!"

They took two cars to Houston—Scott and his cameraman, Steven Stewman, in one, and Kansas and Mariana in the old pickup. They were there at sunset, getting inconspicuous rooms at the local Motel 6. The plan was that Scott and Steven would do the interview, then they would all tie up and drive back to Dallas, where they could package the video. Until the interview was done, they would stay apart. Kansas would supply the truthmaker just before the two newsmen left to meet Macken.

That evening, while Kansas went to get some Kentucky Fried Chicken for dinner, Mariana went to the lobby and placed a collect call to Miguel Juan Santiago at the Ministry of the Interior in Cuba, explaining that there had been an unforeseen development—that apparently the artifacts had drawn the interest of another party and one had been stolen. She would need more time to resolve the situation, but she hoped to have them in her possession within a few days.

"Martinez, you are running out of time," Santiago threatened, the anger in his voice leaving no room for debate. "You have two days. Then I send in another team. Don't disappoint me, Martinez. You've been around long enough to know what happens to those who do."

She hung up the phone slowly, listening to the "click" separate her from the only world she had ever known. Mariana drew a deep breath and exhaled in a sigh. She was rapidly finding herself caught between two worlds. One she had known all these years, that offered safety and the security of sodality—the one in which she knew what to expect, and had made a place for herself—a good place. Her Cuban heart missed the smell and the murmur of the sea, the sound of her language bubbling up from the children in the street, and her friends. This other world was filled with uncertainty. There was no balance in it, none of the structure she had lived with all her life. But it was this new world that held such life about it. It was as if she was seeing in 3-D for the first time. It had brilliant color, and waves of emotion that she had never experienced, and there was a freedom in this strange country that left her enthralled. Then, of course, and most of all, there was this man—this tall, exciting, island man who had somehow found a way through her defenses and left her needy and vulnerable for the first time since the loss of her family. Soon she would have to make a choice, and ultimately one world would be lost forever.

The following morning at 10:00, after getting the truthmaker from Kansas, Scott Mosby and his cameraman arrived at the front desk of the Four Seasons Hotel in Houston. Seconds later they were joined by two large men in gray suits and escorted to John Macken's suite. They were frisked professionally and their equipment was examined thoroughly before they were allowed to enter the room. The truthmaker that Scott had in his pocket was examined briefly, but he explained it was a new voice recorder and his explanation was accepted.

Macken was sitting on a couch in his living room, sipping coffee. His cold, slate-colored eyes fastened on them and he ran a hand through his dark hair as he stood for the introductions. Afterwards, Steven immediately went to work setting up his shoulder camera and Macken returned to his seat. Scott sat in a chair adjacent to him, a coffee table between them, explaining that his cameraman would shoot while they talked. All security personnel had left the room to wait outside the door of the suite. The president's highest security man had already decided that whatever was said here was best said alone, just in case this Mosby guy actually knew something about the truth device. While Steven prepared his equipment, Scott began by saying how much he appreciated the opportunity to do the interview. As he talked, he turned on the truthmaker in his coat pocket. There was that brief hum and the room was splashed for a moment with the subtle vibration. Macken's eyes showed that he caught something, and he unconsciously rubbed the hair on his arms, but before he could say anything, Scott immediately spoke, softly but firmly.

"Now, Mr. Macken, I'm going to ask you some questions and you'll reply to them, not the other way around. Do you understand, sir? You'll reply to my questions."

The man's eyes narrowed and he was about to level a retort when the heat just sort of faded from those orbs, and he shrugged, "Okay, for now." He was strong-willed, and a part of him knew his acquiescence wasn't quite right—not the way he did business. He gently rubbed his high forehead in consternation—an old habit. There was something that only a few people knew about John Macken. He had a metal plate in the front of his skull, a memento from a Bouncing Betty landmine in Vietnam that had killed two of his friends and taken him out of combat. The plate fit over the frontal lobes of his brain. Macken stared at Scott and Steven for a moment or two, then settled his forceful but somehow slightly disconcerted gaze on Scott. "Okay, Mr. Mosby."

Scott trod softly as he moved into the interview, at first asking genuine questions about the security man's history and the challenges of protecting a president. Then he took a deep breath and slipped in a question that would decide the future of the conversation. "Do you think this president is taking this country in the right direction?"

The eyes of the president's top security man hardened and he started to reply sharply, but the words stopped before they reached his tongue. He blinked a couple of times and his mouth opened and closed. His eyes flashed with wariness.

Scott watched the struggle. *He's fighting it. He's an extraordinarily strong man.*

But as always, the will gradually succumbed. Macken sighed, confused and resigned, but uncomfortably so. "No," he said slowly. "No, I don't. It's time for more than just the change he had on his agenda, and he's slowing the process."

Scott's heartbeat double-timed. He couldn't believe it. It was working! He threw a brief, excited glance at the cameraman. Quickly now, hands shaking a little, he continued, stepping off the cliff with the next question. "Do you know of an organization called The Bright Circle?"

Macken's expression carried a trace of shock when he heard that name. His nostrils flared just a touch, and his piercing orbs locked with Scott's, staring hard.

He's still fighting it! Mosby realized.

But seconds later it all finally just melted away. The head of presidential security exhaled softly and started talking about The Bright Circle and the people involved in it. The names he mentioned stunned the two men as they listened. With Scott's encouragement and the carefully chosen questions, Macken told about the organization's intentions to gradually change the form of government in the United States and rearrange the economic structure, moving it to sync with a "New World Order," and finally, the *pièce de résistance*, he told about the influence of Ramone Torreos in The Bright Circle, the plan to assassinate the president, and how the assassination would be used to crush Second Amendment rights and eventually begin a change with minimal resistance from the indigenous population. Most importantly, as Kansas had adamantly required of him, he got to the truth behind the death of the Assistant Director of National Security—how the Director, Congressman Meyers, and Macken himself had set up Kansas and his friends so they could take the truthmaker—this device from another civilization—from them, and prevent America and the world from ever being permitted to live with genuine truth in government, law, or daily life.

Scott Mosby was absolutely beside himself with the revelations he was receiving—the exposé he would break to the public. But in his excitement he failed to notice that while John Macken was talking, a fire burned in the depths of his eyes that had not been extinguished by the truthmaker. The powerful official could feel himself enveloped by its control, but he wasn't lost to it, as others had been.

When the "interview" was over, Scott did as he had been ordered, suggesting to John Macken that he would not remember discussing anything other than the presidential security issues and the upcoming visit to El Campo, and he would feel pleased about the interview. Somewhat apprehensively, Mosby turned off the truthmaker in his pocket and waited for the hammer to fall.

Macken just blinked a couple of times and looked at him, face filled with a combination of confusion and agitation, but acceptance. As his eyes cleared, he fixed Scott with that hard stare. "Okay, Mr. Mosby, now it's my turn. What do you know about a device these terrorists have—the ones who killed the Assistant Director of National Security?"

Scott launched into his preplanned speech. Kansas and his people had decided to provide just enough truth, yet keep Macken headed away from them. The worst that could happen was that he might catch the guy with the other truthmaker. "I have a friend who was in the Florida Keys about three weeks ago and he heard this guy talking at a bar. The fellow was a little drunk and he said he had a device from an ancient civilization that forced you to tell the truth. No one believed him, but the damned guy used it on a waitress there and thoroughly impressed everyone. Could have been a scam, I guess, but the fellow said he knew a guy—one of the people the papers have been showing, Bell, Will Bell, and where to find him."

"You don't have the other guy's name? The guy with the device?" Macken questioned sharply.

Mosby shook his head. "No, just the story."

"You sucked an interview out of me for a piece of shit story like that, with no names, huh?" the chief of security barked angrily. "Pack up your stuff and get the hell out of here. You've wasted enough of my time." He pressed the intercom on the table and ordered his security men back into the room. "Escort these two out of the hotel, now." Then he glared at both men. "Give me the recording of this interview, now—you didn't earn it!"

Macken's sudden demand for the tape sent Scott's blood pressure soaring. *God, no!* He was dead on so many levels if the guy got that! He calmed himself as much as possible, clearing his throat.

"Sir, if you don't want the interview, we'll erase it, but I'm telling you it's a great interview and I believe a powerful, intelligent man like you has aspirations for greater places in our government. It's opportunities like this that show your character and your devotion to what you do that will help take you to those places. Why don't you let me clean it up and bring it to you—let you watch it before we do anything with it. If it doesn't please you, I'll toss it in the incinerator."

Macken paused, thinking, those unemotional, flat eyes still holding Mosby.

"Sir, you can't lose this way."

Finally, the big man grunted in acquiescence. "Okay. But I want a copy on this coffee table by 8:00 p.m."

Scott let out the breath he'd been holding for what seemed like a couple of minutes. "Yes, sir. No problem, sir." His mind was screaming all the while, *Oh, sweet Jesus! The story of a lifetime! The freaking story of a lifetime!*

Scott Mosby and Steven Stewman were absolutely ecstatic as they drove away from the Four Seasons. They had done it. They had the interview that would make their careers. They would be the next Woodward and Bernstein!

Mosby called Kansas at a prearranged telephone booth. "We did it, my friend. We freaking did it!" he said to an astonished and supremely thankful Kansas. "That little son of a bitch worked like a charm. We got everything—enough information to bury Macken, Torreos, and The Bright Circle, and exonerate you and your friends. The story of the century! Meet me at the IHOP on Seventh Street and I'll give you back your gadget, then we're on to the studio in Dallas to package this into a jaw-dropper of a news piece."

Ten minutes later they tied up and Kansas and Mariana got a short version of the interview. Everyone was "on their knees" grateful. They were going to get out of this situation alive and stop a presidential assassination. Scott was so full of himself he couldn't sit still; he had to get going. So, after returning the truthmaker, they all headed toward Dallas in their separate cars. It was a long drive for Kansas and Mariana—up to Dallas then back to Wharton and El Campo—but they had to do it. They had to have this tape in their hands. Mosby said he would call Kansas that evening, when he got to the studio, had showed his producer, and had a Betacam video copy they could preview.

However, when he and Steven arrived at the studio, much to their disappointment, his boss was nowhere to be found, having taken the day to attend a conference in New Orleans. Undaunted, they commandeered the editing room, and in the next two hours assembled an acceptable package of the interview. Scott made three copies on cassettes; one for his boss, one for Kansas, and one for himself. After finishing up, he took two of those with him. *Woodward and Bernstein—damned straight! Make Watergate look like a freaking convenience store robbery. Freaking heroes of the country!*

Unfortunately, while they worked, things were not going so well elsewhere. By late afternoon John Macken was beginning to have more flashbacks than a Haight-Ashbury acid junkie. The device from another civilization, which had performed so well on everyone else, was having less than desired results on the man who had a steel plate in his head. The first vision came as a split-second thing—more like an image of him speaking to the reporter, the conversation unintelligible. He shrugged it off and rubbed his forehead. A few minutes later he clearly heard himself saying something about The Bright Circle. Instantly his stomach knotted and his mind shuddered at the prospect. *That's not possible. It's just not possible!* But a half hour later he got a clean flash of himself talking about Torreos and the meetings. "Jesus Christ," he rasped under his breath, alarmed now for the first time. All the plans he'd made! *Son of a bitch! How could this have happened?* He calmed himself. Maybe he'd just been working too hard. That couldn't have really taken place. *Gonna have to take some time off after this—a week in the Michigan cabin.*

But not long after, in the back of his private jet on the way to El Campo, it came again—clean, loud, and clear—him listening to that reporter telling him that he was not going to remember any of the interview. Macken was sweating and his hands were shaking as he grabbed his new military phone from the console next to him and dialed a number. "Macken here. I have a job for you. Code Rose."

When Scott Mosby got home he poured himself three fingers of scotch, did a celebratory line on the kitchen counter, and put the videos safely away. In the process, he went to his phone and called Kansas at the motel where his friend said he would be staying. There was no answer at the room, so he waited a few minutes and tried again. When there was still no answer, he called the motel in Wharton, where Kansas had told him his team had booked rooms—maybe something had happened that forced his friend back to Wharton. He found Kansas's pre-booked room and when there was no answer, he asked the front desk to let him use the motel's recorded message processor. He wasn't exactly sure why, but he added a few more words to the message—to be on the safe side. Then he did another hit of coke. He deserved it. He was going to be a serious celebrity by this time tomorrow. There was a knock on the door and he smiled—aahh, the pizza he had ordered on the way home. Life was good. Very good.

That evening Wilson landed in Houston. Ralph had, for some reason, taken a hiatus on the plane and Wilson was left on his own throughout the debarkation, baggage claim, and car rental processes. He drove to Wharton, which he was told was about fifteen miles outside of El Campo, where he had booked a room at the Holiday Inn. There were no rooms left to be had anywhere in El Campo. The president's speech was two days away.

The normally glacial Vitor was nearly apoplectic, having lost Wilson/Ralph in the monstrosity that was Houston International

Airport during the car rental ordeal. Now he would have to begin the laborious process of checking motels in surrounding towns. He, too, was aware that there were no rooms available in El Campo. Vitor prayed fervently as he drove toward his hotel in Wharton.

By 5:00 Kansas still hadn't heard from Scott. Unfortunately, he didn't realize that while he and Mariana were in the shower, Scott had called.

Kansas was getting nervous. He tried Scott's home phone twice again and left messages. No reply. They went out for a quick dinner, then returned to the motel. Mariana, in shorts and an oversized T-shirt, was curled up against the backboard of the bed, knees to her chin, trying to remain positive. Something ominous was twisting and swirling in the air around them. They both felt it. Mariana picked up the television remote and turned on the news.

A few minutes later, they sat on the side of the bed shrouded in misery and trepidation—enveloped in an aura of regret and helplessness. Two young men were dead—brutally murdered. Steven Stewman, a cameraman of great potential and an unlimited future, was found in his car in the warehouse district about a mile from where he lived, the victim of an apparent carjacking and robbery. It appeared he had been tortured, as well.

Scott Mosby, for whom life had promised so much, was found tied spread-eagle on his blood-soaked bed, tortured, then shot to death. The newscaster said the apartment had been ransacked, so it was assumed it was a robbery gone sadistic.

Trapped in despondence and guilt, they sat there, no longer hearing the droning television. The normally capable and stalwart Mariana was wiping tears from her face. Kansas's eyes were hollow and desolate, dark as an empty grave. They had involved two more people in their folly—their Draconian, quixotic folly to save the world—and now those two were dead. How many more people would suffer before they gave up and let the inevitable happen? Worse, now they had nothing left with which to stop the death of a president and perhaps, at some point, the elemental change of America. Kansas was as alone as he could remember being, sitting on the edge of a dark chasm, lost to his wretchedness and remorse.

Finally, he sighed and rose. "I've got to call Will," he muttered lifelessly. "They need to know."

When Kansas passed the news to Will, there was nothing but silence at the other end—empty, impotent silence. All the hope they once had lay decimated and decaying; all the faith they had mustered lay dashed and bloody on the jagged rocks of reality. They were alone. No one was coming to the rescue. Like Tennyson's Light Brigade riding into the valley of death, they knew there was nothing left to do but try, their pride and their conscience refusing to allow them to turn away, to seek the warmth and the refuge of cravenness, or the succor of ignorance.

"Will, I'm sorry that I got you into this," Kansas said quietly.

"Like you twisted my arm."

A glimmer of a smile touched Kansas's lips, graced with affection and respect. He knew his friend would see this through with him. Neither man spoke of quitting or running. It wasn't in their nature.

"I'll see you tomorrow morning. We should be in El Campo by 10:00. We've got to figure out how to save a president who thinks we're terrorists. Life's a bitch, ain't it?"

"And if we don't figure out who the shooter is and get him before he gets into that concrete ductwork, you're gonna have to shimmy into that ancient, shitty water line that runs to the junction under the bandstand in El Campo," Will replied, with some of that old humor and confidence returning.

"Who said I have to get in the pipe? You're the skinny one."

"No, no! I'm claustrophobic. I get the heebie-jeebies in phone booths. I ain't crawlin' into a freaking sewer pipe!"

"We'll flip a coin."

"I'm not getting into no freaking sewer pipe. There're probably rats—and spiders big enough to eat half of you there and drag the rest home for the kids."

Kansas's smile widened. "Good night, Spiderman."

A couple hundred miles away Will grinned. "*Buenas noches, amigo.*"

That night Will and his partner weren't the only people who were finding sleep a challenge. In a cheap room at one of the small hotels in Wharton, Frank Benson was struggling with the gods of slumber. His shoulder-length, coal-black hair splayed out on the pillow as he lay in bed, his dark eyes staring at the stucco-swirled ceiling. Less than forty hours—forty hours and he would make history, striking a blow for people everywhere who believed in the power of the individual, the laborer, the workingman—pulling the country back from the edge of this seductive democracy that only served the wealthy and the well-placed. He would end this false message being bartered by the rich snake oil salesman who had been slipped into the White House two years ago. Thank God he found Roberto and his group—individuals willing to make sacrifices for the betterment of the whole. Out of the ashes of this conflagration would rise a new form of government—one that truly served the people, and he would be the Che Guevara this time. He was scared, he admitted, but he was proud to have been chosen as the scalpel that would cut out the cancer and change the future. Besides, if it all went as planned, he'd be living in Cuba by the end of the week—a nice little villa not too far from the water. They had shown him pictures. In a couple of years, when things settled down, he could return to this country the silent hero. It was his reward. They promised him.

In Houston that same night, John Macken met with two of the men from his Code Rose team in the suite at the Four Seasons. The largest of the two handed him a package. "The recordings you requested, sir."

He fixed the men with those cold, flat eyes. "All of them?"

"All there was, sir," the man replied. "Trust me. He gave us all he had."

"I don't trust anyone," Macken barked. "Sure as hell not after this goddamned fiasco!"

CHAPTER 12

There are truths which can kill a nation.

— **Jean Giraudoux**

By midmorning the next day, Kansas and Mariana had arrived from Dallas. They and the others, who came in from the hotel in Wharton, were all gathered around breakfast at Emil's Café in El Campo. Fresh, strong coffee and Texas sunshine bolstered their spirits, and although the tragedy of last night and the dreadful challenge that lay ahead still crouched in the shadows of their consciousness, they had chosen to embrace it rather than succumb to it. Like Teddy Roosevelt, the Earp brothers, and all the other heroes they had grown up with, they wrenched loose the talons of fear and moved on, eyes on the target.

Kansas leaned forward in his chair in a conspiratorial fashion. "First off, we need to find someone who can tell us about the old sewer system. I suggest we start at the water department. One of us needs to become someone writing a book, looking for information." He looked at Cass. "You look like a budding novelist, maybe something that deals with 'the waterworks of the West,' and if it's a guy, you'll get his attention nicely."

She smiled, throwing back her new sable locks dramatically, her eyebrows dancing. "I always wanted to be a famous novelist."

Cass changed into a short skirt and a tight-fitting, sleeveless blouse that emphasized her more perky attributes, then went to visit the water department.

Johnson Mallard was not only the manager of the department, but somewhat of a historian, as well. He had weathered his fifty-nine years well. He still had most of his light brown hair, a twinkle in his blue eyes, and a healthy touch of ego, which made him putty in Cass's slim but firm hands. By afternoon they had fresh, up-to-date schematics of the old sewer system and a complete understanding of egress and ingress points in relation to the presidential bandstand and the water plant.

When Cass returned, she related that the town of El Campo

had grown up around the old water plant, which was a little less than a quarter mile from Friendship Park, where the president was to speak. The new primary ductwork ran parallel to the old in most places, and the actual water flow connections to the old system were still in place. The huge valves, with manually operated wheels in the water plant, were still operational, just tightly closed. Mallard explained that rather than go to the trouble of disassembling the old system, they just left it in place, and using backhoes, filled in and closed off the pipes at specific locations in town so the system was sealed. He said the primary lines running out from the water department to the first series of junction boxes were oversized. The city had gotten a special deal on those, so they used them. Cass had received a personal tour of the water department from Mr. Mallard, and it became apparent that the entranceway to the old, unused ductwork and the first junction box was in the older part of the building in the basement—a perfect, secluded location. The access rose up out of the concrete floor and had a steel cap on it, much like a submarine hatch, which was tightened down with a circular wheel. The water department would be closed the following day, Saturday, when the president was to speak. They realized they'd have to set up at the access point that night and wait for the assassin. It made sense that the man wouldn't get in place until late night or early morning, when the town was quiet and there were no watchful eyes.

Frank Benson had also recently toured the water department, disguised as a federal inspector, with all the right documents supplied by his friends. Tonight he'd slip into the building and down into the ductwork, crawling the quarter mile to the junction box under the bandstand. He had a heavy-duty cordless saw and several masonry-cutting blades. *Just notch out a square at the top, take it out, and leave the dirt and grass in place above it to be removed at the last minute. Then wait there until the next day, at noon, when the president did his speech—his last speech.* He caressed the 9mm Glock pistol with its fifteen-round magazine and large silencer on the bed next to him as if it were a child. "You and me, baby. We're gonna change the world," he whispered.

Vitor had been up with the sun, checking motels for Wilson/Ralph. The Vatican had supplied him with numerous documents for numerous identities. Today he was a detective for the Austin Police Department, looking for an escaped convict. He possessed a relatively good photo of Ralph that he'd pulled from the Key West City Council newspaper article. It was 11:00 when he finally got a hit. The manager of the Wharton Holiday Inn said the fellow had stayed there the night before, but had checked out that morning.

"Did he say anything at all when he checked out?" Vitor asked. "Anything at all?"

The woman at the desk thought about it for a moment, then her eyes lit. "Yeah, he did as a matter of fact. Something about looking forward to asking the president something...I think."

In less than a minute Vitor was in his car and headed for El Campo.

Overnight, El Campo had gone from a sleepy South Texas town to a crowded, bustling municipality, with people coming from across the country to share the president's birthday with him and hear him speak in El Campo's Friendship Park. The restaurants were packed and the main thoroughfares, Jackson and Mechanic streets, were impossibly congested. Street vendors were out in force, selling everything from hot dogs and ice cream to T-shirts and ball caps. Network news vehicles were everywhere and El Campo's small police force had been burgeoned by state and national law enforcement, and of course, the elite presidential guard that cleared, qualified, and interrogated anyone who appeared the least bit suspicious. Eddie said the whole place looked like a John Belushi movie—all the people standing around in dark sunglasses and suits, trying to look inconspicuous. For Will, Kansas, and the others, their research was done and they had a plan in place. The trick was to be at the water department before the killer.

That afternoon they returned to the motel in Wharton. When Kansas and Mariana settled into their room, Kansas noticed a light on the phone was blinking. It occurred to him that he had probably noticed it before, but with everything that was going on, he hadn't given it much thought. Curious, he picked up the receiver and got the office. The manager explained that they had this new system wherein friends and business clients of their customers could leave voice messages. The manager activated the message for Kansas and politely hung up. As Kansas listened to it, his face changed from indifference to profound interest, and finally to what could only be described as guarded euphoria. "Dear God, could it be possible?" he whispered hoarsely to himself.

When Mariana came out of the bathroom, he immediately punched the replay and let her hear it: *Hey Kansas! Just wanted you to know that I've got the videos. What a great recording—I'm gonna be famous! Have to wait until tomorrow to see my boss, but I left him a copy. I'm hanging on to ours overnight. I put one in that secret place I told you about—where I keep my bad habits. Don't know why, guess I'm just a paranoid SOB, but I wanted you to know. I know, I'm babbling a little—I'm just a tad high. Screw you—I deserve it! See you soon!*

Kansas turned to Mariana, a small glint of hope in his eyes. "Hon, do you realize…there's just a chance…. What if it's still there? I've got to get the others."

Moments later they all sat around in the room, everyone having heard the message on the phone. Kansas turned to Eddie after explaining about Scott's secret hiding place under the sink. "My friend, we're going to have our hands full tomorrow, but we need to know about this now. How quickly can you make Dallas with the Goose?"

Eddie mentally calculated for a moment. "Once I'm in the seat, two hours tops, probably less. This is just too killer, dude. Turn me loose, man, and I'll be gone like Burt Reynolds' hair. Don't worry about me getting into the apartment. Eddie got other skills he don't talk much about."

Kansas grinned, feeling like maybe they had a chance again, even with the long odds. "Okay, I'll give you Scott's address," he said, scribbling on a piece of paper at the nightstand and handing it over. "You get to Dallas, get what we need, and get right back here, because we're going to be up to our asses in alligators and we may need your services in a hurry." He paused for a moment, weighing something. "Listen, Eddie, I want you to check one other thing in Scott's apartment. He was a player—got around quite a bit and liked to brag about it a little. He once told me he had a camera in his bedroom, mounted behind the tile art design on the wall. If the paper is right, they killed him in there. That recording would be invaluable in bringing his killers to justice, and tying them to Macken. Check that out, too."

Their one-eyed aeronautical madman nodded solemnly. "Eddie digs. We gonna get them runamuckers." He stood and waved a V of fingers at them. "Peace, brothers and sisters," he said with that lopsided grin, and headed for the door. Suddenly, he stopped and turned around. "Give me the keys to Tabitha's old pickup you've been using. You have to go anywhere, you use the car I rented—give you more room." With the exchange from Kansas, he was out the door and gone.

The stars were just finding their way into the sky, and the western edges of the dark dome above Eddie were still brushed with the last iridescent blues of evening. The old hippie drove the few miles to Wharton's airport, lost in the throes of hope and anxiety. He looked up at the sky through the windshield. "Hey, Big Guy," he whispered. "Don't be bogarting the doobie of luck, now. Give Eddie a hit, *por favor*. Eddie need a couple hits!"

He reached the airport without incident, parked the truck and walked out to the old girl that had carried him through so much. But as he started to release the tie-downs on the wings, he heard footsteps behind him. He turned and found two large men facing him, dressed in gray suits, very official and austere-looking.

"Edward Jackson Moorehouse?" one said. It was more of a statement than a question. "We're with the FBI. We have some questions for you regarding the disappearance of Congressman Stan Meyers, and some associates of yours, Kansas Stamps and Will Bell."

Eddie just stood there like a deer in the headlights. "I...I don't know any of those dudes, man. I—"

"We think you do. You're going to have to come with us."

Eddie's head was screaming. *Holy shit! Not now! Lord, not now!*

So, he did the only thing he could think of. His shoulders sagged and he said, "All right. You win." He stepped up to the closest man and put his hands out for the cuffs to be put on him. The two men glanced at each other and relaxed. One reached behind his back and produced a pair of handcuffs, but as he stepped forward, Crazy Eddie's one good eye got that psychedelic gleam and he kicked the man in the groin as hard as he could. As the fellow doubled over with a surprised grunt, Eddie body-slammed the second guy and started running into the darkness toward the gate. However, the man he'd slammed recovered quickly and drew his weapon. As Eddie bolted as fast as his old legs would carry him, the last thing he heard was the sharp report of a pistol. His brief elation of escape was shattered by one of the heavy forty caliber rounds striking him in the head.

Moments later the two men stood over the body. Edward Jackson Moorehouse—remarkable pilot, loyal friend, and concocter of remarkable rum punches—lay sprawled on the pavement, a small pool of blood gathering by his head.

"Macken is gonna be pissed," one of them said quietly.

The other nodded, glancing around to see if anyone might have heard the commotion. "Yeah, no question. But now we need to get out of here. We'll send someone to check out the plane." They quickly searched the body. The taller man found a motel key and held it up for the other to see. Then they disappeared into the darkness.

It was still early, a couple hours before the rendezvous at the water plant, so Cass and Will decided to go get a cup of coffee at the diner down the street. Leaving the motel, they strolled the two blocks bathed in the glow of a huge moon, which was ripe and yellow as a fresh peach, holding hands like teenagers. It seemed like the only thing they had left in all this craziness was the new romance that was forming amidst the ruins of their lives. It was the only constant—the only thing that made sense—and they cherished it with a passion, allowing all the walls to come down and letting love insulate them from the fear and the anxiety that clawed at them through the bars of the cage they had created around themselves.

It was still and quiet, and the soft breeze caressed them like a soothing balm as they walked, accepting gratefully these few moments of serenity. They never noticed the two big, black Cadillacs that came in from the other direction and pulled into the motel.

Kansas and Mariana were sitting on the bed watching television when the door burst open and four men charged in, guns at the ready. In moments they were thrown to the floor and handcuffed. One of the men stepped forward and nudged Kansas with his foot. "Where are your friends?"

Kansas processed that question quickly. It meant they hadn't found them. How that happened, he didn't know, but he was glad. "I've been told I don't have any friends," Kansas replied. "I'm not a very personable soul."

He got a kick for his glibness.

"You got a better answer than that, or do you want to be kicked again?"

Kansas just glared at him.

The man drew his foot back again, but one of the others stopped him.

"Let's save this for the interrogators. Get 'em up. Let's go."

A half hour later they found themselves in another motel room on the other side of town, being guarded by a couple of men. Their room at the other motel had been searched and the truthmaker was discovered, along with their weapons. Kansas heard their captors talking. They were waiting for "the man" to arrive. They were not to do anything until then.

Macken had been forced to return to Houston for a few hours to attend a security briefing on the president's visit. The meeting lasted well into the evening. He was ecstatic at the news—they had two of them, and apparently the truth device. He already possessed the recordings of the interview, and now he was going to put the rest of this behind him. He would sleep at his suite for a few hours, then his private jet would have him back to El Campo by 7:00 a.m. It was going to be a busy day, on so many levels.

Will and Cass returned to find their motel room door kicked in and their friends missing. The couple quickly grabbed their weapons and Eddie's handheld army radio, which they had hidden well, and were on their way out when a black town car rounded the corner and screeched to a stop in the parking lot, men pouring from it. *They had been waiting for them!*

"Back inside!" Will hissed and he pulled Cass into the room and slammed the door.

A second later several silenced rounds slapped through the soft metal. He grabbed Cass and pulled her into the bathroom, hammering out the small, high glass window with the butt of his pistol. Quickly he lifted her through the portal, then pulled himself through. They barely made the ground before the front door was shot open and their assailants poured in.

They sprinted across the field behind the motel and over a fence into a small subdivision. By the time their pursuers circled the motel and entered the field, Will and Cass had raced through the small subdivision and down the road to an alleyway behind a nearby strip mall. They crouched between two cars bearing a pizza parlor logo, gasping for breath. Soon the sounds of racing cars and men yelling commands grew louder, moving ever closer.

A large dumpster stood about fifty feet from them. Cass took a look at it and grabbed Will's hand. "C'mon, we can't outrun 'em. We're going to have to hide!" The dumpster was nearly full of large plastic trash bags. The odor of rotting food and refuse was almost overpowering. "Perfect," she said with a grimace, as they climbed in and covered themselves with the bags.

They stayed there for the next hour, listening to the search as it shifted and moved around them. Twice they heard men near the dumpster. Once it was opened tentatively, but the smell prompted an expletive and it was quickly shut. They were just beginning to feel safe, that the search had drifted past them, when they heard a final, deliberate set of footsteps. One last pursuer was bringing up the rear when he saw the dumpster. Something pushed that sixth sense button within him and he decided to check. He moved up silently, step by quiet step, and grasped the handle on the top, then threw it open, gun ready. He saw nothing but odoriferous plastic bags. He was about to start pulling them away, but something caught his attention. It looked like a twenty-dollar bill, crumpled a little, resting against one of the bags. More casually now, certain he was safe, he reached down for the bill. It was a bit of a stretch; he had to pull most of his body over the side. Just as his fingers touched it, a hand shot out from under the bag and grabbed him. He issued a burbling, terrified shriek as Cass rose up, dragged him in, then hammered him in the throat with an open-handed strike, quick as a hungry spider. The fellow coughed out a surprised gurgle, his eyes rolled back in his head and he collapsed like a rag doll.

Will slowly stood up and looked around cautiously. There

was no one else to be seen in the dark alleyway. He looked over at Cass, who was disdainfully brushing herself off. "Jesus Christ! You're like a freaking Venus flytrap!" He put his hands up, palms out in supplication. "Would you just be sure to remind me occasionally not to piss you off?"

She grinned. "Let's get out of here. I'm gonna need to bathe for a week."

While Cass and Will were being chased and eliminating some of the competition, Kansas and Mariana were working their own brand of magic.

For over an hour they had sat on the bed, hands in their laps tightly handcuffed, while their two guards slumped in chairs and watched television. One of their captors, a Teutonic blond with austere blue eyes, finally rose out of his chair and stretched. "I'm going down to the lobby to get some coffee. You keep a tight eye on these two. I'll be back in five."

The other one, a heavily built man with a dark tan and dark hair, nodded. "Sure, no problem."

When the blond left, the other, thoroughly bored, stood up and began looking through Kansas's belongings, pausing to have a second look at the truthmaker that they had taken. Kansas's attention was immediately piqued. He glanced at Mariana, who was paying equal attention.

"Do you know what that is?" Kansas said.

"No," the man replied, "but I wouldn't be surprised if it's what my boss is looking for."

Kansas chuckled. "He wants a porn projector? I doubt it."

The guy looked at him. "What do you mean, 'a porn projector'? There's no such thing."

"Where have you been, man, living under a rock?" Kansas scolded. "VHS's are becoming obsolete. This is the latest thing. You press that indentation on the side, and the glass in the center projects a three-by-three-foot screen on any flat surface." He smiled. "Anything you want, from 'Girls Gone Wild!' to 'Naughty Teen Slumber Party' at your fingertips." He looked at Mariana and grinned. "We use it to spice things up in the evenings—you know…"

"You're shitting me," the guy said, but it was obvious his

curiosity had been aroused.

"I don't give a rat's ass one way or the other," Kansas replied with indifference. "All you have to do is press the button to find out."

The fellow looked at him again, trying to figure Kansas's angle on this. Finally, he shrugged and pressed the button. There was, of course, the instant hum that filled the air, and everyone felt the vibration spin through the room like an ancient, whirling dervish. Before the fellow really had a handle on what was happening, Kansas looked at him and said, "You're bored and you're tired, and you're sleepy. Very sleepy."

The man looked at him strangely, and his eyebrows narrowed. "No, I don't think so—"

"You're very tired. Go sit in that chair, now," Kansas droned softly.

The fellow stared at Kansas as if he were crazy. He started to say something. His mouth opened, but nothing came out. Suddenly, he shrugged and without another word sat down.

"You need to sleep," Kansas continued. "You're tired. Close your eyes and sleep, very deeply."

Again the man stared at Kansas, confusion dancing in his eyes, but slowly the confusion faded and his eyes closed.

"You can feel nothing now but deep, peaceful sleep," Kansas murmured as he got up slowly and quietly, moving over to the man and taking his gun from his shoulder holster. But just as he got the gun in his hand, the guy's eyes opened, registering obvious concern. As he started to rise, Kansas bashed him in the head with the gun. "I told you to sleep, asshole. You just didn't listen," he spat.

They couldn't leave without taking down the other soldier. The word would go out and they would be on the run before they'd traveled a mile. So, after undoing their handcuffs, they grabbed their weapons and sat the guard comfortably in the chair, sitting up, head down, with a book in his lap as if he were reading. Mariana and Kansas returned to their positions on the bed, looking as if they were still handcuffed, their weapons hidden at their sides.

Moments later the other fellow came through the door carrying two coffees. He glanced at his friend. "You're not supposed to be reading! You're supposed to be paying attention!" he growled as he set the coffees down. He barely had time to realize his friend hadn't responded when Kansas and Mariana stood up with weapons pointed at him.

Five minutes later the two men were in the closet, locked into their own handcuffs, with strips of sheets binding their feet and socks stuffed in their mouths.

When they got outside, Kansas called Will on his Army radio, explained what had happened to them, and was informed of his friends' plight, as well. "Listen, you're not that far from the motel, right?" Kansas said.

"Yeah, not that far. Why?"

"Because we're going to need transportation to get to El Campo and the last place they're going to expect you to show up is the motel. They're probably long gone from there, anyway. Why don't you try doubling back and see if you can get the car. Eddie told me he keeps an extra set of keys in a magnetic container under the front right wheel well of anything he drives— because he's always losing his keys or getting too high to find them, whichever comes first. We've been held at the Super 8 Motel on U.S. 59, but don't come to the motel, drive two hundred yards past it to the donut shop on the corner, okay?"

There was a pause and Kansas thought perhaps, with all they'd been through that night, it might be too much to ask, too much of a chance.

"Hey, why not? Can you get some donuts? Jelly filled, okay?"

Kansas smiled. "Yeah, jelly filled."

When John Macken heard his prisoners had not only gotten away, but had escaped with the truthmaker, he pistol-whipped the messenger. He decided not to report this to Ramone Torreos right away, fearing he might respond similarly.

By the time the foursome was teamed up again it was 5:00 a.m. and they realized clearly that they had missed the window of opportunity for getting the shooter before he moved into the ductwork. He was certainly in place now and waiting—waiting for the president to stand above him with nothing more than a half-inch sheet of plywood between them. Someone had to go in after him.

"I told you, man, I don't do closed places well," Will explained emphatically as they all sat in the car eating donuts and watching the first rays of the sun crest the horizon, magically turning the gray bands of low clouds into mauves and purples.

For the first time, Kansas realized that his friend wasn't joking. There was a pronounced sense of panic in his voice as he talked about it.

Will sighed, more like an angry hiss. "Look, when I was a kid, some of the bad-assed kids in the neighborhood stuffed me into a fifty-five-gallon drum and put the lid back on because I punched out one of their friends. They forgot about me and I was in there for almost twenty-four hours—all scrunched up in the dark, no food, no water—while the police and my parents tried to find me." He paused and exhaled hard. "I gotta tell you, of all the things that have happened to me, that was near the worst. It had a profound effect on my opinion of narrow, dark places."

Cass leaned over and put an arm around him. She could see the dread in the eyes of this person she knew to be nearly fearless. "Babe, I'm sorry to tell you this, but having seen that ductwork, Kansas just isn't going to have enough room. He's too big." Silence filled the car for a few moments, then Cass sighed. "I guess I'll have to do it. We're too late now to get him outside the pipes. I know damned well that's a fact."

That was too much for Will's conscience and ego—his lady risking her life. He let out a shaky exhale. "No, that's not gonna happen. That's just not gonna happen." He took another ragged breath and exhaled hard. "Okay, okay, I'll do it. I'll crawl into that freaking little, spider-infested, rat-filled pipe, and by the time I get to the end I'm gonna be glad to find someone I can beat the shit out of."

Kansas had to grin. "You can do it. I know you can." Then he became more serious. "I know I'm probably asking a lot, but if you could get him out alive that would sure put the icing on the cake for Macken and his group."

"Anything else you want while I'm in that freaking concrete tube—like maybe bake you a cake, or readjust the axis of the earth a degree?"

Kansas put his hands up, grinning again. "Okay, okay." Then

he added, "On the plus side, Eddie should be on his way back from Dallas by now, hopefully with a video that will bury this whole crew that's been chasing us."

"*Por favor, Dios,*" Mariana said softly but adamantly. "At this point I would consider it a win if we all get out of this alive."

"Amen," Cass added. Then she became more calculating. "Look, I figure the best time to hit this guy in the junction box is just before the president starts to speak. I know that's cutting it close, but anytime before that he's going to be nervous and his senses heightened, and he may be positioned in a way that he's looking at the entrance to the box. The closer it gets to noon, the more he's going to be focused on clearing out his shooting hole in the top of the box and setting up to shoot. His back should be to the entrance of the pipe in the junction box then. That's Will's best chance to get him and survive."

"Glad somebody's thinking about me, and I like the part about surviving," Will huffed. "But, unfortunately, I'm gonna have to be in there just a little early, regardless. This is not an appointment we can miss. If we can stay in touch with Eddie's radios, you can tell me when everything is coming to a head, and I can make my final move," he said, patting his pistol in his waistband.

John Macken's jet was just making its final approach at El Campo. He'd been on the phone with the man himself, Ramone Torreos. He was surprised to find that, very quietly, Torreos and his team had flown in for this occasion, staying at a ranch owned by one of The Bright Circle supporters about thirty miles southeast of Wharton off Highway 60. Macken had been informed of the elimination of the competition's pesky pilot—good riddance. When they passed over the airstrip in Wharton, he didn't see the big aircraft on the field. His people must have already taken care of it. The Chief of Presidential Security eased back in his seat and smiled, appreciating the efficiency. He sometimes felt like a magician. How easy it was to make things disappear.

However, Macken knew that the next part of the show was slightly more complicated. He had been informed that their "man" was in place, waiting underneath the presidential podium with a silenced pistol and several magazines of high-powered, hollow-point ammunition. A team was in place, ready to move in and "discover" the assassin as he came out of the water line at the plant. There would be a gunfight, and unfortunately, the shooter would be killed in the process. It was a nice, tight package. Macken would get credit for killing the assassin, whom he had set up to kill the president. He loved irony.

Vitor had failed to find Ralph/Wilson the day before, and when he returned to their motel that evening, the manager said the room had not been reserved for another night. Ralph had shown up again. The presidential "interview" was tomorrow, and his preservational instincts had encouraged him to relocate. Vitor spent the next few hours checking hotels in Wharton without success, but all was not lost, because he had begun to put all this together. His target had come to the very place the President of the United States was speaking. He began to glimpse the psyche involved here. All he had to do was be in the park where the president was going to speak. His target would be there too, he was certain. Vitor absently ran his fingers over the new knife tucked into the small sheath in his sleeve. It felt good, reassuring. He was looking forward to using it.

CHAPTER 13

The pure and simple truth is rarely pure and never simple.
— Oscar Wilde

By 9:30 a.m. El Campo was bustling like a stick-stirred ant pile. News vehicles were everywhere and thousands of visitors swarmed through the town, filling every service-related business to the maximum. The entire place had the festive exuberance of a carnival—and on many levels, it was.

There had been only a couple hours of uncomfortable rest in the car for the home team. They drove into El Campo, bleary-eyed and wrinkled, then stumbled out of Eddie's rental, found Will and Cass some clean clothes that didn't smell like dumpster, then walked over to The Uptown Grill for breakfast, because, as Will had reminded them in dark humor, "Condemned people always get a last good meal."

After breakfast the group drove to a parking area near Friendship Park, which was less than a quarter of a mile from the water plant. They checked the pistols that they carried, the women concealing them in purses and the men in the smalls of their backs under their shirts, then joined the milling crowds, working their way along the periphery of the park toward the water facility and the fenced area adjacent to it that housed the city's heavy machinery—trucks, backhoes, and bulldozers. They were concerned that there might be Bright Circle people at the plant, but unbeknownst to them, Macken had ordered everyone away from the facility. They would wait until the president had been shot, then move in, making it all appear a natural sequence of events, killing the assassin as he came out of the ductwork at the plant.

Ralph/Wilson had also been up early, and after a leisurely breakfast, had set out for the park. It was 10:30 and he had a little business to take care of. His plan was to use the truthmaker to coerce one or two of the presidential security people into allowing him to be part of the vetted circle of residents who would be allowed to stand up close and ask questions of the president.

Piece of cake.

It just so happened that, as he was entering the park and trying to determine which of the security personnel would best suit his purposes, Kansas and his team were coming in from the parking lot. Mariana, trained to be observant, was watching the periphery when she saw the slightly pudgy guy with the curly brown hair and big sunglasses walking parallel to them about a hundred feet away, milling through the crowd. She paused, putting up her hand to shade her eyes from the bright summer sun. Her face registered surprise and she stared again, hard and careful this time. "*Madre de Dios,*" she whispered. "It is him!" She grabbed Cass's arm. "Cass! Look!" she pointed into the crowd, slipping into Spanish/ English in her excitement. "It is him. *El pequeño bandito* with the truthmaker!"

Cass peered across the crowd. Her face registered the same surprise and she grabbed Kansas.

After a quick glance, Kansas grunted, "Son of a bitch! That's the guy from the motel into D.C.—the one who took the other truthmaker!" He swung around to the girls. "We're gonna have to split up. You take him—get that damned device back! I'll get Will settled into the pipes at the water department. You meet us there, okay?"

Three minutes later the girls had set up a tail on Ralph/Wilson, but it wasn't long before Mariana's trained eyes noticed something. Ralph was being followed by someone else— a tall, austere-looking man in a white cotton shirt and dark pants.

In the park stood the old adobe ruins of the first general store and cotton gin in El Campo. They had been preserved and rebuilt to serve as a tourist attraction, but a tornado had damaged the roof and the walls two months earlier, and the facility was closed temporarily. Ralph was fine, but Wilson always had a nervous bladder and the restrooms were on the far side of the park. Ralph decided to take a chance. He jimmied the back door of the cotton gin and snuck in. *Who's gonna care about a little pee on two hundred-year-old walls, anyway?* The interior of the building was musty-smelling, with lines of sunlight cascading through the open slats in the damaged roof, but the old adobe walls made the place cool and quiet. He went to the corner and relieved himself with a mighty sigh. He had just put everything away and turned around when he saw Vitor standing across the room, staring at him with those disconcerting, unemotional eyes.

"Fark! Fark! Fark!" he hissed under his breath, starting to back up in a room where there was no place to go.

Vitor grinned evilly and took out his new knife.

Suddenly, Ralph just slipped away, gone as yesterday's breakfast, leaving Wilson totally alone in a sun-trellised room with a madman. "Ooohh, sweet Jesus," Wilson muttered, thoroughly terrified, staring at the tall Italian and deflating in surrender. He held up his hands in a placating fashion. "Listen, let's just make a deal. Whatever it is you want, you can have it. Just no cutting, okay?"

Vitor brought the knife up and spun it in his hand like a baton, the light through the battered ceiling reflecting off the shiny new blade. Then he grasped it by the handle and pointed it at Wilson menacingly. "Give it to me. Give it to me and maybe I let you live."

"Hey, no problem," Wilson said congenially. "You got it. Actually, I am getting pretty tired of this game, anyway." He reached in his pants pocket and brought out the truthmaker, thinking he still had one more ace to play. He hit the button, and the room hummed with the ancient vibration. Wilson smiled, his confidence returning some. "Put down the knife. I would like you to put down the knife, now."

But nothing happened. Vitor just stood there, staring at him with those hollow eyes.

"Put down the knife, now!" Wilson commanded.

Vitor just offered an ugly grin and reached into his shirt pocket, holding up a small, Walkman cassette recorder and pointing to the ear molds in his ears. "Opera is the most beautiful music, especially when it is very loud. Are you ready to die now, my friend? It is time."

Wilson backed up a step, then raised the truthmaker threateningly. "Another step and I'll throw it against the wall! I'll smash it. I promise!"

Vitor caught his gist and simply shrugged, offering a bitter smile. "Go ahead. It's what I'm going to do with it, anyway. Go ahead."

"Holy freaking shit. I can't get a break here!" Wilson

moaned. Then he shouted, "Ralph! Ralph! Where are you, Ralph?" He swung around, eyes desperate. "Don't leave me here alone!" he screamed, throwing up his hands, frantically looking around the room. "C'mon, Ralph! C'mon, man!"

As planned, Vitor couldn't hear what was being said. *Don Giovanni* filled his ears and his head with wonderful sounds. He could only see the little fool dancing around and yelling something. It was certainly unusual. Nonetheless, it was time to end this. But all of a sudden the small man in front of him gradually changed his posture. He straightened up from his slouch, his head tilted cockily and his eyes suddenly gleamed with an odd fire. Without a word, the strange little guy abruptly bent down and snatched up one of the baseball-sized chunks of wall that littered the floor, and, before Vitor could blink, he hurled it. It was something no one in the room was ready for, least of all, Vitor. He never even had time to duck. The rock struck him squarely on the forehead and he went down like Frazier in the 14th at the "Thrilla in Manilla," eyes still registering the most exquisite surprise when his head thumped the solid adobe floor.

"There, is that better? Whacked that son of a bitch into next week," Ralph said, adjusting his shoulders.

Suddenly, there was a precipitous slouch to the body for a moment. "Oh Jesus, Ralph, I'm so glad you came back! I'm so glad!"

The body straightened up again and the head tilted, eyes alight. "Well, damn it, I couldn't very well leave my little buddy to get knifed, could I? Ruin a perfectly good body for us. Now just shut up. We're getting outta here."

Ralph/Wilson, having come to some sort of new, simultaneous agreement concerning the body they shared, were headed out the back door at light speed when they caught a straight-arm from Mariana at about head-height. Feet went up in the air and the body came down hard on the pavement, taking the breath away from all concerned. While they lay there, Mariana plucked the truthmaker from their coat pocket and she and Cass hustled away.

For those who would be interested, Ralph/Wilson woke up well ahead of Vitor, and, in a mutual epiphany, decided that a truthmaker was just more trouble than it was worth. They returned to their car, went to the airport, and bought a ticket for Jamaica. They really liked the Caribbean islands—white sand beaches, hot babes in small bikinis, and lots of stupid tourists just waiting to be fleeced.

Kansas and Will reached the water plant. The back door had already been jimmied and they walked in cautiously, quickly moving down the stairs to the entrance of the duct system. With all that had happened to them, they knew they had cut this close. It was already after 11:00 a.m. and the president was scheduled to speak at noon. The hatch to the ductwork stood out about two feet above the concrete base on the floor, with its large, metal submarine lid and the wheel that opened it. Will was sweating by the time they got it open, but not from exertion. He stared down at the pitch-black, forty-inch hole he was about to climb into and thought he was going to throw up.

"Shit! I don't know if I can do this, man," he said tentatively. "God…"

"You can do it, man. You have to," Kansas coaxed softly but firmly. "You have to. This is like one of those bad Roger Moore 'Bond' movies, where the whole world is depending on you. But it really is. You have to."

Will took a gulp of air, then let it out slowly, and at that moment there was an almost imperceptible change in him, but Kansas noticed it. Will got out his flashlight, made sure his pistol was tucked at the small of his back, and his radio clipped to his belt, then he looked at his friend. Kansas had never seen such fear in a person's eyes, but behind it all there was a distant light of determination. There was no question a battle was being waged, but character was winning. He had never admired Will Bell more than at that moment, and although Will didn't know it, Kansas's admiration and pure, honest affection had never been greater for any other man he'd known, except for perhaps his father. He realized that this friend of his was one of those rare people who kept his courage in his pocket, not to be displayed in unnecessary bravado, but held more like an amulet, to be grasped and used when he really needed it.

"Let me leave you with a quote a friend once told me," he

whispered. "'You can measure an individual by the opposition it takes to discourage him.'" Then he smiled. "Go save the world for us, Will."

A minute later, Kansas watched as Will slipped into the hole and began crawling a quarter of a mile in rat-infested, spider-laced, pitch-black darkness toward a fight most likely to the death. It takes a lot of opposition to discourage some men.

Ahead of Will, crouched in a four-by-six-foot concrete box, Frank Benson was preparing to remove the dirt and grass from above the box, having cut away a two-foot by two-foot-square of the concrete above him in the early morning hours. Dressed in a black sweatshirt and jeans, his dark eyes gleaming with anxiousness and his long hair pulled back in a ponytail, he was just waiting for the radio communication from his team, telling him the president was in place.

Outside, the president's entourage was arriving by helicopter at El Campo's airport. As always, there was no delay while he was in the open. They hustled into armored limousines and the cavalcade was underway to El Campo's city hall for a brief ceremony with the mayor, then it was on to the park.

Will was about halfway through his ordeal, moving hand over hand in the cramped, hard, concrete tube. There was barely room for his shoulders, sweat poured from him in rivulets, his shirt was soaked, and fear crawled over him and nibbled constantly at his nerves and resolve. The musty, fetid air was cool, but heavy with the staleness of dried mold. He could hear the twitter of surprised, angry rats ahead of him and occasionally one or two, in their confusion, would scamper over him, clawing and biting and squealing in his ears. Without his small flashlight, he would have already succumbed to the terror of his childhood trauma and danced cleanly into lunacy. His knuckles and the sides of his hands were raw from the rough concrete and his bloodied knees were already a torment of pain with every move. The terror of the confinement and darkness crawled inside him and pulled at his sanity. Spiders dropped on him, crawling into his clothing, skittering down along his spine and finding his skin, releasing their anger and their venom on his shoulders and his back in places he couldn't reach, and it added a whole new dimension to the symphony of panic and horror. Still, he pressed on, clawing and grunting through the darkness, his breaths coming in short grunts and gasps. He was given a slight reprieve in the cramped space near the center of his journey, where the pipe adjoined a small, three-foot by four-foot concrete box with a circular metal lid above it—a manhole probably used to check the water flow in the pipes periodically. As he rested there a moment, he heard Kansas on his Army radio.

"Will, come back."

Turning on his side, he pulled the radio out. "Yeah?"

"You've got to double-time. The president is already here," Kansas whispered in panic. "He's done his thing at city hall and they're on the way to the park! Move, man! Move!"

At nearly the same time Frank Benson's new, state-of-the-art military radio buzzed. The harsh voice said, "He's here. We'll call when position is established."

Will dug inside himself and pushed back his fear and pain. By his calculations he was into the last quarter of the distance. It was time to turn off his flashlight so the shooter wouldn't be warned of his approach. The darkness enveloped him and added new dimensions to his terror. For another five minutes he clawed his way in misery and mind-numbing claustrophobia, then he saw the flickering light ahead. Now he had to prepare himself for a new challenge. He paused and tried to bring his breathing under control so he wouldn't be heard as he neared, then he started moving slowly forward, weapon in hand.

While Will was struggling the final distance, the president was being escorted to the bandstand by his bodyguards. As he stepped up onto the stage, his personal bodyguards took positions on the ground at all four corners, and two more on the stage with him, but at the sides of the bandstand so as not to detract from his image of sureness and confidence with the public. Every inch of ground in, around, and under the bandstand had been meticulously checked earlier that morning. They were confident of the president's safety.

Frank Benson was seriously at work, pulling away the dirt and grass from his opening. The time was finally here! His destiny had arrived!

The president reached the podium and waved. The pre-vetted, specially selected crowd directly around the bandstand cheered and waved, lost to their adulation.

Frank Benson got his second call. "In place. Act at will." He quickly brushed away the last of the dirt and grass, then he reached down for his weapon on the floor, instinctively making sure the extra magazine was in his back pocket.

Will was still twenty feet from the opening, moving as fast as possible. He had just seen the assassin reach down for his weapon. There was furious cheering outside, dulled as it was by his confines. He knew what that meant.

The president quieted the crowd with his hands, and as the audience settled, he spoke. "My fellow Americans, it is with great pleasure that I return to this town to share this birthday celebration with friends and family, as I did so many years ago..."

Benson was now totally absorbed in his purpose. He stood up, bringing his head and shoulders out of the box, above ground now. There was about five feet between him and the plywood floor of the bandstand, and he guessed he was approximately ten feet from the podium—slightly diagonal to the side of it. He was shooting blind, but he was only a few feet away, and the president's voice would direct him. He raised his weapon, aiming, his hands shaking a little. "For America," he whispered, and pulled the trigger.

But nothing happened. In his anxiety and excitement he had forgotten to flip off the safety. With a muttered expletive he quickly snapped it off and raised the gun again. Will was still five feet from the junction box, no longer trying to be subtle. He realized he had taken too long. The president was being assassinated before his eyes.

Benson smiled, brought the gun up with purpose, pulled the trigger twice, and was rewarded with the recoil of the heavy pistol. The bullets exited the gun with nothing more than a spit, tore through the plywood floor with a muted pop, and missed the president's head by maybe an inch. The president felt the wind stream of the bullets and brought up a hand, casually brushing his hair, as one might to shoo away a fly.

When nothing happened, Benson took a breath, taking aim at the voice above him, and fired three more times. Two rounds buried themselves in the upper edge of the hard oak podium not eighteen inches from the Commander in Chief's chest. The other ripped a hole through the waist pocket of the president's suit, missing his hip by an inch and passing harmlessly on. The crowd was cheering noisily to their leader's first words. The security men were busy with eyes on the assembly, watching for any anomaly, and no one noticed the impact of the rounds in the podium. The president felt an odd tug at his pocket and glanced down for a fraction of a second, but he was in the middle of an address and let it go.

Benson was puzzled. Why hadn't he heard the thump of a falling body? He aimed again at the sound of the voice, intending to empty the gun this time, when Will came out of the ductwork behind him like the devil crawling out of Hell. Benson heard something behind him in the box, but his head and shoulders were outside of it and he couldn't see what was taking place. Before he could pull the trigger again, Will had the man's legs, and with a horrendous wrench borne of fear and adrenaline, he jerked the man down and back into the confines of the small concrete box. Benson wasn't a big man, about five-foot-seven, but he was fairly muscular. He turned quickly as he was dragged into the small box and brought the pistol around, getting off a shot that grazed Will's shoulder before Will grabbed the man's gun hand and battered his opponent in the temple with his Glock. Benson was stunned and Will took the advantage, slamming the man's hand with the gun against the concrete wall as the weapon discharged again and again, bullets ricocheting off the hard concrete and zipping through the enclosed space like enraged wasps. Benson's pistol finally tumbled from his grip and clattered across the floor, out of reach. Will, still on his knees in the small chamber, broke the man's grip on his gun arm and viciously straight-armed his opponent in the face with the butt of his gun, breaking the man's nose and knocking him out.

A moment later, Will sat in the dim light of the assassin's overturned flashlight, heaving in gulps of air, listening to the president speak above him and the crowd enthusiastically respond. He had caught his breath for a moment then grabbed his radio. "I got him, and he's still alive, though somewhat banged up."

The relief in Kansas's voice was more profound than his

words. "Thank God, man! You did it! God! I can't believe it! If your hair was longer I'd kiss you on the lips."

"You do that and you're gonna ruin a perfectly good friendship."

Kansas chuckled. "Okay, get him out of there. We need the world to hear his story."

When the assassin had recovered, Will, holding the man's silenced pistol, explained what was going to happen. "You're going to get in front of me and head out of this pipe—"

"I'm not doing shit," the man spat back defiantly.

Will had no time for niceties and was way out of patience. He brought up the gun and blew away a portion of Benson's right ear. The man shrieked in pain and Will clubbed him into silence. A moment later Will shook him awake. "Now, we're going to try this again. You fail to cooperate, and this time I'm gonna shoot off something you're gonna miss a lot more than your ear. Am I clear?"

Benson nodded sullenly, with no bravado now, hand pressed against the ragged remains of his ear trying to staunch the blood that was running down his face and neck.

"You go ahead of me," Will barked again. "I'm going to be right behind you with my gun between your legs. You do anything but crawl quietly and I swear to God you will be pissing through a rubber hose for the rest of your miserable life."

As they began to work their way back, the president finished his speech to a standing ovation and was whisked away by security personnel. Ten minutes later he was in the air and headed for Washington.

Macken was enraged when he heard that the plan had gone awry and the president had gotten away.

"What do we do with our shooter?" the voice on the phone asked.

"You know what to do," he responded coldly.

When Macken was forced to report the botched assassination to his boss, who was still at the ranch just south of Wharton, the typically taciturn Ramone Torreos came apart at the seams. "I would tell you I would take your job for your failures here," he hissed icily, "but I don't want your job. I will take your life. I will take your wife and your children, and then I will kill you. Am I getting through to you? You find those people and you kill them, and you bring me the device they possess, or you die trying. There is no middle ground."

Kansas sat impatiently on a bench in the basement of the water department, waiting for his friend to reappear from the concrete duct opening on the floor before him. There were bound to be some unhappy people, given the end to this story, and he wanted his team out of town as quickly as possible. He sat there, lost in thought, worrying about Will, trying to determine what their next move had to be to stay alive, and wondering how Eddie was making out. *Had he managed to make it to Dallas and get into Scott's apartment?* And most of all...*had he found anything?* Suddenly, he heard something behind him. He turned quickly and found himself staring at two men in gray suits with guns aimed at him. He recognized them immediately.

"Well, look what we've found here," the Teutonic-looking blond said sarcastically. "The fellow with the porn projector. Are your friends around?"

"No, I lost them somewhere. I think they're headed back to Houston."

The darkly tanned man moved in and frisked Kansas, taking his gun and finding the truthmaker. "Well, well, your porn. We'll hang on to this. You just stay where you are. We're waiting for a friend, too."

Kansas was just starting to reply when Frank Benson appeared in the mouth of the duct and crawled out onto the concrete platform that surrounded it. He was still on his knees, blood caked on the side of his face and down his shirt, nose bashed crooked. He looked up at the two men. "I'm sorry, the mission failed. I couldn't help it."

As he shakily stood up, the big blond muttered disdainfully, "Yeah, we know," and shot him twice in the chest with his silenced pistol. But just as he pulled the trigger, Will's head appeared above the rim of the large duct. As Benson dropped dead in front of Will, the blond took two quick shots at him, both ricocheting off the low metal casing around the pipe. Will quickly ducked back down.

While that was happening, the dark-haired man held his gun

on Kansas. His partner kept firing at the opening as he moved forward, and Will was forced to slip back down into the pipe system. When the fellow reached the opening, he fired his last few rounds into the darkness of the duct, but Will had anticipated that and had scurried backwards into the L of the pipe that led back toward the bandstand. The rounds slapped the concrete in front of him, hurling a barrage of shattered concrete into his face as he reversed into the gloom. His antagonist grabbed Benson, who was quite dead, and pushed him into the hole, then closed the lid and wound down the wheel, locking it. He looked at his friend, then glanced at the wheel valve next to the concrete platform. Stepping over to it, he turned the wheel rapidly. Everyone heard the rush of water into the pipe.

"That Mallard guy said it wouldn't take ten minutes to fill this entire section of ductwork. That'll take care of him." He slipped a fresh magazine into his pistol and jabbed the gun at Kansas. "Bring that one. The boss is gonna want to chat with him."

Kansas was dragged up, unable to tear his eyes from the locked valve and the ductwork filling with water. *Ten minutes!* He thought about trying to take them, but they were professionals, one holding him and pushing him forward while the other kept his distance to control the situation. There was no chance. *No chance for Will, either...*

Will Bell found himself locked into the perfect storm of physical and psychological terror. It only took seconds for him to realize what had happened. In moments the water was flowing, sluicing in like a thin river underneath him. Enveloped by the darkness, he quickly switched on his small flashlight. The body of the assassin was wedged into the exit in front of him, water boiling out and around it. He could only go back into the hell that had nearly claimed his sanity before, but now there was the added terror of drowning in the dark. Adrenaline coursed through his veins, adding to the panic that was overwhelming him. It was as if the oxygen had been sucked out of the air—he couldn't seem to get a breath. His heart was pounding with the reckless staccato of a heavy metal bass drum. He began to madly scuttle away from the source of the flow, almost blind with fear.

In less than a couple of minutes the water was several inches deep and he was sloshing as he moved forward. If he could make the concrete box at the park, he could crawl out, but it was an easy fifteen minutes away. Still, it was all he had. The water continued to rise, and in just a few minutes it was at the base of his throat. His hands were bloody and raw from forcing his way along the rough concrete like a madman. His elbows and knees were shredded. The flashlight had taken on water in his mad rush, and was starting to fade. The terror of dying like this crawled into him and tore at his insides. He found himself sobbing in claustrophobic, mortal terror. And still the water rose.

When they got outside the building, the man who was holding Kansas pressed his gun into his ribs and hissed at him, "Just walk normal and don't do anything stupid, or I will kill you, regardless of what the boss wants."

They waited for five minutes while the blond guy called his boss and got instructions. It took a while because the information had to be relayed to "the big man," then the decision had to come back to their boss. Finally, they began to walk along the chain-link fenced yard next to the water department, which held the city's heavy equipment. The party was wearing down in El Campo and the traffic had thinned out. There were still a few people moving toward the parking lot from the park and migrating back into the center of town. Vendors were selling out the last of their wares. The mimes, clowns, bands, and the portable arcades were all packing up. None of this registered with Kansas. He was frantic with guilt and consternation. His friend was dying in a frigging water pipe not two hundred yards from him and he was helpless to save him.

He finally decided it was better to take an impossible shot at this than live with the memory and guilt for the rest of his life. He began to figure the distance between the man who held him and the one behind him. He would have to break the first one's grip and go for his gun at the same time. If he could swing him into the line of fire from the other, he might have a chance—albeit a slim one. He was preparing himself, taking a couple deep breaths, when he saw a clown coming toward them on the sidewalk—the fuzzy halo of red hair, a clown mask, the oversized polka-dotted costume—carrying a trio of balloons.

As the clown casually sauntered by Kansas and the man

holding him, there was just the briefest of winks from an eye behind that mask. Kansas blinked, uncertain. He readied himself. The clown walked past them and when he was almost even with the big blond guy, he slowed and stopped almost in his path, but not aggressively. The zany-looking creature suddenly held out the balloons, like a gift. The blond fellow started to protest angrily, when the balloons got away and lifted into the sky. He paused just a moment and looked up instinctively. With the speed of a cobra, the clown's right hand shot out, fingers folded and hardened knuckles extended, striking the fellow in the throat. His eyes bulged, his mouth fell open and he coughed anemically. His hands came up to his throat as he gagged for air—the gun in one of them. The clown grabbed the man's gun, bent it inward and down and snapped it loose from him as if he were a child. Then the clown hammered him in the head with it.

Hearing the commotion behind him, the dark-haired man turned. That was the opening Kansas was waiting for. He brought his left hand up fast, knocking the pistol way from his body and swinging the man around toward him. He hit him squarely in the jaw with a fierce right hook. The man staggered and tried to bring the weapon around, but Kansas stepped into him, blocked the weapon away again, and hammered his opponent with a monster right cross that literally took the fellow off his feet, leaving him in a crumpled heap on the sidewalk.

The two left standing looked at each other for a moment, then the clown came over to Kansas.

"It cost me a hundred dollars for this piece of shit clown suit," Cass said angrily. "A hundred dollars for a freaking piece of polka-dotted cloth and a crummy four-dollar wig, for God's sake! We saw you come out of the water plant so I made a quick deal with the guy who owned it." She straightened up, eyes wary. "Where's Will?"

Mariana came running up to them and Kansas hugged her, but his face immediately became serious. "Will's in trouble. He's trapped in the duct system and they're filling it with water! We have to get back to the water plant and turn off the wheel valves that release the flow into the ductwork. C'mon! Run like you never have before. Will's life depends on it!"

But in his heart he knew it was probably too late. It had been over ten minutes already. He grabbed the men's guns and took back the truthmaker, then bolted off behind his friends.

Cass had ripped off the clown suit and started to run. In her adrenaline-charged fright she was outdistancing Kansas and Mariana.

As Kansas ran along the fence, he glanced into the heavy equipment yard. Suddenly, he quit running and shouted to Mariana, "You keep going. I've got an idea." He immediately began scaling the eight-foot fence, ignoring the strings of barbed wire at the top that ripped at his hands and chest as he clambered over and dropped to the other side, where a huge backhoe was parked. A backhoe was one of the tools he'd learned to use while working in construction/mining after college—the same place he got his experience with dynamite. He climbed up and threw himself into the seat. In seconds he had the great beast fired up, driving it right through the fence, tearing out a section and dragging it behind him until it succumbed to the huge wheels and was left behind.

Will was lost to horror and madness. The water was high enough now that he was sucking in mouthfuls of it with every breath. He couldn't force his head any higher. He had simply run out of space and time. Panic was overwhelming him and he was growing numb from lack of oxygen. He crawled forward a few more feet and as he did, he felt the contour of the pipe change into a sharp edge. His hands grasped the edge and he pulled himself forward, realizing he had found the three-foot by four-foot concrete square with the round metal manhole lid at the top of it. The box was mounted into the pipe, but was a few inches higher than the pipe, providing a little breathing space. He crawled into the square and gulped in the fetid air. The water was nearly to his chin, but his head was at least above water.

As soon as his strength had returned and his head cleared, he turned his attention to the manhole cover above him. Using his palms, he put his strength against it, pushing up, trying to pop it open. But it didn't budge. At that point his flashlight finally gave out and he was left to total darkness, head just above the water in a tiny concrete coffin. He shoved again, using every ounce of strength he could muster. Nothing.

Is it frozen from age? Or locked from the outside?

The water was still rising, faster now because it had finally reached the collapsed ends of the ductwork in that section, which had been blocked off many years ago by backhoes. He began to struggle maniacally, slamming the lid with the palms of his hands until the bones cracked in his wrists. And still the water rose. He was forced to tilt up his head now to keep the water out of his nose. He cried out in fear and exasperation, hammering his balled fists on the metal plate above him. Finally, he began to realize with a certainty that this was the end. *All that he had failed to do, all the plans he had…Cass…oh God, Cass…*

Just before the water finally rose over his nose, he took one last desperate breath of life. Then the terror of dying like this returned in full and he clawed madly at the metal lid that imprisoned him until his fingernails split and peeled back from the quicks of his fingers and the blood swirled in the black water around his wide, terrified eyes. Finally, the instinctive need to breathe outweighed all logic of survival. His lungs convulsed and he gulped in water. There was a final moment of obscene desperation, then it all stopped. His sightless, wide eyes lost their fear, and the essence of Will Bell, marvelous pilot, extraordinary adventurer, and soul capable of both compassion and mayhem, lifted away. His last sensation was of his body being pulled at by the water, his last thought was…*Cass…*

While Will was dying, Cass was frantically shutting down the water valves, with no knowledge that it was already too late. Kansas had raced the lumbering machine across the periphery of the park to the back of the water plant. When he reached the area where the pipes ran out from the plant, he was forced to make a decision as to where to dig. He had only the vaguest idea where his friend might be, but in one of those rare moments of intellective alchemy, borne partly of intuition and partly of spirit, he saw the concrete square and manhole cover fifty yards away and made his choice. He threw the monster underneath him in gear. But for all his gallant efforts, he, also, was too late.

Will Bell felt himself rising. There was no more fear. A peace had settled over him; a quiet, gentle peace. He drifted into a brilliant circle of light that widened into a softer aura of bright, clear pastels. As he floated into this incandescence before him, he began to make out shapes. The shapes metamorphosed into figures—friends and family who had gone this way before him. They were smiling with such warmth and their arms were open to greet him. It was beautiful. He had never felt more secure, and safe, and loved.

Kansas quickly settled the side supports of the backhoe in place and plunged the bucketed blades of the giant machine into the earth, stabbing and dragging furiously at the dark soil, smashing the concrete pipe just below the surface with a fury and watching the water explode from it, rushing across the ground as he rapidly dug a trench to pull it away from the pipe. He ripped at the concrete duct once more, tearing it completely in half and dragging the rubble away, and when he did, he couldn't believe his eyes. In the rush of water pouring from the opening, Will's body came sliding out, coming to rest face down in the brown, muddy water.

Kansas, Cass, and Mariana were next to Will before the engine of the backhoe quit rumbling, dragging him out onto the grass and turning him over. Cass gasped, terrified when she saw Will's face—eyes just slits, no life in them—but she never missed a beat. Kansas began CPR on his friend's chest, while Cass covered his mouth with hers and began breathing for him, but after a moment or two there was no response. Kansas rolled him over quickly and slammed his back, trying to dislodge any obstructions. They turned him over again and frantically began once more, but in another couple of minutes there was still no response. Will lay limp and lifeless, his empty eyes staring unflinching at the sun. Kansas looked at Cass with a helplessness he had never felt before in his life. There were tears running down his cheeks. Mariana, hands clenching at her sides, was crying, stricken by helplessness. Cass, on her knees next to her love, had begun to sob, salty tears running down her face in rivers of abject sorrow.

Will Bell was finally at peace, something he had struggled mightily to find in life. He was surrounded by an aura of love and he had never felt anything like it before.

Cass Roundtree felt like the life had been sucked from her body, as well, but the fierceness and determination that was so much a part of her rose to the surface one last time. She grabbed

Will by his shirt, screaming at him as she shook him. "You can't do this! You can't die! I won't let you! I swear to God, I won't let you!" She hammered his heart open-handed twice, then threw herself on him again, tilting his head back and covering his mouth with hers, moving beyond the physical, commanding all the mental and spiritual power she could marshal, all the "Ki" she had been trained to command in her martial arts, and she forced the breath of life into his lungs one more time, then once more, and then again. But still there was no response. Finally, in emotional and physical exhaustion, she cried out softly in agony and drew him up to her, to simply hold his body close one last time.

Will was still engulfed in wondrous sensations, but he was aware of a new feeling, almost like flight, as if speeding into the eternal.

Cass passionately crushed her lover to her breast, hating to let go, knowing that when she did, it was over. Finally, she sighed heavily and started to release him, but as she did, Will's body stiffened and he coughed violently, spewing water all over her. He gasped desperately, then spewed out more water. Instantly, both she and Kansas had him to a sitting position, slapping his back and helping him keep his head up. It took several minutes for Will's eyes to clear and for him to be able to speak. He was battered, muddy, and bloody from head to foot, and shivering. He looked up at them and croaked, "What took you so long?"

Cass just laughed with joy and crushed him to her again. "We were busy," she said, tears of gratefulness rimming her eyes. She squeezed him, her voice choked with emotion and gentle rebuke. "What have I told you about being impatient?"

Kansas reached over and gently brushed the soggy hair out of his friend's eyes. Then he grinned. "I'm really over this 'bringing you back to life' crap. Once in The Dry Tortugas, Cat Island last year...it's wearing thin. You're taking years off my life."

Will coughed again and smiled despite the pain. "Next time you get to drown and I'll save. I'm good with that."

CHAPTER 14

He who tells the truth must have one foot in the stirrup.
— **Armenian proverb**

It took a few minutes for Will to be able to stand. They could hear sirens in the background, and knew it was time to get out of there before destruction of public property was added to their growing list of charges. With one arm over Cass's shoulder and the other over Kansas's, Will was carried out to the car that Mariana had brought around. They piled in and took off, but not before they were seen by the two foot soldiers Kansas and Cass had taken out earlier.

The Teutonic blond brought up a military-type radio and rasped through his damaged throat, "Sir, the shooter is eliminated. We've located the group that got away last night. They've got the device. They're headed out on East Jackson, toward Highway 59 in a red Ford Granada. We need units on them, now!"

Macken, still in El Campo, had three vehicles and eight men in the city. He had another two teams in Wharton. If they were headed east on 59, he had them trapped. In the few miles between the two cities, there was no place for them to run.

Kansas really didn't know what to do but run. They were in the middle of nowhere and the ace he figured they always had— Eddie and his airplane—was nowhere to be found. *God, I wish I knew where the hell he was! Probably drunk or high somewhere, or both!* Out of sheer desperation he grabbed his radio and called Eddie again. "Eddie, I don't know where you are, but if you're getting this we need your help, bad. We're headed out of El Campo on East 59 toward Wharton."

Sometimes desperate men grasp at straws that don't exist.

Inside of three minutes, the first of Macken's teams cut them off at the intersection of Jackson and 59. The black Cadillac pulled out in front of them and screeched to a halt in the middle of the road. A rear window came down and a burst of automatic fire stitched across the highway, raking the front of Eddie's rental car as they sped toward the vehicle, cutting a shattered line across the windshield between Kansas and Cass. Kansas threw the Ford hard to the right and virtually slid by the stopped vehicle on two wheels, almost overturning. As he skidded by them he snapped the wheel to the left and brought the car back down hard enough to jar everyone's teeth. They bounced viciously as the automobile settled back onto the pavement. Kansas slammed the pedal to the floor and rocketed forward at full speed. Two more Cadillacs suddenly appeared, coming off Jackson from behind the stopped one, speeding around both sides of it and continuing the chase.

He had turned onto Highway 59 and was headed east toward Wharton along the flat, brown, sagebrush and mesquite panorama, when the first of the cars came up behind them. The shooter in the passenger's seat leaned out the window and opened up with an H & K assault weapon. The back window of the rental exploded in a shower of glass, but by some miracle no one was hit. From the front passenger's seat Mariana swung around with her pistol and opened fire out her window, placing three neat holes in the windshield of the vehicle behind them, forcing their pursuers to exercise a little caution. But everyone knew the truth of this situation—there was no place to hide, and it was only a matter of time.

There were three vehicles behind them now, engaging with automatic rifle fire and occupying both their lane and the oncoming traffic lane, forcing drivers off the road as they closed in on their target. Cass and Will were using their handguns from the back seat, but it was a losing battle—a handful of pistols against armored Cadillacs and automatic weapons.

Another barrage of fire ripped through the car and Mariana cried out, blood oozing from a wound high on her shoulder. Still, she snapped in her last magazine and fired back, screaming curses in Spanish. One more burst and a rear tire exploded. The car swerved sideways and Kansas fought for control, finally straightening it out, but the slap-hammering of the flattening tire told them time was running out, and he had lost his ability to maneuver.

"How much ammo do you have left?" Kansas yelled to his friends, realizing that they may be forced to stop and make a stand, or try to cut across the fields—ultimately suicide, either way. He knew it, but he had to do something.

"Five rounds," Will shouted over the noise of the car's tires and the gunfire.

"I'm out!" Cass said.

Mariana looked at him, blood running down her arm. "Maybe four rounds, *mi amigo*."

Kansas had done the least amount of shooting, and had nearly ten rounds. Maybe he could hold them while the others made a break. He had just started to relay his plan, still trying to keep the shaking, bouncing car on the road, when he stopped talking in mid-sentence. Coming straight at them, about a half-mile ahead and a hundred feet off the ground, was an airplane—a big airplane. He stared hard, squinting through the dust and the glare. The hot Texas sun was gnarling the air, creating shimmering waves of heat across the highway and the landscape, making it hard to be certain. He squinted as another burst of fire stitched the rear of the car and the right taillights exploded. "Son of a bitch," he whispered to no one in particular, his mouth involuntarily curling into a grin. Out of the rippling heat ahead of them came Crazy Eddie's Grumman Goose. Kansas couldn't believe his eyes. It was Eddie's freaking Goose!

Mariana saw it then, as well, and cried out, "*Madre de Dios! Es Loco Eddie! Es Loco Eddie!*"

As the plane soared in at them, Kansas could see the pilot had some sort of gray turban on his head, and a stick (or something) sideways in his mouth. *Who is that?*

Crazy Eddie, head bandaged with surgical gauze and half a roll of duct tape, was high as a kite on Percocet and pot. He had to be to ease the freaking pain in his head. The bullet that struck him as he ran from the two Bright Circle soldiers at the Wharton airport had hit him on the side of his head, cutting into the scalp and gouging a quarter-inch groove along his skull for three inches before exiting. It had knocked him out, and as with any head wound, it had bled profusely, providing the appearance of fatality. He came to an hour later with the mother of all tequila hangover headaches. But, realizing the gravity of the situation, he had managed to stumble over to the airplane and crawl inside, where he promptly passed out again. Two hours later he awoke, gulped down some painkillers and smoked a joint, then cleaned himself up a little and bandaged his head with gauze and duct tape, as tight as he could stand it. Ten minutes later he was in the air—still seeing double, but on his way to Dallas.

Now, with his one eye gleaming psychedelically, a stick of Kansas's dynamite clenched between his teeth like a boarding pirate's blade, and another stick in his right hand, he bore down on The Bright Circle's Cadillacs with the fury of an avenging angel, Meat Loaf's "Bat Out of Hell" hammering the speakers loud enough to flex the walls of the cabin.

He waved the fuse of the stick in his hand over the lighter in his other hand, which also held the yoke, and as it sparkled to life he swooped down over his buddies in the rental car and tossed the dynamite out his side window onto the pavement in front of the first Caddy. The explosion lifted the heavy vehicle into the air as if it had been swatted by the hand of God, shattering the windows and buckling the frame as it rolled in the air and slammed down onto the highway in a crumpled, gyrating heap. It careened into the car behind it and both automobiles were enveloped in a fiery explosion. The third car swerved around the explosion and kept to its purpose, closing on Kansas's battered and exhausted Ford.

Mariana and Will emptied their pistols at the remaining vehicle behind them as Eddie threw the Goose wing-over like it was a crop duster, flight surfaces and engines screaming in distress, cutting it so low he nearly buried a wing in the dusty Texas earth. He yanked it around and came up from behind the last of the Cadillacs. He waved at them as he soared by and tossed the second stick of dynamite fifty yards in front of them. It wasn't a perfect toss, and the dynamite blew up in front of the car, but the driver was forced off the road and into a ditch with sufficient force to invite concussion and fractured bones. The vehicle slammed into the embankment, bounced into the air, and rolled over, sliding a short distance before settling on its back, wheels still spinning furiously.

Kansas and his friends couldn't believe it—snatched from the jaws of death by an ungainly thirty-year-old metal bird and its spindly, whacked-out pilot. Kansas was on his radio immediately. "Eddie! Eddie!"

"Wass up, dude?" his friend slurred back, holding his military radio as he controlled the plane.

"Thank God you showed up when you did! Where the hell

have you been?"

"Long story, dude. Eddie been dealing with some harsh bongs, man."

Kansas decided to leave it there for the moment. They had other fish to fry. "Can you put your bird down on this road?"

Eddie smiled dizzily. "Does a pigeon walk funny? Is a frog's ass watertight?"

Kansas couldn't hide a smile of his own. "I get it. Get the hell down here, now!"

Five minutes later they were all in the Goose and on their way out—Will in the copilot's seat and Kansas crouching between his friends, a hand on each seat. The girls were in the newly installed cabin seats. Cass was cleaning and bandaging Mariana's wound, which had taken out a groove of flesh on her shoulder—not serious, but painful.

Eddie glanced at Will, who still looked and smelled like a plumber who had fought a badger in an overfilled septic tank. He shook his head. "Dude, you know I dig you, man, but you need to work on your hygiene. You look like you just lost a fight with a Veg-O-Matic."

Will chuckled. "Yeah, I know. It's been a complicated day. My mellow has been harshed a little."

Eddie nodded, but suddenly his glazed eye got a concerned look. "Oh shit, man! I been a little busy and forgot about the fuel thing."

Will and Kansas glanced at the fuel gauges, both of which were touching the red.

"We're gonna have to take a chance and try to get some fuel at Wharton Airport," their pilot mumbled. "Eddie got bad memories about that place, but Eddie also got bad memories about crashing planes with no gas."

About five miles ahead of them Vitor was headed into Wharton. After his last episode with the crazy little man, he had lost his lead again. He decided to temporarily give up the chase on him and focus on finding the others. Vitor wound his way around the carnage on Highway 59, realizing he was probably not too far behind them. The Texas Highway Patrol arrived after him and closed off the road. He was a couple of miles outside

Wharton, about to cross the bridge over the river before town, when a huge, amphibious aircraft passed overhead, moving toward the airport, close enough for him to read the N numbers on the fuselage. Something jarred his almost photographic memory about that plane and those numbers. In the dossiers on two of the other targets he read that they had flown into Cuba, and he assumed it was there they had discovered the devices. His memory cleared and he recalled an amphibious aircraft, the suspected pilot of which was a druggie from the Florida Keys. He pulled over, closed his eyes, and concentrated for a moment. *What were the registration numbers on that aircraft?* When he opened his eyes, he smiled. God was still with him.

As the Goose passed over the bridge before Wharton, they could see two more black Cadillacs on the side of the road, waiting.

"Do you wanna bomb those jive turkeys?" Eddie asked eagerly.

Kansas shook his head. "No, let's not draw any more attention than we have to. Let's just get into that airport, get fueled, and run for the coast." Then he turned to the old pilot and asked the question that had been hanging in the air since Eddie had found them. "How did you make out in Dallas? Did you find anything?"

Eddie adjusted the pitch on the propellers and spoke without looking at Kansas. "How important was that? I mean, is it like the end of the world if I tell you no?"

Kansas felt his insides clutch up. *Oohh, Jesus, no...*

Will quickly glanced over at Eddie, his face filled with dread.

"Mmmmm," muttered Eddie. "Important, I take it."

Kansas just exhaled, feeling the world closing in on them. *Without those videos...*

"Okay," Eddie said, starting to grin. "If they're that important, then I got 'em. Both of them—the one under the sink was a Betacam video cassette. The camera he had in the bedroom ran to his digital video recorder in the living room, which was running continuously into a Betacam, as well. I took that, too. Whatever he was recording will be on there."

Will turned to Kansas. "Mucking firaculous! I would kiss

him on the lips if his hair wasn't all taped up like that."

"Don't ever do that again, Eddie, that's not funny," Kansas admonished, starting to smile with horrendous relief. He turned back to the others in the seats behind them, and gave them a thumbs-up. "We got them!" he cried over the engines, and there was a spontaneous cheer—a tenuous lifting of voices in celebration of the possibility of survival.

Eddie had put the tapes in a heavy plastic baggie. He reached under his seat and pulled them out. Double-checking the seal on the bag, he tossed it to Cass behind him. She slipped them down the throat of her heavy Khaki shirt and with a little shuffling, secured them into her jeans waistband. "These little puppies aren't leaving my person!" she said with a determined smile.

The leader of The Bright Circle team at the bridge before Wharton picked up his car phone.

"Sir, it appears they have somehow taken out our pursuing teams. We just had a visual on the amphibious aircraft they flew in on."

"Yeah, I know," Macken spat. "One of the survivors said he saw the plane land and pick them up."

"Sir, my guess is they're going to head for the coast. We have no more resources to stop them here and our helicopter in El Campo can't possibly catch that airplane."

As much as Macken dreaded it, he had to inform Torreos immediately.

The darkness in the silence over the phone when he announced the news frightened him more than any assault in Vietnam. "You have failed me miserably," growled Torreos. "Now I guess it's time I clean up your shit for you."

The line went dead.

Torreos turned to his chief of staff. "Get the Sikorsky ready immediately. I want to be in the air in ten minutes."

His man looked at him in surprise. "You, sir? You will be...with us?"

Ramone Torreos's detached, reserved persona was melting as waves of fury and rage, and just a little uncertainty, rolled over him. *Who the hell were these goddamned people who threatened to undo fifteen years of preparation? He would have them personally. He would watch them die with his own eyes. His honor and his future demanded it.* Breaking all his own rules of being there firsthand on any "wet work," he snarled, "You're damned right I will!"

Torreos owned a specially outfitted Sikorsky UH-60 Blackhawk helicopter, built for the Argentine Air Force as a VIP transport. It was armed with two M-240D machine guns and equipped with modified ports hidden under the stabilizers that could fire two Hydra rockets each. He was able to get around the regulations of a personal aircraft being armed by maintaining its registration with the Argentine Air Force. If you had enough money, you could arrange anything.

Torreos told his pilot they would set a southeastern course for the coast, then swing around and maintain a holding pattern just out to sea to watch their radar for aircraft coming out of the Wharton area and headed toward the Freeport vicinity. Torreos was certain they would run for the water with the amphibian, and probably for The Keys, which he knew from his reports was their home base. He would catch them just out to sea with no witnesses, and kill them—just another airplane crash in the Gulf of Mexico. He also knew he had to be in front of them as they entered the Gulf, because even with the modified engines on his bird, they were almost an even match when it came to speed. He had to surprise them and take them out before they had a chance to recognize the danger and tried to outrun him.

Kansas and his battle-weary team landed in Wharton with great trepidation, not knowing if The Bright Circle people or regular law enforcement would be waiting for them. But the authorities didn't know who they were looking for yet and Torreos had pulled off his last team, setting up his own attack, not expecting the Goose to land.

"I'd recommend everyone get out and use the restrooms," Kansas yelled out over the engines as they taxied off the runway. "We're not stopping again until we hit The Keys."

Eddie seconded that, reminding everyone again that the toilet in the small bathroom stall at the back of the plane didn't work, because "a freaking inconsiderate rat" had chosen to die in the drainpipe. When they reached the FBO facilities, Eddie and Kansas went in to pay for fuel and the girls took Will to the restrooms to clean him up a bit. The old Goose waited patiently for them in the warm sunlight.

While the plane touched down and taxied in, Vitor was just pulling into the parking area, and Ramone Torreos was lifting off in his Sikorsky from the ranch about twenty miles southeast, off Highway 60.

In record time the Goose was fueled and they were in the air again, headed southeast, aiming for the coast between Freeport and Galveston. Eddie planned to run along the coastline to New Orleans, then cut across the Gulf into The Keys. They had the evidence to bury Macken, Torreos, and The Bright Circle forever. The video of Macken was damning enough, and if the recording from the bedroom unit showed what they expected, as macabre as it would be, that would be the icing on the cake.

The only one who wasn't totally happy was Eddie, who kept fooling with the mixture and the prop pitch on the starboard engine.

Will looked at him from the copilot's seat. "What's up, man?"

Eddie shrugged. "Don't know exactly, but I'm not getting full power out of that engine. It's running rough for some reason. Probably be all right to get us home, but Eddie don't want his mellow harshed anymore. You dig, bro?"

Will nodded with a grin that was harried around the edges. "Yeah, I dig."

They couldn't have known at the time, but news reporter Scott Mosby had displayed incredible courage in the last few minutes of his life. As Macken's people cut him horribly, demanding to know where the tapes were, he gave up the first two (but he lied about the location of the one in his boss's office, pointing them to a cassette of last week's news he had in his desk), and never said a word about the other, hidden in the kitchen. Even after they located the one in the house they still tortured him to be sure, but he never gave up the third—or the one that was recording his death. Mosby was an incredible human being. Even as they punished him, he cleverly coaxed them into identifying their bosses, knowing that the camera in the bedroom was recording everything. He never surrendered—even in the end when they put a gun to his head.

It takes a lot of opposition to discourage some men.

They had been flying for about fifteen minutes. The blue waters of the Gulf of Mexico were in sight, dead ahead. Eddie and Will were up front in the cockpit. There were four seats behind the cockpit partition, two on each side of the narrow walkway, one behind the other. Kansas and Mariana sat across from each other, the aisle between them, and Cass sat in the seat behind Mariana.

For the first time in days there was the smallest collective sense of optimism, and each person was actually relaxing some, lost in their own thoughts. The hypnotic drone of the big radial engines on each side of them added to the repose. They were going home, and they had what it took to clear them of any and all charges, aside from the fact that they had saved a president's life and prevented the process of a political coup.

As the vibration of the aircraft numbed their senses and eased the constant vigilance they had lived with for days, no one heard Eddie's latrine stall door open slightly as Vitor peeked out. When he realized the situation—everyone up front and resting quietly—he stepped out without a sound, carrying two sticks of dynamite and a righteous, evil smile.

Vitor had slipped aboard when everyone was in the restrooms or in the FBO at the airport. He quickly searched the plane to see what could be used, or used against him. In the process, he was most surprised to find a small cardboard box containing half a dozen sticks of dynamite, along with fuses. He thought about it for a moment and decided to take two sticks with fairly short fuses, tucking the dynamite into his belt. The beginnings of a plan formed. As he worked his way up front, he found Will's lighter in the console between the cockpit seats. He took that, too. There was a lot of junk strewn about, as well—an old cot in the back, dirty clothes piled around it, rolls of duct tape lay cast here and there or taped to the wall (it was Eddie's favorite tool), a compound bow and a box guitar were tossed in one corner, along with a hefty yellow bundle stenciled with "U.S. Navy" on the side, and stacks of magazines were cast around, many of them obviously containing evil things by the looks of the women on the covers.

When he saw Kansas and Eddie headed back with the fuel truck, he glanced around frantically, looking for a place to hide. He couldn't let them get away this time. His gaze came to rest on the tiny lavatory stall mounted into the wall in the middle-rear of the plane. He hurried back and opened the door. The odor was horrible—like something had died in there. Nonetheless, Vitor sat, waiting, for almost ten minutes before risking a peek outside. During that time he had considered what he might do, and had finally come up with a couple of alternatives, one of which had been in the back of his mind throughout this ordeal. The small glimmer of an introspective smile touched the corners of his lips in the foul darkness of the narrow box. God would be pleased with him.

The tall Italian crept out, straightened up as much as the headroom of the aircraft would allow, and lit one of the sticks of dynamite—the one with the longer fuse—then he tossed it down the aisle, almost into the cockpit.

Kansas immediately saw it as it bounced by him and settled on the threshold of the cockpit. He had no idea how it had gotten there, but his instincts, honed from mining work as a young man, had him on it like a linebacker on a fumble. All eyes fastened on Kansas as he grabbed the stick, ripped out the fuse, and crushed it with the heel of his boot. Vitor moved forward silently, came up behind Cass's chair, and grabbed her by the hair, jerking her head back violently and placing his new stiletto against her throat. As she cried out involuntarily, everyone's attention was drawn to her and her captor. Eddie glanced back, worried, but he was busy flying an airplane with an engine on the blink. He had all the harshed mellow he could handle at the moment.

Will was out of his seat in a flash. Kansas stood up in the aisle and was pulling out his gun—none of the others had any ammunition left. But Vitor yelled, stopping them in their tracks.

"Halt! Do not move any closer or I will kill her!" When he saw the gun come up in Kansas's hand, he yelled again, "Drop the weapon now! Or she dies!" To emphasize his point, he dug the tip of the blade into Cass's throat, just in front of her jugular, bringing it down vertically in front of the vein. Blood coursed from the wound, thin runnels of red trailing down her neck and onto her chest, staining her white blouse. Cass, eyes wide, issued a terse whimper.

Will turned to Kansas, his eyes filled with fear and surrender.

Kansas exhaled and nodded, bringing down his gun, still staring hard at his antagonist. "Okay, okay. You win. Don't hurt her."

"Slide the weapon along the floor to me," rasped Vitor. "Do not do anything foolish or she dies. Slide it now!"

It was a small cabin—less than a dozen feet separated them. Kansas knelt slowly and shoved the weapon across the floor. The Italian stopped it with his foot.

While all this was happening, Eddie noticed a gray and blue helicopter moving in their general direction, on a quartering, forty-five-degree angle. But he lost it to the hazy rivers of low cloud cover. It hardly mattered. There was lots of traffic out there, arriving and departing from Galveston. He didn't give it much thought. He was still busy coaxing an engine that was starting to piss him off.

Vitor jerked Cass's hair back sharply and as she cried out, he quickly reached down, dropped the knife and grabbed the gun. Rising up, still holding Cass by the hair, he shouted, "If you want her to live, if you all want to live, you will now give me the truth device. Give now!"

There was no hesitation with Will, and only a touch with Kansas. Looking at the frenzied zeal in the eyes of their antagonist, they knew Cass's life depended on it. They had seen madmen before. Unfortunately, captured in the heat of the moment, neither gave any thought to the fact that their assailant had said "device" and not "devices" when he made his demand, and they both produced the truthmakers they had been carrying.

Vitor's eyes went wide with shock and revelation when, there before him, were the two truthmakers. *How? Could it be...?* "Where did you get second device?" he growled. "Tell me now or I kill one of you." He pointed the gun at Kansas and pulled the trigger, punching a hole in the cockpit partition not five inches from Kansas's head. The report in the closed cabin was thunderous, and there wasn't a soul who didn't flinch. "Where did you get it?" he yelled again.

"I took it from a man in the park today," Mariana said,

defiantly staring at him from her seat.

Vitor riveted her with a glare. "A small man, curly brown hair?"

"Yes," she said hesitantly, wondering how he knew.

The bloodhound from the Vatican could not believe it. It was truly a sign from God! His eyes burned brightly with triumph and rimmed with tears. God had led him here! This was his purpose—the final, consummate, animus to his life and the consecration of his faith. Vitor suddenly saw it all so clearly. God loved none more dearly than the martyrs. He had all the devices that threatened the citadel of Christianity, and he had those who had found and used this evil, prostrate there before him. In one fell swoop he could preserve all the intimate knowledge that lay entombed in the Vatican that was threatened by this unholy, unnatural device from another time. It was what his masters had chosen him for—to sacrifice himself, to become a martyr. He felt light and free, like a leaf cascading down through the fall air, ending its life with dignity and design. He would be remembered in the halls of the Vatican for a hundred years.

Eyes gleaming with spiritual fervor, Vitor shouted, "Slide the devices to me on the floor, now!" He emphasized his demand by putting the gun to Cass's head. When the truthmakers lay at his feet, he shoved Cass to the floor, tucked the gun in his belt, and pulled out Will's lighter, then snatched the last stick of dynamite from his belt and touched the fuse with the lighter. "May God have mercy on your confused souls," he intoned as he calmly, almost serenely, held the dynamite to his chest. The fuse burned brightly, like a sparkler, dancing inward toward the stick with anxious resolution.

Kansas and Will glanced at each other and their eyes carried the same message. The madman with the gun and the dynamite guaranteed death—better one or two die trying to get to him, and the others live. Without another thought, Kansas charged down the aisle, knowing he'd be dead before he reached the crazy Italian, but maybe Will would make it behind him. Vitor drew the gun and fired point blank. Kansas spun as the bullet hit him, but before Vitor could get off another round Mariana, sitting just in front of him, was out of her seat and on the man with a fury that can only be found in that feminine/maternal instinct to preserve that which you love. She was specially trained in hand-to-hand combat, and although Cass held most of the limelight there, Mariana was almost as good as her friend. She hammered Vitor's hand aside and elbowed him in the face, knocking him backwards. He lost his balance and stumbled to one knee in the open back cabin, but still held the dynamite. He came up again with the gun, aiming at her as she stood in front of the others, protecting them with her body. But at that moment all hell broke loose.

Suddenly, the walls of the fuselage ripped open with furious, staccato popping sounds, machine gun fire tearing dozens of holes instantaneously across the aircraft's soft metal skin, slinging jagged pieces of shrapnel and steel-tipped bullets through the air with deadly indifference. One of those lethal volleys cut through the cabin door and the center of the airplane, driving over a dozen deadly 7.62 rounds through Vitor's body. He danced violently as if he had just grabbed a 220-volt line, and was slammed back against the opposite side of the plane, gradually sliding down, leaving a wide red smear against the wall, his eyes registering profound surprise…and disappointment.

However, there was no time to take satisfaction in small miracles. They were being attacked and there was a stick of dynamite on the floor, its fuse an inch away from completing Vitor's task for him. Mariana, being the closest in the cramped confines of the cabin, was on it instantly. "Get the door!" she yelled over her shoulder as she snatched it off the floor. In adrenaline-pumped frenzy, Will dove over Kansas, who was crumpled in the aisle, and rolled to the portal, slapping down the latch with a single blow. The cargo door was caught by the turbulent, rushing wind and snapped back so hard it snapped off one of the hinges, leaving it slamming violently against the side of the cabin.

Mariana looked at the fuse. There was nothing left. She threw it through the hatch as hard as she could, and almost instantly an explosion rocked the airplane sideways, nearly turning it over. Eddie shrieked blasphemies from the cockpit and fought with the controls as everyone was thrown to one side of the aircraft. As he brought it back, the direction of inertia reversed and everyone was thrown to the other side toward the open door. Kansas watched in dismay as one of the truthmakers slid across the floor and out of the cargo door, disappearing into the rush of air. The other one tumbled across the cabin floor, bouncing off the wall just inches from the open hatch and sliding under the last seat on the right side of the aircraft.

Will managed to grab a chair to keep from going out, but Mariana, who was in the center of the plane, tumbled across the floor and was rolling out of the door feet first when she felt a huge hand grasp her arm above the elbow. She looked up and it was Kansas. Bleeding badly from his side, he had anticipated the opposite roll of the aircraft and had stumbled forward to save his lady. She was halfway out of the aircraft, and the terrible wind was sucking at her, drawing her out inch by inch, but Kansas braced himself, crouching, holding one of the nylon straps near the cargo entrance, his other hand grasping her with a strength borne of fear and desperation. He was badly hurt, but there was a sense of determination in his eyes that said he would go out that door with her before he would let her go. At that moment, he saw the blue and gray helicopter coming at them from the starboard quarter. He could see the machine guns mounted in the nose begin to flash, and once again the plane shook from the punishment.

This time, Macken's pilot and his machine guns found the front of the old Goose, cutting through the wing and the cowling of the port engine and smashing the electronics panel in front of Eddie. Glass and plastic exploded in a hot, jagged fusillade, slicing Eddie's face and neck in a half-dozen places, but the courageous old pilot refused to surrender, shouting curses at the aircraft above him and trying desperately to bring his crippled bird back under control. He cut the power on the ruined engine, feathered the prop, manually adjusted the trim and stood on the opposite rudder to keep her straight and level. The enemy was shooting him to pieces and there was nothing he could do but fly his girl, dodging and weaving until the helicopter killed them both.

Kansas felt Mariana slip a few more inches into the wind stream. She stared up at him, terrified, recognizing the futility of what he was attempting. Her arm was numb from the pain of his grip, and she barely had the strength left to grasp his arm in reciprocation. The ferocious wind clawed at them both like a wild animal. Will had staggered up behind Kansas and was holding his waist to keep him in the plane. Cass was lying on the deck inside the aircraft, reaching out, trying to get some kind of purchase on her friend. If the plane tilted now they would all go out the door.

Mariana looked at her man, at the desperation and terror in his eyes, the blood soaking his shirt. "Let me go," she said. Then louder, over the wind, she cried, "Let me go. You will all die! Let me go!"

The helicopter in the distance turned sharply after its last pass, coming around and moving in for the kill. Kansas saw it, and something inside him snapped. He would not lose his woman like this! A final surge of adrenaline and defiance coursed through his veins just as Cass got a grip on the belt in Mariana's slacks. He screamed, pulling with every fiber of his being, transcending physical strength and stepping into the cerebral energy of pure willpower. The muscles in his legs and arms knotted, the overwhelming pain driving him rather than denying him, and he heaved with every ounce of strength, digging down to the core of his being, and his lady began to slide forward. Against all odds, she began to move upwards, clawing her way in inch by inch. But Torreos's copter was coming in again, falling on them like a hawk, almost within firing range once more.

The wind fought them, refusing to give up its prize, but even the furious wind wasn't a match for Kansas. With a final surge of determination, he dragged his lady into the aircraft and they all lay panting and exhausted on the cabin floor for a moment. Then Eddie screamed a warning and the rain of bullets came.

This time they took out the wounded engine completely, chewing off the propellers and leaving it smoking and in flames. The rest of the old girl was riddled with enough holes to rival the best of Swiss cheeses. Eddie was no longer fighting for flight; he was now trying to maintain a modicum of control in what was going to be a bad crash. His starboard ailerons were sticking and catching—a piece of metal had probably broken off somewhere and lodged in the mechanism. He had almost no instruments left. There was an acrid smoke swirling in the cockpit, burning his eye and all but blinding him. He was flying strictly by intuition and the sense of balance and speed that every old pilot accumulates if they live long enough. And no one knew it, but he was doing it magnificently well, with courage and timing, and faith in his old plane and his own abilities. He was exactly what those who truly knew him considered him to be—the best damned Grumman Goose pilot this side of Hell.

The crippled aircraft was plunging precariously toward the ocean below, smoke billowing from her in a dozen places. Eddie was howling like a wolf, lost to wild abandon, his one eye gleaming fiercely as he clutched the yoke that was bouncing in his hands as if it were alive. The water was coming up way too fast. Kansas and Will were trying desperately to get everyone in a seat before they hit. The helicopter was turning and coming at them again.

Everyone in the cabin had just finished a frantic game of musical chairs and had buckled down when the plane hit the water. She had come in much too fast, and the old Goose slammed the fairly smooth, blue water ferociously, cracking the port wing and snapping off its pontoon with a sharp report that sounded like cannon fire. Inertia lifted the old bird free from the clutches of the sea once more and it sailed, crippled wing askew, for another fifty yards. It plowed hard into the water, ripping the damaged wing completely from the fuselage, spinning the plane almost sideways and nearly burying the hull in the water. It popped upright a moment later, but its boat hull, fractured and riddled with bullet holes, was already taking on water.

Miraculously, no one was seriously hurt, but there was no question that they only had minutes before their faithful ride would disappear beneath the waves. If that weren't enough, the helicopter had moved in on them and was slowing.

Eddie came stumbling out of the cockpit, his face and neck laced with cuts, his head wound bleeding again, but still Eddie. "Dude, what a gas!" he muttered. Then he smiled. "Any landing you walk away from...or swim away from..." He glanced toward the back of the plane. "There's an old Navy life raft back there— the yellow rubber square. I'm thinking maybe we're gonna need that." But his words trailed off as he saw the helicopter hovering about a hundred yards out.

Torreos sat in the copilot's seat. He was a former Argentine military helicopter pilot and he was quite comfortable being in on the chase. Actually, he was enjoying it. His cold eyes gleamed with satisfaction, a grim smile touching his lips. "Activate the Hydra rockets on the port side, and set yourself up for the kill," he said to the pilot, unable to keep the triumph out of his voice.

Will saw the ports slide open under the left stabilizer and he knew what was happening. The Goose was beginning to list, and although the water hadn't reached the inner deck yet it was only minutes away. He turned to his friends. "Get out of here, now!" he shouted. "Get into the water! He's going to fire a rocket!"

No one needed any prompting, except for Kansas, who was desperately looking for something—actually, two things. The others were already jumping into the water. Suddenly, Kansas's eyes lit up and he raced to the back of the plane, dragging out the compound bow and arrows that his cousin had given him in Arkansas. He staggered across the cabin, and grabbed a roll of duct tape en route to the cardboard box of dynamite. He snatched out a stick and shoved a short fuse in it, then quickly bound the dynamite to the arrow with duct tape. Stringing the bow, and hooking it over his shoulder, he clambered his way back to the hatch and pulled himself onto the top of the plane.

The pilot in the helicopter had taken a few seconds to position his aircraft and activate the rocket. The active light had stalled for a moment, but was finally coming on when they both saw the big man below climb on top of the sinking aircraft. He had a bow on his back and an arrow in his teeth as he drew himself up. He stood quickly and readied the bow and arrow, then did a strange thing. He drew out a pack of matches that he'd taken from their hotel room, struck one and touched it to something on the end of the arrow.

"I'll be damned," muttered Torreos, his pale gray eyes narrowing as he suddenly realized what the fellow was doing. "Take him out," he barked sharply. "Take him out!"

The pilot needed just a moment to zero in with the bird, but in those few seconds, the man below brought up the bow, aimed, and fired.

Actually, it was little more than an act of sheer defiance. Even the case-hardened tip of a hunting arrow wasn't going to pierce the metal skin of the Blackhawk helicopter. The only chance was to get the arrow into the rocket's port, or have the dynamite explode the same instant the arrow hit the copter. But with the Blackhawk still moving somewhat in hover, it was, at most, a desperate fool's effort.

Kansas's arrow missed the port by a couple of feet. It hit the upper nose on the copter and ricocheted upwards toward the glass windows. Unfortunately for Torreos and his pilot, Blackhawk helicopters have large windshield wipers with thick rubber blades, similar to those on automobiles. The arrow glanced off the metal nose and its razor-sharp point slapped the lower part of the windshield, hitting and penetrating one of the large rubber wipers, driving itself through the hard rubber, and lodging on the windshield.

The pilot, who was just pulling the launch trigger, flinched instinctively as the arrow came at him and slammed against the windshield, distracting him. His rocket screamed out of the port, sweeping in at the foundering aircraft, but the distraction had thrown off the pilot's aim and the missile darted over the fuselage by about three feet and buried itself in the ocean fifty yards behind the Goose, exploding in a maelstrom of water and shrapnel. Torreos couldn't believe his eyes at the miss, but in a split second, all of that was dismissed as inconsequential. Horror and disbelief filled his countenance as he looked down at the dynamite lodged not two feet from his face on the windshield. The fuse crackled furiously for the last inch, and slipped burning into the stick. Torreos and his pilot looked at each other, impotency and death dancing in their eyes for a second, then the explosion turned the copter into a ball of fire. An ear-splitting thunderclap sent a compression wave hurling over the surface of the sea and flaming pieces of metal soared across the sky, splashing into the ocean and sizzling out clouds of steam. Rocketing plumes of smoke sailed out in plummeting white trellises, and what was left of the tail boom and the rotor gyrated away like a mortally wounded dragonfly, to bury itself in the water several hundred yards away.

Kansas viewed the whole sequence with as much disbelief as Torreos and his pilot had, but with considerably more satisfaction. "Impossible," he muttered to himself. "Freaking unbelievable."

His friends were cheering from the water around the sinking

plane. Will was already climbing back aboard, going after the raft—and one other item. He quickly located the rubber inflatable raft, tore off the cover and tossed it out to those in the water. Mariana immediately found the pull cord and with a high, compressed-air squeal, the rubber boat began to inflate. She and Cass crawled in, then helped Eddie aboard. They were all greatly relieved to find an Emergency Landing Transmitter built into the life raft, and Cass quickly confirmed that it was on and operating, and sending out a signal. This close to land, they knew there should be someone along quickly to rescue them.

The water was already a foot deep in the cabin of the plane. Miscellaneous buoyant objects were bobbing around on the surface. Will was down on his hands and knees, scrambling through the water, feeling around the floor with his hands, and as the depth in the cabin rose, he plunged himself into the water, splashing around like a demented seal.

Kansas swung down from the roof painfully, the wound in his side still bleeding. The bullet had cut into his side muscles just below the ribs and come out on the other side, tearing an ugly hole, but it hadn't hit any vital organs. He had lost a lot of blood, and with the adrenaline now fading, he was beginning to feel it. He looked down at Will. "I don't think you're going to find it, and it's been under water for five minutes."

The flying boat was beginning to list badly. Water was rising quickly and the plane was going down.

"C'mon, Will!" Kansas yelled. "Leave it. It's not worth dying for!"

At that moment Will popped up, gasping, a look of jubilation on his face. "Got it!" he shouted, raising his hand, holding the last truthmaker, water draining from its front vents.

A few minutes later they were all in the raft, weary to the bone both mentally and physically, but they were alive. Mariana was working on Kansas's wound with bandages from the airplane's medical kit, while Cass redressed Will's wounds. They watched as the proud old Grumman Goose groaned and rolled onto her wingless side, her intact wing pointing defiantly at the sky. Slowly the sea claimed the aircraft, with the wing gradually sliding downward, out of sight, until, with a final, gurgling gasp, she was gone. There was silence in the raft, and there were tears in Eddie's single, sad eye.

Will reached over and put his arm around his old friend in comradeship and commiseration. "I'll find you another one, Eddie," he said quietly but confidently. "I promise."

Within the hour they saw search helicopters coming toward them, working search patterns, and an hour later they were being treated by emergency personnel at Brentwood Hospital in Galveston. Their names, of course, threw up a bevy of red flags and they soon found themselves handcuffed and detained by National Security personnel, followed by several hours of explanation. Both of the videos that Cass had so diligently protected throughout their escape from the sinking airplane— Macken confessing information on The Bright Circle, and the one of Scott's murder—were being processed by the FBI and National Security. During their interrogation, no one mentioned Torreos and his helicopter. It would have just complicated matters. They simply said their airplane crashed after engine failure, which was actually true.

Ultimately, the Macken recording cleared them of any wrongdoing. The disappearance of Congressman Meyers was a little more complicated, but by prior decision the group had agreed to say he had been taken by Bright Circle personnel during the raid on Greg and Tabitha's place in Arkansas. The authorities were not happy with them—they had been the focal point of an international manhunt, but the people in charge were beginning to realize the width and depth of the plot they had uncovered and foiled. The arguments ran from just trumping up something to charge them with, to giving them medals in a public ceremony. In the end, they just decided to let them go quietly. Twenty-four hours later, everyone was released and their belongings were returned to them.

The truthmaker was discovered on Will, but no one was really certain what it was, because no one had actually seen one (and those who had were no longer alive). Security personnel had studied it, found the button on the side and pressed it, but nothing happened—nothing at all. It was assumed to be non-functional, whatever it was, and they returned it to its owner.

During the following twenty-four hours, U.S. Marshals and FBI personnel were at the doors of some of the most influential and important political figures in the United States, including John Talbot Macken, Chief of Presidential Security.

Macken watched from the balcony of his suite at the Four Seasons Hotel in Houston as the U.S. Marshal vehicles pulled up below. He had already received calls from his associates— Channel 11 News was running their copy of his "interview." He took a drag of his cigarette and sighed out the smoke, then turned and went inside. He sat down on his couch in the living room and looked around once more at the luxury and position he had attained. Macken exhaled, crushing out his smoke in the ashtray on the coffee table, then he slowly reached over, took the pistol from the table, and put the barrel in his mouth.

The courageous Scott Mosby and his feisty cameraman Steven Stewman would be remembered as the Woodward and Bernstein of network news reporting. Their strength of conviction and spirit had literally saved the country. Hell, they "made Watergate look like a freaking convenience store robbery." They reminded the United States and the world that it is not simply ideals that make a nation great, it is the people and their willingness to make sacrifices that propel a country into greatness and continue to maintain that status through trials and tribulation.

The president survived a coup and an assassination, with no knowledge of either as they happened. The grand experiment in democracy continued to limp forward, and if at some point this remarkable political philosophy was to ingloriously fade into something else, it would at least not be tomorrow.

Kansas and Will bought another Grumman Goose for their good friend, complete with an actual latrine and a top-of-the-line stereo system installed in the cockpit, which Crazy Eddie thought was "far out, bitchin', and psychedelic."

They all looked forward to cooler times and less "harshed mellows" for a while…

You dig?

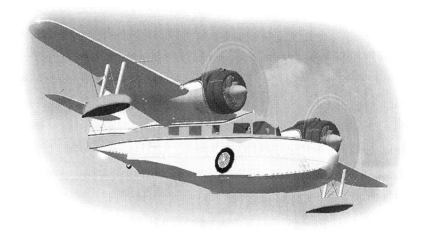

EPILOGUE

The lace and calf's hair bonefish fly soared through the air in a graceful, slow motion loop, plopping soundlessly on the surface of the still, aquamarine water of the backcountry. A wisp of a satisfied smile brushed Kansas Stamps's lips as he pulled the slack from the cast with his left hand, watching for movement in the water where the fly settled, and carefully observing the line for a change in tenseness.

The morning sun was just cresting the horizon, turning the mirrored waters to a golden incandescence, and the silken morning breeze caressed the surface tenderly. A second fly settled expertly on the water a dozen feet from his, and he turned and smiled at Mariana, standing on the stern platform of the bonefish skiff. She had become quite the avid fly fisherman, challenging his ability while complementing his pleasure immensely on these morning outings. She had made her decision a few weeks back, contacting her superiors in Cuba and informing them she would not be returning, while applying for political asylum in the U.S.

It had been approved almost overnight—the government owed them a favor.

She smiled, thinking back to the incredible journey that had taken her to this point, exhaling softly. "Life is an adventure, is it not?"

He nodded, understanding intuitively. "Sure is, hon."

"It is too bad about the truthmaker, though. But perhaps it was just fate."

The last truthmaker was rendered inoperative by the saltwater. Cass had taken it to some of the big electronics people she knew in California and they had studied it, using x-ray and ultrasound technology. There appeared to be no way to open the casing and no one was ready to dissect the device yet. Their opinions of the interior workings of the artifact were that it operated on a technology totally foreign and contrary to anything they knew. One of them said, disappointed and almost angrily, that their studying it was the equivalent of giving a Walkman to natives in New Guinea.

Kansas had mounted the truthmaker on a fan of flat white

coral, surrounded by a mahogany frame with a glass front. They got it six months of the year, and Will and Cass the other six months—an heirloom, a memento of a remarkable adventure none of them would ever forget.

"But you know, you don't seem as disappointed as the others," she added. "Why is that?"

Her lover and friend gazed out at the water introspectively, drawing in a little of his line and giving the fly movement. "Well, I'll tell you. I ran into an old buddy of mine the other day—that crazy, mystical Rastaman, Rufus, who has pretty much been responsible for most of the wild adventures Will and I have had since we moved to The Keys. I was having a regulator worked on at Underseas Dive Center and suddenly there he was, standing behind me. It's like he appears out of thin air. Same as always— old T-shirt, worn shorts, beat-up sandals, dreadlocks down to his shoulders. With little more than a nod, he says, 'Don' worry 'bout what you lose in life, mon. Dey always be another mango on da tree.' Then he gets this strange look and says, 'Relax mon, catch your breath. You and your buddy got plenty interesting adventure comin' up—sort of reward for being little balls in great pinball machine of life recently.'"

Kansas reached up underneath his long-brimmed cap and wiped a bead of sweat from his forehead, then continued.

"It was weird. Rufus grinned, big white, overly spaced teeth looking like bright tombstones, eyebrows bouncing up and down, and he said, 'You got 'golden future,' mon! May your life egg break cleanly and the Great Tortoise grant you a moonlit path to the sea.'"

Mariana turned toward him. "What does all that mean?"

Kansas smiled and shrugged. "With Rufus, you're never quite sure. But I'm betting it's gonna be interesting."

Acknowledgements

I owe a debt of gratitude to a number of people for the success of this novel. For their proofing talents and valuable suggestions, which made *Along The Road To Key West* a better book, thanks so much to Mark Medford, Tabitha and Greg Booher, Marcia Hodgson, Diane Marosy, Robert Simpson, and Bill and Linda Snell.

I also wish to offer a special thanks to Kathy Russ for her exceptional "final eyes" edit on this, and last but certainly not least, I'm so grateful to my editor, Cris Wanzer, for her unflagging efforts to make this book all it could be.

OTHER BOOKS BY MICHAEL REISIG

The Road To Key West
Book I

The Road to Key West is an adventurous/humorous sojourn that cavorts its way through the 1970s Caribbean, from Key West and the Bahamas, to Cuba and Central America.

In August of 1971, Kansas Stamps and Will Bell set out to become nothing more than commercial divers in the Florida Keys, but adventure, or misadventure, seems to dog them at every turn. They encounter a parade of bizarre characters, from part-time pirates and heartless larcenists, to Voodoo *bokors,* a wacky Jamaican soothsayer, and a handful of drug smugglers. Adding even more flavor to this Caribbean brew is a complicated romance, a lost Spanish treasure, and a pre-antediluvian artifact created by a distant congregation who truly understood the term "pyramid power."

Pour yourself a margarita, sit back, and slide into the '70s for a while as you follow Kansas and Will through this cocktail of madcap adventures—on *The Road To Key West.*

Back On The Road To Key West
Book II
The Golden Scepter

From the best-selling author of *The Road To Key West* comes a sequel guaranteed to take the reader even higher—another rollicking Caribbean adventure that will have you ripping at the pages and laughing out loud.

Back On The Road To Key West reintroduces the somewhat reluctant adventurers Kansas Stamps and Will Bell, casting them into one bizarre situation after another while capturing the true flavor and feel of Key West and the Caribbean in the early 1980s.

An ancient map and a lost pirate treasure, a larcenous Bahamian scoundrel and his gang of cutthroats, a wild and crazy journey into South America in search of a magical antediluvian device, and perilous/hilarious encounters with outlandish villains and friends along the way will keep you locked to your seat and giggling maniacally. (Not to mention headhunters, smugglers, and beautiful women with poisonous pet spiders.) You'll also welcome back Rufus, the wacky, mystical Jamaican Rastaman, and be captivated by another "complicated romance" as Kansas and Will struggle with finding and keeping "the girls of their dreams."

You're in for another rousing medley of madcap adventures in paradise with *Back On The Road To Key West.*

The New Madrid Run

The New Madrid Run is a tale of desperate survival on an altered planet. In the aftermath of a global cataclysm caused by a shift in the earth's poles, a handful of survivors face the terrible elements of a changed world as they navigate a battered sailboat from the ruins of Florida into the hills of Arkansas via a huge rift in the continent (the New Madrid fault). They survive fierce storms and high seas pirates only to make landfall and discover the greatest challenge of all...

The Hawks of Kamalon
Great Britain, Summer, 1944

A small squadron of British and American aircraft departs at dawn on a long-range strike into Germany, but as they cross the English Channel, the squadron vanishes.

Drawn thousands of light years across the galaxy by Kamalon's "Sensitive Mothers," ten men and eight aircraft are greeted by a roaring crowd in a field before the provincial capitol on the continent of Azra; a distant land in desperate need of champions.

About the Author

Michael Reisig has been writing professionally for almost two decades. He is a former newspaper editor and publisher, an award-winning columnist, and a best-selling novelist.

Reisig was born in Enid, Oklahoma. The first son of a military family, he was raised in Europe and California before moving to Florida. He attended high school and college in the Tampa Bay area. After college, he relocated to the Florida Keys, establishing a commercial diving business in which he served as the company pilot, traveling extensively throughout the southern hemisphere, diving, treasure hunting, and adventuring.

From there he turned to journalism, putting many of his experiences into the pages of his novels and columns, then going on to manage, then own, newspapers.

He presently resides in the Ouachita Mountains of Arkansas where he fishes and hunts and writes his novels, and occasionally escapes to the Caribbean for further adventures.

Made in the USA
Lexington, KY
01 November 2015